A noise at the front of the tavern distracted Yor. Through the double doors strode a barrel-chested cougarand, a puss in boots, muscles and thick tawny hair bulging from his half-buttoned waistcoat. The cougarand went straight to the bar and exchanged soft words with the bartender.

The bartender gestured at Yor.

Uh-oh!

Purposefully the cougarand turned toward the black-clad cavalryman. The feline eyes brightened, but no smile graced his lips, only a shallow frown that made the ends of his drooping beard whiskers arch like hairy tusks. The cougarand walked toward Yor and stopped two feet from him, folding his immense forearms over his chest, revealing a death's-head tattoo on each biceps.

The cougarand looked Yor up and down. "Are you Count Yor? The craven coward sired by the mating of slime worms in a condemned dung pit? A bugger of baby zux, a cheater at cards, a writer of bad poetry, and the clumsiest lover in the Six Estates? The man whose tailor jabbed out his own eyes rather than see what—"

"What?" croaked the enraged adventurer, rising to full height in a flash, the last insult being by far the most telling. "Who wants to know?" If I live, Yor vowed, when this tale is retold, I'll have much more clever repartee!

# Other TSR® Books

# Captains Outrageous

*Or, For Doom the Bell Tolls*

Roy V. Young

# CAPTAINS OUTRAGEOUS
## OR, FOR DOOM THE BELL TOLLS

First Printing: May 1994
Printed in the United States of America.
Library of Congress Catalog Card Number: 93-61471
ISBN: 1-56076-855-X

9 8 7 6 5 4 3 2 1

TSR, Inc.
P. O. Box 756
Lake Geneva, WI 53147
U. S. A.

TSR Ltd.
120 Church End, Cherry Hinton
Cambridge CB1 3LB
United Kingdom

For Brian and Ashley, who made it possible;
for Dean, who still likes the first draft the best;
but mostly for Bob and Ed, of course.

# PROLOGUE

Not without fear did the winged lizard seek.

The dream vision! Firefang shuddered as he flapped his argent wings to gain altitude. So real! Does she mean to end the Game itself? Doesn't she realize I will perish, too? I have not molted gold yet!

The thought sent a shiver clattering through the dragon's silver scales, causing him to drop sharply down through the low-hanging clouds pinned to the mountain crags. A surge of leathery reptilian muscle stabilized his precipitous descent, turning it to a smooth glide through the windless sky as he coursed over the titan forest below like an arrow loosed from a yeoman's bow.

*I will have an answer! Yes, I will!* his mind shouted.

*Will you, my son?* the dragoness replied in his mind. *Five moltsleeps have you survived. Not one in fifty makes it that far, O mighty Firefang! But I have survived six!*

*Mother!*

She laughed, and he felt shame. Following a downdraft, the dragon floated lower, then veered uneasily back up toward the highest ridge crest, a brooding line of trees speckled with immense grey boulders. Can any silver truly comprehend a gold? he worried. Is she as far above me as I am above a red?

Fanning his silver wings majestically, Firefang streaked through the Darkling Mountains, scanning, sniffing as he soared by the green-cloaked rocks. Anxious for the scent, he dipped low over the mountains, sweeping past lair after lair, gathering in his senses the recent gossip, then climbed higher toward the sharp, brooding pinnacle where he knew she must dwell.

Up there . . .

Long-forgotten images emerged; the dragon's emotions occluded. He alighted on a rock by the mouth of the aerie. Below, a bearcat growled up at him in warning; then the huge carnivore dragged its furred kill into the deep, dark shadows of the forest. The one-eyed saurian ignored the bearcat; there would be time for food later. Mind pounding, he crept toward the cavern mouth, as awkward on the ground as he was graceful in the air. A thousand dooms trumpeted in his mind, twisting threads together into intricate patterns, all of which cast ashes on the future of Leiblein.

Hesitating, he peered into the dark lair with draconic caution. *Perhaps I should spellguard first. . . .*

*Go, coward, go before your scales fall off from fear!*

*Taunt me not, Mother! One more molt! That's all I need until I can truly fly! Until I can soar between worlds as easily as you do! Just one more molt until I'm gold!*

*If you think the next molt will be easy, my son, think again! Not one in three survives it! The pain you will know is beyond your ability to comprehend!*

Gathering his courage, the silver dragon plunged through the cavern opening and crawled into her lair, his scaled skin prickling in nervous fear. Powerful indeed was the one-eyed silver dragon, first among his molt, a creature whose sight alone caused the natural inhabitants of Leiblein to tremble in terror.

But she was gold. She opened her auric eyes, lighting up the underground grotto with an almost holy glow. A cruel smile crossed the gold's crusted lips, a smile that struck terror in the silver.

*Have you really given the dust to that court wizard, Mother? Did you really tell him of the Bell and promise to—*

*Silence!* she dictated. *Vows made to the creatures of this world are not promises at all! You will not question me, whelp!*

Her mouth twisted, and she loosed the glyphs of power from deep in her soul in horrid, grating shrieks; the spell exploded over the silver dragon and sundered his own counterspell.

When Firefang awoke, he was on a mountain a hundred leagues away, and her unearthly laughter was still ringing in his mind.

# CHAPTER ONE

It was his move now, and they knew it.

Calculating, Yor peered across the tavern table at the well-armed duo of ruffians: a red-bearded barbarian and a tall, broad-shouldered loremaster—veteran villains, men who meant to do him ill before this night was over.

Stone silent, the two men stared back.

Not good . . . not good at all . . .

Yor lifted his flagon chin high, careful not to let any foam fall onto his glittering, expensive black shirt, its distinctive gold passementerie twinkling in the tavern light. The aroma of malt ravaged his nostrils with a husky scent; he drank deep, a desperate plunge into the frothy brew.

There must be a way out of this mess! thought the Bretilyan agent. Using the tankard as a shield for his striking blue eyes, Yor glanced at the bench to his right, confirming that his flintlock—loaded, but not yet cocked—remained an innocent lump below his neatly folded green cape. The feel of cold metal on his thigh reminded him that his rapier was also close at hand.

A noise at the front of the Dreaming Dragon drew his eyes. Tensing, Yor examined the newcomers. Two men: the local cooper and his apprentice, the latter part owl by the look of him, with curved claws and widely set eyes.

Harmless.

Cautious, Yor surveyed the whole alehouse again, daring once more to look past the immediate challenge of the two swordsmen seated opposite him. Who knew what other cutthroats might show up in the Dragon at any moment? Enemy spies certainly knew his favorite watering hole; there were enraged wizards, vengeful monsters, unpaid creditors, jealous lovers. . . .

Quickly he assessed in precise strides the distances to the oaken bar; the chandeliers; the empty fireplace; the gabled windows, one of which shone crimson with the image of a winged dragon deep in moltsleep; the front door, a yawning chasm away. The rear door, he knew without looking, was two short steps behind him and one to the left.

The red-beard cleared his throat ominously, a certain summons to action. The barbarian's right hand wavered as if to drop down below the table for some purpose, but then he thought better of it and returned the hand to the table's edge.

Yor guessed what was concealed below the table and glared defiantly over the top of his mug at the Norlander. Unflinching, the black-clad adventurer gulped down another draft of the hearty fluid and poised the mug in a subtle counterthreat.

I will not be rushed; do as you dare! Yor smiled tauntingly back at the red-beard.

The barbarian's face ruffled; his thick, rusty eyebrows coiled up like a firemander's tail. Impatient, the Norlander reached down again, this time without pausing. He dragged an enormous briar pipe into view, then struck a straw shaft unerringly through the exact midpoint of a nearby candle's flame. Waving the fire pole above the pipe bowl, he puffed one prodigious breath after another, spewing a noxious haze, wave after hostile wave of fumes, across the table.

The barbarian snubbed the glowing straw ember unsubtly between his bare fingers.

Yor coughed, gagging. "Worse than wizardry!" he shot back.

The red-beard grinned back vilely, confident that in this one action he had strengthened his own position while weakening both of his opponents.

Eyes watering, Yor looked away to the left. Seated

catercorner to the barbarian, a head taller and somehow
even less benign, was a lithic pillar of sinew, emotionlessly
scrutinizing Yor's every motion. There was a scent of pungent
herbs clinging to the man-mountain of muscle, an esoteric
aura reeking of unseen strengths that rivaled his physical
prowess and foretold his true passion: lore. Beside the loremaster was a massive two-handed broadsword, formerly
belonging to the Overtoad himself. Few had the strength to
heft such a blade, but the towering loremaster could wield it
with the precision of a foil.

The red-beard: Dword Ecklundson; the loremaster: Captain
Trebor Blackburn. Yor knew them both all too well!

Dword. Born in the cold, unyielding ice forests of Norlandia,
where men were weaned on warfare against the elements and each
other, flensed by the winter wind until they were bad-tempered
steel. Until a dozen decades ago, Dword's forefathers had roamed
the Northern Sea as if it were their own private pond, marauding
from Kor to Westphalia, holding thrall over all the northern
coast, bullying the Brets and all others who failed to prostrate
themselves before their fjordboats. Dword overcame the worst of
situations with the minimum of effort; often his stare alone was
enough to squelch a conflict.

Trebor. Strong was not a potent enough adjective. Yor had
seen Trebor pull up a dormant wood paladin, one of the sentinels of The Grove, and shake the tree-man until its hiber-
bark fell off and the bloodsap flowed, bringing it back to the
motile phase. Trebor then thrashed the wooden warrior over
an indignity that a bad-tempered wartslogger—a redundancy
in terms—would let pass even in the rutting season.

Something about a dog-eared book page . . .

Decisions: which one to strike at first? By the blessed bard,
this is a tight one! Perhaps I shouldn't have poisoned the
queen! Cursing beneath his breath, Yor drained the flagon
with a mind-boggling gulp. True, my king is now free to
marry again, free to wed the Lady Green, a ripe prize with her

swollen coffers, her horde of loyal soldiers, and the formidable Castle Slystone, all badly needed if the tide is to turn.

But Trebor's prelate now blocked the road.

Gears clicked in Yor's skull. The convent gambit? Testing and discarding ploys in swift succession, Yor raced silently down the avenues of attack, searching for a badly needed flash of inspiration. Could the royal marriage be pressed now, with the queen barely cool in her grave? And what, pray tell, might the clergy have to say about that! The potential loss of prestige could be fatal. . . .

Clerics! Damn them all to hell! What's Trebor up to this time? He's never favored clerics before! That was more Dword's style! And speaking of Dword, he's now consorting with wizards!

Across the table, the loremaster tapped the tabletop with his huge right hand and stroked his square, smooth chin with the other. "It's time," the man-mountain said, shifting his beige surcoat. "The night wanes. . . ."

"And only one of us can win," added the red-beard stiffly.

Set jaws.

A chill swept over Yor. Yes, it was time to make a move. Somehow the Lady Green must be lured to court. . . . Ah, but wait! Perhaps it's not necessary to grab her just yet! There might be another way!

Precipitously the black-garbed cavalryman slammed his flagon to the rough-hewn table in heavy metal thunder, startling his two deadly opponents. "If it were done, 'twere best done quickly!" Yor palmed his cards with deft celerity, thumping a pair of his most potent pasteboards down on Trebor's prelate.

"Holy rite card! Your prelate is required at Cathedral Dour! And behold! The poisoned wine card! The blackguard dies!"

"What?" chortled the Norlander, his pipe nearly dropping from his teeth, since he, too, stood to profit from Trebor's misfortune. "You dare murder a priest in his own sanctuary?

Oh, foul! First your own queen, then a man of the gods! Woden's mummery! Such egregiousness!"

"They do not poison love who do poison need!" Yor replied, quoting the blessed bard and savoring the counterattack. He leaned toward his red-bearded friend and leered sinisterly. "'Ware, wizard-lover! You're next!"

"I can wait for a spell. . . ."

Yor groaned, shaking his head in punishment, but Trebor was unfazed. His steel-grey eyes settled hard on the cavalryman. "So," he rejoined, "our alliance is broken! I expected as much!"

"Broken?" Yor countered. "'Twas broken when you moved that accursed prattler—"

"Prelate!"

"—between me and my queen-to-be! You were going to whisk her away to a nunnery, and the clergy would then claim all her worldly possessions! The prelate must pay for his master's treachery!"

"There'll be hell to pay if you fail, knave! Roll!"

Grabbing up the many-sided die, Yor shook it menacingly. With a dramatic flourish, he released the icosahedron. . . .

"A seventeen!" Dword announced cheerily. "More than enough! The prelate dies. . . ." Cocking an eye at his opponents' treasuries—including the gold markers he'd seen Trebor slip up his sleeve, arguably a violation of the house rules—the red-beard tallied the expected income from Yor's estate, Trebor's collection, and his own alchemistry; deducted the cost of royal taxation, bribes, assassin's wages, monster's depredations, castle upkeep, and magical expenses; then added the root mean square value of the probable treasure to be recovered from quests likely to be completed in the next round, barring event cards, bad weather, and royal edicts.

I'm still ahead!

Faster than the eye could follow, Yor's terrible swift hands closed about the doomed prelate figurine.

"Hold!"

Trebor hoisted his cards up to his imposing chest; he studied them meticulously, verifying that they were as remembered, then plucked one out and pitched it, with a nasty sneer, atop Yor's clenched fist.

"Antidote card!"

Yor paled.

"You lose the rest of this turn."

"And the next!" Dword injected gleefully. After all, he also gained when Yor suffered! He began an immediate reassessment.

"Plus two die prestige points!" the táll Bret loremaster proclaimed with haughty bravado. "And as a penance for your heinous attempt at clericide, I require—nay, demand!—the prelate's weight in gold, or else face excommunication, wretch!"

"Putrid ogre pus!" Yor swore. "No luck! No luck at all!"

"*You* never get any luck?" Trebor huffed. "My bishop died of the pox last turn! A bishop with the pox! I lost a hundred prestige points on that event card!"

"A pittance!" Dword revolted. "My sorcerer supreme was eaten by a seaslime! I may never recover the Orb of Awfulness!"

"And just what was he doing way out in the Seething Sea anyway, eh?" Yor goaded the barbarian. "It wouldn't be the old 'lost continent' strategy again, would it?"

Blustering like Kleshan vulgars over a live one, the trio spewed a rancorous torrent out from the rear of the Dreaming Dragon. If the noise disturbed the other customers in the dramshop, however, none complained, at least not out loud, not against the three most dangerous men in Bretilya, men whose exploits on behalf of King Derek were already the stuff of minstrels' supsongs.

Max, the tavern owner, looked back at the tempestuous trio and sighed. What could he do? They virtually lived in the Dragon when they were between escapades. Though it was rumored legions of bill collectors sought them, the outrageous captains always paid Max in cash, and Max had to admit there were those who came to the tavern with the hope of seeing Trebor's renowned, mesmerizing sleight-of-hand tricks or hearing Dword's latest madrigal. Ah, such a voice and such a story spinner!

But alas! This was not one of those nights!

There was one who remained undeterred by the trio's reputation. Shirley, Max's daughter, oldest of the three barmaidens serving in the tavern, strutted purposefully past her two sisters to the ruckus in the rear. "Are you wastrels going to blather all night?" she blared, her buxom blonde body heaving indignantly. "If you are, then off with you! Make room for some drinking men! This is a business 'stablishm'nt, not a ward for wayward warriors!"

Stunned, the trio looked at her, back at each other, and then again at the well-endowed wench.

"Shirley!" Yor protested. "You jest!"

"You've got rooms—such as they are!—don't you? So if you're not drinking—and you've nursed that one all night, Captain Trebor Blackburn!—then find some other tavern to collect dust in!"

A boyish grin lit Yor's face. Swiveling, he planted his costly, flashy boots—made from firemander skin and imported from decadent Gormus—on the table and made a sweeping gesture of conciliation to the rest of the tavern. "My fellow sots!" he boomed. "You have my sincerest apologies if my good friends and I have disturbed your hard-earned drunken reveries! A drink, sirrah! One for every man and woman in the room! Shirley! Goodie! Merci! Let's have a round to good King Derek's health!"

He paused and leaned suddenly forward, lecherously ogling the blonde's sumptuous decolletage. "And another for the three most luscious lasses that have ever watered a man's dreams!"

Howls erupted all around the tavern. "Hear, hear!" passed

from tongue to tongue in rambunctious agreement. Max's two other daughters, less brazen than their older sister, blushed. But not Shirley. She bent precariously forward, exposing a titillating expanse of perfumed bosom to the cavalryman's eyes. "In your cups again, are you, Captain—or is it *Count*—Yor?"

The taunt made Yor blush with embarrassment. His eyes veered to the Norlander and the loremaster with an I'll-get-you-two-later glare, then returned to the soft female mounds heaving delightfully before them. "Well flaunted, hussy," he conceded, then exploded loudly, "but by the boisterous bawd, I'd rather be in your cups than in my own! Mayhap you'd like to see my sword collection anon?"

Catcalls hooted around the tavern, but Shirley held her ground. "That'd be 'short' swords, wouldn't it?" she sassed back. "And your speed is legendary!"

Yor flushed with a wry smirk, gesturing politely in defeat. Pivoting abruptly, Shirley deprived the greedy male stares of the view of her bounteous cleavage and sashayed past tables toward the brew barrel, eluding a playful grasp by one of the patrons, in a salacious promenade that riveted attention to yet another salient aspect of her pulchritude.

The tavern roared; mugs clamored for more.

In a trice, Max's three daughters circulated with pitchers of ale. When the blonde reached the trio's table, Yor tossed her a small silver, which disappeared down the front of her dress. "A fine tittup," he said with a smirk, emphasizing the first syllable.

"You should know." She winked as she jiggled to secure the coin's lodging. "Your horsemanship is also famous. I've never heard of any of your mounts complain. . . ." She paraded away, devastating the Bret cavalryman with a look that could have steamed up a Valdrician frostblight.

"There have been fewer of them than you think," Yor confessed, too low for her to have heard. "Well," he sighed, bemused, "I guess that's enough gaming for tonight."

The loremaster frowned. "Quit? Now?" Dword and Yor evaded his glower. "I'll record it," Trebor persisted. Rummaging through his bag of tricks, past the stoppered vials and bundled plants, he fetched a blank parchment, a quill, and a bottle of ink. Gazing at the board, he listed the strengths of the various factions in a patient script.

"Not smoking tonight?" the red-beard queried.

Yor shrugged. "I forgot my tobacco."

"Here. Try some of mine."

There was a clay pipe at the end of the table—the better taverns provided them gratis—but having failed to bring his own trusted blends, Yor warily eyed the proffered twist. Dword had a penchant for mind-quavering, room-emptying blends, and this helix, blacker than a dragon's heart, was surely the red-beard's favored fire-cured mouthslayer from Pangrim. Mustering as much enthusiasm as he could, Yor finally replied, "Thanks," and took the twist, setting it aside for the moment. He picked up the clay pipe, inspected it, banged it against his palm to loosen the dottle.

Oh, no!

A tar-soaked flake fell out of the pipe and onto his velvet shirt. With controlled hysteria, he flicked the offending shard off as if it were one of the deadly spiders of Hra. Gingerly he stroked the golden embroidery on his chest, restoring order, and assured himself that the rest of his perfectly creased clothes remained unsullied.

Sigh.

Yor gave the Norlander an accusing glance, then pulled his dagger from his boot and sliced a few rings off the twist, rubbing them until they were loose enough to pack into the pipe. Evoking fire, Yor lit the tobacco and sucked in deeply.

"*Gagh!*"

"It'll put hair on your chest."

"From the lungs out, I fear!"

"Then don't inhale."

"I didn't!"

The barbarian shrugged. Puffing a perfect smoke-ring vortex, Dword launched it with a playful archer's artistry; it hooped Trebor's bottle of ink.

Annoyed, the loremaster flapped it away.

Ink pinwheeled.

Yor dodged like a greased pickpocket.

Zounds and double zounds! The loremaster gritted; Dword took a sudden interest in the ceiling. A single blot lay on the parchment. It was not on any of the writing, but . . .

Trebor scowled. He got another blank and started over.

A lull settled over the trio. Yor fell to smoking, drinking, and making a mental list of the morrow's activities, which principally consisted of grooming his horse. A block of briar appeared in Dword's hands, and he began to whittle, absorbed in his quiet craft, the pipe already half done. Trebor finished his scribing and, seeing his friends evince no urgency to leave, refilled his mug and dipped into his tunic for a book. The tome, *A Concise Treatise on Mycology and Mithridatism as Practiced by the Lords of Kor (Upper and Lower)*, bore the embossment of the Library of the League of Loremasters, from which he had borrowed it without authorization. Content, he burrowed into the book, abandoning the realm of the tavern.

Ten minutes drifted by. . . .

The rear door parted almost noiselessly.

Alert, Yor felt the warm summer breeze on his neck, and his hand flew to his cached pistol; it was hard in his palm even before he twisted to see through the open portal.

Shadows in the alley. Five . . . six. The stench of lathered horses; the clink of mail and sabers: The Royal Guardsmen.

Yor released his weapon. On either side of the rear steps poised a teal tunic, the red and white entwined roses of Bretilya embellished on their surcoats. The two guards stared back but made no move to ascend the steps.

A silent salute.

A slender lass walked into view, her delicate skin coming alive in the candlelight. She was about average height with straight auburn tresses, and the whiff of her perfume immediately identified her class: noble. Hesitating at the foot of the steps, she peered up into the Dreaming Dragon, her green eyes flashing over Yor with a tremble.

"Milady?" whispered the leader of her escorts.

"Wait here, Lord Gregolan," she said softly. "I'll go in alone."

The steward nodded, knowing that the trio was the best protection she could have. He motioned to two of his men to go around to the front; then he and the remaining soldiers faded into the shadows. The princess pulled her cloak tightly about her; the hood forced her auburn hair into a veil across her forehead and green eyes, obscuring her identity. Ready, she climbed upward.

Three steps. She crossed the threshold and slipped in alongside Yor, glancing once at each man and then dropping her eyes to the floor.

"Ah," Trebor murmured low, his gaze still locked on his book, "the plot thickens. . . ."

Princess Janine! Yor's curiosity roused like a cat from a nap, stretching and yawning, trying out each of its rested muscles. Excited energy buoyed the cavalryman, the same rush that came with the onset of each new adventure. What would it be this time? Off to vainglorious Munflenchia for some rabble-rousing? Did some mischievous monster need chastising? Perhaps a brave beauty to be rescued from an odious oubliette in a distant realm?

This feels like a good one!

Misinterpreting the heated intensity of his cobalt blue eyes, the princess blushed with a surge of heat, momentarily losing the reason for being here. Nervously she fidgeted with her cloak, and it parted, exposing a silken gown, turquoise with black and magenta trim.

Yor put on a mask of duty. Careful not to reveal the royal

identity of his guest, he said in a low voice, "Welcome, Lady. To what do we owe the honor of this visit?"

Demurely she faltered, wondering how to begin the awkward tale. "I need to talk to you—all of you. There's been trouble at the castle."

"Trouble?" Yor echoed in delicious anticipation.

"It's Bosamp," she said sadly, her eyes shrinking away from his gaze. "It's difficult to explain. You probably heard about the scandal at court this spring. . . ."

Indeed they had. The handsome new court wizard had been wooing two of the ladies-in-waiting at the same time. When they found out about each other, there had been a terrible fight, but after it was over, the two women decided to get revenge. At the king's birthday party, they toyed with the young wizard, making him run back and forth through the gardens, from one to the other, with less and less clothing on, while half the nobility watched from hiding. Finally they confronted him and . . .

The princess flushed modestly, though plainly she hadn't been there at the time.

"Yes, we heard about it," Dword said, sparing her the necessity of reciting the sordid details. "What's Bosamp done now?"

The princess breathed deeply, steadying herself. "Poor Bosamp! He was so humiliated. He went into seclusion after that and refused to attend any of the court functions or to perform any spells."

"Unprofessional," Trebor grumbled succinctly.

She nodded, but not without a gentle sympathy. "He would go up into his tower late at night and sing these sad songs about broken promises and unfaithful lovers. . . ."

There's no fool like a young fool, Yor thought.

Wince.

Kathy!

Yor's breathing halted; then he forced air and memories down into his body. Reflexively the black-clad Bret drank deeply, savoring the cold Bretilyan ale as it flowed down his throat.

"We've heard about that, too," the loremaster said, urged on by his aroused sense of propriety. "Bosamp acts more like the court jester than the court wizard! He's not half the sorcerer old Wendom was! It was a black day for Bretilya when that roc devoured Wendom! I think the Guild snubbed us by sending us Bosamp as a replacement! Wendom was one of the Circle of Seven Sevens—and likely to ascend to the Council of Seven."

Trebor paused, visualizing the structure of the Guild as interlocking juggler's rings, groups of seven wizards from which the most powerful was also a member of the next inner ring, with the core ring the Council of Seven. He continued by pronouncing, "Bosamp's just come from the Guild Workshop, a rank beginner!"

"Everyone has to start somewhere," Dword allowed. "And it's happened before, you know. Westphalia got a first-timer, too, and he's turned out quite well. I heard Bosamp did exceptionally well on his exams; he's been posted to the Ring of Forty-nine Sevens."

Trebor snorted. "Tests are not the real thing." Relenting, however, he motioned to the princess. "Pray continue, Lady."

"It went on until midsummer," she said. "Then Bosamp seemed to come out of it. Where before he had seemed so aimless, so lost, now he seemed to have some dark purpose. He sent off to the Guild for scrolls. He must have been trying to learn new spells, because strange sounds and odd smells came from his tower, especially at night."

Trouble! all three thought at the same time.

She bit her lip, hesitant, and folded her gloved hands. "Then yesterday Bosamp came out of his tower. He was shouting at people and acting very unusual, even for him. He said terrible things to the scullery maids and to the stable boys."

She looked at Yor quickly, then pointed her eyes down to her lap and straightened the seams of her gown. "Then Bosamp came to court. He told everyone they'd be sorry they had laughed at him, and he started calling them awful things. Daddy ordered him removed, but when the guards started after him, Bosamp reached into his robe and threw a scroll in Daddy's lap! Before anybody could figure out what was going on, Bosamp said, 'I quit,' and ran out and went back into his tower."

Trebor pounced. "The scroll . . . what did it say?"

She paused, intimidated by the loremaster's fierce scrutiny. "Well . . . it was hard to follow. I didn't actually see it, but I heard that the handwriting was really bad. Every other sentence seemed to be 'doom to you' or 'cursed be you' . . . things like that. The Royal Sagemaster couldn't figure out what it meant, so to be safe, he burned it."

"He *what?*" the loremaster erupted in disbelief. "He *burned* the scroll?"

Trebor's outburst made the princess cringe. A naturally shy teenager, she had lived in the sheltered shadows of her protective older brothers and fussing servants. The last day had been an experience for her, but despite the dread of it, she guiltily enjoyed having something out of the ordinary happen at court. And being here in the tavern with the realm's most feared protectors raised the level of her emotions in a way she would not have missed. She looked to Yor for reassurance; he smiled at her, and she felt warm all over.

"Now, Trebor," Yor said gallantly, "let's not jump on the messenger because of the message. Pray, onward, milady."

Something about his words disconcerted the princess. She blinked, then managed to continue. "The scroll didn't make any sense at all," she said with more animation, her eyes brightening with confidence. "Really! It was just a lot of odd stuff about a prophecy or something. Daddy was very angry. He gathered up Prince Cedric and a few of his knights, and they went to Bosamp's tower to get him and throw him out of the castle."

She looked at Yor for his reaction, but the black-clad

adventurer's thoughts were galloping ahead alone. "Bosamp and Daddy argued with each other, with lots of threats. Then Bosamp spell-sealed the door to his tower and refused to come out. Daddy told him he was going to ask the Council of Seven to discipline him, maybe even get him banned. Bosamp said something like, 'Steal a loaf of bread and they put you in jail; steal a castle and they make you king.' "

"The sacred scribe!" Yor exclaimed, open-jawed. "Quoted out of context! Inexcusable! Fie on him!"

"Daddy called Bosamp a coward," the princess recalled. "He said that Bosamp wasn't a man at all, that he was afraid to face life. Bosamp got very red in the face." Her voice dropped down low; she trembled. "Then Bosamp said, 'The true test of courage is not how you face life, but how you face death!'

"And then he threw a firewand at Daddy."

"He threw a *firewand* at the king?" three voices echoed.

"Not actually *at* him," she corrected. She paused and flushed at the pleasurable sensation of having three such men hanging on her every word. "It didn't hit Daddy or anyone else. But when it exploded, it made this awful cloud of smoke that spread across the bailey and into the main castle keep. It went everywhere. Nobody could see anything for hours! The smell was dreadful! It made everybody sick! Some people passed out; others were covering up their faces trying not to breathe the fumes, but the smoke got into everything. It ruined some of my clothes."

She shivered, momentarily unable to say more.

The trio looked at each other with somber glances.

Yor prompted her to resume. "Then what happened?"

The delicate skin of her face grew taut even as her eyes grew bigger, lips pursing. "Everyone was running around, coughing. It was dreadful! Bosamp must have cast another spell. It was hard to hear in all the confusion. But this big boulder appeared out of nowhere and hurled itself at every-one! It rolled up and down the castle steps, through the kitchens and the court. Several people were knocked down. Nobody was seriously hurt, but Lady Greymoor and some others were bruised pretty badly."

"A rolling stones sigil," Trebor interrupted, and all eyes turned to him for further details. The tall Bret loremaster read every tome on the sorcerous arts he could get his hands on, including every volume on legends and legerdemain, every grimoire on the preter-, super-, and unnatural forces loose on Leiblein. He was a self-taught loremaster.

Okay! Trebor thought to himself, his mind disappearing from the conversation to argue with his inner prosecuting barrister. So I'm not an accredited member of the League of Loremasters! There's the paltry matter of dues—unconscionable!—and that pathetic exam, which I could surely pass—and that little contretemps with the stackmaster at Ravenscrag! I would have brought the books back! He needn't have been so huffy about it!

Seeing three pairs of expectant eyes on him, Trebor's mind rejoined them, and he resumed. "Or possibly it was an attack rock. That's not beyond Bosamp's feeble skills. His magic seems to favor the earth element over the others. But go on."

The princess nodded and continued. "In all the confusion, Bosamp slipped out to the stables and stole one of Daddy's best horses and rode out of the castle. The guard was mustered, but it was almost dark and nobody seems to have noticed him after he crossed the bridge."

She paused, searching her memory for anything else that might be of value to them.

"And the king wants us to bring him back?" Yor deduced.

She nodded. "He's supposed to be brought before a Guild tribunal."

The trio looked at each other.

Well, it didn't seem like too tough an assignment, Yor thought. We've bested better wizards than Bosamp! But thank the gods they weren't all as bad as that last mission!

The Great Miasmal Swamp! The Glass Dome and those purple frogmen with their warped word contests! It's a good thing that we know just about every dirty ditty, off-color limerick, bad pun, and ridiculous riddle making the rounds, or we'd still be stuck in the swamp!

"Oh!" she said suddenly, laying her hand on Yor's arm to get his full attention. "Bosamp made this curse or vow or something to the Royal Sagemaster just before he got away."

Big trouble! all three thought simultaneously.

"What exactly," Trebor demanded, perhaps a bit too brusquely; he immediately regretted it and altered his tone in midsentence, "did he say?"

The royal lass hesitated, trying to remember Bosamp's words. "I don't know *exactly*. . . ." She quivered. "We were all trying to get out of the smoke and away from that crazy boulder! But it sounded like some kind of vow, kind of like the words in the scroll the Sagemaster burned. I didn't understand most of it—I wasn't all that close, and it was foreign or something—but I do remember one word." She looked at the loremaster hopefully. " 'Bell.' Bosamp definitely said something about a bell."

"Bell?" three bewildered voices echoed in unison.

"Yes, that's what he said." She looked at Yor and held his gaze for a full heartbeat before breaking her green eyes away.

"Bell . . . hmmm . . . maybe," Yor mulled aloud, "it was 'hell.' "

"That sounds more like Bosamp," Trebor said.

"No," she insisted firmly, looking from man to man with determination to sustain her point. "I'm certain it was 'bell.' I heard it very clearly. 'The bell on top of the girl' or something like that."

Pause.

"Well . . . whatever it was," Yor said finally, "the king wants us to get Bosamp back, and we'll be glad to do it. You can't have demented, lovesick sorcerers running around making threats. There's no telling what kind of trouble he might cause! Even a novice like Bosamp can be grief to a lot of innocent people!"

"He'll have to be brought back to the Guild tribunal," Dword said, then locked his eyes on the loremaster as he continued. "Alive, if possible. Stealing horses and assaulting kings is bad business, but the Guild is very fussy about policing their own kind."

"The Guild!" Trebor snorted. "Most likely they'll let him off with a warning! At the worst, they'll revoke some of his privileges for a while, then send him off on a contrition—disposing of some toothless old critter, no doubt! But privately—" he paused with disdain—"privately they'll slap him on the back and say what a dandy prank it was and how they all wish they could have been there! A plague on sorcerers! Varlets all!"

Loremaster against wizard, the League against the Guild, the sages against the Council. Ever bitter was the rivalry between the students of the natural sciences—astrology, alchemy, metaphysics, healcraft—and the wielders of the glyphs of power. Lore and sorcery were antipodal, immiscible, and had been since the day an eon ago when the first golden dragon came to Leiblein and taught those with the innate talent how to summon the glyphs of the Sortilege into this world.

"Well," Yor said, turning to the princess and giving her his best boyish-charm smile, "don't worry. We'll bring him back before he can cause himself—or anybody else—any trouble. We'll set out with the dawn."

"It might be a good idea," Trebor noted, "if we have a look at his tower first. We might find some clue as to what he's been up to all these moons."

The princess stared wide-eyed at the trio. "Isn't that dangerous?" she worried. "Won't there be curses and traps and things like that? The Sagemaster wouldn't let anybody go near it."

"Yes, there's danger," Yor said cavalierly, quickly cutting off the jeer forming on the man-mountain's lips. "But if it wern't dangerous, would the king have sent for us this late at night?"

Her eyes wavered downward. "No . . . I guess not." She glanced at the cavalryman once, then looked away. "Well, I'd better be off now. . . ."

They rose. Deftly Yor opened the door. "Tell the king we'll be coming up to the castle on the morrow to look at Bosamp's tower." He bowed courteously. "Good evening, my Lady."

"Good night . . ." she said, fluttering. Reluctantly she turned and stepped down the stairs, where a sea of teal-caped guards swallowed her up.

"She likes you, you know," Dword said softly as they watched her ride away.

Disquieted, Yor gathered up his belongings. "You're reading too much into it."

"Anyone could have come," Trebor noted matter-of-factly. "The Lord Chancellor or Prince Sean would have been far more logical choices. Even with the turmoil at the castle. I can't believe the king's first choice was his only daughter. Not to the East End. Not at night. She must have asked to come."

"Some of the millinery shops and dressmakers are out this way," Dword guessed, trying to reason out how she pulled it off. "She did mention her clothes were ruined. She might have told the king—"

"They're closed this time of night," Yor protested.

"Do you think the king knows that?" Dword wondered. "And even if he did, you know there's not a shop in the city that wouldn't fling open its doors even at midnight for Princess Janine."

"Don't be ridiculous," Yor said casually, concealing the horrifying realization that his friends might be right. I shouldn't have flirted with her at the last pageant, he scolded himself. Idiot! Princess Janine's quite a bit younger than you are! She's only—

Kathy was even younger.

Cold sweat filled the cavalryman's palms as unwanted memories surfaced. A specter of the past was loosed in his mind as the vision of his long-lost lover crept forward to claim a hold on his heart.

His fist clenched. Witch! I haven't forgotten you! He shoved the succubus back into its inner tomb before the tide of emotions could drown him. Shaken, he took one more swallow of ale, washing away the emotional residue of the past and recorking the memories of the Lady Katherine Lee. He clasped the stay of his cape and let the green felt hang loose on his taut, athletic upper body.

"Yor?"

The word broke his trance. "I don't think King Derek would appreciate it much," the black-clad dandy said, "if a hired sword paid court to his daughter. The princess is way out of my league, as you scoundrels well know. Now, let's go. We've a mad magician to run down and a lot of things to get done before we can leave."

He felt stares, and he met their linked gaze. "Bell?" he feinted.

"Beats me," Trebor said.

Dword frowned briefly, as if there were something he should be remembering, but whatever it was, it wasn't where he was looking for it. The Norlander shrugged and began to kill the fire burning the briar in front of his ruddy beard.

"Dawn, then?"

Sighing, Trebor mournfully shook his head. "Why does it always have to be dawn?"

Two laughs.

The three most dangerous men on Lothar had work to do.

# CHAPTER TWO

"Stay!" the trim young wizard barked for the third time at the king's magnificent charger, which in fact had remained entirely still since the first time he had growled the command. "Hold still, you worthless pile of mobile manure, or I'll stake you out for bearcat bait!"

Snarling, Bosamp struggled clumsily with the reins, tangling them in the metal hoops of his armillary sphere as he tried to line up the celestial position of the newly risen moon Zelaven in the constellation of the White Snake with the tiny ceramic twin in his lunar model. In order to take the sighting, everything had to be just right.

The itch demanded attention: wriggling, galling, abrasive.

Like the sucking, gnawing grate of a meatborer.

Like the cold, citric grip of hellspawn.

He tried to ignore the itch in his right side, determined to complete the astronomical sighting, but he couldn't keep his hand from rubbing at his side. He swore and surrendered entirely to outright scratching. In rapid strokes, he clawed at his orange robe just above the embroidered symbol for the glyph <#!@>, unable to directly access the itch through the durable council cloth, a costly weave made exclusively for the members of the Wizards' Guild by the Council of Seven and whose properties included weatherproofing, resistance to spellcraft and blades, and an automatic adjustment for external temperature, thickening and thinning with the seasons.

The sturdiness of the material, however, was a frustration to a man trying to get at an inflamed chancre. Wild thoughts flashed through Bosamp's mind, thoughts like taking a dagger and hacking the festering flesh from his side, but the itch of the new scaly patch of skin was not quite severe enough to make such a thought an action.

Yet.

He lost his grip, and the celestial contraption slipped free, tumbling. "No!" he shouted in a fumbling attempt to regain control of the metal instrument, but he failed. Startled, the equine whinnied, then reared as the armillary bounced off its flank and rolled clanking down the road. The sound of the armillary's escape clattered for several seconds in the dark and then ended with a disheartening plop.

Nearly pitched from his saddle, the sorcerer held the reins in panic and pounded his fist on the horse's neck. "No! No! No! Be still!" When the horse calmed, Bosamp ranted profusely against the fates and dismounted. Yanking the reins, he dragged the exhausted horse to a bush and tethered it maliciously tight.

Now—where did the sphere get off to?

Running his hand through his thick black hair, the cleft in his chin deepening with his frown, Bosamp surveyed the road in the direction the device had taken, but it was nowhere to be seen. "Mangy beast!" he said, slapping at the horse's head and rattling the painted pots draped around its neck. It was a hard slap, for the virile young wizard was rather athletically inclined and not at all the image of the grim greybeard conventionally associated with his craft. "They'll be after me soon, won't they? But nothing must stop me! Nothing! I'll ride you into the ground if I have to! To think my destiny is tied to such a pathetic creature as you!"

He struck the horse's ribs, unconsciously trying to transfer the itch from his own side to the horse's; this did not happen, but at least the sorcerer had the satisfaction of knowing that it, too, now felt almost as much pain as he did. The itch! He lifted the robe, pushing it up until the folds nearly gagged him, and peered at the wound in the dark. The patch was growing! It was as big as a coin now!

A cry of silent fear froze on Bosamp's lips. For a moment, he thought back to the blundered tongue twist that had transmuted his simple sigil, a rudimentary combination of the glyphs of power, into whatever foulness it had become.

"One small slip of the flinking lip!" he cursed. "Just one! I've read the complete journals of the Twelve Great Ones! Nobody ever mentioned anything like this! It's not fair!" The sorcerer shuddered as he remembered the explosion that had hurled him against the ceiling. He had blacked out; two hours later, when he woke, he first felt the itch and found the tiny scabrous growth, a small reddish purple dot halfway down his right side.

That screech must have caused this! he theorized. That was no known sound from the Sortilege I ever heard before! It must be a new rune, one the dragons held back from us! And I found it! Not the Council! Not any of the Twelve Great Ones! The thought made the itch almost bearable—that is, until he conjectured that the vile morphogenesis was going to consume his body, turning his flesh into some sort of scaly hide, something lizardly, like a newborn dragon hide, though they were born brown or green and never, as far as anyone knew, purple.

And there would be months of itching . . . agonizing months.

"I passed all the tests!" he fumed indignantly to the horse, his dark eyes glowing. "I was at the top of my class! It's not fair!"

Suddenly a thought struck him and he felt giddy. He laughed feyly, dizzily, roaring at the night's tapestry of light and void. "Oh, what the blorg does it matter? Once I've found the Bell, nothing will matter!" he said out loud. Clasping his hands together in rapture, holding them clamped until they hurt, he tried to force the itch from his mind, but it did not abate. Instead, it elbowed into his delirium, turning the ecstatic smile on his face to a contorted grimace of soul-scalding agony.

The itch!

There was one thing he knew worked. Hastily he unpacked his brazier from the saddle, setting it up on an outcropping on the Wolds, inflaming the coals with a shrieked rune cry that made the horse panic in terrified fright.

"A king's destrier, are you?" he said, sneering at the horse. "But you shrink from real power, don't you? Craven plow puller! I shall be rid of you at the next stable!"

He turned away. Reverently he lifted the sachet on the chain around his neck up into his hands, fondling it. He removed a pinch of dust, carefully lowering the pouch back down the front of his robe, and dropped the glittery flakes onto the fire.

*Fwomph!*

"Ahh . . ."

A flare of brimstone smoke and yellow hellfire crashed over him like a tidal wave, flooding him with energy, taming the pain in his side.

Yes . . . yes . . . yes!

A feeling of invincibility, of great penetrating insight, overcame him, and he bathed in the brazier's eerie glow. Smiling at his earlier fears of failure, he saw the world now as something beneath him, a smudge of moss-infected dirt, misbegotten, unworthy.

World Shaker! World Breaker!

The night sky beckoned, and he stared joyously at it, exhilarated, elevated. He danced alone in the moonlight, swirling his orange robe about him like a Korian skipdancer, shouting the glyphs of the Sortilege one after another like a child reciting the alphabet, waving his arms in a phantasmal fugue.

"My name will echo through all the stars for all eternity, just as Drachshiska promised! World Shaker! World Breaker!" He saw her golden wings soaring in the heavens, soaring, soaring to a world his own to rule, just as the dragoness promised. . . .

He breathed deep again, exhaled, and glanced furtively about him. *I need a diversion to gain some time, something to throw them off the track.* . . .

\* \* \* \* \*

Morning: cadmium comets, the first shafts of the new dawn, blazed through the gauzy darkness and set the high clouds above the royal city afire with their prismatic heraldry. The dry stillness of the air augured a hot afternoon, as if a potter had left the door to his kiln open overnight, baking away the morning's coolness. The city stirred sluggishly, rubbed its eyes, and groaned in protest at the thought of rising to face such a sweatmaker.

Not everyone could bury himself back into the bedding. On the tree-bracketed green in the East End, three men toiled purposefully in the shadows, critiqued by bister furballs bounding noisily above, who were none too happy about having their rest disturbed.

Like them, Captain Trebor Blackburn was in a bad mood. "Fly fecula!" he mumbled. "Would midmorn have been so bad?"

Grumbling, bleary-eyed, the loremaster walked from the lodge with his saddle sacks and spied Yor sharpening his rapier on a whetstone. It had been the Bret dandy who had shaken him awake an hour ago; the sight of Yor's gold-trimmed shirt flashing in the dawn reminded Trebor of how it had blared in his face when he first opened his eyes and found Yor rattling his cage.

And again fifteen minutes later.

And yet again another five minutes later, with the last arousal including a shout right into Trebor's ear that went something like "Beware the rack monster, O mighty snorer!" followed by splashed water and yanked pillows.

*I can't stand people who are cheerful in the morning.* . . .

Yor watched Trebor mumbling to himself and laughed quietly. Returning the whetstone to its pouch, the Bret cavalryman hoisted his rapier and eyed its shaft; satisfied, he thrust it back into its scabbard. Adjusting the sword's sheath on its leather baldric until it was comfortable over his black shirt and the chain mail below, he tied his sabretache to it, then looked to the yawning Bretilyan man-mountain.

"Got everything?"

Trebor gurgled and stopped, unhearing, or rather hearing but not absorbing. "What did you say?"

"I said, 'Have you got everything?' "

"Ah, well, that's not an easy question," the loremaster said. Loading the back of his mount with bags, he tightened his horse's tack as he talked. "Just where are we going? How long will we be gone? What perils await us? And—"

"Are you absolutely, positively certain," Yor dared, "that you have an entirely adequate supply of paper, writing implements, and books? Especially books?"

"If he doesn't," Dword said as he joined them, "he can always sneak into an archive along the way and grab a few more—like that time in Caswellsex!"

"Right!" Yor agreed heartily. "What's one more livid librarian anyhow? After the first dozen, they all start to look alike!"

"Not so fast!" Dword protested to Yor with hand held high. "You didn't have to fend off that last one! Woden's rut! Could that little bookworm kick! My shins were bruised for a—"

"That," Trebor stuffily informed them, "was neither a fully-certified League stackmaster nor an insect tome-eater; he was, in point of fact, a rather supercilious old geezer known as the Bibliophile of Logomachy, and he—"

Their chuckles made Trebor cease. Harrumphing, the broad-shouldered man-mountain decided they merited no further explanation of the incident and resumed stowing his gear on his horse with characteristic attention to detail, slowed even further by the uncivilized earliness of the hour and the snickering of his friends.

Yor wasn't quite through, however. Sinisterly smooth, quiet as a grey mouser, the cavalryman sneaked up behind the loremaster and said in the voice of conscience, "I've heard that the League's put a price on your head. . . ."

"Not his head," wagged the red-beard swiftly, "just his hands!"

Trebor grimaced. The only thing worse than one cheerful person in the morning was two of them! Stolidly the loremaster finished packing for the quest, lashing the last pouch to the saddle rings, ignoring the amusement of his two companions.

Satisfied all was safely secure, he began putting on his armor, and the activity brought him awake. Bending, he buckled on his chausses, twisting each of the leggings until it felt right, tight on his feet and loose at his knees. He then put on his grey hauberk, tying the chain longshirt's sleeves at the wrist, not too tight, but snug enough so the day's ride wouldn't chafe. Over the hauberk he pressed his steel cuirass, a relic from his days in the War of the Six Saints. It bore the oak heraldic insignia of Croswall, the province on Bretilya's southern coast where he was born. Finally Trebor slipped a plain beige surcoat over his head and belted it with a thick horsehide strap.

"A trifle hot for all that, isn't it?" Yor questioned.

"Better hot," the loremaster replied flatly, "than deathly cold." Across his back, he attached his famed sword, a massive metal virgule that made him impossibly seem even more formidable. The sword hilt was inscribed with the emblem of the Overtoad, from whom he had wrested it in combat. On his right hip, Trebor stuck his seldom-used main gauche, and next to it, a small hand axe. Last, he burrowed his flintlock, the mate to Yor's—the matched set had been given them by the grateful Poohbah of Fusistan—into his belt, snugging it between two belt pouches.

Almost ready . . .

Placing a helm over his dust brown hair, Captain Trebor
Blackburn, hero of the raving of Castle Hod by the storm
wraiths, survivor of the carnage at the Battle of the Crater,
tied his bag of lorecraft by its braided drawstring to his belt.

Wizards beware!

"All set—but you aren't, soldier," Trebor asserted as he
eyed the cavalryman with an exaggerated squint, mimicking
a parade inspection, for which he was feared far and wide.
"Your right epaulet is unbuttoned. Give me ten."

"Don't have an epauletic fit," Yor rejoined, nailed by the
remark. He reached up and did the button.

Both Brets then turned expectantly to the Norlander.

"Just about . . ." the red-beard said defensively.

"Last again!" the chorus chimed.

Reddened, silent, the barbarian led his sorrel up beside
Yor's grey and Trebor's bay. One by one, he placed his packs
on his steed and tugged to satisfy himself that all was secure.
This done, he reached into his trousers and pulled out a coiled
argent armband. As he slid it up his bare, bristling left
biceps, it gleamed in the dawn's incipient rays.

"Can't you use coins like everybody else?" Yor begged.

"Nobody's complained yet."

Yor grinned and shook his head in amusement. Dword followed—when it suited his purpose—the customary Norlandic
approach to the bothersome concept of money. The barbarian
would take his poniard and cut off an exact length of the
notched silver snake—usually with the coil still around his
arm! Merchants were loath to argue with him, perhaps because
the idea of actually paying foreigners for anything was still such
a relatively novel notion for the raiders from the north.

Dword pushed his hands into his mail gauntlets, flexing
his fingers. He checked the hang of his screamsax, a barbarian
sword that was a full forearm shorter than the loremaster's
awesome broadsword, but wider by half.

Just one more thing . . .

He put on his brigandine, pulling hard on the sleeveless
jacket and making the metal-studded leather creak as he
stretched it to latch the stays.

"Ready!" he cried magnanimously.

"Pipes?" Trebor huffed.

"Of course!"

"Tobacco? Flints?" Trebor continued.

"Here," the red-beard replied, patting his belt pouch.

"Flute?" Yor demanded.

"You don't think I'd leave without it, do you?"

"No."

But as Yor relaxed, Trebor leaned forward to inspect at nose
length the most minuscule mote on Dword's chest.

"What?" the Norlander trembled.

"Helmet?"

Well . . . no. The Norlander sighed, wheeled, and tramped
back to the lodge, mumbling in his mother tongue.

Yor noted, "He hates wearing it."

"It saved his life in Wormawk," Trebor said.

A moment later, the red-bearded freebooter returned. Under
his arm was a short, pointed, dented helm. On its forehead,
emblazoned in cloisonné, was a diving sea hawk, talons
extended, wings spread in the same shape as the island continent of Norlandia. With pomp and circumstance, Dword lowered the helmet and turned it until the nose guard was centered.

"I *hate* wearing this thing."

"It keeps your nose from getting sunburned," Yor said,
"but you could use a new one at that. Maybe you should get
one of those horned ones that your ancestors used to wear."

Dword made a rude noise. "We never wore those into battle! Can you imagine what would happen if someone hooked a
halberd on one of the horns? He'd rip your whole head off!
We only wore those at religious ceremonies. Or," he added
devilishly, "just to scare the Bretilyan peasants. You people

are so easily intimidated, and there was no real risk of serious combat."

The two Brets snorted back unsociably; Dword turned his back on them and did a quick double-check of his tobacco stash.

"Well," Trebor drawled, "Yor may be right. You've had that one a long time now, and the dent is rusted."

"I got it that time in Wormawk," Dword said sheepishly.

"Why don't you buy one of those fancy ones? You know, the kind Yor was looking at last week."

"Humping hoarmaidens!" wailed the Norlander in horror, whipping about to eye the black-clad dandy as if he had the festering plague. "Not one of those with the roc feathers in them!"

Two loud chortles.

Reddening, Yor sniffed. The truth was he didn't wear armored headgear at all. Most horsemen found them more of a bane than a boon, something that had to fit perfectly or a steed's bouncing would leave you brainless. Instead, he favored a fashionable gold-hued plaid tam, a subtle hat that matched his embroidered blouse. Of course, a glory plume was traditional for the members of the Fairfax Light, Yor's unit in the war, but good roc feathers were hard to come by. He had given his last one to a lady spy from Munflenchia. Grinning as he remembered the episode, he asked, "Shall we go?"

"Forsooth!" Trebor replied merrily. "Avaunt we posthaste!"

Dword beamed ear to ear and sucked in a deep breath.

Aghast, the two Brets cried, "Don't!"

A wild, rebellious, randy howl pierced the morning quietude of the East End, a yell that was the traditional companion of the Norlandic doomhorns of yore. The entire neighborhood sat up sharply in bed, mortified; women pulled covers up over themselves; men gulped and fumbled for weapons they didn't have; dogs barked; birds took wing; the bister furballs kicked tree pieces down at the trio.

"Do you *always* have to do that?" scowled Trebor.

"It brings good luck to begin a new adventure this way!"

"What it brings," Yor said with a smirk, "is angry neighbors! *Now* can we leave?"

"But of course."

None too soon were they mounted. All around them, windows were flung open and fists were being shook, accompanied by terse jeers.

"Let's hope it's a long trip," Yor sighed.

Like hounds to the hunt, the trio took off. They rode west through the green and lunged out of the East End into the cramped, winding avenues of the royal city. The roads thickened with the day's ventures. Bakers' carts piled with oven-tempered bread blocked the way, filling the morning air with mouth-watering aromas; fishermen returned from the Severwye with barrels of finny fare; cobblers and wainwrights opened their doors; cutlers and blacksmiths; coopers and candlemakers. The city hummed and whirred and plunked. . . .

Off again! Yor reveled silently, eyes absorbing the city sights. The feel of a horse gliding below me! The smell of oil on burnished steel! The sound of leather straining and spurs jangling! The blast of wind in the face! Gods, I love it!

Within minutes, they arrived at the Cross. There were two ways into Castle Atalanta, the thronestone of the Bretilyan monarch: an impregnable gate set into the steep western ravine, or a bridge at the foot of the fortress's promontory. The bridge was closer, so they made straightway for it, cantering through the streets with a stirring sense of urgency.

Before the sun reached the rooftops, they went up a ridge that ran like an inverted keel through the royal city. The Severwye unfurled in the daylight below them. A light, phantomy fog had risen off the river; it hung suspended in the treetops, giving the castle on its distant hillock the illusion of floating like a proud, regal raptor hovering over the city and the morning mists.

Under this shelf of white was the bridge. A tower stood on each side of the Severwye; each had a stout, metal-plated door facing the landward side and a drawbridge over the water. At midriver was a third tower, with two drawbridges of its own, each able to open a gap in the bridge, isolating itself in the dread event that either side of the river fell to foes. But in peace, only the last stretch was raised, and then only at night.

The trio rode across the bridge over the Severwye, the clopping of hooves on the wooden planks echoing off the grey stone ahead.

"Ho the gate!" Yor cried out.

The tower commander peered down from the battlements. His face lit up cheerily when he saw the trio. "Ah, Captains! We've been expecting you!"

"Has there been any news about Bosamp?" Yor yelled up.

"No, not yet," the commander replied. "Patrols were sent out last night and again this morning, but there's been no news." The commander's voice grew heated as he remembered the previous day's events. "I was here when he came through yesterday. He told me that the castle was on fire—we could see the smoke from here—and that he was on his way to get the Guild firewarden. It all seemed natural enough at the time. Then he ordered my men to form a bucket brigade up to the castle, which we did at once. When the wind shifted, that foul stench hit us. . . ."

The commander stopped, too angry to continue.

"By which road did he leave?" Trebor asked.

Pointing along the river's course, the commander stretched his arm northward. "He rode that way, on the river road, toward the Wolds. It didn't occur to me then, but the Guild's to the east, isn't it?"

"Yes," Trebor said. "About half a league."

Yor nodded and looked up to the tower again. "It seems likely that we'll be coming back this way shortly, within an hour or so. Can you arrange for some fodder for our horses?"

The commander nodded. "Of course, Captain. Oh, by the way, the king sent a messenger down here this morning. King Derek wants to see all of you before you leave the castle. Something about a favor he wants you to do."

A favor? The three men glanced fearfully at each other. What could be so awful that he couldn't order them to do it?

Guiding their horses through the tower, the trio passed through the outer walls of the royal fortress and into the lower bailey of the two-tiered battlement.

"North?" the Norlander mused, looking down the river toward the unseen Wolds in the distance. "Why would Bosamp head north? You'd think he'd try to get out of Bretilya as quickly as possible. Toward Munflenchia. Or even the Guild keep at Thorl. For sanctuary."

"Both of those make more sense than north," Trebor agreed. "Maybe we'll find the answer in his tower, though I sorely wish that purblind Royal Sagemaster hadn't burned the scroll! There must have been a clue in it!" he snorted. That there was no love lost between the titular head of the Bretilyan League of Loremasters and Trebor was hardly news. It seemed their every opinion was at odds.

"Bell?" Yor said pointedly.

"It doesn't ring a—" The man-mountain stopped, feeling silly, and failed to complete the metaphor. "I mean, it could mean almost anything. Or, more likely, nothing."

As they rode away from the Severwye's banks, the ground sloped sharply upward, through grainfields and fruit orchards, finally leveling off on top of the promontory's sheer bluffs. They followed the road up to the inner stronghold, to the castle proper. Here the roads parted; north led toward the main keep and castle ramparts, west toward the outer annex area.

"We should search Bosamp's tower before we see the king," Yor said. "We may find something to tell him."

"Bosamp's tower will be on the west side," Trebor explained, "on the skullrock that the spellcasters prefer."

They turned away from the main keep and rode through the west gate. Then, a few minutes later, they passed through a low tunnel, coming at last into the upper bailey annex area. As they emerged into the morning glare, a slim cylinder brooded on their left, as smooth and lustrous as polished azure crystal. Rising high above the castle walls, it was of surpassing beauty, wondrous, mysteriously elegant, a sleek and terrible ceramic rod probing high into the blue Bretilyan sky.

Yor's flesh tingled. There's power there, he thought. Real power! This may not be so easy. . . .

"No," the loremaster said, following Yor's thoughts. "That is—was—Wendy's tower." Trebor bobbed his head to the right, where stood a ramshackle wooden structure with a parapet—well, more like a two-story shack with a balcony. Nearly obscured by the castle gardens, the tower had a crumbling facade blackened with soot. The timbers were beveled improperly, the boards were warped and getting worse, and there was a noticeable lurch to the right.

Cheap material, shoddy workmanship.

"*That*," the loremaster said with arm extended, "is Bosamp's tower."

"That hovel?" Yor wondered absentmindedly. "I thought Bosamp moved into Wendy's tower when he came here."

"He didn't dare," breezed the loremaster. "Remember, Wendom, god rest his cranky bones, was one of the Circle of Seven Sevens, in Glyndwr's ring, Glyndwr being the link to the Council of Seven, of course. Now, as the new court wizard, Bosamp could use any of Wendy's stuff he wanted to—by law, it belongs to the realm—but he couldn't live in Wendy's tower."

"You lost me."

"Then allow me to review," Trebor said, seizing center stage.

Oh, gods! Yor thought. What have I done?

"As you may recall, the Circle of Seven Sevens is, mayhap, a misnomer of sorts," Trebor began like a patient professor in a lecture hall full of students for whom he cares not a whit whether they pass, fail, or even stay awake. "At any given time, there may actually be forty-nine members of the Circle. In practice, the number fluctuates higher or lower depending on the vagaries of birth, war, fate, the rancorous state of Guild politics, and the survival rate of new spell research, which is, as you know, the primary prerequisite for admission to the Circle, a hair-whitening, life-shortening requirement."

"Yes, it all comes back to me now," Yor said hurriedly. "I don't believe—"

"Bosamp is a beginner," Trebor explained. "A jackleg apprentice, albeit a promising one, out on his first assignment. The Guild protocol is very specific as to just exactly how high its members can erect a tower, depending on their stature in the Guild. If Bosamp had been brazen enough to live in a tower a single cubit higher than deemed appropriate in *The Wizard's Companion*, their official handbook—I believe the blue cover is the most recent edition—he would be subject to censure, or worse, all the sorcerati above his rank might take offense and blast his belfry to bat guano!"

"Thorogod's thunderbuns!" the Norlander remarked. Unlike Yor, he rather liked Trebor's lectures, possibly because he was more than a bit of a storyteller himself. "They sure take little things like that seriously, don't they?"

"You betcha."

Wary, the red-beard inspected the dilapidated tower with a jaundiced eye. "Is it safe? It doesn't look too sturdy to me. I think I'd be more worried about getting out of it than into it! It'd be a shame if the final stanza of the 'Ballad of Count Yor' was—"

Oops!

Quickly Dword shut his mouth and stared with total absorption at Bosamp's domicile, whistling a telltale ditty, then balked at his compounded *faux pas*.

Yor's eyes bored holes in the Norlander's back. "Count" Yor

indeed, you prevaricating songslinger! Insults leaped like eager volunteers into his mind, jostling for position, each a sharp barb ready to hurl itself at the barbarian, but before Yor could choose one among such a fine mob of enthusiastic javelins . . .

"Bosamp's just starting out," Trebor hastened, trying to divert the subject. "He hasn't had many fees yet; he can't afford anything better!" An odd feeling oozed through the loremaster as he realized that he was taking up for a magician! "Anyhow, no matter what it looks like, it could be dangerous. Those door runes . . . I'd better have a closer look at them. . . ."

The Bretilyan man-mountain slid from his saddle and noted a dusting of ash and the lingering, nose-wincing aroma of the previous day's debacle. *Blech!* It'll be weeks before they can get the smell out of everything, he thought. When we catch him, we'll make the blackguard clean it all up.

Trebor walked to the tower and reached in the right pocket of his tunic and retrieved a small, well-kept pamphlet. Pacing cautiously, he checked the poorly carved glyphs on the gaudy veneer against those depicted in the pamphlet.

"Well?" Yor said nervously.

Trebor peered intently at the door, then at the pamphlet, thumbing through the illustrations, trying to match the marks against those shown in Morrison's *Doors of DOOM!* [sic], flipping through the compendium of known door curses. Some mavens of lore, of course, preferred the more chatty *Portals of Peril* or Eric the Loud's beautifully scribed *More Than a Bad Feeling*, but neither, Trebor averred, was as authoritative as *Doors* was.

He stopped, frowning, and prepared for the worst.

"It's not in here."

"Wonderful!" Yor ballyhooed, still irked by Dword's gaffed reference to the song that had caused the cavalryman endless grief and embarrassment. "An unlisted curse! Methinks you can get your name in *PLY* again—if we live, of course."

Trebor looked back with a stubborn jaw. He was proud of

his contributions to *Popular Lore Yearbook*. Gritting his teeth, he said slowly, "Most likely it's some old adage or wizardly greeting—maybe just 'gone wenching,' for all I know! Not all runes are magical; in fact, most are just part of the Guild's secret language, a thinly veiled attempt to keep common folk from realizing just how easy spellcasting is, if you have the innate ability! Not nearly as difficult as healcraft, for example, or even holycraft—"

"Or even, say, lorecraft," Yor drawled.

Trebor stiffened his lip and pressed on. "In any event, the runes are not among the known door wardings."

Dword shook his head in dissatisfaction, not comforted, not at all. He dismounted, as did Yor, and stomped up beside the loremaster, peering and scowling. "As I recall," he chided Trebor, "neither were the runes on the portal to the Cavern of the Invisigoths!"

"Surely you can't hold that one against me!"

"You aren't the one who had the invisible . . . ah, member!"

Trebor deflated. What do they expect from me? he thought silently. Wizards keep making up new spells all the time! It's darned hard to keep current! Book knows, I try!

Ingrates . . .

He stuffed the pamphlet back in his tunic and faced the red-beard. "Well, it was only for a fortnight, wasn't it? A minor inconvenience."

"Tell that to *your* lady friends! This time you go first!"

The loremaster smiled graciously. "But of course! It is, after all, my turn." Trebor's blade rasped gleefully from its scabbard; behind it came the yelp of a loosed rapier and the squeal of an impatient screamsax.

Iron wands, iron nerves.

They walked to the door. The loremaster held his two-handed broadsword waist high; the Overtoad's filigreed blade waxed gleefully in the sunlight. Like a divining rod, Trebor's weapon pushed at the door. . . .

The auspice of iron.

*Snick! Cropple! Pap!*

Puffs of blue smoke erupted at the metallic touch; the magician's runes crawled to malevolent life, writhing like serpents over hot rocks. One by one, the sinuous glyphs whined and hissed in hair-straightening ire as they sought to escape the cold pain of Trebor's ferric prod.

*Krizz! Rispee!*

At the sound of sorcery, Dword and Yor whirled and stood with their backs toward the loremaster, forming a tritusked creature, ready for action.

"Zounds!" Trebor cried. "I didn't expect that!"

"No! Of course you didn't!" Dword brayed.

Caged to the plane of the door, the animated runes writhed and regrouped, forming into a new glyph; then they sizzled into the wood and left a new symbol.

Pregnant pause.

"Trebor?"

"Nice effect, I'll say that. Transmuted into a completely different glyph. It'll keep most tax assessors out."

"But what is it?"

"Looks familiar . . . I could check the book, but—"

The loremaster pulled up short. The sickly sweet scent of sulfurous clover wafted about them, more powerful than the residual stench of the firewand. The new smell shocked the sinuses, as if some blinkard had left a vent into the surreal world open.

"You know," Trebor said, his interest keening, "I bet this spell works like a lock tumbler. If the wrong combination is entered, then a safety catch operates and a trap is sprung, you know, like poisonous snakes or spring-loaded blades." He thought about it and was satisfied that he had solved the puzzle. Brightening, he added, "Yeah, that makes sense. The glyph has re-formed into a new spell, with some sort of safeguard now in operation."

"We're delighted to hear it!" Yor said.

Almost on cue, a voice thundered nastily, "I am the fiend Furbelow, master of the truly awesome Flail of Flesh Acid. I serve the mighty Bosamp—all hail my great and powerful master! We dance in the pits at the merest mention of his name! Fall to thy knees, verminous interlopers, and sing ye long and loud mighty praises to my omnipotent Lord Bosamp posthaste, or know hence the true nature of your feeble mortality!"

They looked to the door. Then north. South. East. West.

Then the door again.

On a hunch, Yor looked up, but no swooping death hung over them. Quickly he inventoried himself and his two companions on the outside possibility that one of them had been ensorcelled.

Nothing.

"Come again?" Yor said politely.

"Ah, precisely so, O punious, soft-shelled, inflammable ones!" boomed the unseen voice. "The prodigious Bosamp—huzzah!—is not here at the moment! Leave your piteous entreatments in duplicate, and then go away, whilst youst stillst clingst to yourst wretched essencesths!"

"Umm . . . where are you?" Yor said with a taint of doubt.

"Behind the door, O tiresome, hard-of-hearing one!"

"*Behind* the door?" Yor scoffed, his eyebrows askance. "Umm, shouldn't you, ah, be in front of it, O ferocious Furburger?"

"Completely unnecessary! And the name is Furbelow, whimpering whelp! Be grateful that my benevolent master Bosamp—oh, happy day!—has seen fit in his infinite wisdom to spare you the certain death that would result from the merest glimpse of my too-appalling visage! Total horripilation! Forests wither! Stones weep! The nightmares you would have! A thousand years must you give thanks to the exalted Bosamp—callooh, callay!—for his self-sacrificing mercy!"

"Okay. Right you are: behind the door," Yor said. "Trebor?"

The man-mountain pondered it, lowering his sword, his eyes never veering from the door. "Well, it's a trifle unorthodox—and bad form, if you want my opinion—but basically, I guess I don't have a problem with it. If the intent is to bar our entrance, as seems likely, then it hardly matters which side of the door it's on. Though it is out of the ordinary."

Yor remained unconvinced. "Come out here and fight like a man!" he challenged.

"Non sequitur! My patience grows thin! Your suffering will be manifold, doubter! Persist not in this foolhardy denigration, and make swift supplication to the awesome Bosamp!"

Impulsively the black-clad adventurer reached past the loremaster and tried the door latch, tugging stiffly.

Ugh. Not a chance!

"Let me try it." Trebor gestured for Yor to back away, which the cavalryman did. The loremaster stuck his broadsword forward and leaned the whole weight of his titanic body behind it, increasing the pressure rapidly until his face went purple from the exertion.

Force: enough to dislodge a stubborn blobolink from its power spot; enough to make stone whine.

The door budged not a whit.

Trebor frowned, vexed. "Could be spell-locked. Even Bosamp can manage that. And perhaps some razzle-dazzle like the voice to go with it."

"Maybe it's just plain locked," Dword offered. "You haven't even tried to pick it yet."

The loremaster stared at him incredulously, then swiftly glanced at the door in panic, only to have his confidence restored.

No lock.

"Or maybe not," Dword recanted hastily.

"Poltroons!" the voice behind the door rejoined. "You have sealed your dooms! At this very moment, I am entering your names onto the List of the Eternally Afflicted! Lucky for you I have the most exacting penmanship, so should you choose to turn and run away even now, despite the aspersions cast on mighty Bosamp, you might just barely escape deaths of unimaginable, drawn-out agony! Flee now or pay later!"

"Shoulder down and full speed ahead?" Yor proposed.

"Suits me." Dword shrugged, then looked right and left. Possessing a substantial skill in woodworking himself, the Norlander was appalled at the lack of effort and talent that went into the construction of Bosamp's hut. "I wouldn't be surprised if the whole thing fell over."

"Jambnation!" Trebor quipped.

Surging forward, the three men lowered their shoulders collectively, forming a fearsome battering ram of breathtaking fury, and charged willy-nilly.

*Whomp!*

The walls of the wizard's abode trembled spasmodically, shaken to their feeble foundations, rattling precariously. The entire building quivered and swayed; the rafters groaned; the building resonated with an ear-splitting screech.

The door, however, remained entirely unmoved.

The trio, on the other hand, slid and slumped to the ground. As the pile of muscle untangled, sitting on the ground and expelling their breath in frustration, they looked at each other contritely, nursing bruised shoulders and bent backs.

"So much for the subtle approach," Trebor noted.

"Do you think it moved?" Dword volunteered.

"No!" the two Brets replied.

"Not even a little? I think it did."

"Cretins! Your doom comes! As soon as I finish the painstaking details of your present addresses, birth dates, next of kin, religious preferences . . . be astounded at your continued existence! Would that my master, mighty Bosamp, were not so scrupulously forthright about the scrollwork! Even now my flail moans for the taste of your meat! I—"

"Look!" Dword exclaimed. Staring at what would have been knee height if the trio had been standing, he pointed at a small hole in the door. "What's that? A peephole?"

A bright yellow orb darted away from the hole.

"Aha! I saw it!" the red-beard announced. "It looked like a mophead with yellow eyes! That's no fiend. I don't know just what it is, but it's no fiend!"

"Ignore that creature! That is only . . . my pet! Yes, my pet, and deadly in its own right! So don't try any more of your tricks! That ludicrous assault made me laugh so hard—hardee-harharhar—that I completely forgot to strike you down! But I warn you, you'll only hurt yourselves severely if you try that again! Dislodged shoulders! Lifelong back pain—no laughing matter! So beware, defilers! Potent indeed is the thaumaturgy of the great Bosamp! Truckle you now before his palace—"

"Palace?"

"Truckle?"

"—or suffer further bone-busting mishaps!"

"Bosamp is getting farther away by the minute!" Yor muttered. "Enough of this folderol!" He struggled up to his feet, dusted himself off, and took a deep breath. Eyeing the tower quickly, he decided to reconnoiter and made a hand signal to the other two. They nodded.

Yor paced around the wooden structure. As the tower wasn't more than two rods in diameter, the Bret adventurer completed the circumnavigation in less than a minute. When he returned, Trebor and Dword were up and ready for whatever came next.

"Well?" Trebor asked. "Anything promising?"

"No windows and no other door. No other way in," Yor said, "or at least nothing visible . . . or is there?" He looked up, a grin spreading over his face. The balcony! Where there's a balcony, there's a way to get to it from inside!

The decision was made in a heartbeat. Wordlessly Yor walked to the wall and sprang, his mailed claws grabbing at the wood and catching on the molding between the first and second floor. He kicked his legs frantically, jackknifing, and scaled the ill-fitted planks, finding enough unplaned joints and protruding nails to grant him footholds. Perched on the flimsy cornice below the balcony, hanging shadow-silent, he considered his next move.

Now what, O punious one? he jeered at himself.

The earthbound duo conferred.

"You know," the red-beard noted, "that door is not properly hung."

"Neither, by all reports," Trebor irresistibly injected, "was Bosamp."

The barbarian squinched, wishing he'd thought of it first, then continued. "The hinges are on the outside—bad thinking! Not only that, but they've used nail diamonds to attach them, rather than screws as any craftsman knows they should. I'll bet we can pry the door hinges right off!" He looked expectantly at the loremaster. "I'm sure it moved."

"I doubt it," Trebor mused, "but I also doubt the spell, whatever it is, extends to the nails and hinges themselves—a flaw in its design. They are, after all, made of iron and should be immune to sorcerous mutation. It is—dare I say it?—ironic."

"I'm just going to have to steel myself to your remarks," Dword retaliated. He was already proceeding with the idea; his poniard was out and pointed toward the rune-infested door.

"Desist at once!" whined Furbelow. "My master will return very soon, and he will not be amused! Stop, I say, or I shall be forced to spread unsavory falsehoods about your personal habits! You'll never work in this town again!"

Picking up a handful of dirt, Trebor smeared it over the peephole; the yellow eyes darted back out of sight. He drew his main gauche, paused momentarily to admire the fine edges, and then surrendered to the notion that after the demeaning work ahead, several hours of sharpening penance would be required.

Dword popped out the first diamond-shaped nail from the hinge and went onward with enthusiasm. The idea of demolishing the building brought unexpected pride; something inside him warmed to the idea of removing the eyesore that was Bosamp's tower, and the barbarian considered finding a career in the challenging field of building inspection should their escapades lose their thrill.

"You'll be sorry!" the yellow-eyed thing warned. "I take no responsibility for the unspeakable fate that awaits you! I did my part, but you didn't heed me! It's not my fault! I warned you, but you didn't listen!"

"Oh, be quiet," Trebor said. "It's fight or flight time."

Meanwhile, Yor searched for a route to the roof. In an instant, he bounded upward and grabbed at the cornice. He caught himself with a firm handhold, but then his arms snapped taut, strained by the weight of his body and armor. His legs flopped unsupported, boots flailing at the smooth planks of the wooden walls, unable to get a foothold.

He paused to catch one breath, then shimmied sideways along the cornice until he came to the large knot in the timber he had spied from below. The knot was waist high as he hung; he released one arm, and with a bold rap of his fist, he knocked the knot inward, precariously hanging on a one-handed grip. He repeated the pounding, fatigue infecting his muscles.

The knot yielded.

Arms aching, he held tight to the cornice, bent, and pulled himself up until the toe of his boot stuck in the knothole. With this as a brace, he hurled himself higher, in a frantic effort to get to the railing above.

Got it!

The sweet taste of success was not to be savored, however. The railing creaked a ghostly creak, unable to bear his weight.

*Crack!*

Maniacally, a scared kitten raking for a hold, Yor scrabbled up and caught the edge of the roof where it slanted down past the balcony, his legs dangling into eternity. . . .

* * * * *

*Déjà vu*: Castle Fairfax.

He hung just below the bartizan, below the rim of the west parapet, having used his last peg and run out of rope. Far below, the Fairfax River rushed loudly over its rapids, calling for his blood. The river that was his childhood friend was now a cold, heartless executioner waiting for his head to hit the watery block. Sweat beaded on his forehead, leaked off his matted brown hair into his eyes. He gasped, holding on high above the rocky, watery death.

The Lady Katherine Lee, Mistress of the Fairfax.

The image of his former lover stabbed his eyes; her perfume teased his nostrils; her laugh assailed his ears. . . .

Rage and pain.

How can you hope to defeat her? he tormented himself. She has tricks inside of tricks! Secrets inside of lies reflected off mirrors! You're no match for her cunning, her guards, or her sorcery!

Flame, ice.

She took the talisman!

He hung on desperately, but part of him wanted just to die. He remembered the night on his sixteenth birthday when his father and his uncles had passed the talisman on to him. In a solemn ceremony, they told of those who had carried the talisman before him, following the instructions left by mysterious Kantar, Yor's great-great-great-grandfather, who had wrested the red dragon's eye from its owner. His vows echoed in his head as he placed the talisman about his neck and took responsibility as the sixth steward of Firefang's eye.

I've failed them all! he reproached himself. It would be so easy just to let go. . . .

Daring to look down, he gazed at the raging river, now illuminated stunningly by Leiblein's three risen moons, their iridescent moonbows shining in the watery spray from the boulders, an awesome vision of dangerous beauty embedded forever in his mind. The sound of the white water called him, a lullaby offering an end to the pain of failure. . . .

\* \* \* \* \*

Here and now, the railing collapsed in his grip with a ruinous crack that obliterated the flashback, if not its drift-wood emotions. Then, as now, Yor faced down his fear of falling; he summoned his inner resolve and held on, swinging sideways to gather momentum.

Only one way out: up!

*Snap!*

The shattering railing scraped him as it broke apart, exposed nails ripping at his flesh like a zirii's talons, trying to drag him down with it. He twisted at the waist in midroll and uncoiled both boots, kicking the toppling, grasping woodwork away from him as it cascaded by.

All or nothing!

He launched himself vertically. The shudder of the railing as it hit the ground coincided with his landing on the balcony. Rolling uncontrolled, he collided with the wall, balling himself up in a bruised wad.

Made it!

*Whomp!*

The pair of metal-enhanced shoulders blasted into the tower door, and the building vibrated like a twanged string.

"Ah!" Trebor pronounced. "Just as I suspected. The door cannot be opened per se—not in the usual sense of the word. Bosamp's used the Alekhine variation. The spell forces the door to remain upright and rigid, but it can be displaced horizontally—an obvious oversight!"

"Just as you suspected?" Dword ahemmed.

Above, Yor unraveled from his heap and reassembled himself, checking all the moving parts, shaking his head to clear it, then looking about the balcony.

A hatch!

He smiled in triumph and pounced on it. It's not over yet, Kathy! he thought now, as he had on that ill-fated day seven years ago. I'll find a way, somehow, someday, to regain what is rightfully mine! The cavalryman moved like an angry cat to the hatch and laughed. Not barred! Bosamp apparently never considered the possibility someone might try to get in this way!

It's just another second-story job. . . .

Bemused, Yor threw the hatch back vigorously and peered into the wizard's habitation. Light flowed into the room through the open hatch. Farther below, as he looked past the second floor to the ground, shafts of light escaped around the displaced doorjamb, illuminating the darkness. He stuck his head through the hatch and let his eyes adjust to the dimness.

A rope ladder!

*Whomp!*

The charging pair made the wizard's tower spasm and reel; Yor wobbled like a man on a tempest-tossed deck, grabbing the roof to steady himself in the swells as the blow struck by his two true friends dispersed from the sorcerously fortified door to the rest of the tower-hut. The First Law of Magic, Yor remembered, also known as the Conservation of Reality: Natural forces must go somewhere! Kathy said . . .

He reddened. You've taught me a thing or two, witch! But not necessarily what you meant to!

On the floor where the rope ladder ended, something moved with agitation through the dust-filtered light. "You're all in a lot of trouble now!" the mophead squeaked shrilly, eyestalks twitching back and forth.

Yor looked around quickly, then dropped down through the

hatch and caught his feet on a rung of the rope ladder. Descending viscerally, he stood on the second floor and drew his flintlock. His cobalt eyes darted about, his blood in full fever.

A bed . . . a desk . . . bookshelves . . . nothing obviously—

*Whomp!*

The tower rocked, almost throwing Yor off his feet. He bounced spryly toward a post and held on as things began to fall off shelves and the desk and roll around on the floor. "Once more into the breach, dear friends; once more!" he heard Dword shout encouragingly to Trebor. "It definitely moved that time!"

Yor started for the ladder, but his feet tripped over a spittoon, which he kicked inadvertently down the ladder well. It landed behind the door guardian. Alarmed, the mophead scurried under the rope ladder and tilted its eyestalks up at the cavalryman. "Eeek!" it wailed in panic. "They're here! Help me, Dalibosch! Save me!"

"You down there!" Yor shouted with a voice that froze the mophead. "Halt!"

*Whomp!*

The building trembled, shuddered; Yor was pitched to the side, dizzy, off-balance; the boards creaked ominously; and it seemed as if something crucial, something wooden, snapped irrevocably.

"That did it!" Dword shouted. "We can squeeze through there now!" The Norlander slipped into the gap between the still upright door and its frame.

"I'm done for!" the mophead moaned, wagging its red tail in timorous frenzy. "I surrender! I yield! I capitulate! I give up!"

"Hands, er, tail up!" Dword shouted, screamsax pointed at the yellow-eyed, red-tailed, bony-spined mophead. What the heck is that thing? he pondered. "And don't move!"

But just as the loremaster squeezed through the narrow opening to waltz up beside the barbarian, a scaled gold and green tail reared up through the floorboards, materializing through the wood and hovering in the lower chamber. It was as thick as a man's arm and just as pliant, but unjointed. On its end was a sharp, barbed tetrahedron that looked as if it could pierce armor as easily as a Xedic mace. The tail paused in a question mark.

"Dimension hole!" Trebor swore. "That blathering wretch of an imbefool Bosamp ran off and left a dimension hole open! That irresponsible, moss-brained spellslinger! Thank the lucky star it's only a small hole, or—"

"Furbelow!" a stentorian tenor vomited sulfurously. "How many times have I told you not to play in the real world?"

"Back!" Trebor roared unnecessarily, and the man-mountain flung himself with uncharacteristic speed beyond the range of the creature's tail. A fifth-rank surrealist, he wagered as he rolled to safety and got up on one knee. Or possibly an over-grown fourth with a—

"It's a dimen!" he warned loudly.

"Mortals!" boomed the surrealist from beyond the palette. "Unhand Furbelow, or I shall deal with you harshly!"

"It can't see us!" Yor shouted out intuitively. "And it can't get anything but its tail through the opening!"

"Seeing things as they really are is entirely unnecessary!" it barked back, tail darting.

Yikes!

As the tail swirled around in widening circles, Dword and Trebor retreated quickly, swords *en garde*, well aware that the touch of a stygian barb on the end of that prehensile lash meant disaster.

Slash! Dodge! Whap! Weave! Jab! Duck! *Riposte!*

The tail drove the twosome for cover, rising and diving until it finally reached its target. Wrapping roughly about the fear-frozen mophead, the tail pulled it through the still-open hole.

"No privileges for an eon!" boomed through the unseen pit.

"But it wasn't my fault!" whined Furbelow.

"We've got to close the dimension hole!" Trebor urged. Possessed of purpose, the loremaster rushed forward to where the cusp to the surreal world must be, though to the eye, the floor appeared unblemished, completely ordinary. Taking his broadsword, he probed, sizing up the unseeable outline of the cusp.

"We have unfinished business, O punious, soft-skinned, inflammable ones!" boomed through the floor. "The penalty for bullying Furbelow is death!"

" 'Bullying'!" scoffed Trebor vehemently. "I'd hardly—"

The dimen's tail shot out at the loremaster—"*Argh!*"—grazing his leggings, cutting them cleanly but not reaching the skin. The loremaster recoiled but was off balance.

Yor's flintlock roared, lead burrowing into the tail. The yelp of pain was gratifying if grating. Ice pink ichor spurted from the wound, forming frozen crystal flakes on contact with the air. The tail snapped in anguish and wavered, then lunged in blind fury. Dword leaped forward and grabbed it, pulling it back from the stumbling loremaster's chest. Struggling, the red-beard wrestled with the thrashing appendage, his hands firm about the base of the tetrahedron, the deadly barbs almost in his face.

"Hurry!" the Norlander howled. "Seal the hole!"

At once the loremaster recovered. Using his broadsword as a stylus, he began to etch in steady, smooth strokes a six-sided geometry around the spot he had probed. Hmmm . . . the size of the hole should be directly proportional to Bosamp's skill and should give us a figure of merit on how much he's learned burning the midnight oil! Now, what was the formula for this particular shape again?

"Hurry!"

Encumbered and taken by surprise, the serpentine tail was not happy; it struggled to wriggle free from the red-beard's grasp, but the barbarian's grip was resolute. Instantly the tail changed tactics. With raw strength, it rose from the floor, carrying Dword along effortlessly.

"Woden's trumpery!" the Norlander shrieked as he soared up, his head banging into the ceiling. The tail began to wag from side to side, pounding Dword into the floor.

Yor stowed his flintlock, and in one smooth blur, palmed his dagger and jumped off the rope ladder, flying, intercepting the tail in midwhip. He grappled it with a hug, adding his mass to the dynamic tail-and-barbarian metronome.

All three crashed to the floor with a numbing thud, Dword taking the worst of it as he ended up cushioning Yor's fall. Yor's dagger talon sank through the wound his pistol shot had made in the flesh.

A sound like the wail of a soul being wrenched from its marrow came from the tail's owner, and it writhed with convulsive pain.

"O punious, soft-fleshed one, *we*," Yor said savagely and paused for effect, "are the dimens in *this* world!" He twisted the dagger with malice, and his grip on the surrealist's flesh was nearly unbreakable.

Nearly. Thoroughly peeved now, the vengeful tail outmuscled both assailants and pummeled them back and forth and side to side in rapid, effortless, full-stroke swishes.

"Hump-(*bang!*)-ing (*bang!*) hoar-(*bang!*) hoar-(*bang!*)-maid-(*bang!*)-ens! (*Bang!*) Hur-(*bang!*)-ry, (*bang!*) Tre-(*bang!*)-bor!"

The loremaster stepped lively. Concentrating, he timed the upside-down pendulum's uneven, overloaded swings and crossed over to complete the six-sided floor etching.

"There! Hex all gone!" he proclaimed.

The tail vanished in the middle of the air; Dword and Yor fell free and landed on the hard wood.

"No problem," Trebor said blithely.

"None whatsoever . . ." Yor moaned.

"Woden's hairy . . . sphincter!" Dword gasped. "I'm glad Bosamp couldn't open a hole any bigger!"

Yor sat up, elbows on knees, panting. "What *was* that thing?"

"It was a dimen," the loremaster said.

"I know that!" Yor said. "The other thing!"

"Oh, that . . ." Trebor said. The vast catalogue of his mind opened, and he thumbed through for an answer. "It was a mophead with yellow eyes," he decided wisely.

Two stares.

"Well, that's a relief!" Yor said, spreading his arms wide like a black bird. "By the vaunted vagabond! For a moment, I was afraid it might have been a mophead with yellow eyes!"

"Or worse!" Dword added with equal sarcasm. "It might have even been a red-tailed mopthingie!"

"What's more important," Trebor countered, serenely confident as he sheathed his fabled sword, "is what it wasn't! Now, let's—"

"Wait a minute!" Yor said. "What was it that it wasn't?" Halting, he began to wonder if he had phrased that right.

"Dangerous!" Trebor responded glibly. "Now, shall we have a look around this drabbery?"

The loremaster found some candles and lit them, passing one along to each of them; they used those to light the others placed about the wizard's den. Slowly the dingy, musty chamber congealed into recognizable objects. The first floor had the appearance of a workshop: benches, tables, chairs, bottles, loose paper. There was no obvious project in progress. Mostly, things seemed to be piled up as if they had just been unloaded from cartons and no particular home had been assigned to them—scrolls and scroll cases strewn about haphazardly, beakers of unknown fluids now dried out, sealed glass jars with their labels peeling off and containing magicians-knew-what, shelves bloated with odd, arcane devices.

Dust, dust, and more dust.

"Do you think he ever cleaned any of this?" Yor asked rhetorically as he sidestepped something that looked like a threat to his boots.

"I'd say it's about typical," Trebor replied.

Fanning out, the trio poked among the claptrap with discriminating speed. They looked in the corners and trash piles, sifting through the refuse, scrutinizing the bizarre decor and the thaumaturgical paraphernalia.

*Creak!*

"What was that?" Trebor asked.

"Just house noises," Yor said. "People hear them all the time and think they have ghosts."

"Doesn't sound right to me," Dword said. His ears perked up quizzically, but there was no immediate repetition of the sound.

"Ah! Scrolls!" Trebor said suddenly. "Maybe there's a clue here." The loremaster plowed into the muddled morass of scrolls, his eyes agleam. One at a time, he unrolled them and scanned swiftly, like a pirate rummaging through a treasure chest, sorting the prizes from the baubles.

Gazing at the runes wasn't as dangerous as many believed, he told himself. While it was certainly true that occasionally a zealous warlock might spell-trap a scroll, this wasn't a common practice. Unlike gold or gems, parchment wasn't easy to ensorcell and often lost its magical imbuement through dissipation. A greater danger lay in releasing the spell itself. Not one in a hundred was born with the ability to summon the glyphs of power, and fewer still actually mastered them, yet more than one victim had discovered his unknown talent the hard way, by compulsively forming the soul-wrenching glyphs while casually perusing a scroll.

Chilling envy gripped the loremaster. For all he desired it, he knew that he lacked the birthright.

"Find anything?" Yor asked.

"No. Standard stuff. Guild meeting notes, mostly."

*Warrrrp!*

"Nothing here either," Dword said from across the room as

he once again heard an ominous house noise. Trying to quell the foreboding in his stomach, he looked in the bottles, opened and unopened.

"There's a desk and some bookcases upstairs," Yor said.

"Sounds good."

It took but seconds for the trio to ascend the rope ladder. As they looked around, the light from their candles cast the upper chamber in eerie shadows, giving the furnishings an inauspicious aura. Death masks of inhuman species hung behind Bosamp's desk; on another wall, an ancient map of Leiblein stared at them, frayed and faded; adjacent to the desk was a chart on the phases of Leiblein's three moons. The desk itself was small but of good quality and therefore seemed out of place. On it, a small orrery lay cocked, its planets loose on their wires. Five or six open books were stacked together, along with a pile of banded scrolls, crumpled parchments, writing tools, a gnawed greening sausage next to a lump of what was once must have been bread. . . .

"Not much for housekeeping, was he?" Dword sniffed, trying to forget the nauseating sight he had just seen.

"It looks like he left in a hurry," Yor said. "He didn't have time to gather up much."

Trebor nodded. "It appears that what happened yesterday was only partly planned. He must have assumed the king would be too awed by his pronouncement to do anything about his arrogant behavior. I'll bet he was really surprised when the guards came. He reacted without thinking, though it's clear he was about to leave anyway."

*Crrrreeeeeeeak!*

"Are you sure this place isn't haunted?" Dword asked.

"No," Trebor said.

" 'No' you're not sure, or 'no' it's not haunted."

"Whatever."

They spread out. Yor went to the bed. The hide of a large nondescript mammal covered the sorcerer's bed, over which hovered a gallery of nude sculptures and some posted pieces of illegible writing—poetry? Yor poked about the mattress, looked under the frame, and . . .

What was that? A flicker? The hair on Yor's neck ruffled in warning. He stood straight up and stretched his arm to hold the candle as far in front of him as he dared.

There! On the nightstand!

He leaned closer. The glittering increased sporadically, growing brighter, as the scintilla from some faint layer of silvery powder gave off tiny flares that danced hypnotically.

The smell of burnt honey, brimstone, and clover.

Yor forced himself to turn away, a feeling of dread punching him in the gut. "By the blessed bard!" he swore solemnly. "Trebor, is this what I think it is?"

"Where?" The loremaster stiffened at the sight of the shooting starlets. "Don't touch it!"

"Don't worry! I won't!"

Dword pivoted. Even from across the room, he could see the brilliant mini-lightning sparks. "Dragon dust!" The barbarian bard blanched. "Woden's wonders! Where did Bosamp get dragon dust? The stuff is as rare as it is dangerous!"

Yor shook his head in disbelief. "I wonder how long he's been using it."

"Once is too often," Trebor said righteously, "but wizards will do a lot of reprehensible things to enhance their power! This could explain a lot of things, such as his sudden change of—"

*Crack!*

The splintering of stanchions, though never before heard by any of the trio, was a sound they nevertheless immediately recognized. "Do you suppose," Dword began, sucking in a short breath and looking around quickly, "that three grown men—"

"In full armor!"

"—have ever stood up here before?"

*Wreeeeeeak!*

"Run for it!"

A stride ahead of Dword, Yor reached the rope ladder and started up, deciding in a split second that their best hope lay in getting out of—but more importantly, above—the imploding tower. Boards belched; dust and cobwebs jumped through the air; rafters rent. Even before he reached the balcony, the unforgiving shatter of strained timbers resounded in his ears, a crescendo of ligneous doom.

*Crack!*

The tower quavered, wobbled, fluttered, throbbed. Bursting through the hatch, Yor turned and clasped his arm to the Norlander's, helping him through the orifice.

There was no one behind Dword.

"Trebor!"

"I'm coming . . . aha!"

*Crack! Crack! Crack! Creeee . . .*

Pound, pound, pound, leap.

The tall Bret's head popped into view, but his feet slipped on the lurching ladder; Trebor grimaced as he held on, trying to find a place to lodge his big boots.

*. . . eeeeeak!*

The tower sighed, buckled, and rolled right, deflating like a house of cards.

*Kaboom!*

A thick billow of dirt rose in eulogy over the morass of pick-up-sticks. Coughs and groans. Yor crawled out from under the debris, shoving aside a plank. Several seconds later, he extracted himself from the wooden web and looked around.

"Dword? Trebor?"

The barbarian burrowed out next, his red beard soiled, a second dent in his helmet. "Alive . . . mostly."

An arm poked out, with a loremaster attached to it. Trebor emerged soon thereafter. "No problem . . ." he gasped.

"Last again!" Dword chimed.

Slowly three chagrined figures perched on one akimbo timber, discovering each other as the haze settled.

"I don't much like the way this is starting out," Dword said.

Yor grunted. "Now we'll have to dig our way through this woebegotten woodpile and try to find something that will tell us where Bosamp went! Another day lost! Filthy verbiage!"

"Perhaps not . . ."

They looked askance at Captain Trebor Blackburn, who, brushing an unkemptness out of his surcoat, produced a tome, likewise doffing the dust from it.

"I found this in Bosamp's desk. It was in a locked drawer, but . . ." The man-mountain grinned profusely and held the tome up close to his eyes, peering like a gemsmith appraising a mysterious stone. "Hmmm. *Savage People, Savage Tales*, subtitled *Legends of the Northmen as Translated by the Incomparable Ritardando Shirr and Edited by Sunny N. Shirr; First Printing* . . . fah!" Trebor critiqued, interrupting himself. "The man's a rumormonger . . . a whoremonger . . . a costermonger! I doubt seriously if there's a single syllable of truth in the entire volume!"

"Our legends?" Dword wondered nervously. "Why would Bosamp be interested in them?" Suddenly the barbarian quaked with misgivings, red on red.

Woden's wayward wastry! Not *the* Bell!

Trebor parted the book at Bosamp's mark, then uncreased the page with churlish disdain—not that the scurrilous Ritardando Shirr deserved better treatment, but a book, after all, was still sacred! "Amateurs . . ." he mumbled, smoothing down the sheet as he read it. "Ah, yes! 'The Tocsin of Terror'!" he announced.

"What's that?" Yor asked.

"Hmmm . . ." The loremaster scanned down the page hungrily; then his head bolted out of the text. He stared accusingly at the red-beard. "You people!" he bleated.

"What? What!" Yor implored.

Suavely the loremaster said to Dword, "It's your legend. You tell him!"

"But it's only folklore," the Norlander protested. "You know, the kind of stuff you use to keep the little ones in bed at night."

"What?" Yor insisted. "What!"

An apologetic smile waxed over Dword. Besieged, he settled in. Spying the wizard's door, still erect through the cataclysm, he leaned his back against it and prepared to tell the whole story, noting Trebor's cocked ears and watchful eyes perusing the book like a schoolmaster adjudging a pupil's recital.

"Well, as I recall—and it's been a few years since I've heard this particular myth," Dword began, with a heavy emphasis on the word *myth*, "one of the Skolgods—not the ones we worship today, like Woden, but the creation pantheon—anyway, one of them, D-Ray, I believe it was—"

"Zepolinirt," Trebor interrupted, forefinger to the text. "It says here 'Zepolinirt.' "

Dword's visage screwed up quizzically. "That can't be right. D-Ray, or perhaps it was Om . . ."

"I'm just reading what it says."

"Trebor, will you let him tell the story?" Yor said impatiently. "Follow along in your hymnal if you must, but let the man tell his story!"

Dword took the opening. "Well, anyhow, one of the Skolgods left this magical bell far to the north, at the top of the world. The legend says that if the Bell is rung three times true, then the world—all of it—will be destroyed."

"Destroyed?" Yor squinted, then looked at Trebor.

"Destroyed," the loremaster confirmed.

"But why?" Yor asked. "Is there some specific reason?"

The red-beard shrugged, nearly falling off the battered boards, then repeated the gesture in a more subdued motion.

"Who knows the ways of the gods? Besides, it's only a legend."

"That Ritardando Shirr sees fit to repeat it," Trebor concurred, "means there isn't the slightest chance of its being fact!"

"The Bell at the Top of the World?" Yor nagged. "The Tocsin of Terror? Bosamp has gone off to destroy the entire world?"

"More or less." Dword shrugged again.

"It's not quite that simple," Trebor elaborated. "It says here that only the Hammer of Zepolinirt can chime the Bell."

"You mean the Mallet of Doom," Dword corrected.

"No, that's not what's written here. Look!"

The Norlander looked. Appalled, he said, "That's not a very good translation. And it should be D-Ray. That's just not right. I don't—"

"The Mallet of Doom?" Yor interrupted and fell into his stage voice. "I prithee, kind sirs, what manner of thing is this?"

"Not to worry," Trebor replied. "Getting the Hammer is no easy quest. I quote: 'The humongous, horrific Hammer lies in a fiery caldron of burbling lava, a lascivious inferno that the lust-crazed, mead-soaked, vair-cloaked savages of Norlandia—' "

"Savages!"

" '—call Vangberg the Volatile, Vangberg the Vagarious, Vangberg the Vatacide, Vangberg the Venous, Vangberg the Verrucose, Vangberg the Verijuiced, Vangberg the—' "

"Argh!" cried Dword. "Mercy!" He reached desperately for the book, but Trebor had anticipated the red-beard's lunge and turned deftly just enough so that Dword overextended and fell forward off his perch.

"*Now* I remember Ritardando Shirr!" Yor raved. "The man opens his dictionary at random and copies every adjective he sees! He should be publicly flogged!"

"Worse!" Dword said as he resumed his seated position, accurately flicking a splinter from his brigandine directly across Trebor's nose as a warning shot. "He should be tied to a chair while I read his own book to him!"

"At the very least!"

" 'Alas,' " Trebor continued, ignoring the chattering and warming to the narration, " 'not even the erstwhile savages know how to'—"

"Savages!"

" '—to enter into the sulfurous bowels of the vociferous volcano wherein the fell Hammer lies secreted, awaiting Doomedsday, protected'—"

"Doomedsday?"

"Savages!"

" '—from theft by the dreaded fireflies'—"

"Fireflies?"

Even Trebor could not stomach reading further. "A vastly overwritten style," he said, evading the barbarian's suspicious glare.

Not at all happy about the look in the loremaster's eyes, and not at all sure just whose style he had heard, Dword stuck his hand out. "Let me see that!"

Trebor stuffed it inside his cuirass. "It's not a very good translation," he said blandly.

"So," Yor imposed, trying to forestall another round, "just where is this vaunted Vangberg?" He turned to the red-beard. "Norlandia, obviously, but that's a lot of ground."

"It's about a hundred leagues north of Hjarstad, on the edge of the Frozen Wastes," Dword said, one eye on the lore-master's beatific expression. "Nobody much goes there . . . a few hunters in the summer, maybe. It's a long ride over rugged terrain. . . . Savages!"

Cherubic smile. "I didn't write it," Trebor protested mildly. "Besides, it doesn't sound like Bosamp's going to be able to handle all this; he's only a novice, after all. Still, I don't recall that I've ever heard of anyone trying to do it."

The two Brets accosted the Norlander with stares.

"Well!" Dword answered indignantly. "None of us *savages* has ever tried it!"

"Woden's turpitude!" Yor gibed. "Well, at least we know now which way Bosamp went."

"North for certain," Trebor said. "Probably to Axiom to get a boat."

"That's at least a fortnight's ride," Yor pointed out. "We should overtake him long before then. And there's not a moment to waste. Up, me hearties! Let us eloign from here! Let there be much eloigning necessatudity!"

Dword and Trebor exchanged glances, but absolutely refused to ask. "We're not letting him go to any more of the blessed bard's plays," Dword suggested conspiratorially.

Ignoring their prattle, the cavalryman rose and clambered over the shattered structure. "Last one to Norlandia is a lust-crazed, mead-soaked, vair-cloaked savage!" He ran and jumped into the saddle, a showy move that his groin regretted almost at once.

"You forgot," Dword said.

"What?"

"We have to go see the king."

Oh, no! The favor!

# CHAPTER THREE

In the Great Hall of the castle sat King Derek, not on the Sapphire Throne of Bretilya, but in a nearby nook at an expansive, officious table, inundated with petitions, entreaties, appeals, and proclamations. On his right stood the Lord High Exchequer, a prim, bloodless stalk feeding documents by the handful to the beset monarch. Beside the exchequer toiled a squad of high and low clerks, checking and double-checking spelling, signatures, and dates, and then rolling up and dispensing documents as appropriate.

Boots reverberated in the hall; halberds crossed with a metallic clink barring the entry to the nook. Looking up, pardoned from the drudging necessities of rule, King Derek the Third, eleventh monarch of the sovereign realm of Bretilya, slowly smiled, his first of the day, and then stood up, for the first time in an hour. "Captains!" he cried, not waiting for a formal announcement, waving to the trio and motioning for the guards to part. "Don't stand on ceremony! Come in, lads!"

The trio approached and bowed.

"You wished to see us, Your Majesty?" Yor said.

The king nodded, hesitating as he reordered his thoughts. A bear of a man in his midfifties, Derek's brown-blond mane was now graced with silver strands. For twelve years he had ruled Bretilya, through war, jealous nobles, feuding factions, and the Famine Frost, and it showed in his eyes.

"Yes, Captains," he said. "There's a personal matter I need to discuss with you. But first, I understand you searched Bosamp's tower this morning."

"Ah," Yor said, grappling for just the right way to put it.

"Yes, but the tower has met with an unfortunate accident. It . . . fell down."

The monarch suppressed a laugh, settling for a subtle grin. "Well! I see! I can't say I'm sorry to see that sorehead's eyesore go! It's been a real blight on the castle grounds . . . not like old Wendy's spire." Wistfully Derek stopped to spend a moment remembering a cherished friend. Wendom and he had been together for many years, starting long before Derek became king. Wendom's passing had been more of a loss for Derek than anyone else, which made Bosamp's antics even the more unpalatable.

The king resumed. "Well, gentlemen, this is another fine service you have done us! Now we shall have ample firewood this winter. Isn't that right, my Lord Exchequer?"

"So it would seem, Your Highness."

What a boor! Yor thought of the cadaverous lord. How awful to be penned up with that dry-blooded fop all morning! Clearing the thought, Yor went on. "We managed to find some indication of where Bosamp has headed and what he intends to do. He rides north, for the coast; the port at Axiom would be our guess. And beyond that, it appears he's headed for Norlandia."

"Norlandia? Hmmm. I should have thought he might have headed for Munflenchia or for the Guild keep. . . ." The Bretilyan crown considered it for a moment, then turned to Dword. "Seeking refuge, perhaps?"

"Not exactly," the barbarian hedged, biting his tongue. "We wouldn't give it to him anyway. But the thing is, there's this, ah, legend, sort of. . . ."

"We'll catch him long before he gets to the coast," Trebor injected, cutting the red-beard off.

"Long before," Yor echoed.

Relief showed in the monarch's face. "Well, good! I'm glad to hear you say that! After all those pronouncements of doom yesterday and that horrible smoke—I don't think the smell will ever come out of the clothes I was wearing—"

"I've had them buried," the Lord High Exchequer broke in.

"—and we'd be just as well rid of Bosamp, too! But we can't have him terrifying the good citizens of the realm, can we?"

"No, my liege, we can't," Yor agreed. "We don't envision much trouble catching up with him, despite his lead."

"No!" the king agreed. "I didn't think you would! Not you three! My captains courageous! A dull chore for you this time, eh? Ah, well, they can't all be as much fun as the last one, I'm afraid!" Derek beamed at the trio with genuine affection. "What would I ever do without you all? The kingdom would never survive! And I was pretty sure you'd feel that this was an easy one! That makes what I'd like to ask you a little less worrisome! I'd like to ask a favor of you. . . ."

A lump came to Yor's throat. Here it comes! he girded. This must be worse than that time with the Demiurge of Birse at the Eisteddfod! I don't think I've ever seen so many wigs at once! To have Wendom cast an animation spell on them was the height of lunacy! It took us three days to get the last one out of the keep!

The wall of fearful, blank gazes daunted Derek with guilt. Rushing, he blurted it all out too quickly: "Wouldyouplease-takemysonwithyou?"

Yor flinched. "Prince Colin, Sire?"

Prince Colin, the heir apparent, was a skilled soldier and accomplished athlete in his early thirties. Blond and virile, he was a handsome man, aging well, and though somewhat of a rake and party hound, he never shirked when duty called. He had a presence of command and was able to take advice judiciously when he needed it. The realm rejoiced at its good fortune, for it was often said that if any man were able to fill King Derek's beloved shoes, it was his firstborn son.

The Lord High Exchequer stretched his thin lips forward in an expression of sanctimonious superiority.

Dotard! Yor berated himself. Send the heir apparent out on an errand like this? Are you daft?

"He means Prince Sean," Trebor said, covering Yor's embarrassment glibly. "A good choice for this enterprise, my liege. I'd welcome the opportunity to compare lore with him."

Slender and dark, like his mother, Prince Sean was as lean and swift as an arrow. But his renown was his great intellect. Versed in history, theology, and philosophy, he was a gifted planner, the king's principal counselor, but unlike many with great genius, he was affable and friendly, so that even the lowest felt at ease with him. As fit to rule as his older brother and completely lacking in the jealousy second sons of kings sometimes fell prey to, Sean was selflessly content to serve his older brother Colin, when the time came, in the same capacity as he now served his father. And Sean had once voiced an interest in riding with the trio on one of their escapades.

The Lord High Exchequer sniggered uncontrollably, rending his red and black plaid doublet. Worse, his twin rows of clerks echoed his assessment of Trebor's surmise.

Derek winced awkwardly, fumbling for words. "No . . . not Sean. His wife is due any day now."

Trebor whitened. Stupid! You knew that! Prince Sean, indeed! Not with Princess Debra heavy with child! He'd never leave her for this trivial pursuit!

There were two choices left. Grabbing at the longer straw, Dword tugged, fearing what he was now certain must be the dreadful truth. "Cedric?" he pleaded.

The third son, in his late twenties and the same age as Yor, Prince Cedric was a bull, a slab of sinew without guile or tact. A natural huntsman given to cups, dice, and carousing, he was valorous to a flaw, a brawler and a braggart. That he envied his two older brothers was ill concealed, yet he had fought valiantly in the War of the Six Saints, earning the respect of his soldiers for his willingness to share their dangers and their deprivations.

A good sword to have in a tight spot! Yor thought hopefully. Not that there'll be any tight spots this time, but . . .

The Lord High Exchequer glared smugly, clucking his tongue in amusement. Checkmate! He looked at his entourage of clerks, and the body of them tittered quietly.

King Derek plunged onward in a croak, "IwantyoutotakeRoddie!"

Augh!

Gulp!

Woden's whimsy!

"Oh, not as a king commanding loyal subjects," the king said softly. "I can find a legion of eager flatterers to do that! But as a father asking a favor of dear friends. The boy needs to get away from the castle, to get away from the fawning servants and the toadies at court."

Reflexively, all four glanced at the Lord High Exchequer, whose elated sanctimonious humor evaporated.

"Rodney needs to see a little of the world—not from a coach, but from a saddle! He needs to be with men of action!" The worst of it out on the table, King Derek relaxed enough to smile again. "A trip with you three, an adventure—a short, easy adventure—would do so much for him!

"And," he insisted forcefully, "I don't want you to show him any deference, not a whit! While he is with you, I order you to treat him as you would any commoner. Make a note of that, Lord High—not as a prince of the Sapphire Throne, but as any other citizen of the realm. Think of him as your younger brother, whom you've taken under your wing! Show him the ways of the world—how to ride, how to hold a sword, how to gut and dress a wild boar!"

The thought made the Lord High Exchequer's knees weak; he touched a perfumed handkerchief to his lips and leaned against a desk for support.

Derek smiled weakly at the trio, his face full of sympathy. "I know this will make it more difficult for you. He's clumsy, he's headstrong, and he's not much of a rider. He's liable to slow you down. You might not make it back in time for St. Tuhy's Day. . . ."

Gagged consternation.

The patron hagiarch of the obsessively fastidious, St. Tuhy's order of insufferable monks were devoted to keeping everything imaginable neat and organized beyond all semblance of sanity. Once each year, however, for one day, they were released from the madding strain of their vows and they ran amok, making a mess of everything in a mind-boggling frenzy, a berserk, contagious debauchery that likewise eroded everyone else's self-imposed inhibitions.

People had been known to get up off their deathbeds for it.

"No!" the monarch suddenly revolted. "By thunder, you'll not miss it! Lord High Exchequer, by royal decree, there shall be no Feast of St. Tuhy this year until these three return from their labor for the crown! You will send this word out at once!"

"But it's—"

"Now!" the king insisted. "Go! Do it!"

Stunned, the Lord High Exchequer lost what little color there was in his hollow cheeks. He walked, then ran from the Great Hall, though to where, he was not yet certain, while his equally stunned clerks froze, unable to decide how to proceed.

Feeling really useful for the first time all day, Derek beamed. "What's the point of being king if you can't do a few things for your friends?" he roared happily. "The prince will be ready shortly. Sir Dudley will accompany him and take care of attending to the prince and the other minor details; you won't be bothered by them. They'll meet you at the bridge gate within the hour."

"You honor us, Your Highness," Yor said. He meant it sincerely, but was unable to attain the appropriate emotional equilibrium to carry it off with bravado.

A teary glaze settled on the king's eyes. He looked forlornly at the waiting pile of petitions. "It's not like it was before

King George died. There was a kingdom to carve out then, a kingdom to defend against our archenemies. That brought us all together. Nowadays, I . . .

"You know, I wish it were me going with you."

We wish it were you, too! three minds thought in unison.

* * * * *

Here it comes again!

The sorcerer held his hands before him, fingers spread wide, put the force of his mind into the floating glyph bubble, and uttered a sound so vile that the grass wilted around him.

The warwing dived, its scythe-edged feathers slicing against the magic dome, flapping, its taloned legs grasping. On contact, two horrid sounds erupted, one from the aerial predator, the other from the wound in the translucent shell.

*Caiii!*

The warwing swept upward in renewed agony, crying throaty shrieks of frustrated rage. Bosamp cringed at the blood cry. He watched the warwing soar up into the air over the meadow. Three times now had it tried to wreck the bubble; three times had both been wounded.

But the magic shield held . . . so far. Evoking fresh guttural glyphs, Bosamp formed them in the air like clay mist and sent them to patch the holes in the dome, merging them with mind-sapping concentration.

How much more of this can I take?

While the warwing circled, resting on the wing, looking for a weakness in the dome, Bosamp looked for an escape route. His eyes passed over the morass that had but minutes before been his conjured feracat, now a twisted, inanimate pile; he had watched the warwing slice it to pieces.

That's what it wants to do to me!

He shuddered and looked behind him, at the tallest tree on the edge of the meadow, where lay the rent body of the warwing's mate, raked with his feracat's claws. But that had been in the nest, by surprise and stealth, not out in the open, where the warwing had a fighting chance. Bosamp clenched his teeth, the taste of the thieved eggs still sweet on his tongue. If only it hadn't been a warwing's nest! If only the mate hadn't returned so soon!

If the shield goes . . .

He shuddered with fatigue. His back and limbs were sore from riding, an unfamiliar enterprise, and the drain of wizardry left him with barely enough vitality to sustain the hovering dome.

I thought warwings were extinct! Bosamp chafed. The scrolls say they were all wiped out at the Siege of Ravenscrag in the last War of Lore and Magic! Old Kla told me the siege would have succeeded but for the warwings! They destroyed the firebolts! Those damned oily feathers of theirs are immune to that kind of magic!

That was thirty years ago! Bosamp shivered. Before I was ever born! The warwings were supposed to have all perished along with the birdsages when the aviary fell! But some of them must have escaped into the wilds! They're breeding again! And the Council doesn't know about it! I must . . .

He stopped, laughed.

Why tell them? What good would it do? In a few more days, it won't matter!

*Caiii! Caiii!*

The warwing called to its dead mate from aloft. The cry made Bosamp's horse fractious; it whinnied and strained against the reins. "Damn you!" Bosamp howled as he tried to steady the nervous animal, his voice cracking. Foolishly he whipped the reins across the horse's face, as if slapping a clumsy servant. "Stay put or I'll—"

The horse bolted, running through the misty shield.

No! Not out in the open!

Startled but thinking quickly, Bosamp leaped off, tumbling on the ground. The wands strapped to his side bruised his flesh; his staff slammed against his temple. Stunned, he crawled for the salvation of the dome.

The warwing dived.

Both arrived at the shield at the same time; partway through the shield, Bosamp felt the warwing slash his side through the robe. "Gah!" By a twist of fate, the sharp-edged warwing bit into the blotch on his right side. Stiffening electrically, the warwing's entire body wrenched with thrashing convulsions, unable to control a single muscle.

Bosamp growled in pain and passed through his runewall, stripping the warwing from him as he went. He sat, holding his bleeding side, spewing new glyphs to patch the dome. From safety, he watched the warwing thrash about, caroming over the meadow. As fate would have it, it fell beside its mate and soon ceased struggling.

Bosamp waited a long time before dispelling the dome.

"Sorcery supreme!" he sermonized. "Thus be it ever to those who serve lore!"

The horse was no longer around to hear it. Flinking horse! he mused. No better than the king's pathetic steed!

Say, I wonder how that ruse is going . . . ?

# CHAPTER FOUR

Midday was now a memory.

"Where is he?"

Yor tapped a polished boot into the dirt, dulling the gloss—a sure sign of his impatience—then folded his arms over his chest, only to unfurl them in black-streaked fury. "We're wasting time! Bosamp could be halfway to hell by now! If we have to wait any longer, we won't be able to get through the Teckwood before nightfall!"

He glanced from comrade to comrade, waiting for a response, but since this was the third repetition of that same despondent observation, it was slow in coming.

"It'll be all right," Dword said finally, pausing with his knife in one hand and a block of briar in the other. "How much longer can it be? The last courier said he was almost ready, just a few last items to pack. And it was rather short notice."

"But it's been hours!"

The red-beard shrugged and resumed whittling. A mound of wood shavings crouched at his feet, the sands of an emptying hourglass.

"Do you want to leave without him?" Trebor said.

Yor almost answered truthfully but relented with a sigh. "No. We can't do that."

"Then we wait." The loremaster burrowed back into his book.

Yor sighed. I was lucky to get that much out of Trebor! he thought. Nothing seems to tax his patience, not in all the years I've known him. Yor looked back from the bridge across the bailey, assuring himself that nothing was about to happen, then took the luxury of daydreaming.

It was the War of the Six Saints, nine years ago. He had just turned nineteen, right after the clash at Toqutte. Then came the Battle of the Crater. . . .

* * * * *

In a crisp new uniform, Yor sat on his steed and watched impatiently. The war was going well. In a series of quick marches and sharp battles, the duke had outmaneuvered the Munflenchians and rolled them back across the border, though without a decisive engagement. Now the Bretilyan army thrust directly at the enemy throne city of Lopach, a bold stroke to skirt around their flank and fall on the enemy rear near St. Glissade, the last defensible position before the Munflenchian city.

Horse-bound, waiting for something to happen, Yor reviewed in his mind the march two nights ago and the battle at dawn when the Bret cavalry column struck, routing the Munchies back across the river. Before a decisive blow could be landed, however, the enemy regrouped, rallying quicker than expected, and made a stand on a ridge opposite the road into St. Glissade. A trampled farmer's field lay between the two ridges. Peeping over the enemy ridge were the tall steeples of the fabled Cathedral of St. Glissade, decked now in the fiercely proud green and black flags of the Munflenchians.

Eager to get into the battle, the men of the Fairfax Light Cavalry and the other regiments of horse soldiers stood far to the left of the Bretilyan formation, astride the muddy, rutted road, waiting on the ridge opposite the enemy lines. Below them were ranks of archers, and below them a brigade of pikemen; this force was defensive, intended to secure the road and not expected to be committed to the coming battle.

"Dragon's breath!" Yor moaned loudly. "Stuck with the

reserves! We'll miss the whole war! The army'll be in Lopach by nightfall, and all I'll be able to say was that I guarded the supply train!"

As far as he could see to his right, Bret soldiers had formed up for the attack. It won't be long now, he realized. Within the minute, the cry "Forward!" went up, and Bret footmen marched out from behind their makeshift redoubts, forming into a **V** aimed at the opposing ridge. Couriers dashed back and forth between units, like bees collecting pollen. The swarm of units grew, their colorful uniforms making a living quilt in the shallow valley between the two ridges, a valley that was green a day ago but was now a muddy field of broken plants and caltrops, the latter tossed like a child's jacks on the paths up the ridge to impede the horsemen.

Suddenly glyphs of power sundered the air; a burst of sorcery sizzled to his right as the Bret wizards began the assault. Sigils formed in the air, horrid sounds that startled the horses. Yor reined his horse tightly. Calming the frightened beast, he looked to the knoll where the cluster of Bret wizards had gathered. The creek that flowed down from the enemy flank now was transformed in a gushering geyser by their spellcraft; hot water spewed over the Munflenchian soldiers, its steamy mist concealing the advance of the Bret army.

Trumpets sounded the attack; the duke shouted, "For King Derek, lads!" The words themselves could barely be heard above the noise of ten thousand men marching. The Brets loosed a battle cry and rushed over the ground uphill toward the Munchie line. Enemy archers appeared, stepping out of the trees at the crest. They loosed a furious volley, but it fell mostly behind the onrushing Brets.

Even before the attackers' vanguard hit the Munflenchian barricades, the enemy line broke, peeling away from the sorcerous stream in confusion. Caught up in the excitement, the Croswall Guard and other units that had not yet been sent forward—the entire Bret center, in fact—surged out of formation, running across the valley floor.

"Hold fast!" shouted the colonel of the Light. "Our orders are to guard the road! If it all goes well, we'll get the chance to round up the stragglers!"

Stragglers! Yor whimpered. The decisive battle of the war, and all I'll be able to say is that I rounded up stragglers!

Up the ridge rushed the Bret soldiers. The Munchie archers got off one effective volley, but it failed to slow the advance. When the first of the Bret infantry reached the crest, the Munflenchian lines disintegrated. With a roar, the Brets plunged after them into the forest, running, cheering.

They were soon out of sight, if not out of hearing.

I won't even get to see it! Yor swore.

Fifteen minutes went by, then thirty. The roar of combat receded, muffled by the distance and the woods. Sounds came now from the left—a counterattack? Another ten minutes passed. The sounds of the fray were distant and muffled by the interceding ridge and trees.

"Horse pudding!" one of Yor's companions spat glumly. "We've missed it, mates."

But then there was a silent flash of orange and blue light. A low murmuring moan like the wind being sucked out of the sky came from the woods, a basal tone at first but rising in pitch and timbre until it became a soul-freezing wail, like the laugh of Old Red Bones himself.

Yor's skin crawled in terror. Horses whinnied and shied; some bolted. Yor struggled to control his mount.

"What's happening over there?" the cavalrymen muttered among themselves. Smoke and dust bellowed up over the woods; like a black fog, it swept down off the ridge and over the Light. The wind had turned and brought the sounds of battle directly to the Bret cavalry; shouts and cries penetrated the haze, along with the clank of metal on metal.

The sound and smell of death.

Ten nervous minutes went by. The smoke thickened until

the enemy ridge was obscured. Suddenly a lord Yor had never seen before and would never see again emerged from the smoke and rode up to the Light. His face was withered with horror; a gash on the side of his face where an arrow had removed his ear was a red streak; his left hand was missing, and the bloody stump was wrapped in lace, obviously his lady's token.

"The battle's turning!" the nobleman yelled. "Come forward at once!"

"For the Fairfax!" the colonel shouted. The mounted soldiers set off at a trot, but the mood was less than jubilant. Down the ridge they rode, joined by other regiments and by a clutch of knights; into the thick smoke they rode, quickly losing sight of each other.

Where is the army? Yor wondered. What's happened?

An enemy skirmish line cut across their path.

"Charge through!" the colonel ordered. "Don't stop to fight here!"

The Light obeyed, slashing, blasting, sabers cleaving through the thin enemy rank, plunging farther into the woods. The formation disordered in the thickets behind the fruit grove, a stand of trees so thick they could only get through in ones and twos. Smoke was everywhere, tasting of burned meat. The battle clamor grew louder with every yard, but they could see nothing of the fierce melee ahead.

All at once the ground opened up before them, and the Fairfax Light was rushing down, down, down into an immense depression, a seething caldera of men and horses, smoke and holyfire.

The crater.

"We've been tricked!" Yor shouted to his squad.

He tried to halt his horse on the slope, but the forward pressure of the horsemen behind him blew them all down slope like leaves in a waterfall. A wall of heavily armored pikemen closed in behind them. Enemy archers lined the heights above, and a battery of white-robed Munflenchian clerics poured wicked streams of holyfire down into the pit. Screams tore at Yor's ears. A fireball broke over the crater, and the horses stampeded in every direction, the Light broken into shards, scattered about the enormous smoke-shrouded caldron of death.

Mortar and pestle.

Units mingled, mangled in the rain of arrows and holycraft. The Brets charged this way and that trying to escape, unable to climb up the steep sides of the crater.

Men died and died and died, vying for a place to fall. . . .

* * * * *

My horse was killed, Yor remembered soberly. I had to fight on foot and fell in with a group of the Croswall Guard. We tried to fight our way back upslope, but we faltered. Then a Bretilyan wizard appeared out of nowhere, hanging in the air above the enemy lines. With a sound like the gates of hell opening, the sorcerer exploded, a sacrifice that blasted hundreds of Munchies down into the pit, making a hole in their lines.

It was then Trebor and I met. . . .

"The prince is almost ready, sirs."

Yor looked up. The courier's uniform startled him; for a moment, he wasn't sure where he was.

"Just a few minutes more, Captain."

Yor nodded. Once the courier was out of hearing, the black-clad dandy ranted, trying to incite a conversation to shake the grim images of the Battle of the Crater from his mind. "We've given that blorging Bosamp a whole day's lead now! If this keeps up, we'll never catch him this side of the channel! We'll have to go across to Norlandia to nab him!"

Dword looked up, ears perked. "That wouldn't be so bad. It's nice there this time of year! After we catch him"—he licked his lips lecherously—"we can stop at my mom's home and look up a few lively ladies I know. . . ."

Yor's eyes lit with mischief. "Sure, why not? I've heard about your women! Your forefathers stole our prettiest lasses! I'll bet they're desperate for some real men by now!"

Dword scratched his ruddy beard, his red eyebrows knitted in deep thought as his pale blue eyes squinted. "Hmmm . . . that's *really* odd. I don't recall any of them trying to get back to Lothar, especially not to Bretilya. . . ."

"We'll see about that!" Yor vowed.

"Don't count on it," Trebor said, without looking up from his book. "Bosamp won't make it even to Axiom. We'll run him down before the next Juggler's Moons or I'll wrestle a two-headed werezombie in my mother's old housecoat! Blindfolded!"

"Don't say such things!" the red-beard admonished. Mortified, he made a complex three-fingered anti-hex gesture and glared aghast at the loremaster. "Don't you know better than to tempt the Three Weird Sisters of Destiny? They hear everything! Haven't you learned your lesson yet?"

"Fah! Superstitious prattle!"

"How can you say that? Remember that time in Frore when you swore that nothing short of a ten-foot albino wharfbat could keep you from—"

"Happenstance!"

"You call a ten-foot—"

"Closer to nine-foot!"

"—albino—"

"More like chalky!"

"—wharfbat *happenstance?*"

"No!" Yor butted in. "He called him Fred—but, hey!" He stopped, suddenly wondering about the grammatical structure of Trebor's oath. "Which one of you is going to be blindfolded? And how are you going to get a werezombie in your mother's old housecoat? No self-respecting—"

The blare of a clarion blew the conversation to a halt. A

herald stood statue-stiff and announced prissily, "Sir Dudley of Manchester!"

They looked up. The man of Manchester, a thin, white-haired knight in somewhat dated panoply, rode toward them, towing a packhorse. They recognized Sir Dudley at once. Half past his impressive glory days, Sir Dudley had been a fixture at court from before any of them had been born. The trio also knew that he now held the office of Shield of the Prince, that is, he was Prince Rodney's personal bodyguard, mentor, cook, confessor, and valet. It was considered a plum appointment by most, but a demeaning post by those who preferred action to responsibility. The senior knight, however, bore the honor with grace and without complaint, characteristics that marked all of his long and faithful service to the realm.

Their eyes focused on the pack horse; it looked like a West-phalic peddler's pony with its sacks and baskets attached to a wooden frame, jangling. The pack horse was bowbacked with gear; every conceivable eventuality seemed to have been accounted for: food, clothes, shoes, fardel cakes, blankets, rope, pastries, tools, wine flasks, and even a small wicker hutch with a quartet of clucking hens.

Hens?

"Welcome, Sir Dudley!" Yor said warmly. "I hope this means the prince is ready?"

"Aye, Captain. He comes now," the elder knight replied. "I must apologize for the prince's tardiness. We did not receive the word until this morning, and we were not ready to make such a sojourn. I hope the wait has not been too tiresome."

Before Yor could speak, the clarions fanfared with regal pomp.

"His Royal Highness, Prince Rodney!" the herald heralded.

A callow teenager trudged into view, if it could be said that someone on horseback trudged. The morose expression on the prince's face left no doubt as to his opinion of the situation.

"Welcome, Your Highness," Yor said, bowing much too

unctuously. "We're positively delighted you were able to honor our humble enterprise."

The prince, a portrait of adolescence gone awry, said nothing. Realizing his predicament, Rodney gnawed the last bit of nail off one finger and sniffed his swollen nose, a centerpiece that demanded constant attention. His legs were too long and his feet too big; his shoulders slumped out in front of the rest of his gangly frame, and his hair zoomed off in all directions in a flaxen fountain that redefined the word *unkempt*.

And this was not the worst of it.

"What happened to his face?" Dword winced.

"Poison acne," Sir Dudley whispered sadly. "He fell in a patch of it when he fled the castle yesterday, trying to get away from the Bosamp's smokewand. It was quite hectic there for a while."

Even Yor's anger waned into sympathy. "Shall we away, then?"

"Aye, Captain; we're ready."

"Prince?"

No reply.

Ignoring the prince's lack of response, his foot to the stirrup, Yor's spirits rose with his ascent to the saddle. His horse picked up his mood and pranced a few fancy steps before settling into a brisk trot toward the bridge. Maybe this isn't so bad after all! he thought optimistically. Sir Dudley's a good man . . . still has a decent sword arm and a wealth of experience. Having him along relieves us of the responsibility of watching over the prince every minute, cancels him out as it were.

"Beware, wizard!" Yor said suddenly. "The wolves are loosed now! There's nary a safe hidey-hole anywhere for you! Not from the three most—"

He stopped and jerked his head around, already knowing what he would see—Trebor's nose buried in a book!

"Trebor!"

"Last page . . ."

\* \* \* \* \*

Cursing with his every step the horse that had deserted him, the wizard walked to a farmhouse, overpowered the farmer's daughter, and stole a plow horse.

I could be a month in the saddle! Bosamp lamented. Why did they have to put the flinking Bell so far away?

\* \* \* \* \*

Low on the horizon, the sun hung derisively over the Wolds, laughing in reds and purples, like a bad-tempered manservant at his master's long-awaited deathbed.

"Dragon's breath!" Yor grieved. "Dusk already!"

A nameless dread touched him as he watched the sunset ribbons of color streaming through the cloudy sky. The air was heavy with an unsung dirge; the Wolds were a charcoal sketch: beautiful, terrible. Fretting, he scanned around for some reason for his uneasiness, some source of the foreboding. Everywhere were the mounds, bumps on the rolling green-clad countryside; he felt as if they were pressing in on him, inch by inch, with the failing light. Even now in the lush swell of summer, the Wolds seemed in mourning, more like ancient raised graves than dunes of verdant earth.

Yor shivered with a flash of intuition. We've been here dozens of times, but something's different now; it feels like a long forgotten battlefield.

We've got to get out of here before it gets dark. . . .

He looked down the road, considering the only exit. Ahead were the woods of Teck, looming vulturine over the road in the gloaming. In his mind, he thought he heard the rustle of small creatures scuttling through the forest underbrush, leaving the shadowy trees for the Wolds, preferring even those sepulchral mounds to the perils of Teckwood.

Trouble. Either way.

He turned to the cause of this dilemma. Who would have

believed anybody could eat that slowly? "Has the prince finished his dinner?" he asked Sir Dudley too sweetly.

"Are there any more tortes?" Prince Rodney burped.

"No, Your Highness," the grey knight answered. "I only brought the four."

The prince threw down his sixth-course lace napkin in disgust. "Well, then, I guess I'm done."

Immediately Sir Dudley set out with efficient speed to gather up the spread of demolished comestibles, sorting out the various containers and packets and stowing them back on the packhorse. Aware of the lateness of the hour, his eyes met the cavalryman's. "Only a minute more, Captain."

"Not quite," Prince Rodney grunted. "Bring the chair, Sir Duds. . . ."

The chair it was. The knight escorted the young prince behind a mound.

*By the sacred scribe!* Yor chaffed. *Another delay! I'd hate to think we're all going to die because—*

The loremaster jostled the cavalryman's shoulder and bobbed his head in the direction of the forest. "We're not going to make it through those woods before dark," Trebor said pointedly. "You know what that means. Mayhap we should camp here on the Wolds tonight."

"No!" the cavalryman recoiled, surprised by the strength of his own response. "This is no place to be . . . not tonight, in any event."

The strangeness of Yor's voice paralyzed Trebor; his nerves tingled. He stared at the black-clad adventurer, waiting for an explanation. "I know of no lore involving the Wolds," he finally prompted. "The dangers here are all natural . . . the usual creatures of the night."

Yor didn't move. Something inside shivered, stirring restlessly. At the edge of his soul, harsh alien sounds fomented, flowing up to hover near the tip of his tongue, ready to leap to his need. *No! Not that!* He forced the unworldly sigil back down into the recesses of his existence and relocked the cage.

He stood on the brink of unreality and looked at the laughing sunset. "I'm not sure what it is," he said at last. "It's as if tonight is special in some way. Some sort of . . . of . . . something . . . a force not of this world." He glanced at the duo, unable to express it any better. He grimaced, a sour aftertaste in his mind. "We have to get out of here."

"But Teckwood?" The loremaster frowned. "At night?"

"I know, I know." Yor looked away from him and up at the sky, drawn by instinct. The last sliver of sun was sinking below the horizon, and he trembled. The night's first starlight was already a pinpoint on the eastern sky, a harbinger of the darkness to come.

He tranced.

He saw the star pattern not yet revealed, masked by the sun's dying glow. The confluence of two ancient suns formed an eerie glow that seemed aimed at the Wolds from across the millennia. They will fight here again, Yor foresaw, as they have every confluence since their own worlds perished: soldiers from distant stars waging a forgotten war on a distant outpost, lost in time and space. . . .

He shuddered. "We must go."

"Then we shall," Trebor said. Long had he trusted the voice inside Yor, even when Yor himself doubted it. They would go, even through Trebor's own insatiable curiosity demanded that they stay and investigate. Of course, they didn't necessarily have to leave right this very moment. . . .

"The woods aren't that deep," Dword said with resignation. "Only a few leagues. We'll make some torches; we'll get through. We've done it before, you know."

Yor gazed down at his shadow.

It flickered.

But it wasn't his shadow.

An elongated shape had attached itself to Yor's boots, a fantastic creature with bilateral appendages and some kind of

chitinous carapace with curlicue horns. Looking around, he
saw that Dword's shadow, too, was not right. It had arms like
animated antlers and cloven hooves and tentacles, each holding a ghostly flaming pike, whirling like a pinwheel in heat.

Trebor's was even more grotesque.

"I believe," the loremaster said, gaping as he followed Yor's
gaze to the ground, "that I've seen enough to formulate an
entirely satisfactory working hypothesis." His heart pounding
in horror, he sucked in his breath, his feet already moving
toward his horse's stirrups. "It seems apparent that as soon as
the last iota of light is gone, we will be possessed by our shadows—whether physically or noncorporeally is moot—and
then perforce be forced to participate in some unspeakable
rite that we cannot possibly hope to fathom. . . . Don't just
stand there! Make torches!"

When the prince and Sir Dudley returned, several nearby
bushes were burning brightly, highlighting their bizarre
shadows. The three men were mounted, and each held a burning stick in his hand.

"Hey! Aren't we going to make camp here?" the prince
asked.

"No. We're riding through Teckwood. Now."

"Are you senile?" Prince Rodney guffawed, honking. "Ride
through Teck? At night? You must be joking! Nobody in his
right mind would do that! Even the village idiot knows—"

"Look at your shadow."

"What? I don't see how—*aaiii!* Get it off me!" The prince
hopped up and down, but each time his foot landed, the
shadow reattached itself, and his was arguably the most ferocious and ugliest of the abominations, particularly the tentacled thing in the center of its face.

If that was a face.

The prince was on his horse before his howl stopped echoing in the Wolds. Later, when Dword added the new stanza to
the "Ballad of Count Yor," he would say that the prince

leaped ten feet vertically, turned, ran without touching the ground, and dropped down into his horse's saddle. And for once, not even Trebor would contradict him.

"Let's go, ho!" the prince urged. "Beat feet! Move it or lose it! Oh, gods! I'm too young to die!"

"*No one* is too young to die," Yor stated grimly.

They fled the Wolds, galloping down the road toward the dark woods of Teck. Within minutes, they were out of the hillocks and into the grassy meadows bordering the forest proper. At the forest edge, they stopped to gaze into the woods. In the dusk, the lanky limbs of the sinister trees stretched out like grasping, leaf-feathered claws, the thick trunks as inhospitable as cold castle towers. The air was damp and clammy, carrying the scent of overripe fruit and mossy bark. There were no sounds of branches swaying or birds nesting down for the night, but the woods were not still.

*Buzzzz . . .*

The trio looked at each other knowingly.

"Teckwood isn't fit for human beings!" cursed the Norlander. "Where I come from, the winters are cold enough to kill these things off! Frieda's fishing hole, I hate these tropical climes!"

"Tropical climes!" his Bret companions chimed.

"Well, compared to where I come from!"

"Compared to where you come from, the heart of an icewight is a blazing inferno!" Yor retorted. The observation brought him up short; he added quickly, "Stay close together! Whatever happens, don't go off the road!"

"Humping hoarmaidens! Here we go again!" the red-beard muttered unhappily.

And so they rode toward the dark corridors of Teckwood. The forest umbra silenced them. Holding torches high, the riders plunged into the fell palisade, following the road, which seemed to shrink down to a slender wisp, a tightrope from which they dared not fall.

"Button all your garb!" Trebor warned. "And make use of your torch! They're better than swords for this!"

Oaths and prayers.

As they went deeper into the timber, the trees seemed to creep closer to the road, edging nearer a root at a time, encroaching on the safety zone until they oppressed it, corrupted it. The riders had the sense of being in a place that was very much aware of their presence and glad to see them—for the wrong reasons!

*Buzzzz!*

The treetops riffled with arousal. Dart-long shapes began to swoop down from the trees, scarlet bolts as sleek and as pointed as dirks.

Twos. Fours. Dozens.

One brushed by the royal heir.

"*Augh!*" Rodney shrieked, swatting at it. His hand made contact, flesh on wing; he retracted his paw as if it had touched a hot kettle, whining, "Vampire beetles! They're all around us! We'll all be killed! We've got to make a run for it!"

"No!" Yor pulled up alongside the teenager, gripping his horse's bridle so that the prince's fear wouldn't stampede his steed. "It's too far! The horses can't make it through all of Teckwood in one gallop! You must pace them! We've got to get as far into the forest as we can, until the beetles are as thick as we can possibly stand, and then—and only then!— we'll make a run for it!"

"Remain calm, Your Highness," Sir Dudley said to his youthful charge. "These gentlemen have done this before. If we don't panic, we'll make it."

Probably, one or all of the three thought.

The prince paled. Instead of allaying his fear, their words confirmed it. He unsheathed his dagger and held it jittery in his left hand; the torch was already making his right arm ache.

"Form a diamond with the prince at the center," Yor ordered. "No more than an arm's length between us."

The horses were herded together. Yor took the point and
Sir Dudley and Dword flanked the prince, while Trebor
guarded the rear.

"Good," Yor remarked. "Remember to hold your reins
tight. Don't let your horses have their heads. They're going to
be even more afraid than we are!"

Impossible! the prince quailed.

*Buzzzz!*

The whirring grew. At first, it was almost subconscious, more
imagined than heard, but it heightened with each furtive furlong until the mind could hear nothing else. The night filled
with fluttering wings. Red shapes launched themselves from
their mother-hive trees, eager to bring back flesh blood to succor
their arboreal queens. They went whizzing past the concerned
riders, keeping their distance from the flames, scouting the riders one at a time, a few seconds apart, but as their numbers
swelled, their frenzy rose to bloodlust.

Knot tight, the riders advanced into the depths of the malig-
nant forest. The trees overhanging the road were so close now
that neither starlight nor moonlight was able to penetrate their
wicked limbs. Even the torchlight seemed unnatural in the
shadows of Teck, in the turgid darkness, stifled, eclipsed of
hope, evoking thoughts of the finiteness of life. . . .

*Buzzzz!*

"Try to ward them off with your torches!" the loremaster
exhorted. "And don't panic if they bite you! They're not ven-
omous, and it will take more than a few of them to cause you
any serious blood loss."

Blood loss! The prince felt faint.

Scores.

Grosses.

The airborne throng descended, a red buzzing cloud. Daring the wedge of torches, the beetles dived on the riders from
every direction, smacking against armor, ricocheting off horse
and man. Some caught fire in the flames, fizzling with a hiss,

while others became strings of fire, miniature meteors shooting through the trees.

The stench of burning beetles profaned the air.

"This is worse than Bosamp's stinkwand!" wailed the prince, whose nose, despite its susceptibility to allergies, had an uncanny range and sensitivity. "I think I'm going to—"

Just then, a red dart flew straight into the prince's face, alighting on his nose.

"*Gah!*"

The beetle tasted the royal youth, spat, then fled that acned protuberance in insectoid terror, chittering a high-pitched cry, but the frightened youth overreacted and struck out frantically, clumsily, with his torch—and lost it. He made a grab for it, but the burning brand fell to the ground.

Unarmed. The vision of thousands of beetles covering his body, like a second skin, sucking the life from him, was more than the royal teenager could stand. "I'm doomed!" he cried.

Beetlemania.

Rodney dropped his reins and waved his hands frantically about himself, failing to note that the beetles were suddenly giving him wide berth as the buzz of his inedibility spread.

"Pick up the torch!" Yor shouted.

"I'm getting out of here!"

"Wait!" Dword cried. The barbarian bounded off his horse, grabbed up the fallen torch, and remounted rapidly. But before he could hand it back to the royal youth, the prince gave his horse a kick and the distressed equine responded all too eagerly, tearing free from the group, dashing pell-mell down the road.

"Rein him in, Prince Rodney!" Sir Dudley called out. Then he, too, urged his steed to speed, chasing after his charge with a loud "Ha!"

The trio's own horses rankled into panic. Unlike their riders, they were unarmored and helpless to evade the swarm of blood-sucking red darts now covering their flanks with hungry mouths.

The diamond disintegrated.

Yor gritted his teeth and let his horse run. It could do more harm than good to try to hold them back now. God help them when their mounts tired! "Keep to the left at the fork ahead!" he cried out.

Through the vile woods they galloped, slapped by tree limbs, stumbling over stones, splashing across a cold stream, racing breakneck through Teckwood. Behind them, the cloud of beetles pursued, angry at the sudden departure of dinner.

Hot breath, white foam.

A league later, the adrenaline died. Exhausted by the head-long rush through the torturous forest, the horses faltered, slowing to a walk. In a few seconds, the group was back together. For the moment, they had outrun the beetles, but even now they could hear the buzzing of newly aroused inhabitants of the woods, fresh beetles emerging from their tree hives, ready to feast.

Yor looked ahead and behind; soon they would be besieged worse than before. "Keep together!" he growled. "Keep the horses moving! Drop the reins if you have to and grab a weapon! We're in for a fight!"

*Buzzzz* . . .

"Use two torches!" Dword suggested. He stood up in his saddle and drew his screamsax, chopping off a branch and igniting it with his torch. He passed the new firebrand to the prince.

"Here! Wave it in a circle above your head, slowly, so you don't tire, and unevenly so they can't time it."

*If only we had a way to draw them off for a while,* Yor thought desperately. *It's not that far to the end of the woods. Maybe the three of us should drop back and draw them off while the Prince and Sir Dudley get away. . . .*

A cackle of poultry panic pierced the air.

Five pairs of eyes looked at the packhorses. Much of the gear had fallen off in the wild flight through the woods, but not the coop.

They all had the same thought at once.

The elder knight gazed at the trio evenly. "This is my responsibility and my decision," he announced and wheeled his steed about.

"Not the chickens!" Prince Rodney protested halfheartedly. "They won the pulleteers' prize last spring!"

Sir Dudley paid no heed to the prince. With a stroke that still carried authority, he cut the straps binding the crate to the packhorse; it fell to the ground, accompanied by a fowl diatribe. With another stroke, the aged knight sundered the hutch, releasing the hysterical hens.

"Have a run for it, ladies," the knight said, feeling distinctly unchivalrous.

No urging was required. Like ghouls with their heads cut off, the freed birds scattered, clucking frantically, four feather-flying zigzags knifing through the insect-infested forest, searching for cover in the brush.

*Buzzzz!*

The first pack of beetles caught up with the five riders again, making the air thick with furious bloodthirsty streaks. The gathering storm of beetles paused, and, choosing discretion as the better part of valor—or perhaps just looking for a quick appetizer before returning for the main course—the bulk of them veered away from the wall of flame and steel stalwartly arrayed against them, and after dividing into smaller balls of humming red, chased after the hens.

"They shall not have died in vain!" Yor cried heroically. "Ladies, I salute you!" Howling, the black-clad adventurer brandished sword and firebrand in a windmill fury. "Onward!"

They made their way forward, their desperation daunting even the beetles. Slashing, burning, enduring bites and giving back a score for each, they littered the road through Teckwood with flaming beetle hulks as they fought their way through the forest.

Another furlong.

And another.

Fatigue crept in, overtaking the prince first, then the elder warrior. Finally even the trio tired, their arms and backs aching. One by one, beetles penetrated their defenses and drew blood, each bite sapping the men's diminishing strength. But just as their arms were too heavy to swing anymore, their swords and daggers too coated with insect ichor to cut anymore, the forest border came into view.

"Only a little farther!" Yor encouraged.

Spirits reviving, the horses trotted out of the shadow of darkness into the marshy pasture of Grant's Field. The beating wings of the airborne armada welled up behind them and hesitated on the edge of the meadow. Far ahead, silvery grey in the tri-moonlight, was a stone house. The inn stood like a veritable fortress in the distance—a long distance.

"We'll never make it!" the prince whined. "We're done for! You rogues have been the death of me!"

"I think not," the loremaster stated tersely. "Look!"

All about the meadow, bright yellow stingers emerged from their ground nests, summoned by the sound of the buzzing, shooting up into the evening like fireworks—

A yellow rain in reverse.

"Reinforcements!" Trebor said heartily. "Go get 'em, yellow britches!" Though never particularly fond of insects in the past, the loremaster now decided to find a good book on the subject at the next opportunity.

Straight for the beetle crimson tide the yellow wasp bolts went, vengeful and ravenous, pitted once again against their arch rivals. When the first of the fierce stingers broke into the red cloud, the beetles scattered in panic.

The hunters became the hunted. Trilling in terror, the beetles fled back into the murk of Teckwood; the stingers pursued doggedly into the forest.

"God bless these tropical climes!" Yor yelled unabashedly.

The inn beckoned, but the battle was not yet ended. They had the hangers-on to deal with, dozens of beetles still clinging greedily to flesh, especially to their horses.

"Don't try to pull them off or pry them with your daggers!" the loremaster warned. "You'll cause more harm than good that way! Their jaws can rip the skin, making the wounds worse than before! Heat your blade and press it on top of them. They can't stand that, and they'll drop right off!"

They needed half an hour just to clear the horses, killing the bloated beetles one by one. They had to strip off Sir Dudley's armor to get the last one.

The prince had suffered only the single bite to his nose.

With concern, Yor inspected their horses. "They won't be much good tomorrow . . . or the next day," he said. "They've got cuts from running into tree branches, torch singes, beetle bites. . . . This is all Bosamp's fault!" he swore. "But for that madman, we'd all be snug in some warm bed this night! You'll pay in full, Bosamp! I promise!" Still smoldering, he looked to the loremaster. "Have you got anything for the wounds?"

"Not much. Just a philter for minor cuts. I'll get right on it." Trebor opened up his bag of lore, hunting through the bundles of dried plants, the vials, pouches, special stones, and—

Aha!

The man-mountain went to work, uncorking a small jar of dried herbs. He made a slurry of the powder with some wine, then applied the poultice to all the wounds, rubbing each until the skin around it turned green with stain. "It could have been worse," Trebor concluded. "It *was* worse last time. Undoubtedly the diversion with the chickens helped."

"Hmmm . . . saved by chickens . . . à la king," the red-bearded bard mumbled, his mind racing creatively. A new stanza for the ballad! He whistled a few bars of the well-known ditty just a tad too playfully, getting its meter fixed in his mind. "I feel an inspiration coming on. Where's my flute?"

Yor, bloodstained and wild-eyed, stared daggers at the Norlander. "Don't you dare!"

The inn was as cozy and warm as they had expected. So tired were they that not even the serenade provided by the prince's virtuoso nose was able to penetrate the depth of their slumber.

\* \* \* \* \*

The young court wizard hid off the road in a hollow tree as befits a man who has made enemies from sunrise to sunset. After stealing the horse, he had butchered and barbecued one of a shepherd's flock, leaving the sorcery-stunned lad trussed and at the mercy of nature. Later, he had robbed a miller's bread and money to buy another horse—the one he had stolen had been ridden lame. Shortly afterward, he had zapped a sheriff with a blindness spell and taken his saddle to replace the ill-fitting one on his new steed, and late in the day he had used a waterwand to escape from a group of deer poachers after he had assaulted them and stolen their kill.

Best to stay out of sight until morning, he decided. Hunger churned within him; he tore off a chunk of bread and bit into the strips of deer meat, chewing heavily. On impulse, he sprinkled a few glittering grains of dragon dust on the meat.

A warm feeling of superiority came over him.

Clods! Not worthy of my potent magicks! Hah!

Of course, he realized, it won't be this easy for long. The word will spread. I've got to keep ahead of it!

Suddenly he was certain someone was watching him. He felt eyes on his back. The touch was far away, but it disturbed the psychic ether. He felt exposed, naked to this new threat. Someone is after me! And not just the local constable! No, someone, or something far more dangerous.

There is a way to find out: the dreamwalk!

He shuddered from head to toe; his trim body spasmed in

trepidation. I've never done that spell before! It will take every ounce of my power; it will be days before I'll be able to conjure again. Very dangerous! But the dragoness said the dust would help me, would give me a better channel for summoning, and quicker recovery from the effort.

The foreign flesh on his side twitched, itching suddenly.

What if I lose my way in the dark? All these trees look alike! What if someone comes along and moves my body and I can't find it? Or what—

He chewed his lip; then his whole body clenched tight.

You do or you don't do. There is nothing else!

He wrapped his hands about a cold iilyrum charm, a touchstone that brought luck and helped him concentrate.

Now!

Trembling, he found the scroll and unrolled it. The light was bad, but he had copied the spell in glow ink against just such a possibility. He was smugly satisfied at the phosphorescent aura that lit the runes.

A world of my own to rule! The dragoness promised!

He took a deep breath, gripping the charm as he read the scroll carefully, the first electric glyph vomited out from his soul, rending the night's peace. Foul, guttural glyphs followed in careful cadence, flowing galvanically, harshly from his innards, forming supernaturally in the air. Ten runes there were to this sigil, each a cat's claws rasping across his throat. His lips parched and cracked as hot, dry air spewed from his lungs, and he squeezed the charm tighter as the blue smoke of magic filled the night air.

Unbidden, the urge to choke his own throat popped into his mind, and his arms moved to comply. Beyond all control, his hands flew to his neck and gripped. No! Down! Down!

He continued with the spellcasting, shrieking each new glyph through the constricted orifice of his mouth. When he finished, he collapsed, inert but aware. A rumble of thaumaturgic thunder, a low moan, rippled through the woods as the assembled runes melded into sorcery, precipitating into the complete sigil. Bosamp felt ripped in two; his skin stretched tight with rigor mortis as his spirit was cast from his body, hovering in the night just outside the log.

He viewed his inanimate body with terror.

Then came elation.

I did it!

Dreamily he considered the lifeless hulk of his body lying in the log and resisted the desire to destroy it so that he might never again be chained to that feeble flesh. The exhilaration was soul-wrenching; he wanted to soar skyward and fly around the world; he felt that he could be anywhere he wanted to be—all he had to do was fly there.

Remember! The grimoire said there's maybe a few hours at best before it's too late to return! Now—who seeks me? Who dares to thwart my destiny? Let's go find out. . . .

He flew down the road, sniffing the psychic ether, following the scent. But when he floated near a village, he spied two young lovers in a tryst and stopped to watch. Drawn by his own lust, he found to his delight that he was able to mingle his spirit with their inflamed bodies, jolting their own arousal and pushing it past the brink.

He experienced both of their passions.

When it was over, he realized with a start that there was precious little time left, so he hastily returned to his corporeal existence.

# CHAPTER FIVE

Despite his immense size, the chrome dragon glided through the jagged, twisting cavern gracefully, a purposeful saurian shape parrying all obstacles effortlessly. When he saw her, he realized she was not surprised at his coming; no doubt the entire dragon mind net was trilling with the news of his presence. The ancient chrome's wizened eyes lacerated the gold, but the dragoness's composure was undaunted as she drew serenity from the sanctity of her own lair.

Psychelink was inevitable; he was gratified to see she understood and did not try to block his probing in her thoughts. He searched her memories with propriety and without resistance; the gold was proud and arrogant, and not yet afraid of his coming. He soon found what he wanted. It did not enlighten him; it merely confirmed that of which he was already certain.

The oldest dragon on Leiblein was emotionless in his judgment. *Honor . . . there will be honor at any cost!*

*I have not broken any of the Rules!* Drachshiska replied haughtily. *You cannot say that I have! I have not dishonored the Game! This matter then is beyond your jurisdiction!*

Her protest gained her no leverage with the chrome. *You made promises to your pawn that we both know you will not keep! And—*

*The Rules are clear on that point! Promises made to humans are not binding!*

*—And you gave him the dust to aid his quest!*

*Not specifically a violation!*

*If he succeeds, this world will be destroyed! No life below gold molt can hope to escape the holocaust of the Bell! How many dragons will perish because of your interference, their chances sundered because of your unjust actions? Their lives cut short before they can reach Threshold, before they can fly to the safety of a new world?*

*I care not what happens to mindless eggspawn! And neither does the Game!*

The chrome roared an angry sigil, spewing glyphs dramatically, like an outraged artist creating a mural in the lair, venting his spleen with feral hissing, his metallic tongue flicking through the air like a master swordsman's fencing lunges. The gold had her own sorcerous craft, augmented by the power stones she had cached in her lair against just this moment, and her spell rose up to meet the chrome's harsh phonemes. The two forces converged, collided like opposing tidal waves, but the gold watched with shocked dismay as the chrome's power simply crushed her own sigil as easily as a man blows out a candle.

She collapsed to the rough floor of the cavern, unable to rise against his will, a muscleless heap, bound and helpless. *Six moltsleeps have I survived!* she thought as the pain and danger of each flashed through her mind. *And the depredations of men and beasts! And the mating fury! And still he can do this to me!*

Can any gold ever really hope to understand a chrome?

With a short hop, the chrome moved forward and took her face in his claw, holding it up so that her auric eyes could not avoid his righteous fury.

*You led him to believe you would save him! Would he have gone had you not thus promised? Were you not gold, I would simply hurl you into the sun!*

*But they are nothing! They will all die anyway! I've done nothing wrong!*

*You risk bringing the wrath of the gods on us! The Bell is their artifact! Did you really believe there would be no consequences for your actions?*

The chrome raked his gleaming sharp claws across her face, leaving scars in the golden scales, scars that would never heal, inflicting pain, mental as well as physical.

*We will remain here in this cavern until this matter is decided.*

His pronouncement staggered her. Unless the eddies of chance flowed over them, both the gold and chrome might reasonably expect to live forever, since none of the so-called natural causes would ever overtake them, but having a mountain fall on oneself was not a natural cause.

*It is a death sentence! For both of us!*

She writhed in agony as he flailed her mind relentlessly. Then the chrome breathed deep and regained his composure.

*You will recite the Rules.*

*I am no whelp! I am gold! My feet have touched the moons! You can't—*

*You are nothing! Nothing!*

Then he roared a sound she had never heard before, a tone so terrible that her every fiber screamed in anguish, an agony beyond anything she could possibly have imagined. At length, when she knew total humiliation, he deigned to make the terror even more severe.

*I am the Gamesmaster! Your fate—and mine!—are now in the hands of the same insignificant nit you have chosen for this shameful enterprise! If we do not die outright in the carnage he may yet unleash, then I will torment you for as long as it takes for this mountain to erode away! We will await the verdict of the die you have seen fit to cast!*

He stopped and raked his talons across her face again. The desire to tear her limb from limb flooded him, but he fought it down.

*We are the chosen at the whim of the gods, you foolish ant! Pray! Pray your pawn fails!*

His gleaming chromium eyes drilled holes in her draconic soul, and she knew pain beyond belief. He paused, lost in thoughts she could not interpret, his alien mind beyond her comprehension.

*Without honor we are nothing! Merely pointless echoes in the endless vacuum of time and space! Now, repeat after me . . .*

\* \* \* \* \*

"He . . . hit . . . me . . . with . . . his . . . staff," the fainling said. A spot of ichor showed on the fainling's head. Its slender limbs were contracted now, wrung together in a gesture of restraint under pressure. Those same limbs were capable of extending, thinning until they could comb seed spores from ferns, or hardening into scuttles for carving stone to make niches for their gardening. The gentle knee-high creature's fawnlike eye drooped in timid sadness, not a pitying of the injustice done to itself, but sorrow instead for the karmic disaster that would befall any that harmed one of them.

"He hit a fainling," Dword said, troubled. "I can't believe Bosamp would sink that low. . . ."

"He's changed, Captain," Sir Dudley said to the red-beard. "He's not the same man he was when he first came to court. I remember thinking what a hale fellow Bosamp was when he first arrived. A smart lad, rather handsome, and he had a jolly sense of humor. In the beginning, he did the kingdom good service, such as when he cleared the new road through to Virgate. But he's all twisted up inside now, a knot that maybe cannot be untied. 'Tis a shame."

"We'll catch him," Yor asserted to no one in particular. Inside, the Bret cavalryman burned as he remembered how they had lost a day chasing the *faux* Bosamp. Clever of Bosamp, he grudgingly admitted. Realizing the Fairfax Road was the obvious route, he took the highlands route instead. To throw us off his tracks, he sent the king's horse up the Fairfax Road with an illusion of himself riding on it. The townspeople we talked to assumed it really was him, though it did seem odd that he never spoke to anyone and he never stopped. He must have spell-bound the horse, something only the lowest slime weasel would do! If I hadn't noticed that the tracks at the stream crossing weren't right for a horse carrying a rider—too shallow and too evenly weighted—we'd still be on the wrong road! With the day's lead he had to begin with and the added day we lost backtracking, it's taken a week for us to make up the ground and get close again! But even with the prince as ballast, we're going to get him before the day's over; I can feel it in my bones!

Lost in thought, Yor's gaze drifted to the jarth stone, a massive upended megalith that had been placed at the road junction before the Fall of the Elders. He was fascinated by jarth's immense majesty; the fainli had carved a rock garden into the jarth, filling it with lush ferns, oddly beautiful fungi, and iridescent mosses. As tall as the nearby trees, the jarth radiated eldritch power, power that regulated the weather in the immediate area, power that healed, power that nurtured, but a power that had failed to affect Bosamp.

How long have the fainli lived in this jarth? Yor wondered. A thousand years? Longer? Were they here when the stone was set in place, when the Elders ruled before the Fall? We know almost nothing about the fainli. . . .

"He . . . stole . . . fungi . . . and . . . ate . . . them. His . . . eyes . . . were . . . yellow . . . and . . . he . . . was . . . not . . . sensitive. Was . . . he . . . diseased?"

Trebor replied, "No, he was not diseased. Or at least his sickness is not contagious."

"He . . . is . . . not . . . well. You . . . must . . . stop . . . him. He . . . took . . . the . . . north . . . fork . . . toward . . . the . . . Escarpment."

"We'll not lose him again!" Trebor vowed warmly. "Is there anything I can do for you? I have some herbs and such." He patted the bag at his side and considered the possibilities.

"It . . . is . . . unnecessary."

"Then," Yor said, breaking his daydreaming, "we must get after him before he can do any more harm."

"You . . . must . . . come . . . again . . . when . . . you . . . return. We . . . may . . . be . . . able . . . to . . . cure . . . him . . . when . . . the . . . yellow . . . eyes . . . are . . . gone."

"We'll come back this way," Yor concluded. "Perhaps you may be able to salvage his soul."

The fainling community cooed, a purring sound that whistled through the jarth with eerie beauty, an empathic casting to soothe the troubled consciences of the men. A feeling of well-being swept over them as they passed by the jarth and headed up the east fork.

Once out of sight of the jarth, however, the tranquil mood did not linger.

"How could we lose Bosamp now?" the prince declared with a sneer. "He's leaving a path a blind man could follow in his sleep!"

There was no argument. After finding the wizard's real trail at Curtalax, they had heard tales of Bosamp's infamy from his victims at every village and crossroads on the road all the way to the fainli community. The errant court wizard was on a rampaging beeline north, no mistake about it: north, to the coast and Axiom.

"We've got him now," Yor noted confidently as he reviewed a mapskin. "You can see that he only got from Kirby Downs noon three days ago to Creekfork by last evening, not twenty leagues total. He's not making very good time at all. We're only a few hours behind him now, and the gap is closing!"

Even with the prince! the gold-trimmed cavalryman mentally added. Rodney's so slow! And he doesn't ride very well! If we didn't have to drag him along . . . sigh. As he rolled up the mapskin, something drew his eye hypnotically; he paused to stare at the region of north-central Bretilya for a moment, then carefully rolled the map and stowed it in its leather case.

The Darklings, he mused. The source of the Fairfax.

And we'll be there soon. . . .

Onward they rode in the early morning mist. Rising above the stiff, lordly trees lining the road, mountains poked up into view, until only a few leagues down the road from the jarth, the front range of the Darklings rose to loom over the endless hardwood forest like a series of grey carbuncles bulging up from the shoulders of Lothar, the world-girdling cummerbund that wrapped around Leiblein's bulging midsection like a bloated serpent—the belt on which the jewels of Bretilya, Munflenchia, Thunbia, and the other civilized realms were set.

Legend held that the tailor who stitched the continent of Lothar threw all the odd-lot cloth scraps and rugged remnants of his craft in one place: the Darkling Mountains. From Thunbia in the west all the way to the Great Miasmal Swamp in the east stretched the Darklings; from Ravenscrag in the southwest, the power spot of the loremasters, to the towering pinnacles of the northeastern peaks where the higher molt dragons dwelled. The Darklings evoked powerful and primordial emotions—not a malevolence, but rather a deep-rooted feeling that the Darklings served an older world, the Leiblein that existed before the Fall of the Elders, hoary, an uncatalogued domain, one full of raw magic and power stones and demigods.

Soon they began the ascent into the foothills. The Darklings' western highlands brimmed with sparkling streams that cheered the riders on, tossing bright red and blue flowers in their path and making them feel lighter in the saddle. The untamed swath of silvery granite peaks grew with every league northward, hovering above a brood of steep streams full of surging water and thick braces of large grey-trunked trees cloaked in deep green foliage, both guarded by garlands of adoring waxy-leafed thornbushes, their brilliant yellow berries as deadly as they were lovely. The grandeur of the dark mountains and deep woods made the riders' fateful quest seem like a pleasant holiday outing.

The road into the foothills wasn't difficult at first, but their pace slowed as the riders began to conserve their mounts for the rigors ahead. The road grew less formal as it cut between mountains; then, after another league or so, it was no longer possible to avoid steep inclines. They were well away from the settled lands of Bretilya as they wended upward toward Surridge Lookout, the next major landmark on the road.

Yor's blood stirred as they went higher in elevation. Surridge Lookout! he rhapsodized. It should be a fine day for it! A feast for the eyes!

For the next few leagues, the lookout loomed ahead of them. The road climbed steadily as it wove around the foothills. It was near midday before they reached the last leg of the upward slope, a straight shot to the top of the ridge that marked the beginning of the Darklings' inner sanctum.

Yor stopped at a creek that rambled over the road and looked along the ground. "He's been by here," he said. "Judging by the tracks, I'd say about an hour ago."

"He dumped some trash over here," Dword said as he looked along the creek banks. "He must have stopped for lunch."

"Again?" Trebor mused. "He stopped before he reached the fainli village. If that wasn't lunch, what was it? Brunch? He sure seems to be eating a lot. . . ."

"Riding makes you hungry!" the prince said. "In fact, I'm getting hungry again myself. Maybe—"

"No," Yor said. "Eat while you're riding if you have to. I'd like to catch Bosamp before he gets to the Escarpment."

"Aw . . ." the prince complained but gave it up quickly.

They continued uphill in silence. Slow going it was, but not difficult. The road bent alongside a ridge, then rose straight up the side of a gradual incline that lifted up to the tableau of the Darklings. The climb was without incident, though not without exertion, so that when the road finally leveled off, their horses were sweating.

They reached the lookout and paused. Peeping through a grove of tall timber, they saw the Gorge of the Fairfax, an amphitheater of rugged mountains where the celebrated river was born.

"Hold here for a minute and let the horses catch their breath," Yor said. "We can't be that far behind. Maybe we can catch a glimpse of Bosamp from the lookout."

The riders formed a line along the north edge of the road and peered out into Fairfax Gorge and the surrounding mountains. Far below, a short trestle bridge spanned the turbulent river. Above the river's rabid rambling rapids, ethereal mists hung suspended, a tapestry for oblique sunbeams to frolic in, a stained-glass water window shimmering with dewy phantoms, wavering shapes that stoked the imagination.

Yor looked beyond the river's gash, scanning up the road, trying to see through the veil of trees and mist, but he couldn't spot their quarry. He stood in his stirrups, desperate for a glimpse.

"I see him!" Dword blared suddenly, breaking the group's intense scrutiny of the gorge and the road below. An orange dot blinked once between gaps in the immense wood cover, then quickly again. "Over there!"

"Where?" the prince asked. "I can't see anything!"

As the red-beard raised his arm to point, the orange dot flashed out of sight, disappearing over the rim of the next ridge line. "He passed over the ridge," Dword said with a sigh. "You can't see him now."

"Well, hey!" the prince voiced enthusiastically. "Maybe this whole dumb trip will be over by nightfall! Then I can get a decent bed and a good meal! Let's go!"

The riders waited for Yor to lead, but he remained unmoving.

"Go on ahead," he told them. "I'll be along shortly."

"Nature calls, eh!" the prince chortled. "Want to borrow the chair?"

Yor didn't respond. Dword and Trebor looked at Yor for an explanation, but he offered none, content to let them accept the prince's interpretation. With Trebor in the lead, the four riders carefully picked a path down the road, mindful of the steep drop-off that awaited the careless.

"Don't be too long," Dword said as he rode by the black-clad cavalryman. He gave Yor a knowing look, but withheld his suspicions.

As they vanished around a bend on the way downhill, Yor dismounted and tied his horse to a bush. To the edge of the precipice he hiked, the need to look overcoming his fear of heights. He climbed down a few yards to a small ledge that offered a better vantage point and sat hunched over quietly on a shelf of rock, a black carrion bird on a perch.

The sunlight found him; the warmth on his shirt was a welcome friend, glittering off his golden passementerie, bouncing beams off him like a many-faceted gem. The sky was clear, just a few far-off clouds. He saw that of the three moons, only Zelaven had not set yet. The largest of the three moons was wafer thin now, a crescent earring for the sun.

He gazed across the horizon. The Darklings spread out before him, grand and glorious granite slabs, majestic, unfathomable, trimming the broad vista before him. The mountains struck a chord of harmony in him, and he observed their aeries with soul satisfaction, squinting childlike with the hope-fear of seeing a dragon on the wing or a glacier field glistening in the sun, but neither vision came to him.

Nature does indeed call me, he mused. . . .

His reverie turned downward. Below, crashing downhill through a confined, stone-strewn canyon, the Fairfax River trumpeted, the centerpiece of the setting, a white-water woman coursing passionately, freely, dauntlessly. The distant roar of the river called out a promise of coolness. In his mind, he traced the river through the Darklings, down into the Fairfax's highlands, then through the moors as it gathered strength and breadth, and finally into the rolling farm country of the province that took its name from the river, to the village where he was born.

Annandale.

It's been a long time since I was home. . . .

Home? chided his inner demon. Have you forgotten? All the land north and east of the bridge belongs to her! Crimson, he gazed eastward. Seventy leagues into the sunrise, Castle Fairfax was beyond any man's vision, even from Surridge Lookout. Lord Lee is dead! the inner demon jabbed. It all belongs to her now: the Mistress of the Fairfax! But for the king's intercession, you'd be an outlaw in your own province, a wanted man with a price on your head!

The thought coursed through him like the torrent of rushing water below. His mind's eye saw the castle as if it were sitting on the next hill; he wavered on the brink.

Kathy . . .

They could handle Bosamp without me, he thought. I could turn off before the Escarpment and take the old miner's road. In three days, maybe two, if I rode all night, I'd be there. . . .

He swallow hard, tried to gulp down his thoughts, but his mouth had gotten very dry.

No . . . I can't leave them now. Duty calls.

His fingers formed into a ball so tight it hurt; the pain helped to free the grip of unsated desires.

Another time, my love!

Fairfax Gorge called in his ears as he scaled the rock back uphill and mounted his horse. He felt a guilty pleasure at being able to enjoy the sight alone, even though there was work to be done.

Sometimes I just need to be alone. . . .

He rejoined them below on the north slope of the Surridge

Decline.

"Everything come out okay?" the prince snickered.

Yor ignored him. "There's no good place to stop until we reach the river, so keep riding and watch for slides," he advised the party, feeling the need to say something. All of them, except perhaps the prince, had been down this road at some time in their lives, he realized, and he felt awkward at stating the obvious. "We'll have a proper meal and rest the horses in the meadow past the bridge."

Yor resumed the lead, glad for the focus that scouting at the point would provide. The sharp, meticulous decline to the trestle bridge granted a breathtaking panorama of the mountain gorge and the serpentine river writhing through it. In one place, the road shrank to a trail, then to a treacherous path, and they had to dismount, but though the ride downward was strenuous, the day was perfect and the knowledge that Bosamp was just beyond the next hill kept them moving without complaint.

Down.

Finally the party emerged from the tree line into a small clearing at the south end of the bridge and saw the cairn. Rusting weapons and broken pieces of armor littered the mound, charred from the funeral pyre of a dozen years ago. Rimmed with shattered rocks, the burial knoll had been salted so that no grass or weed would grow where the brave Brets now rested.

The cairn.

The Year of the Thogs, Yor brooded.

In a single glance, the sight of the rock monument took away all their high-spirited good humor.

They stopped solemnly. There was no marker. None was needed. The five riders paid silent respect, but one of them was more intense than the others.

"My brother and my best friend lie there," Sir Dudley said, his voice failing to a whisper, his eyes damp and dim. "I was with the earl's column, headed for Castle Fairfax. The thogs barricaded Surridge; the road being narrow and steep, we couldn't bring much of our army to bear. Many men fell pushing the thogs off the lookout, but push them off we did. Then we came to the bridge, and the thogs decided to stand fast.

"Four times did we charge the bridge; four times did the thogs throw us back! In the first charge, my brother Eric was struck down; in the third, my boyhood friend Malcomb died. The thogs hurled the wounded into the water, letting them drown in their armor. Soon men and thogs dammed the rapids in death. The Fairfax ran red and green with blood that day. . . ."

The veteran knight paused, remembering with a somber shudder. "Then as the daylight began to fade, we feared the advantage darkness would give our foe. A council was held, and the earl gave dire, desperate orders. All the remaining knights were formed up into a **V**, with the wizards right behind them, and the rest of the army fanned out up and down the river to try to cross above and below the bridge itself. Into the midst of the thogs we knights charged, with the earl leading the way.

"What a sight the earl was that hour! A brave knight at the peak of his vigor and his valor! He became a conduit for the combined power of all the wizards. His armor glowed with sorcerous import, and his morning star whirled like a ball of glorious blue, bolts flying from it, flashing through the massed thogs! He broke through them and was engulfed in their ranks. He drove on alone into their rear, while we pushed steadily over the bridge. All around him, the thogs fell like wheat before a scythe! The thogs couldn't hold us back. . . ."

Sir Dudley paused for moment of respect. "Struck down finally, the earl fell from his horse and disappeared from our sight. Maddened, we charged onward, and the thogs fled, only to be caught in the ravine over there by the pincer movement of our footmen, who had forded the river by using the very bodies of friend and foe alike as stepping-stones. Not one thog escaped that crucible of steel. When we found the earl, his armor was empty; his body had been consumed by the powers that flowed through him! Three of the wizards also vanished. But the road to Castle Fairfax was open."

Sir Dudley trembled and closed his eyes, then opened them slowly and looked at the cairn again. He raised his sword in salute.

Memories stirred in Yor, too. Without looking at anyone, the black-clad adventurer urged his horse onward. "I was in Castle Fairfax . . ." he said in a low voice and pointed his steed toward the bridge.

Thogs! Absorbed in the dreadful past, Yor remembered with a grim shiver that night of horror when the thogs marched through the province of Fairfax. Visions flashed through his mind: burning farms, looted village shops, animals butchered and eaten raw, men and women bound and carried away back to the vile nest of the invaders in the Great Miasmal Swamp. Thogs! His hand went to his rapier hilt, ready to reap justice. Ghost-racked, he stared blankly at the wooden trestle bridge.

Don't!

A wrongness jolted Yor, wiping away the memories of the Year of the Thogs. He tingled, coming alive, his inner power jumping to its feet, ready to spring.

The bridge? What could be wrong with the bridge?

Wary, Yor stared at the wooden structure even as the horse plodded toward it. It looks the same as it always did, he thought, but uncertainty rippled through him, spreading out from the core of his being, a premonition of danger without an observable cause. He paused his mount at the end of the wooden planking and sought a reason for his internal rumblings. But when no insight came, he tightened his hands on the reins and urged the horse forward cautiously.

*Fizz!*

As soon as his horse set its last leg on the bridge, the air howled, and a bright flash of blue burst like a firecracker, blinding Yor. A set of sigils appeared over the center of the bridge, then exploded. Crackling flames flared up in front of him, a hungry fire looking to feed. "*Yooorrr . . .*" the blue wall of flames moaned at him, beckoning him to come and play in hell.

"Look out!" yelled Trebor.

The blue blaze spat from the timbers of the trestle bridge and enveloped him with fiery malice.

The air around him transformed into flame, scalding Yor's skin. His face felt as if it were lashed by a whip, burnishing his exposed flesh. Blinded, he waved a hand in front of his face and sought to fan the flames away with a silent scream.

"*Yooorrr!*" the flames crowed gleefully.

"Get out of there!" Dword yelled behind him.

With a whinny, Yor's horse reared, preparing to bolt across the bridge, deeper into the jaws of the inferno.

No! Not forward!

Quicksilver. Concealed from the others by the sorcerous holocaust, their frantic shouts muted by the bellow of the blaze, Yor was out of his saddle, his boots battering the wooden planks, his hands gripped to the horse's bit. "Back! Back!" he shouted to his steed.

He wrenched the hysterical, rearing beast around, forcing it away from the inferno. Back! His arms tugged hard on the bit; the panic of the horse was transmitted through his arm and joined with his body. The fire sizzled his skin like meat on a spit. His face went red, and the air was sucked out of his lungs. The pain seared him mercilessly.

Something deep down inside Yor leaped up like an unchained monster. His throat warped as the bizarre tone of the Sortilege rune escaped from his shocked lips, as if the sound were leaping directly out from the center pit of his soul. A dark blue aura suddenly formed around him, mingling with the aquamarine flame, canceling them out, neutralizing them in a screeching wave of unworldly noise. The aura flickered, blue on blue, cooling him at the same time as the fire burned him, magic against magic.

Possessed, he yanked the horse back like a poker from a blazing inferno, the force of his desire so strong not even the adrenaline of the frightened beast could prevent his taking control.

"*Yooorrr . . .*"

A second glyph vomited up past his lips, a horrid sound that hurt his ears and made his tongue taste of ashes, but this glyph he did not try to hold back. Stronger because of his cooperation, the rune blasted through the bridge fire, parting the licking flames before and behind him, making a path to walk through while the sorcerous flames whined in deprivation.

His horse bolted toward safety, back through the channel of parted flames that had formed between Yor and the near end of the bridge, knocking Yor to the ground as it went by. A blast of flames engulfed him and was countered quickly by his own aura. He bounced up and staggered back until he was finally clear of the blue inferno.

"*Yooorrr!*" the cheated flames complained behind him.

As he reached the end of the bridge, his knees buckled before anyone could reach him. The others surged forward toward the toppling Bret; Sir Dudley gathered the reins and steadied the nervous horse; Dword and the prince clasped Yor's shoulders, pulling him gently up, while Trebor searched his sacks for something to counter the burns on Yor's exposed flesh.

"I'm all right . . ." Yor said and then fainted.

"Balderdash's boner!" the barbarian cursed as he supported his friend. "Bosamp did this!" The Norlander gaped in horror at the magical inferno. Like spilled oil, the conflagration spread the length of the bridge. It danced over the trestles playfully, a fumeless, heatless blaze that enveloped, but did not consume, the framework.

"It's wizard's fire," Trebor explained, half cursing, half enrapt. Already his lore satchel was open as his frantic fingers sought a vial of herbal salve. He filled his hands with the tincture and began smearing it all over Yor's face and head. "The fire adheres to wood, but it burns only flesh, a property certain sorcerers find delightfully useful."

The loremaster quickly finished applying the salve. "That ought to help some."

"It had better," Yor said dazedly as he regained consciousness. "It smells bad enough." He motioned them away from him and stood on shaky legs. Gingerly he touched his inflamed skin. Flakes of singed hair fell off his mustache; his face and ears were tender to the touch, but no worse than a severe sunburn.

"Are you all right, Captain?" Sir Dudley asked with concern.

"I guess I am. The clothes must have protected me," the cavalryman replied. "They won't burn in witch fire either." Steadying, he took his waterskin and drank a thoughtful gulp. The cool fluid felt good on his throat; he splashed some on his face.

Out of the corner of one eye, he saw the blue flames gamboling on the bridge, and his curiosity stirred. The exuberant fire still ran up and down the bridge span, but the numinous tingling inside that had overwhelmed him moments ago was gone.

Empty.

He shuddered in loathing at the queasiness in his stomach and soul. Sorcery! I promised I wouldn't use it! But it all happened so quickly! I vow you'll not get free so easily again!

Yor breathed a few deep breaths to regain his composure, bending over with his hands on his knees to prevent himself from passing out. He righted himself slowly and turned back to his companions. "That spell was set for me . . . by name!" he declared. "How could Bosamp have known I was after him?"

"He knows," the loremaster asserted. "He may only be a thaumaturgical tyro, but he knows. Prescience is part of the talent."

Dword joined in. "Isn't it obvious that the king was going to send somebody after him? Who else would it be? Anybody could have reasoned it out."

"You three do have reputations," Sir Dudley noted. "That song Dword wrote has spread pretty far."

Yor grunted and shot an I'll-get-you-for-that-ballad-someday look at Dword. "It's a good thing I went first," he said slowly. "I'd hate to think what would have happened if any of you had been on the bridge ahead of me."

Trebor shook his head. "Don't assume it was set for you alone. That spell," he proposed, "was almost surely set to go off for any one of the three of us. The first to set foot on the bridge would have tripped it."

"Gah!" Prince Rodney blanched. "I'm not going first any-more!" In fact, he had never gone first, but nevertheless he backed his horse up a good rod from the bridge.

"What now?" Dword asked as he cast a fretful glance at the still-burning bridge. The flames danced up and down the length of the planking, leaving not a mark, neither soot nor blackening. "It could be hours before the fire dies, and Bosamp's pulling away from us!"

It was a truth they all saw at once: gnashed teeth.

Can we cross the river anyhow? Yor wondered. He walked to the rim of the gorge, well away from the bridge, seeing the blue fire reach out for him, and looked down into the river, then followed its banks in both directions searching for a ford. The raging water was swift and high, and the sight of it filled Yor with doubts.

"We might be able to climb down to the river," he said, looking along the banks with a frown, "and we might be able to jump from boulder to boulder. . . ."

"*Gah!*" said the royal youth, and he backed off to an even

safer distance. "Deal me out!"

"We might even be able to scale the opposite bank," Yor continued. "But not with our horses. We'd have to leave them here. We'd lose too much time walking to the next village; it's quite a ways to Dowddale. So we'd as well turn around and go home now if that's our only choice."

"Oh, hey!" the prince commented enthusiastically. "Well, it's been fun. A real outing, eh, what? Well, I'll tell Pops you did the best you could, and—"

Their stares shut him up.

"We could go back to the jarth and take the west fork to Crwth, then cut north for the coast," Dword offered sourly, then took it back. "It's quite a few leagues out of the way, though, and we'll lose Bosamp's trail altogether if we do that. No, it's probably better to just sit here and wait."

"We need lunch and the horses need rest anyway," Trebor said. "And the fire can't burn that long; Bosamp's just not that good of a wizard."

Blocked.

"I suppose it's our best option," Yor said glumly. "And we were so close I could almost smell him!"

"We'll catch him," Trebor said. "This is only a minor setback."

"Well, then, lunch it is!" the prince said. "Yo, Dudsy: the grog and victuals!"

The elder knight looked at Yor; Yor shrugged back helplessly. "We might as well. When the fire does burn out, we're going to ride hard. There'll be no more stopping until the sun sinks. Or even after it sinks!"

Seeing agreement, the dutiful Sir Dudley began to gather lunch from the packhorse.

"I didn't think Bosamp was capable of this," Trebor murmured as he watched the flame imps parade along the wooden planks and mock them with funny faces, obscene gestures, and even annoying imitations of the party, especially Yor. "Do you recall how badly he botched the pyrocasting at the sorcers' smoker last spring? A thoroughly shabby performance! I was taken aback when they sent him as a replacement for Wendom."

"Poor Wendy," Sir Dudley sighed mournfully. "None of this would have happened if that roc hadn't eaten him. Stuck on the top of his tower, between a roc and a hard place, as it were."

Yor and Trebor looked quickly at each other.

"Come on now," the Norlander countered the unspoken exchange between his two friends. "You don't really know that the Council found out Wendy was making flintlock powder for you."

"Flintlock powder?" the prince said nervously. He looked at the two men fearfully and resolved to back off a few more steps—after lunch, of course. "I thought the Council banned that a few years ago. Didn't they put a spell on the powder to make it blow up if you tried to use it?"

"We think that they did," Yor said, his wrath rising as he remembered. "A few years ago, when the Council was still selling the powder to anyone who wanted it, they added a warning that the formula had been 'misplaced,' and therefore they couldn't be sure that they had it exactly right anymore."

"And charged a usurious price for it, at that!" Trebor vehemently interjected. "Gold-grubbing blackguards, the lot of them!"

"Then about two years ago, without explanation, they stopped selling even the tainted powder."

"Oh, they explained it, all right!" Trebor inserted. "They said the powder was too dangerous now. They were ever so sorry they'd lost the original formula, but they couldn't take the responsibility for it anymore. Prevaricating imbefools! Do they really think we're so dense as to believe that lame manure? There's more to this than we know—yet."

Yor waited for Trebor to finish his broadside and then

resumed. "There aren't a dozen flintlocks left now. Trebor and I have the last in Bretilya. And we needed powder."

"But only the Council knows how to make the powder," the prince said, perplexed. "Wendom wasn't on the Council. So I don't see how—"

"Wendom stole the formula from Eikos."

"Eikos!" The prince gasped, stiff with horror. The most powerful warlock on all Leiblein! The head of the Council, Eikos was so dangerous that none had even dared to question his right to rule the Council. Vengeance was the trademark of his life, so if Wendy . . . that means . . . yikes!

Prince Rodney backed off even farther, checking the sky for possible bolts of lightning or winged monsters.

"But you don't know that Eikos found out!" Dword protested. "Why hasn't he done something to us if that's true? And besides, you know that rocs have been gulping down wizards for as long as there've been rocs!"

"For as long as there've been *wizards*," Trebor corrected, then paused, suddenly unsure of exactly which had come first. "But perhaps you're right; there are other explanations that don't involve the powder or the dietary quirks of rocs."

The man-mountain gathered in their looks before proceeding. "Wendom was powerful enough to ascend from the Circle to the Council, and that was bound to be trouble. There are only two ways to get on the Council: wait until someone dies and get voted in, or challenge one of the sitting members to a duel.

"Maybe one of the Seven—Golgothagon? M'bababaa? Thunkja? El Rukgeyser?—decided to get rid of Wendom before he got tired of waiting for one of them to die."

They mulled over the loremaster's words for a moment.

"There's another possibility," Sir Dudley said as he spread the picnic blanket on the ground. "Wendy told me once he was more worried about the Circle than about the Council. He had the next opening on the Council sewn up. They didn't dare *not* elect him, for then he really would challenge one of them! Wendy was more afraid that one of the other members of the Circle might have decided to increase his own chances for that opening by assassinating him."

"They're like that," Dword agreed.

Cold thunder boomed in Yor's mind.

Kathy was one of the Circle of Seven Sevens now!

And Eikos had been her mentor!

Yor whipped around and stared at the burning bridge, goose bumps forming on his skin as he watched the flame imps turning cartwheels on the trestle, motioning for him to join them.

Is Bosamp really good enough for this? he asked himself caustically. Perhaps he has been showing more talent than we expected, but this?

Cold, cold, cold.

His thoughts tumbled like the glass in a kaleidoscope, and he stared at the bridge. He stilled himself and listened to his inner voice, trying to think as she thought, trying to visualize what would have made her expend so much power and pay the cost to maintain it over so many leagues.

Cold certainty.

You are right to fear me, witch!

"The thing that galls me the most," the loremaster fumed, unaware of the thoughts bouncing around inside his companion, "is that I don't even think the powder is magical. I think it's a natural phenomenon that the Council stumbled on to, something more properly in the realm of lore than sorcery. But for some reason, the Council came to fear it. I wish I knew why. There's some secret here, mark my word."

"Pardon me, Captain, but lunch is served," Sir Dudley said graciously. The sight of a senior knight of the realm standing like a waiter over a blanket spread on the forest floor may have seemed demeaning to the others, but Sir Dudley's countenance was serene, without evincing a slight of any kind. He had discovered that he secretly enjoyed preparing and presenting food, and it had, in fact, become one of the few joys of his office. "Come and sit on the blanket, Your Highness."

Trebor jumped up like a Fusistanian horned gnorlox in heat. "Blanket?" He stared at the wizard's fire. "Blankets!" the loremaster repeated loudly, laughing at his own folly for not seeing the obvious much sooner. He fingered Yor's garments and drew a reflexive hostile stare from the cavalryman, still too embedded in his own dark thoughts to have heard a word Trebor had uttered. "It only burns flesh! Your clothes didn't even singe!"

Rapidly the tall Bret calculated the length of the bridge and figured the number of blankets in the party. There are two for each rider. . . . Hold on! The prince has three extra! The ground is too hard for his royal back, remember? He makes a mattress of them! Four extra, if I count the one being used for lunch!

Trebor grinned the grin of the man who has someone by the codpiece. Enough, I think! Once the horses are over, we can pull the blankets back off the bridge from the rear! We don't even have to leave them! It'll be a tad close for comfort, but . . .

"Eat fast," Trebor said nonchalantly to the prince. "I'll need that blanket in about ten minutes."

"Huh? What? Were you talking to me?"

The man-mountain stalked off to his horse and unrolled his bedding.

"Trebor?" Dword said.

Reveling in mysteriousness, the loremaster said nothing, knowing all eyes were now on him. He walked toward the bridge with his blankets, unfolding them as he went.

Aha! the barbarian thought.

Before Trebor reached the bridge, the red-beard was humming a scandalous roundelay that penetrated even Yor's trance, and unraveling his own bedding as he rushed up beside the Croswall captain. "Brilliant," he said to the loremaster.

"It was the prince's idea."

"Of course. Let's see: 'With a blanket, they passed/the bridge's fiery planks;/'Twas a princely idea/that bested the wizard's foul pranks.' Hmmm . . ."

Trebor threw his blanket on the bridge, parting the blue fire. The flames stretched out for him in blue tentacles, but the blanket smothered them and kept the loremaster just out of their incendiary reach.

"After you," Captain Trebor Blackburn invited, gesturing.

"Youth must be served," Honorary Bret Captain Dword Ecklundson replied. He stepped out over Trebor's first blanket and laid his own carefully beyond it. "Second verse same as the first?"

"Of course."

The flames crackled in irritation; the blue flame imps were no longer so jolly. They tried to hurl themselves at the duo, but the smothering blankets formed a barrier they could not trespass. Enraged, they lined up on the trestle handrails and made an acrobatic formation approximating a well-known hand gesture.

No matter . . . lore triumphed over sorcery.

By now Yor had broken away from his trance, smiling and shaking his head at the loremaster's ingenuity. He caught up with them as the duo were coming with the second helping of blankets.

"By the blessed bard! You've done it again!"

"It's the prince's idea," Dword espoused.

"Naturally. May I help?"

" 'Twould be an honor, my Count!"

Yor almost smacked him for the gibe, but he took Dword's proffered blanket and strode over the existing coverlet to lay his own blanket on the bridge, extending the blanket pathway another man's length. The flames were incensed at his insult, reaching out as far as they could, but they couldn't quite get to him. They whined piteously.

"Beware, witch!" he said, very low. "Don't overreach yourself! One day soon I'll be coming for you. . . ."

The flame imps fell back in fear.

The loremaster walked to the bridge with another load of bedding. "Bosamp's going to beat us to the Escarpment," Trebor conjectured with a frown, stroking his clean-shaven chin.

"Seems likely," the red-beard agreed, mocking the Bret warrior by stroking his own furred chin, then abruptly stopped to pick out a piece of something unknown that had lodged in the wiry red mat of his renowned beard.

"And he'll wait at the bottom . . . a perfect place to ambush us," Trebor concluded. "He'll be able to see us coming a long way in advance."

"Hmmm . . . there is that . . . but no one promised you a rose garden," Dword said.

"And I didn't get one."

"The Escarpment will slow Bosamp down to a walk," Dword calculated slyly, his eyes twinkling. "He'll have to dismount unless he's completely crack-brained. He'll spend a couple of hours on the face of the cliff. It's a thousand-foot drop if it's a rod, and there are almost a dozen switchbacks. My guess is we'll see him there long before he gets to the bottom."

"But we'll have to dismount, too," Yor said as he joined them, handing his blankets to Trebor, who was supervising the bridge bed-making. "We won't be able to go much faster than he will."

"Oh, yes, we will."

Skeptics, the two Brets peered at the red-beard. Dword winked conspiratorially at Trebor, then grinned at the cavalryman. "Yor and I are going to rappel down the Escarpment. We'll beat Bosamp to the bottom, and he'll be trapped between us."

"*What?*"

"Trebor!" Dword scolded with shock. "Didn't you tell

him?"

"I was waiting for a more propitious moment," the lore-master said drolly.

Tongue-tied, Yor mumbled, "We'll talk more about this later. . . ."

Much later! Next century maybe! Rappel indeed!

When they crossed the bridge and left Fairfax Gorge, the sorcerous fire still clung to the trestles, jealously unsatisfied.

\* \* \* \* \*

Seventy leagues away, a sultry green-eyed beauty felt a chill on her winsome body. Rising from her chair in the tower overlooking the Fairfax River, she flinched quizzically, experiencing a brief weakness, as if some portion of her power had been sapped momentarily.

An inexplicable feeling of loss stabbed through her; she tried to find a reason for it, but the cause seemed distant and did not answer her query. Disturbed, the Lady Katherine Lee went to the window that faced to the west and closed it.

# CHAPTER SIX

"Why did they have to put the blorging Bell so far away, anyway? You'd think the flinking gods would have made it a little easier, wouldn't you?"

The horse didn't answer him. Grumbling, cursing, walking with the horse in tow, Bosamp's brown eyes glared as they ferreted out the road ahead, scouting it. A note of concern sounded in him as he saw that a section of the steep ramp descending the Escarpment had been eroded by water runoff from the sheer slabs of granite stone. He realized with a heart-stopping gulp that one misstep on the sandy footing here would be fatal. Resolute, he tugged the reins and started through the precariously slender stretch of road etched into the face of the cliff. Leaning as close to the rock wall on his left and away from the yawning abyss on his right as he could, he stepped carefully through the washed-out section, using his staff as a brace as he went.

In ten steps it was done. The youthful wizard sighed in relief and paused by a large bush with red berries, one of the few plants that could find a foothold on the Escarpment, which ran mostly northwest. He mopped his brow with a bright plaid handkerchief, one he had pilfered from somewhere along the trip, pushing sweat-wet curls of dark hair off his forehead as he daubed them and dared look out toward the northern horizon. From his vantage point high above the Bretilyan coastal plateau, he could see a score of leagues, well beyond the next village and the river strapped to it. Mentally he traced the tiresome road meandering through the geographical pastiche spread out before him. He imagined hopefully that the shimmering blue at the horizon's edge was the Bretilyan Channel, where lay Axiom. But the channel was still a good three dogged nights away; he wishfully mistook the light play in the heat waves for his desired goal, a mirage in the acute afternoon sun.

"And I haven't even reached the coast yet!" he said, continuing his list of complaints as he resumed walking. "This is going to take weeks! I'll be a worn-out old man before I get to the Bell!"

Bosamp subconsciously began to scratch at his side, a mistake that reawakened the itch and aggravated his hunger.

*Groouwl!* his stomach interrupted. *Groouwl!*

"All right! All right!" Abruptly he stopped to service the tummy tantrum, but the horse, head drooped, ears flat, failed to notice and bumped into the wizard from behind, a more-than-playful nudge in the worst possible location for it.

"*Aaiii!*"

Overreacting to the unexpected shove in his rear, Bosamp floundered, arms and legs flapping out of control. He teetered on the brink of disaster, white with terror, while the Escarpment leered at him. His feet *rat-a-tat-tatt*ed on the road edge, a staccato gavotte, kicking dirt and small stones into the abyss before him. Even though he had made good progress down the face of the cliff, it was still much, much, much too far to fall.

"Ohhhhno!"

Just when it seemed likely he was going to slip over the side, having parlayed merely ajar into total discombobulation, an updraft caught him, billowing his voluminous orange robe up into his face, preventing him from seeing the oblivion awaiting him . . .

. . . and hurled him back against the rock wall.

"Mother Mordred!"

Crazed, steadied, safe, Bosamp angrily wrestled the bright orange garb back into place. Breath pumped through his lungs in terrified gasps as he peered off into the abyss. Sigils leaped to military attention and saluted, but finding no immediate use for his sorcery, he regained control of his fear.

Then, furious, he stared at the culprit in his brush with death.
"Oat-brain! I'll flog you later for that! Just watch where I'm
going from now on, and maybe I'll spare you!" He reached out
and swatted the beast's nose. "Stupid! Stupid! Stupid! You must
have been trained by flinking sages! I'll be rid of you at the next
stable! Of all the wretched horses I've had to put up with on this
trip, you are the worst! I should—"

*Groouwl!*

"Oh, all right! If it's not one thing, it's another."

A steady stream of scatology gushed from the starving sorcerer. He found it vexing that he could eat, eat, eat and never
seem to quench the hunger pangs, not even when he had stuffed
himself until he was too bloated to stand. By trial and error, he
had concluded that what seemed to dull the raving craving best
was to eat about half a meal every other hour.

And the time was up.

Hissing, he reached into his knapsack and tore the wrapper
off a brick cheese he had thieved. His eyes lit in amusement as
he remembered how he had acquired the heavy dairy product in
Kirby Downs. *I bet that milkmaid thought I was groping her,
the harlot! Probably the biggest thrill of her day! Maybe her
whole life! Peasant hag! She wasn't nearly pretty enough for me!*

He tossed the cheesecloth over into the abyss; catching an
updraft, the cloth fluttered, then glided downward, falling,
falling, falling, and finally draped itself over a blooming clifflass
in a cranny below, shutting off the sunlight to the fragile plant,
dooming the unlucky virgin flower. In a rocky nook only a foot
away, her cliffbeau would now wither away forlornly.

The wizard chomped and smacked like a Korian lovedog,
wolfing down savage chunks whole, unchewed. Defiant to the
last, the cheese nonetheless was overcome by Bosamp's
onslaught. Normally the comestible would have sufficed a small
family as a bland, nourishing meal on a hard winter's night—
about the only time the rock-hard cheese was ever called upon,
and then only if there was bread and ale and dried fruit to kill

the taste of the unpopular but durable cheese, which never spoiled and was occasionally used as a substitute for building materials or doorstops—but in a few seconds of the wizard's voracious attack, the entire brick disappeared into the bottomless pit of his stomach.

Not bad! Bosamp burped loudly. Flavorless but filling! It ought to hold me until I get off this blorging cliff!

Curious, he peered downward. His heart pounded at the sight of the sheer sides below, pounded at the sight of the narrow path that zigzagged in great slashes across the Escarpment's daunting vertical decline. Whose idea was this accursed road, anyway? It's not fit for man or beast! It has no commercial value! You couldn't get a cart up and down it if you tried! And what the hell would happen if I ran into anyone coming up?

His criticisms were unjust. For one, the road had never been more than a post road; most traffic went west on Fairfax Road, as he well knew when he had decided to risk the Escarpment Road. For another, most stretches were wide enough for horses going each way, and in the past, when it was maintained regularly, the road offered a shorter, though more arduous, route to west central Bretilya than the Fairfax Road. But several decades ago the Escarpment Road had been abandoned, mostly for the reasons Bosamp had recited, and it was slowly decaying into ruin as slides and erosion took their toll.

The wizard sighed and relaxed. Another hour, perhaps. I should make it down just about sunset. But I can't trust that dull-witted animal with my life on this road! If only I had learned how to fly. . . .

Jealous frustration.

The vein of sorcery running through him was strongest in the earth element and the spells that aligned with it. The air element, however, was directly opposite the earth element on the spoked sigil wheel, making it unlikely he would ever master anything but the simplest levitation or flight spells. Not the best place to experiment, is it? he thought, looking down at the rolling plateau far below.

Sulking in a bad humor, he trudged onward. But the horse remained planted to the spot where he had hit it. Bosamp reached the end of the reins. "*Augh!*"

The stubborn, contrary equine pulled the wizard's feet out from under him; he landed hard on his posterior, jumped up, wheeled around, and stared, face a-rage. "Fodder farter!" he seethed, tugging at the tether, whipping it against the horse's face. "Can't you see that I'm moving again? Get your horse's ass in gear!"

The sun blinked. Twice.

"What was that?" the orange-clad conjurer said and gazed above. The sun was lined up with the cliffside, making it almost impossible to distinguish anything in the glare.

A golden flash . . . a black dot.

What is that? A roc? No, too small, thank good— A man? Wait! There's two of them. . . .

"Nobody's that crazy!" he told the horse, then looked back to confirm that his eyes were not playing tricks on him. He could barely discern the sunspots, but it appeared that two addlepates were rappeling down the slope, vertically leapfrogging on the Escarpment. "Bandits?" he thought. "They'll fall for sure! Too bad for them!"

Then his heart skipped a beat or three as his eyes raced over the cliff to the top. "More up there!" he related to the horse. "I can't tell . . . Great sigil! That's Blackboard at the top! No mistaking that pompous plate cleaner!"

The thought cogged in the wizard's brain. Of course! The king has sent those three overrated fops of his after me! Captain Blackboard and that barbarian brawler friend of his, the minstrel what's-his-name—Dwarf? Yeah, that's him. And the third one, the pretty boy clothes-horseman, Count Gore? That's not right. . . .

Bosamp's mouth fell open as he spied more of his pursuers. "Sir Dumbly and Prince Rotnose! Hah-hee-hee-hee! This is not to be believed! Who would be stupid enough to think that blorge-nosed babycakes could ever . . ."

Comprehension: a slap in his face.

"My sucking stars! They're trying to get below me! I'll be trapped between them!" He stared in fascinated amazement, trying to imagine what would drive anyone to try this hard to catch him.

So . . . think!

Meanwhile, far above, Trebor minded the ropes and fretted as he watched the distant wizard, realizing with a sinking feeling that they'd been spotted. Gadzooks! What do we do now? "He's seen you!" the loremaster hollered down the hill to the two rappelers.

"Woden's wicked whip! We're as naked as a baby zux out here!" Dword shouted back to Trebor as he paused in his descent and latched his hold on the rope. His head swiveled and looked downslope to Yor; he urged his companion insect, "Don't look down! Look straight out!"

Below, about halfway down between the top and the wizard, the black and gold fly stopped bounding and set himself in the face of the rock. Hesitating, a blot eclipsing the sun, Yor looked down anyway and nearly swooned. About a hundred yards below and far to the left, he saw the orange blotch of the wizard. "This is insane!" he mumbled to himself. "We're in for it now! How did I ever let myself be talked into this one? Hanging on the side of a cliff while a lovesick sorcerer tries to decide which of his diverse options will provide the optimum in entertainment when he blasts us to smithereens!"

There's only one hope! When in doubt, take charge!

"Bosamp!" Yor ejected with an authoritative roar, pressing his expensive boots against the wall of rock. "In the name of King Derek of the Sapphire Throne of Bretilya, to whom you owe fealty, I order you to stop this deranged quest of yours! Your crimes to this point, though numerous, have been petty! Yield now and there will be mercy for you! Stand out in the open with your hands up, and we'll put in a good word with the king for you! If you cooperate, there will be mercy; if not, there will only be harsh justice! You cannot hope to escape us!"

Bosamp boiled over indignantly. "Justice?" he shouted back up the Escarpment. "Slaughtering an innocent traveler in broad daylight like uncouth brigands? Oh, most foul! The land weeps at the touch of your blighted feet! The sky mourns at the stench of your passage! To think of all the favors I did for that ungrateful king! Turn back or face my wrath! Count your blessings while you still can!"

Something clicked in the wizard's mind. "Count your . . ." Ah, yes! Now I remember him!

Coolly Bosamp gauged his sorcerous options. I'm not risking any of the hard stuff up here! I could trance and fall over the damned cliff! No, I've got to use something simple, something oaf-proof. . . .

"This is your last chance!" Yor warned, then felt foolish threatening someone well out of reach, someone also significantly more prudent, in that Bosamp's feet were solidly safe on the road, while his own were planted perpendicular to reality. "King Derek didn't say *how* we should bring you back! You're hopelessly outnumbered here! Surrender now before we're forced to use force!"

Brilliant phrasing, Yor scolded himself sarcastically. Real poetry! The stuff of legends! Let's just hope there's time for a sequel, or at least a rewrite. . . .

"I knew it!" Bosamp told the horse as he turned to face it, waving his arms to demonstrate his great patience in the face of such villainy. "Blackguards, the lot of them!" Leaning out so he could see better, he waved his fist defiantly and howled, "Come and get me, fancy pants!" With that, he ducked back quickly against the rock wall and considered which spell to use.

Fancy pants? Who, me? Yor wondered as his striking blue orbs searched about for someplace to alight his feet. Fancy shirt, maybe, but not pants! The boots, well, they may be a bit much, bright red firemander hide, but pants? No way! These are hand-sewn of fine . . .

"Dword?" he asked, wiping the thought away as he glanced back uphill at the red-beard. "Any ideas?"

"Thorogod's thunderbuns!" Dword growled. "He wasn't sup-posed to see us this soon! Maybe the others can keep him busy somehow! I'm going to drop down to the road; you're too far past this switchback to make it. You'd better try to lower your-self to the next one down."

Below, hidden against the cliffside, Bosamp did some quick calculations. They're a long way off yet; they'll probably run out of rope. . . . No, wait! They've got spikes with them, for sure! They'll tie up, and that blorging Blackboard will drop the ropes down to them to be used again.

Rope?

Rope!

The wizard threw his head back and shrieked a joyful noise, laughing at his own cleverness as he decided on a sigil to cast. An old crowd pleaser, suitable for fairs and carnivals and not much else! But in this case, it's just perfect! His eyes weaved from side to side, looking for a place to brace himself. He chose a small pocket in the stone, where he tied the sash of his robe to the branch of a bush.

That ought to hold me. . . .

Her shut his eyes and concentrated, visualizing the runes of power one by one, then gave himself over totally to the casting, feeling the electric surge of power through his frame as the glyphs of the Sortilege erupted from his mouth, pouring from his throat and echoing off the bluff like Norlandic doomhorns. His amusement nearly ruined the first tone, but he continued spitting the glyphs like acid, each unnatural weird cry rending reality, sundering the idyllic peacefulness of the Bretilyan coun-tryside as each escaped from the pit of his being.

Birds took to wing, scattering like a hail of arrows from the face of the cliff; small creatures dived for their burrows;

Bosamp's horse whinnied in fright.

Dword yelled down at Yor, "Drive spikes in! Hurry!"

Yor shuddered. I knew this was a dumb idea! Kicking his heels into a crease in the rock and clamping one hand tight to the cord that linked him to the solid world, he hammered quickly at a spike with his other, pounding it with his mailed fist into the rock, not having much success at it.

Then Bosamp's spell wrung through the air; glyphs swept past the two rappelers in a howling gust of blue smoke. Their ropes went taut with a jerk and became hot in their hands, then spasmed, yanking back and forth, twisting, squirming, thickening, chaffing.

"Woden's tumescence! The rope's alive!"

Yor's curse-scream was even louder than Dword's.

Louder still, Bosamp's laugh could have curdled glass. "Hope you'll drop by real soon!" he yelled at the top of his hoarse lungs. "Who would have dreamed that the biggest braggarts in Bretilya could be killed by something as ordinary as the old rope trick? Next time—and there isn't going to be a next time!—the king should send men, not children!"

*Thump! Thud! Rumble! Thud! Thud!*

"Yikes!" The sorcerer's mirth transmuted into distress as Sir Dudley's boulder bounced downhill, popped up, and whizzed over Bosamp's head like a warning shot. Panicking, Bosamp pressed against the cliff and watched a shower of dirt follow in the wake of the crashing boulder, covering his robe and face with dirt.

Captain Trebor Blackburn's mighty tenor voice boomed, "Who would have believed that the biggest jackass in all of Leiblein could be obliterated by something as trivial as a rock, and I don't mean the avian kind! But Sir Dudley's was only a small boulder! You should see the one I've got! In fact, I'll let you see it right now! Happy travails!"

"I've got to get out of here!" Bosamp paled, trembling, fumbling to untie the sash as he explained to the horse, which was steadily backing away from him, intuitively knowing which of the two of them was the real target. "They've got the high ground on us! We're as exposed as a strumpet's breasts!"

*Thud! Thump! Bing!*

"Flink!" The youthful sorcerer dived and hit the road, eating dirt as Trebor's huge bounding calling card leaped up over his head. The suction of the boulder's passage pulled the thaumaturge toward the abyss. Only the quick use of his staff prevented catastrophe.

When the dust settled, Bosamp decided he was still alive.

Missed me! Still on his belly, the orange-clad wizard looked down and computed his chances. It's still a long way till I'm off the Escarpment! I'll never make it! They'll get me for sure! Like a cornered carnivore, his yellowish eyes darted around. Wait! Down there, where the next switchback starts! There's a way station under an overhang! I can hold them off from there!

The sorcerer ran to the nervous horse and grabbed a few crucial items, including the backpack he had stolen from the farm girl. He stuck both arms through it and whipped it around to his back. Then, loaded down with the tools of his trade, he left the horse to its fate, and vice versa.

Above, the secondary avalanche triggered by Trebor's mighty boulder followed a chute in the cliff toward Yor. Dust and fist-sized stones ricocheted off him; he coughed violently. By the sacred scribe, Trebor's going to get me as well! Yor worried.

But this was the least of his troubles. The rope was alive in his hands, twisting and tossing, trying to break his grip. It snapped like a plucked string and slammed him into a hard slab of rock, crushing his scabbard against his hip.

"Dragon's breath!" Before he could get his foot back on the spike, the rope-snake pitched him back into the air, and he hung in space, his tortured hands bleeding inside his gauntlets, his back aching with the struggle. I can't take much more of this! Desperate, the black-clad cavalryman glanced around for the nearest place to jump-drop-fly; he looked down. The road below was waist-deep in doom, but just maybe . . . Say, is that a ledge down there?

Maybe . . .

"Try to climb back up to the last switchback!" Dword screamed helpfully. But the barbarian had his own problems. As he worked hand over hand along the rope, the rope-snake resisted, spinning the Norlander around like a carousel, making him dizzy, disorienting him. The rope-snake bucked and twanged madly, but the red-beard's grip held firm, and he continued to slip down toward the road that lay below until he reached a sharp, jutting . . .

Frieda's hot crockpot! The rope's fraying itself on the rock!

It broke.

"*Argh!*" The red-beard's hands spaded the cliff; his boots got a rock under them, and he broke his fall with his groin. The pain was awesome. His mind blurred, Dword was at last free of the rope-snake, which had fallen and was still falling. He plotted a course and resumed moving down the sheer stone, using the fissures as footholds, toward the road, his beard filling with grit.

Safe.

It wasn't easy, but somehow he reached the narrow road. He heard Sir Dudley call down to him, "We're coming down as fast as we can!" Dword stood and looked over the edge for Yor. The sight and sound of the Bret dandy banging against the rock made Dword wince; he felt helpless, unable to do anything to help him.

If Yor dies, he'll never forgive me!

Safe?

Dword's rope-snake had split in the middle; the other end now dropped down on the Norlander like a Pyssite choker. It wound itself quickly around his throat.

"Humping hoarm-m-m—"

"The rope!" Trebor screeched in horror, seeing the anchored end of Yor's rope untie itself from the tree and let go. He grabbed . . . too late!

"Yor!"

Free-fall . . .

The ledge!

Transition.

Not much later, after exchanging of rounds of ineffective boulders and spells, after wrestling with ropes and managing to survive, they became acutely aware of the sinking sun, which made it hard to see in the thickening gloom. Clouds flowed over the top of the Escarpment, and an ominous rumble of distant thunder echoed.

Emboldened by desperation, Bosamp sneaked out from under the overhang and made a decision. That flinking horse has gone over to their side! They'll get me if I stay here! I'm doomed!

Unless . . .

I need a recharge before I try it!

He snapped open the snuffbox and inhaled the scintillating power powder. Ah! Fortified with dragon dust, he gathered up everything he could strap somewhere on his body, shoving his staff snugly but awkwardly through his sash, leaving his hands free.

No one said it was going to be easy!

World Shaker! World Breaker!

Hurling the multicolored, fickle dice of chance, he attempted to conjure an aerial servant, a rudimentary spell but difficult for one of the earth sign and dangerous for one in his drained condition. The glyphs failed to materialize into the sleek bird he desired; instead, they formed into a winged glyph, which hovered obediently before him.

Impulsively he grabbed on to the floating rune and leaped away from the Escarpment, only to discover that the glyph wasn't strong enough to support his weight. By then it was too late to turn back, as he was hundreds of feet above the ground and too far from the road to get back. The glyph, however, held together; it sank slowly in a glide, albeit a poor one, that carried the wizard far out over the coastal plateau.

Bosamp hung on for dear life and tried to steer. Off in the darkness he veered, soaring wide from his intended target, the friendly fires of the next village. Instead, as his arms ached and the staff pressed into his vulnerable crotch, he drifted westward. Eternal minutes later, the multisided dice of destiny stopped spinning and showed a saving throw; as luck would have it, he landed with a benign plop in the River Jonney, within three easy strokes of a grain barge, laden and languid.

Near dead with fatigue, almost drowned by the encumbrance of his gear, the trim-bodied sorcerer climbed quietly onto the barge and crawled under a tarp of watervard skins. Ravenous, he gorged himself on raw kernels of grain, eventually falling into an immobilized stupor.

Later, as he lay half passed out under the tarp, he overheard a barge hand say the boat was bound for Axiom.

Back on the Escarpment, well after moonrise—the Three Scimitars this night—it began to rain, a steady, soaking drizzle. Yor spent a miserable night cramped on the narrow shelf, one slip away from death, unable to risk sleeping and barely able to stay awake.

At dawn, they finally got Yor off the ledge.

The first thing he did was strangle Dword, of course.

Soon after, they realized that they'd lost Bosamp's trail.

* * * * *

At the end of their hard ride lay Axiom, a sailing city teeming with hearty gents and lively ladies, with trade and intrigue, with fortunes made, bribed, squandered, and embezzled. Axiom was the preeminent port on the Bretilyan Channel and therefore all the Northern Sea, outshipping rival Hjarstad to the north and lowly Lopach to the east. The former was the gateway to the spread-eagle island continent of Norlandia, while the latter was the Munflenchian capital and the armpit of the world, a stain on Lothar, a cesspool where pleasures and lives were cheap.

Dragon's breath! Yor scowled. A harbor full of ships, and all I can find is these three saltines: two hollow-legged Fishies and an unflappable Thunbian! Better to barter with the Bête Noire herself!

Yor glanced away from the three sea captains and out the window of the Sigh of the Sail Tavern and down into the harbor, trying to tame his mood. Below, rows of boats were docked, canvas furled as dark-limbed porters hustled cargo off one vessel and onto another. The wharf was thronged with barks and barges, with fishing dories and windjammers, a collage of masts and keels and canvas that enchanted the eye and made the mind drift idyllically.

Westbound through the channel came spices and fine cloth from Pangrim's distant bazaars, delicacies from Fusistanian kitchens, gold from aristocratic Upper Kor, gems from bourgeois Lower Kor, and metalmagic and leathercraft from decadent, slave-fueled Gormus. From the opposite compass point came Westphalic power stones and ore, Thunbian livestock and silverwork, and Kibquez loreware and glasscraft. Overland from Bretilya's interior arrived grains and the smoothest ale on Lothar; from the south and west came Menomian weaponry and the fine arts of Celgaetia; from the channel itself, a rich repast of seafood; from across the channel, Norlandic furs and woodstocks.

"Missed him by an hour!" Yor pronounced, trying to provoke some response in one—*any* one!—of the three inert, gassy skippers. Amazing, he mused sardonically, that men can be that comatose and still continue to chugalug drinks down their throats without spilling a single drop!

Well, perhaps not all of them are men, Yor considered. He recalled Trebor relating that the League of Loremasters had a standing committee whose sole purpose was to try to decide which Thunbian sex was which and how to tell them apart. Complicating matters, a few sages believed that Thunbians were unisexual, and there were even those that believed there were three sexes! And with a name like "Hatu Iks," Yor hadn't the faintest clue as to the sea dog's gender.

"Almost had him on the Escarpment!" he continued. "Did I mention what he did to the fainling? The man is dangerously deluded, I tell you, more than you can possibly know! He's a movable plague that has to be stopped! He's not just a Bretilyan problem; he's *everybody's* problem!"

He slammed his fist on the table to punctuate the point.

The three pilots lunged for their mugs before a solitary tear of gratis grog could be shed.

"Too bad you missed the tide maxima," one of the Fishies said with a smirk. "Only one each day, you know. The rest of the time it's two moons against one. But lessers run out till sunset; you can catch the next greater at dusk, if the price is right." The Fishie smiled and showed off rows of yellow, ribbed teeth, then gulped mead.

This is harder than picking lint off a felt cape! Yor bristled. Why couldn't there have been a fast Bret cutter ready to . . .

There was one, his inner demon poked back with glee, but Bosamp commandeered it, remember? The crew didn't know Bosamp wasn't still the court wizard! It's not their fault he got away! If you hadn't panicked on the Escarpment . . .

Panicked! I almost died! I spent all night on that treacherous ledge in the dark and the damp! Enough time to review every bonehead mistake and miscalculation I've made in all my years!

Hah! his inner demon jeered heartlessly. Not nearly long enough for all of them! Why, just the affairs of the heart alone would—

Enough! His ire attached itself to the three sea curs. Fishies! Yor snarled a silent blasphemy. A pox on them! Why don't they take their boat city back to Kor where they came from?

The short, oily, heavyset Fishies were nomadic seamen without a homeland, possibly because no one could tolerate them, particularly not their unique and inexplicable sense of humor, one that universally offended. When the Norlanders ruled the

Northern Sea, the Fishies had stayed away from the rich channel, but now that the long fjord lord war boats no longer raided with impunity, the Fishies had moved their floating villages to the western bays of the channel.

They say they can talk fish right into their nets! Yor sniffed doubtfully. Blowhards! I'd rather ship out with a seaslime in a leaky clamshell! And Thunbians are only slightly better!

"Ten gold!" Yor offered, doing the best he could to restrain his mounting indignation. "Top jack! Ten for five passages to Norlandia with the next greater tide!"

Amused blinks.

The Thunbian trilled his throat as if the cavalryman had just made the most horrendous breech of etiquette known to polite society.

Yor reddened with rage. Typical!

Surrounded by towering peaks with sky-high passes that had rendered every would-be invader gasping helplessly for breath, Thunbia's tall, fair, birdish inhabitants were Bretilya's neighbors to the northwest. Conventional waggery suggested they had resulted from an incompetent cleric's spirit casting and an unlucky flock of seagles. Roosted on a vast, isolated plateau high above everyone else, aloof Thunbia was forbidden to outsiders, and its inhabitants seldom condescended to mingle with other cultures. It was said the Thunbians had a society based entirely on gamesmanship, participating in never-ending tournaments of one sort or another, at which were awarded "status" chevrons. Thunbians wanted only one thing from the lower civilizations, as they viewed the rest of Leiblein, and that was firk, the rare land coral entirely absent from Thunbia, whose impurities made it appear in many stunning colors. Firk was a hard and beautiful gem when polished, and the Thunbians made the tokens and badges necessary to display their chevron rankings from firk only.

The rest of Leiblein agreed *en masse* that the Thunbians were way, way, way out of their trees—not dangerously so, but bird-brained nonetheless, and the Thunbians cared not at all what people devoid of status chevrons thought.

Unless they possessed firk, of course.

Thunbians, Fishies, Munchies, Menomians—how did we noble Brets get saddled with such riffraff for neighbors? Curse the Three Weird Sisters! Somebody owes us an accounting someday!

"Ten gold, with two more as a bonus if we beat that rabid runatic to Hjarstad!"

"With him on the tide and a half-day's lead, eh?" scoffed the first Fishie skipper. "Do you think we're—what is your word for it?—deft? Flotsam on your bonus! You pay Old Red Bones's ferryman up front, eh?" The Fishie eyed his fellow captains and laughed in strange sounds that made Yor clench his teeth.

If this is the best the world has to offer, maybe we should let Bosamp go! Exasperated, the cavalryman looked across the tavern at Trebor. Alone by the window, where the light was better, the loremaster was deep into a new tome, one adorned with a slavering sea wolf, and completely unconcerned with the bargaining debacle.

Sensing Yor's stare, the man-mountain glanced back, then out the window. He saw no sign of Dword and the others, who sought a place to stable their horses until they returned from Norlandia. Their loyal steeds were played out; they would get fresh mounts in Norlandia and be better off for it.

Don't see them, Trebor shrugged back.

Yor sighed and returned to the boat captains. "You win! Twelve gold, but not a silver more! This is a matter of the gravest urgency for all of us! The future is watching you, gentlemen, watching and hanging on a thread!"

"'Tis a long way to swim, is it not, Salmon Dave?" Fishie number one said.

"Most terribly far, Shad N. Jeremy!" replied Fishie number two.

The two Fishies snickered again. Yor's face grew redder until his temper was at the end of its not-especially-long fuse.

"How much longer is this bickering going to go on?" Yor exploded. The black-clad dandy's right hand settled meaningfully on his flintlock, lingered for dramatic effect, then had to be forcibly pulled back. "Twelve gold and four silver. That's my final offer! Tomorrow eve, there'll be fifty ships putting out!"

"Fifty on the next maxima? Hoooo! Perhaps more," the Thunbian clucked. "But only we three this evening. Twenty is my price. Norlandia is—hoooo!—out of my way, but if the future is watching . . ."

"Twenty?" Yor wilted, flabbergasted. "Piracy!"

"My price is twenty also," the first Fishie said.

"A good number," the second concurred. "It is also my fee."

All three tossed down the mead Yor had provided.

Blackguards! Yor ruffled. They've rigged this tightly! I'd need a meat cleaver to break this deadlock!

Where was Dword when you needed him?

A noise at the front of the Sigh of the Sail distracted Yor. Through the double doors strode a barrel-chested cougarand, a puss in boots, muscles and thick tawny hair bulging from his half-buttoned waistcoat. The cat-man had the smell of an easterner from Pangrim; the falchion protruding menacingly above and below his hide sash marked the cougarand as a warrior. From the stranger's furry right ear—the left was missing—hung an emerald gargoyle with bared fangs.

The earring . . . I know that earring. . . .

Walking past Trebor with a lifted eyebrow, the cougarand went to the bar and exchanged soft words with the bartender.

The bartender gestured at Yor.

Uh-oh!

Purposefully the cougarand turned toward the black-clad cavalryman. The feline eyes brightened with eagerness, but no smile graced his lips, only a shallow frown that made the ends of his drooping beard whiskers arch like hairy tusks. The cougarand walked toward Yor and stopped two feet from him, folding his immense forearms over his chest, revealing a death's-head tattoo on each biceps.

"Assassin!" one of the Fishie skippers exclaimed, gagging.

The cougarand glanced once at the speaker, and the Fishie blanched. Choking on their mead, all three sailors pushed their chairs back from the table and evaporated into the woodwork.

The cougarand looked Yor up and down. "Are you Count Yor? The craven coward sired of the mating of a slime worm and werepiss in a condemned dung pit? The man known to have the largest mouth and the smallest cock on all Lothar? A bugger of baby zux, a cheater at cards, a writer of bad poetry, and the clumsiest lover in the Six Estates? The man whose tailor jabbed out his own eyes rather than see what—"

"What?" croaked the enraged adventurer, rising to full height in a flash, the last insult being by far the most telling. "Who wants to know?" If I live, Yor vowed, when this tale is retold, I'll have much more clever repartee!

"I am commissioned." The easterner placed a gold coin on the table. "The choice—"

Finding a welcome and unavoidable outlet for his frustrations, Yor uncoiled and, with a powerful shove, flipped the table over, sending the pitcher and mugs spewing over the cat-man in a shower of mead, soaking the cougarand's clothes and fur. One of the Fishies, maybe both, swore.

Yor felt a brief, really brief, twinge of guilt about ruining the cat-man's rather fashionable attire, then taunted, "Get on with it, litterbreath! By the way, I really hate the smell of wet cat. I'd rather stick my head in a barrel of rotting stinkworms than spend another second downwind from you, you soggy, snaggle-toothed hair ball!"

That's more like it, Yor thought. I can die with that on my lips. . . .

"*Harrr!*"

Feline fast, the cougarand's sinuous arms shot forward.

Lightninglike, Yor sidestepped. The two bronze meat hooks, intended for his neck, flailed; one gripped Yor's left shoulder instead, clenching deeply. The claw extended to bite through Yor's chemise, to the chain mail below. A ripple of pain jolted his left side, from his shoulder to his feet, strangling half his body.

But only half. Before the pain could reach his toes, before the assassin could wrench him around to deliver a killing rake, Yor struck back.

*Whap!*

*Youch!* Yor's fist crunched against a tough sheath of stomach muscles, then buckled in pain. The cougarand flinched briefly and continued with his own downward stroke. Frantic, Yor rolled forward quickly, bumping against the cat-man forcefully, grinding his boot on the assassin's open sandals.

*"Harrr!"*

The maneuver deflected the skull-shredding swipe, which whizzed down the side of Yor's head, grazed off his ear, and pounded on his shoulder. The impact staggered Yor; his knees trembled and his ear throbbed.

Two huge claws sought his throat.

A blur, Yor simply dropped low, lunged in, then shot back up and slapped the surprised cougarand's empty paws away with a blinding outward thrust. Spread-stanced, the two combatants faced each other with a bit more respect. Recovering more quickly than the agile cat-man, Yor twisted around to the side and kicked straight out, driving his firemander boot into the cougarand's shin.

*"Harrr!"*

Off-balance, Yor didn't have time to be alarmed at the feeble response to what must have been bone-wrenching agony. The cougarand cuffed him soundly on the chin, a punch that made Yor bite his lip until he tasted blood. Circling right, the two parted and warily sized each other up. A thin trickle of red dribbled off Yor's lip; he wiped it away with alacrity, but the assassin's nostrils flared, his diamond eyes widening with bloodlust.

*"Harrr!"* the cougarand cried, bounding toward the

black-clad adventurer.

Yor turned, but he didn't quite make it. A sinewy left arm caught his right side and dragged him around. At close quarters, the cavalryman and the cat-man exchanged quick jabs, darting and shuffling for position like two rutting rams, dodging, shoving, ducking.

*If I can just get to the wall. . . .*

*Crack!*

Yor backed into the upended table. Surprised, half-pinned, off stride, he bobbed downward immediately. Air *whoosh*ed past his face as the assassin's murderous punch missed by hairs. Instead, the blow connected with the table leg.

*Crack!*

*"Harrr!"*

The fluid Bret charged into the opening and whacked back with a fast, solid hook on the tabby's nose, one that made the cougarand grunt with intense pain, but before Yor could follow it up with a knockout blast, he tangled his feet in the mead pitcher and his arms windmilled haphazardly.

The assassin loosed a roundhouse left.

*"Ooof!"*

Yor became intimate with the hardwood floor, rolling, tumbling, and finally crashing against the bar. Without waiting for a report from all the new aches, scrapes, and sprains, Yor went with the flow and continued to roll, finally stumbling up to his knees in a corner, dazed, groping. . . .

The cat-man pounced after him, bronze pistons extended, leaping for his stunned victim.

An instant too late, the assassin recognized the ruse. Up faster than a blink, Yor pivoted and launched upward at the cougarand's midsection, a two-fisted wallop into the cat's gut. Accentuated by the assassin's forward momentum, the blow purged the air from his lungs, stopping him dead in his tracks. Before the cat-man could inhale, Yor repeated the attack, doubling the cat's agony. Then the Bret cavalryman uppercut the cougarand on the chin with a blow so fast and hard that the cat-man was lifted clean off the floor.

"That was for my tailor; a finer man never lived! And this—" Yor's forearm smashed across the easterner's forehead, leaving the impression of chain mail on the cat-man's soft skull—"is for the anatomical references!" For good measure, he smashed the assassin's forehead again as he retrieved his arm to his side.

Flat-footed, glazed, the cougarand toppled forward, hitting the floor chin-first.

*Crack!*

Even Yor winced. He waited a few seconds, but the cat-man remained motionless.

"By the way, there's nothing wrong with my poetry. . . ."

He bent and removed the cougarand's falchion. Then, adrenaline still flowing strong in his veins, he stood and, pacing cautiously for a few needed breaths, watched the inert creature. Freed from their vows of silence, the various parts of Yor's body began to flood his brain with complaints of abuse. Huffing, he tested the split lip and checked the rivulets of blood coming from his shoulder. Sighing, the black-clad dandy dusted himself off, a sure sign he was going to be all right, and mournfully examined the rips in his blouse.

Not too bad. I'll leave it here to be mended. But that means I'm down to my last half-dozen. . . .

Finally deciding the cougarand wasn't going to get up any time soon, Yor reached down, glaring at the Fishie who had casually set his foot over the gold coin and threw the skipper's boot off it, claiming the prize without a fight. He set the table back up, picked up the pitcher and put it on the table, righted a few chairs, then crossed the tavern and planted himself by the window.

His striking blue eyes flensed the loremaster. "Hi! Remember me? I sincerely hope that all of my bouncing off hard objects and trying not to die didn't in any way disturb your studies."

"It was a fair fight," Captain Trebor Blackburn of the

Croswall Guards judged. He paused in his reading to look over at the fallen cat-man, shaking his head sadly. "Glass jaw. Never a doubt . . ."

"I—"

"And besides, somebody had to keep an eye out in case he wasn't the only one Bosamp hired."

Oh.

"If there'd been any real trouble, you know I'd have stepped in."

"Never a doubt!" Yor mocked. "Bosamp, huh? I suppose so. But"—he emphasized his words with a vile leer—"we have so many enemies! Librarians, for example. And shopkeepers . . ." Satisfied that he had galled the loremaster, he gestured at the motionless cat. "I wonder why he didn't try to use his sword."

"He's a Kundi, though I've never seen a cat-man do so before," Trebor replied.

"The earring!"

"Certainly. That was a dead giveaway. As you know, they have a strict code. They're not back-alley backstabbers like some of the lower societies of assassins. He announced himself, issued you a challenge by insult, and if you had let him finish, he would have told you that you could choose either to fight or to yield and accept disgrace. Then he would merely have broken both your arms and legs as painlessly as possible, although you'd never heal properly."

"How chivalrous!"

"It beats a broken neck or a slashed throat!" Trebor retorted glibly. "In any event, since the challenge was his, by code, the choice of weapons was yours. As you never made a move for your sword, he was honor-bound not to use his." Trebor paused and considered the motionless assassin. "You should have seen the relief in his eyes, by the way. He knew you'd have cut him into tiny pieces. There is no one faster than you are."

Yor shrugged, checking his left arm for contusions. "Well, if he's Kundi, then we'll get no more out of him."

"Not a word. He'd kill himself before he'd tell us who hired him."

A defiant glow lit Yor's boyish smiles. He stared at the lore-master until the man-mountain froze defensively.

"Count Yor?"

Trebor gulped in fear. I'd hoped he'd forgotten that!

Yor toyed with him, acting as if he would bray full blast, but holding back. True-blue Trebor! Honest-to-a-fault Trebor! Captain Truth stuck me with that erroneous epithet! Yor remembered. . . .

It was five years ago, on the road to Bilox. The trio had fallen prey to Menomian bandits, caught with their guard down. Whose fault that was had become one of those two-brew arguments that would recur until the last of them was in his grave. Taken without a drop of blood spilled! Oh, shame!

Trapped, faced with almost certain death, faithful Trebor, loyal Trebor, told the Menomian cutthroats that Yor was Count Yor, a Bretilyan noble with a vast estate on the southern coast, worth far more in ransom than the paltry pocket change they were carrying on them.

The greed lights went on in the brigands' eyes. Trebor then explained that he and Dword were but the count's bodyguards, hired to escort him home from winter court to the Bilox Con-clave. Yor's gagged protest and his lavish attire convinced the Menomians. And Dword—curse his mangy hide, too!—let on that they were none too happy with their skinflint master; they might even be willing to assist in ransoming him.

For a cut, of course.

Avarice ruled. Both "bodyguards" were released to secure the terms, unarmed naturally, and accompanied by three disguised bandits for good measure.

Bilox was but a day's ride. . . .

The remaining Menomians had time to kill. They camped in Glen Frey, hidden away from the eagle-eyed Bret patrols that roved the Menomian border. Someone, after a round or two of wags' swill, remembered the tale, often true, that Bretilyan peers hid caches of treasure outside their castles against the day they might have to flee hastily.

The look in their eyes! Yor remembered with a shudder. He told them what they wanted to hear, but much too quickly. They didn't believe him; they decided to torture him to get the truth out of him; there wasn't much else to do, so . . .

It was the second worst day of his life.

Later that night, after the bandits fell into a drunken doze from the premature celebration of their great wealth, Dword and Trebor returned. The fracas with their own guards had left both of them badly cut up, but like necromaniacs—those returned from the graves to right a wrong done them—they wreaked vengeance on the camp and freed a battered, unconscious Yor.

If only they hadn't repeated the story so often! Yor swore silently. Worse, that blasted red-bearded poetaster composed that abominably catchy ditty! Half the minstrels on Leiblein are singing the "Ballad of Count Yor" now! In every bawdy house and bistro! And worse, they're making up their own verses! Reciting all our exploits, real and imaginary, embellished and exaggerated, until now sometimes even I can't remember what's fact and what's fiction!

Yor whimpered. Twenty-five stanzas, by the last tally, including the illicit refrains, the three part harmony for . . .

"Thanks," Yor said through a gritted smile.

"Don't mention it."

Dword appeared in the doorway and glanced once around the tavern, eyes landing on the bedraggled cavalryman. "What's happened here? Can't I leave you alone for a minute? Lodi's lechery! Whose daughter was it this time?"

"Don't lecture me about daughters, you slick-tongued button buster!"

Just then the cougarand moaned. Moving slowly, he pushed up from the floor on all fours, batting his bi-lids to drive out the blurs. Unsteady, he rose. Yor tensed, but the Kundi gave no indication of hostile intent.

Wobbling, he padded toward Yor, then paused a few discreet paces away, bowing, but not too steeply, since he was still dizzy-headed. "I am Ali. By the code, you have defeated me, and my commission is therefore discharged." The cat-man bowed again. "It is a great pleasure to have finally met the distinguished Count Yor, though I could have wished the circumstances to be more gracious. Be assured I would have eaten your liver and buried you with the highest honors; I would also have been equally proud to be among your servants in the next world had you slain me."

The Kundi managed one more bow. "My cousin Elizabeast speaks well of you."

Elizabeast! Blood-curdling, white-eyed panic seized Yor. By the vaunted vagabond! When *is* her next heat? Sweating, Yor grunted, reserving wholehearted friendship, but he did a grudgeless warrior's curtsy and handed the Kundi his falchion. "Well fought, Ali Cat-Man. My sword sleeps, but *don't* give my regards to Elizabeast! Please!"

The cougarand grinned knowingly; sex with the female of his kind was typically fatal. Yor was one of the few known to have survived, which, of course, meant that Elizabeast would be hunting him down again. "My sword sleeps," the cat-man echoed the warrior's farewell. Nearly fainting, the assassin bowed one last time, then straightened his proud shoulders and left.

"A Kundi!" Dword said. "Woden's whimsy!" He watched the cat-man leave and turned back to Yor. "You did well! If you had insulted him after defeating him, he would have had to kill himself, you know. It's not a dishonor to fail a commission, especially if the adversary is worthy, but if you had shamed his failure, he would have been doubly disgraced! The code would have demanded immediate suicide!"

Yor tapped his swollen lip. "Lucky for him he hit me in the

right mood. And lucky for me I didn't kill him. I would have had to eat his liver, and I hate liver."

"Don't belittle a fellow creature's religion," the loremaster defended staunchly. "Ours must sound about as silly to them."

The black-clad dandy suddenly whipped around to the skippers. "Now then, which of you three hollow-legged, rapacious barnacles is going to give us passage to Dword's homeland? He's liable to take your obstinacy personally, as I already do! He does *so* want to see his native shores again!"

Cued, Dword gazed out the window toward the distant fjords, which were, of course, far beyond the horizon.

"You didn't get a real workout yet," Trebor mentioned offhandedly to Yor. "It's bad for you to stop now. The muscles will stiffen and you'll get sore. And you know, I could use a stretch myself." Ominously the man-mountain closed his book. He stood at full height and flexed.

"Home! I want to go home!" Dword wailed plaintively.

"His father was Ecklund Rusthair, prowman for Olaf Fyddish, fjordlord of the Hardan!" Yor advised. "You must have heard about the raid on Gormus eighteen years ago!"

Indeed, who hadn't? Though the glory days of the Norlandic marauders had ended almost a century earlier, Olaf Fyddish and his men had undertaken to relive them. Their epic daring raid overwhelmed the fat-cat Gormousians. And Olaf Fyddish's prowman would be the first off the boat—only the bravest, boldest, strongest, meanest warrior could be prowman!

Yor waited for the words to register. "Thirteen gold, or you can barter with that one!" he roared, flexing his arms ominously.

"Thirteen!" Dword sputtered with indignation that was not even close to feigned. "For one way? Outright bill larceny! What's happening here? Am I going to have to get personal?"

"Never get personal with a chicken," Trebor said from afar, though even he had forgotten where the silly expression had originated.

The trio of skippers trembled. Norlanders were the world's

most argumentative hagglers. They would bluff and bluster tirelessly; they would say mean things about your sister over the merest sliver of silver.

The three salts conferred urgently.

Trebor rolled up his sleeves and hoisted a huge oaken chair; Dword, who happened to be sitting in exactly that chair, calmly took his poniard and cleaned his nails, blithely humming a Norlandic battle song while Trebor raised and lowered him a few times.

"What? Only four reps?" Dword protested. "You're badly out of shape."

"I'm in good enough shape to lick, say, any three disagreeable scoundrels in this room single-handed," Trebor avowed.

"Not a chance!" Dword scoffed. "I'd have to break open at least two of their skulls for you!"

"Not more than one."

"Says you."

"Prove it."

Coins passed between the pilots; the Fishies nodded.

"I believe—hoooo!—that something can be arranged," the Thunbian said.

At that moment, Sir Dudley and Prince Rodney arrived, laden with bags of what were surely pastries. "Did you find a boat?" the elder knight asked Dword.

"I believe so."

"A short trip to Norlandia might prove amusing," the Thunbian chirped. "Twelve—hoooo!—and the bonus you mentioned earlier."

"Bonus!" the red-beard thundered belligerently. "Bonus?"

# CHAPTER SEVEN

"But I want a sword like his!"

The prince stamped his foot, his gangly frame quavering, and pointed at the loremaster's fabled blade. Envy filled the royal teenager until he felt as if he were going to burst. The gush of emotion made his nose run and his acne twitch. Worse, they weren't paying him any heed, and what might have just become a prolonged sulk was now overflowing into a full-blown snit.

"I want that one!"

The loremaster looked up from methodically scraping congealed undead ichor from his broadsword. Vertical, its tip embedded in the main deck of the Thunbian sloop *Obol*, the filigreed hilt of Trebor's potent tine danced with the arcane symbols of the Overtoad in the sunset.

Yor smiled weakly, counting to three, and then two more, just for good measure. Slowly he said, "Yes, Prince, I understand. It is a magnificent weapon—beautiful, terrible. But Trebor is much stronger than you are. In fact, he's much stronger than I am. And Dword. And Sir Dudley. And you. His sword requires great strength to be wielded properly; it would just tire you out, as it would me, so I think—"

"Did you see the way he hacked up that werezombie?" the prince reveled as he recalled the skirmish on the docks at Axiom. "Wow! That weird thing just jumped up out of nowhere, wearing that tattered shroud or whatever it was! Scared the lunch right out of me, but old Trebs, he just whipped that sword out and hacked it to pieces! Snickersnee! Really neat!"

The remembrance of the incident made Trebor blush to the point that he felt Dword's reproof on his back. The Three Weird Sisters indeed!

"I want to try it with his sword!" the prince repeated. "I'd be real good with it, I just know I would! Chop! Slash! Wham! Take that, varlet! And that! And this, sirrah!" The royal teenager pranced around the deck, waving an imaginary two-handed sword, slaying pretend werezombies by the legion, some of which had even three heads.

"Prince," Sir Dudley said, "I think in this case you should listen to Captain Hotspur. That is no ordinary sword. The blade has some sorcery to it, properties—as Captain Blackburn himself has noted—the extent of which not even he is certain. You might hurt yourself."

"No! I want that sword!" the prince insisted as he pointed at the blade. He folded his arms over his sunken chest and set himself on the deck intransigently. "I'm a prince of the realm, and the rest of you are nothing but chatelaines! There's not a bit of noble blood in any of you! Forswear me, knaves, and I'll have all of you flogged and thrown into the deepest dungeon!"

This raised even the normally accommodating Sir Dudley's dander. "Your Highness," the elder knight not so patiently persisted, "you know that the king"—and he emphasized the word so that the point would not be lost on the prince as to whose instructions would reign supreme—"told them to show you no special treatment. For the duration of this enterprise, you are under their aegis and authority. Now, Captain Ecklundson has been gracious enough to make you a training sword to practice—"

"No!"

"It's the same length as my screamsax," the Norlander pointed out. "Just lighter, that's all. I learned with a sword just like that. There's no—"

"No! No! No!"

Yor exhaled in frustration. "It's not the size of the wand that counts; it's the magic of the wizard! You can kill—"

"But I'm a prince! I need a sword like that!"

"You can't handle that thing!" Yor barked in a tone that shattered the prince's posturing. The teenager's attitude touched a nerve in Yor, and his temper writhed. Noble indeed! As if there were any way to distinguish the social class of dead, dried bones! "You can barely manage the trainer! In a duel with any experienced fighter, you would be food for worms in the blink of an eye! You've ignored all the training Sir Dudley has given you and decided to act out some fantasy! You'll be dead wrong! You must learn the moves first! You have to fight with your whole body, not just your arms and your thick head! Now, watch me again. . . ."

Yor stood *en garde*, his rapier pointed up ship. He bounced up and down lightly on the pads of his feet, and Dword set the muffin swinging on its chain behind the black-clad dandy's back.

Whirling, Yor lunged.

Spitted!

"That is the way you must learn to fight! Agility and accuracy, not brute butchery!"

Trebor's eyebrows arched as he continued to clean his sword. Truly unlucky, he thought abstractedly, that a pennant came off the rigging of a nearby ship and blew over my eyes during the fight with the werezombie on the docks. Not that it mattered. Just how did a werezombie get on the docks, anyway? You'd think somebody would have noticed it! And was that really a second head it had, or just a cancerous growth on its shoulder? Ah, well . . . it all happened so quickly, and since most of it fell into the water, there wasn't enough left to figure out.

He shivered once. Just what *was* that thing it was wearing?

"You'll never have the muscle to wield a broadsword, never!" Yor noted forcefully. "You must choose a weapon that accents what skills you have, and a style of swordsmanship that covers up the ones you don't! There are no second chances in combat! Being royal means nothing at all to cold steel! Noble blood flows just as quickly as peasant blood!"

The tirade slackened Yor's anger, but he counted to three and began all over with an upbeat note. "Now let's try it again. Your stance is too tight; it needs to open up. Spread your legs to give yourself balance when you thrust; stay on the balls of your feet like a—"

"No!" The prince threw the wooden trainer sword to the deck and formed the formidable pout-scowl that had always sent quaking servants scurrying. "Captain Trebor Blackburn, I, Prince Rodney of the Sapphire Throne of Bretilya, Defender of the Obsidian Order, command you to give me that sword! On your knees, peasant, and do homage to your rightful lord!"

Trebor didn't blink. It wasn't that he pretended not to hear; he heard well enough. One quick, scathing censure was all he deigned to give the royal youth. Then he returned to chipping off the werezombie entrails encasing the broadsword's edge. *I wonder if Mom's missing any of her clothing. . . .*

Captain Yorick Hotspur, vanquisher of the Grimwarl, hero of Cranreuch, and survivor of the siege of Castle Fairfax in the Year of the Thogs, snapped, "You are not in charge here! I wouldn't follow you across an alley to dump in a chamber pot! And neither would anyone else here! Now, you listen to me! We are sailing within the hour! And Norlandia is not a civilized place like Bretilya!"

Dword's eyebrows bent a notch.

"It's a rough place, with lots of dangers. Your lineage means naught there; you're not a prince, just a potential meal for some wandering monster! This could be the last chance you'll get to practice before we catch up with Bosamp again or before we run into creatures far more deadly than that popinjay! We may not always be able to—"

"No!" The prince sulked, pointing a finger at the lore-master. "If I can't have his sword, I won't practice!" The lad bolted toward the forecastle door. "I wish this stupid trip were over! I hate all of you!"

Slamming the door behind him, the lad disappeared.

"Great . . . just great!" Yor sighed with a flap of his black-draped arms. " 'Like a brother,' the king said! But by the blessed bard, if he were my brother, I'd kick his butt across the deck and into the channel, then kick it out so I could kick it back in again!"

"I'll have a talk with him, Captain," Sir Dudley said.

\* \* \* \* \*

"I'm going to the boat tail . . . alone!" Bosamp growled at the Bret skipper, one Captain Harms of the Bretilyan cutter *Jaguar*. "No one is to follow me or to disturb me! Do you understand?"

" 'Boat tail'?" the Bret naval officer replied sharply. "You mean the aft deck?"

"That's what I said! Are you deaf as well as dumb?"

"Yes, your wizardness!" Captain Harms rejoined coldly. "I mean, no! By all means, go to the boat tail! I'll see to it that absolutely no one disturbs you!" As if anyone would want to! thought the cutter pilot. There's nothing I could have wanted more than the absence of your presence!

"No one is going to share my sweets!" Bosamp sneered as he strode down ship; the sailors backed instinctively away and let him pass unhindered. Squirming, festering, unable to enjoy the brilliant display of sunshine backlighting the clouds as the sun plunged toward the ocean, the young wizard sat down at the boat tail, legs under the railing, high above the sea spray.

Gritch!

The itch is unbelievable! he thought as he set the sizable bag of candy down and scratched with both hands.

Gritch!

It's creeping into my armpit and down into my crotch! There's only one thing to do! he thought. Furtively he palmed the neck sachet and put a pinch of dragon dust directly on his tongue. Might as well enjoy what little time this world has left . . . ahhhh!

Wildfire menthol raced up and down his throat, cool and hot at the same time, sweet and sour, flushing his gaunt cheeks. His eyes watered with pain-pleasure.

*Groouwl!*

The hunger! The orange-clad conjurer finally stopped clawing at his side and clutched the heavy sack of bonmoes, a liqueured candy sweet enough even for a honeydipper.

*Groouwl!*

Vengeful, he pitched a handful of bonmoes into his mouth and crushed the syrup out of them, then snickered viciously. He gobbled the bonmoes one by one, salivating excessively, licking his fingers and lips. His belly filled with candy, gushing with confectionery overdose, gurgling its gratitude.

Ah . . . vengeance is sweets!

Bosamp the World Shaker! Bosamp the Bell Ringer!

The dragoness's vision filled his mind now, just as it had when she had come to him and given him the dust. She conjured an image of the possible future and showed him flying away to a new world on her back. It was a marvelous place, with lush greenery, gorgeous ladies, and friendly creatures. He was the natural leader in such a place, and they welcomed his coming with a feast. Unfettered, the young wizard's imagination imploded with sensual fantasies of voluptuous female bodies frolicking in liquid mounds of sugary syrup. . . .

A world of my own to rule . . . and revenge on this one!

But the swoop of a waveskimmer, diving into the waves

after prey, interrupted his daydreaming; he tranced with a premonition. Loping swiftly over the waves, eyes blazing with cobalt blue light, a dark angel streaked up in front of him. "Bosamp," the cruel beast howled, "I'm going to catch you! I'm not going to rest until I do!" Then the apparition stretched out a dark tentacle and gripped the lizard flesh on the wizard's side, squeezing hard on the scabrous growth.

The pain was excruciating.

"*Augh!*" the wizard screamed and clutched his abused side.

"This is but a sample of the agony you will come to know!" the dark angel cheerfully told him. "You shall not escape me, madman!"

The wizard reddened with delirious rage. Compulsively, glyphs poured from his mouth; his arm spasmed and pitched a bonmoe into the sea. Like a summoned sea monster, a wave rose up and surged outward toward the dark angel, shoving it back, rippling it across the sea southward.

But the dark angel came forward once more. "Kill yourself while you still can!" it laughed harshly. "I come for you, and I will not be merciful!" Again it jabbed at his new flesh in drooling glee.

Maddened with the pain in his side, the wizard threw another bonmoe over the side of the boat. A wave rose and waited patiently for his command. "Get him!" he yelled to the water servant.

Again . . . again . . . again . . .

\* \* \* \* \*

Five leagues out from Axiom, a cry of alarm rent the air like the screech of a wounded surfdragon. They ran from the commons cabin onto the deck of the *Obol*; all eyes veered up to the lookout's post.

"Life Master Iks!" the sailor above shouted, confused,

excited. "Hoooo! Come quickly! There's trouble headed
our way!"

* * * * *

Up . . ; ; ; ;
And down ; ; . . . .
Up . . ; ; ; ;
And down ; ; . . . .
Up . . ; ; ; ;
"Woden's . . ."

Unable to finish, Dword sprang from his chair and streaked
from the commons cabin. Just in time, the red-beard thrust
his head over the side of the Thunbian sloop. Spasms jerked
through his midsection; his shoulders shuddered, every muscle aching as his lunch quaked violently.

Up and out.

Down ; ; . . . .

Timidly he clung to the rail, purplish around his gills,
waiting.

Up . . ; ; ; ;
And down ; ; . . . .
Again.

"Gross!"

Finding another source of amusement, King Derek's fourth
son abandoned throwing ballast stones at the hovering
waveskimmers, which had gathered after Dword's post-break-
fast eruptions and were waiting for lunch. Morbidly curious,
the prince watched.

Again.

The waveskimmers cawed, diving down to the boat's wake.
They feasted hurriedly, eyes on the royal youth, wary of his
well-aimed stone barrages.

"You're making me sick, fuzzface!" Prince Rodney gloated.
"I thought Norlanders were the world's greatest sailors! It

looks like what they really are is the world's greatest pukers!"

Dizzy, the red-beard moaned. He closed his eyes to keep the world from whirling around him. *It's not fair. We've all taken turns here, but the prince hasn't suffered a whit. The only rational explanation is that his body is so badly out of kilter that . . .*

*Rational explanation? You want rational explanations in a world at the mercy of the Three Weird Sisters?*

*Rumble!*

Again.

Prince Rodney tittered with delight. "You're supposed to be heaving to, not ho! And your stance is too tight! Spread your legs a bit and remember to balance on the balls of your feet. . . ."

*Not fair at all!* Dword rose carefully, shivering, feeling better but unstable. *Bosamp!* he thought. *Two days of these accursed waves! I'll peel his hide off with dull tweezers! Oh, to be on solid ground again . . .*

Again.

*Ohhhh . . . that's got to be it. . . .*

He took a deep breath and held it.

*One . . . two . . . three . . . four . . .*

*Nothing. Whew!* Relieved but weak, Dword mustered his pride and ignored the princely applause, striding back to the commons cabin.

Bored once more, the teenager threw the last of his stones at a waveskimmer and was rewarded as the bird failed to evade his shot. It fluttered about fitfully, but eventually regained its flying form a healthy distance leeward. *Nice toss!* he congratulated himself.

Elated, he returned to the cabin. "You should have seen Dword this time! Five times! A new record! That beats your highest score!" the teenager taunted Trebor.

Stiff, the man-mountain ducked the gibe. Unfortunately, he had no lore to use against this situation; he added it to his list of things to research on his next trip to the archives. "Any better now?" he asked his suffering companion with compassion.

"For the moment," the red-beard bravely replied.

"Hoooo! I've never seen such waves in all my born days," the Thunbian skipper Hatu Iks muttered. "It's unnatural, 'tis! There should be rain and wind with the waves—hoooo—but, no! The sky is clear and the breeze is at our backs, but still the swells come, wave after wave, day after day! Hoooo!"

"Bosamp's not enough of a sorcerer to do more," Trebor said blearily. "He can't evoke all the flash and thunder of a full-fledged gale like the Council could. All he can do is make waves."

The bow tilted; Dword's eyes rolled; he grabbed the table.

Everyone froze.

Nothing.

Five silent sighs of relief!

"Bosamp!" jeered the prince. "I never liked him! Nor Wendom either, for that matter. When I'm king, I'm going to have a witch for a court magician! I hear they do their spells in the nude!" He brightened gleefully. "I'm going to get a pretty one! One with big—"

"Prince Rodney!" Sir Dudley admonished.

"You'll see, Fuddyduds! Things will be different when I'm king!"

It was a stupefying possibility; collectively, the trio prayed that the prince's older brothers might live forever. Then Dword emitted another paralyzing moan.

"Here, mate," the Thunbian skipper said. In an act of nonpareil courage, he slid his chair over to the barbarian and passed a bottle to him. "Try some of this—hoooo! It's Crosby Stills' Young Mash, an elixir of singular properties."

The loremaster snorted loudly and hoisted his own bottle of sack. "Best to keep to the simple stuff. Any port in a storm, I always say. . . ."

The *Obol*'s skipper blinked and turned cockeyed, then resumed his discourse to the Norlander. "This will settle your giblets, or else you soon won't care—hoooo!"

Desperate, the Norlander pulled the cork, lifted the bottle, and drank. Dword's eyes bulged wider than a Gormousian banker's at the sight of a bare coin. Coughing, he slapped the table hard with the palm of his hand. He gasped for air, blinked, and rocked back in his chair.

"Frieda's fabulous fishing hole!" he wheezed through his scorched esophagus. "This stuff would melt a glacier! It's good, though!"

"Well, then, how about a story to pass the time—hoooo?" Captain Iks asked, having grown jaded with thrashing Yor and Trebor at cards. The Thunbian Life Master gathered in the pasteboards and set them aside, his firk epaulets, chevrons, and buttons shimmering with satisfaction. "Perhaps—hoooo!—this legend I've heard you all talking about? That is, if it's not too much to ask . . ."

Dword nodded. A minstrel must pay for his potables! He glanced at his companions for fear of revealing too much, but Yor and Trebor shrugged acquiescence, realizing that the Thunbian must have heard most of it anyhow.

And, they all thought in unison, if a story would take Dword's mind off his troubles, then on with it!

"All right," Dword replied. Priming himself with another swallow of the fiery fluid—Lodi's short leg!—he cleared his throat and sat back in his chair, stroking his ruddy beard, hearkening back to that evening by the saga fire when, as a young pup, he sat on his father's lap and heard old Feol Loose-jaw spin the creation edda. Ah, yes . . .

"Well, now. This is the saga of the first epoch, of how our world came to be, of Magnus Lifeshaper and D-Ray Doomgranter and the other Skolgods in the time before Woden ascended. It is a tale of wondrous beginnings and of childhood's end!"

He paused to suck them in, his face full of the tale to be told, his pale blue eyes glowing. Picking up his pipe, he relit it in a single puff. The smoke hung in the air and seemed the perfect set for such a primeval topic as the creation of the universe.

He had them.

"Time began with a bolt of lightning and clarion thunder and the smell of sulfur! Nightfall was everywhere! No light shone in the caves of steel, and all was silent and still. . . .

"Then the Skolgods awoke. Ah, the Skolgods! Eternal and immortal! As different from each other as the visions from an enchanted kaleidoscope! Some of the gods were jeweled and scaly, like Om, the spade-footed toad god; some were molten fire, like Aga Fireskin; some were horned, like Kluute of the Nine Tusks; some could soar, like Daedsiluap of the Many Wings; others were tall and beautiful, like Allinir and Magnus, fairest of the fair!

"Born at the end of eternity, in the first flash of time, birthed full grown, they crawled out of their primordial shells and found themselves at the center of the universe, on an island in the sky, on a world as big as a thousand continents, surrounded by whirling gases so thick and so hot that no man could live there! And all the rest of the universe was empty, dark, and devoid of features. . . ."

He puffed the pipe to let them visualize it, just as he himself recalled old Feol's pausing to let his briar bellow forth in imitation of the creation blast. For a flash, he sat on the floor as a child again in the long hall of the Hardan that held the warboat *Hardansclaw*; the carved figures on it were images of the gods. Seen through the mist of Feol's pipe, it was as though he stood among them himself. . . .

"In time, the Skolgods came together and forged the primary elements: earth, water, time, air, fire, and motion! From these, they built Skolholm, their great city, and they dwelt in awesome splendor, each in a tower of metalglass a league high! Long did they remain in Skolholm, pondering, seeking knowledge, exploring the fountains of paradise. . . .

"After a time, they learned to shape things from the gases with just their thoughts! This aroused them, for after an eon, they had grown tired of Skolholm and hungered for more! Thus they came to fashion the firmament and the first and second foundations, filling the currents of space and the black sky with lights!"

He stopped to sip and puff before continuing.

"It became a game for them; each tried to outdo the others, creating new celestial masterpieces, greater and grander than the last. Stars they made in numbers unimaginable—lucky stars, clusters of stars, pinwheels of stars, spiral star-cases— and in all sizes and shapes and colors, making the stars like dust in the heavens against the fall of night!

"Then came comets, then planets, then moons, tossed like pebbles into the sky, decorating the universe with things that will last to the end of eternity. . . ."

Dword needed to relight; he inserted a straw into a candle to keep the fire in his pipe going. The flare of light and smoke caught the fancy of his words, and the others thought they saw a newborn star forming. . . .

"Then Magnus, the greatest of the Skolgods, discovered two more elements previously unthought of: flesh and spirit. He cast a spell that evoked a small fraction of the first flash when time began. The other gods trembled and shook in the fury of his thunderbolt!

"When the smoke subsided, Magnus discovered he had created a living creature: a snow tern."

Dword paused and took another deadly gulp of the Young Mash. His insides seared; his forehead grew damp; his eyes faded out and in.

"Take care that the cure is not worse than the disease," the loremaster murmured.

Dword shrugged and resumed his narrative.

"Now, Magnus was quite pleased with himself, as gods are

wont to be. He repeated the spell often, varying it a little and getting new creatures with each casting, which only increased his pride and his bragging. He placed his creatures all over the universe, from here to the other end of the sky! Like living sculptures, they began to multiply and spread while Magnus boasted, regaling in his achievement.

"The other gods were stirred, and the harmony of the old, friendly competition faded! Some of the gods joined Magnus and launched into their own orgy of life-making, trying to outdo him. Thus did all the myriad creatures come to be. . . ."

Pulling the smoldering pipe from his mouth, Dword took yet another swig and dropped his voice to an ominous whisper.

"But many gods were jealous, offended by Magnus's pride and alarmed at his creations! They came to believe that it was wrong for there to be any other living things but the gods themselves, wrong to force the burden of life on anything without its permission, particularly since what had been created—even the dragons, Magnus's finest work—were so perishable in the cosmic scale of time. They decided to destroy what Magnus and his followers had wrought, to blot out all the new creatures great and small, to forbid them forever!"

Dramatic pause.

"Bitter was their war! For an eon it raged; there were floods and fires and great magicks beyond comprehension! Comets careened! Stars exploded! Planets tumbled to the foundation's edge, never to be seen again! There was a fall of moondust across the galaxy. . . ."

He halted for effect, but only briefly. "But Magnus stood between his creations and the blasts of gods' blows so that, though many kinds of creatures perished, many others still survived. Finally was fought the Battle of Vollkyrishavndon, when a galaxy of stars was ravaged and Skolholm utterly destroyed. It became clear that neither side could win without consuming all that had been created! Thus did the two sides agree to a compromise: Life was to be confined to one world—Leiblein—and the creation of new life forms was forbidden!"

"Hey!" the prince blurted out. "Wait just a second! The dragons aren't confined to Leiblein! They weren't even here until just before the Fall!"

Dword made a not-to-worry-all-will-be-revealed-in-due-time gesture as he sipped once more the Thunbian's killer liquor. "That's another edda, Prince," he said, "but you're right: Magnus ultimately found a way to bend the rules so that the dragons could roam from star to star at will."

"Not quite," Trebor injected. He started to recite from the Bretilyan *Book of Legends*, but decided instead to give the Norlander full rein. It was, after all, only a myth.

"One of the Skolgods," the red-beard resumed, "D-Ray—"

"Or possibly Zepolinirt," Yor baited.

Dword stared a beat before continuing. "D-Ray, one of those who opposed Magnus, took pity on us. While the other gods were off restoring the damage done by Vollkyrishavndon, D-Ray forged a huge Bell, which cannot be moved or destroyed, and placed it at the top of the world. If the Bell is chimed three times truly, all creatures on Leiblein will be rid of the wearisome burdens of life. . . ."

He paused and puffed, allowing it to sink in.

"But D-Ray didn't want to make it too easy, so he also made a special hammer to chime the Bell. Only the Mallet of Doom can ring the Bell and sound the end of the world! D-Ray hid the Mallet at the bottom of Vangberg, on an altar in a lava grotto, and left the deadly fireflies to watch over it—"

"Bosamp will never get by them," Trebor assured.

"—to keep anyone from—"

"What?" Prince Rodney's eyes dilated, and he stared at the red-beard, then the loremaster. "You mean to tell me that silly hammer thing is buried at the bottom of a volcano and guarded by monsters that Bosamp has no chance of getting by?"

"Well, I wouldn't go so far as to say that, but—"

The prince erupted, unhearing. "I don't believe this! I'm stuck on this dumb quest with a puker, a know-it-all, a has-been, and that peacock, and all for nothing? I—"

"Watch your tongue," Yor warned.

The prince pointed a bony finger at the black-clad adventurer and guffawed. "You're the worst of the lot! You wear prettier clothes than my sister does! Lord Wendell says—"

"Lord Wendell," Yor said with cold dispatch, "is a crapulous cretin who couldn't hump his way out of a Kleshan bawdy house! Best you shut up now before I shut you up."

"Help! Help!" the royal teenager shrieked, rising with flailing arms. "I'm a Bretilyan prince, and I've been kidnapped! Somebody save me! I'll—" Yor lurched out of his chair at him, but the prince ran out of the room and down a corridor to his cabin, where he slammed and barricaded the door.

Wearily Sir Dudley stood. "I'll see to him." The aged knight smiled wanly. "Don't think too harshly of him, gents. He's had a tough time lately, with the poison acne and all the other problems of his age. His brothers have always outshone him, and the king's been too busy to give him much guidance. Try to remember what it was like to be seventeen."

Yor glowered resentfully. "Tough? Seventeen?" He pointed at the man-mountain. "When Trebor was seventeen, the storm wraiths attacked Croswall! Do you remember what the Winter of the Rats was like?"

He gestured next to the barbarian. "When Dword was seventeen, the Festering Plague decimated his village! He built his father's funeral boat and set it on fire! He had to leave home to make a living for his mother and his sister!"

Yor seethed with memories. "And when I was seventeen," he said through gritted teeth, "it was the Year of the Thogs. They came early, remember? Five years earlier than they had ever come! The dike walls were undermanned; the thogs were across the Fairfax like locusts, killing people and eating them!" He gagged on his anger, crushing his fist on the table. "My brother James would have been just about the prince's age if the thogs hadn't gotten him."

Limp with disgust, the black fury plopped back down. His face turned toward the porthole as he fought back tears. "Keep him out of my way."

"I'll have a talk with him," Sir Dudley said. He paused a moment, then felt it necessary to add, "By the way, it may not be all that apparent to you now, but he does look up to the lot of you. You're heroes to him. But I suppose it's easier to know your heroes from a distance. . . ."

Awkward glances.

Yor hesitated for a second, considered it, and yielded to a higher emotion. He nodded to the senior soldier and said with honest sincerity, "He'd do better to model himself after you. The world needs another man like you more than it needs more men like us."

Silence followed Sir Dudley's departure.

Yor stared moodily out the porthole, waiting for the inner gale to subside. Trebor propped up a book on the table. The Thunbian reshuffled the cards and played solitaire.

All accounted for but one.

Dword moaned, head lolling. Lightheaded from the liquor, which rested on a gurgling empty stomach, his earlobes throbbed and his vision darkened.

Not again!

He started to rise but lacked the strength. The room spun, so he closed his eyes to prevent further nausea, gripping the table and sticking his face downward.

Ohhhh . . . Will I ever be well again? . . . Will I ever see the Hardansfjord again? . . . Will I ever see my sainted mother again? . . . Will I ever *see* again? . . .

Nothing.

Still nothing.

"That's strange," Dword said.

Everyone noticed it at once.

"They've stopped!" the Thunbian captain said. "Hoooo! The waves have stopped!"

Trebor glanced out the porthole. "They *have* stopped!" the loremaster boomed joyously. "Bosamp must have gone ashore or grown too tired to maintain the spell! It's over!"

The Thunbian Life Master stood, brightening. "Hoooo! We'll catch that shiftless wizard yet!" He burst from the cabin and yelled to his crew, "Full sail, mates! And get the long oars! Hoooo! We'll be in Hjarstad before the next tide! Three red status points to each sailor if we catch him! Hard to! Hoooo!"

Yor's gloom broke; he grasped at the possibility of action after the endless inaction, anything to forget the horrible past that could not be changed. "We'll soon have good horses below us and be galloping over the countryside!" the cavalryman swore. "We'll ride hard and fast, like hellhounds to the hunt! We'll ride all day and all night if we have to!"

"Ohhhh . . ." moaned the Norlander, not at all thrilled at the thought.

"Cheer up, Dword! You're almost home!"

# CHAPTER EIGHT

*Groouwl!*

Gritch!

Not again!

Bosamp halted his steed at the mountain summit just as the first pangs of need rippled in his legs and arms, craving relief from the hunger and the dreadful itch. In the days since he had left the boat at the fjord's end, the itch had become fiercer and the hunger more urgent. His sacks now bulged with food, particularly sweets, mostly from a confectionery shop he had ransacked after zapping the owner and his wife with a stun spell.

Barbarian fools! Resistance is futile! They should thank me that they still have their wretched lives!

The thought of the shop's pastries made him salivate. Sweets seem best at countering the hunger, he thought. He rubbed his hand over his scraggly beard; his chin felt bony to his touch. Can it be I'm losing weight, even with all I've been eating? Hmmm . . . must be all the outdoor exercise. Ah, well, there'll be time enough to rest up later. Just wish I didn't feel cold all the time. . . .

Something about the latter bothered him, tugged at his mind, but it escaped as he absentmindedly brushed his hand over the side of his Council cloth robe and scratched at the itch below. At the first contact, the itch flared, stinging anew, and he realized he was going to have to stop and take measures again.

"This is a good place to spend the night," he said to the lathered horse as he dismounted, expecting it to be appreciative.

Hurrying, fumbling, he set up his brazier, igniting the coals with a single glyph. Hands shaking, he took his dust sachet and threw a handful of silvery grits onto the coals.

*Corkle! Sporf!*

He stuck his face down into the hail of shooting stars, eyes open, letting the scintillas flail across him like the disciplining whack of a Korian lovemaster. The dragon dust crackled through him, a bolt of power energizing every sore muscle, swelling his limbs until he felt as if he could lift a hilltop in each hand. The warmth flowed through him, and he felt renewed.

So good, so very good! Relaxed, supreme, he sucked in another breath of smoke and held it in his bursting lungs. Flushed, he turned and surveyed his new kingdom. The ride up Skandsala had been exhausting but worth it, he decided. From here, I can see leagues in all directions. Ah! Let's see . . . north is that way . . . and is that Vangberg?

He blew the smoke from his lungs, coughing as he did so. Walking to the horse, he unfurled a local map, purloined from some idiot cleric yesterday, then returned to the brazier and poked his head down toward the fire to draw another lungful of dragon dust.

Rising up like a balloon from the fire, he looked northward again. No . . . that can't be Vangberg. Still a few days off. Exhale. *Cough!* Great view from here, though. Let's see, that tall peak there must be . . . Odskag? Inhale. Yes, Odskag! The last barrier to the Wastes! It's a long way off, though. . . . Exhale.

Look at me, world, and know fear!

Giddy, he looked around the pass. It's going to be dark in an hour or so, he thought. There's fresh water from that stream over there, and the boulders will block the wind . . . a perfect place to camp! Hey! I'm getting good at this! I must have covered a dozen leagues today! They're probably still floundering around in the channel!

*Groouwl!*

I could eat a full-grown gnorlox right now! Hmmm . . . I wonder if there's one around?

*　*　*　*　*

A red-haired shadow glided downhill through the boreal evergreens on Skandsala and emerged into the twilight, standing by the road's edge, eyes twinkling with success.

At last! Yor realized. We've caught up with Bosamp!

"He's at the top of the pass," the barbarian reported, grinning with an enthusiasm equal to the cavalryman's. "He's built a fire in a ring of boulders west of the summit . . . appears like he's planning to camp there for the night. Oh," he added quickly, turning to Trebor, "looks like he set a pole in the center of the road near the crest."

"A pole?" the loremaster repeated, worried. "Could you tell what kind it was?"

"No. I didn't want to risk getting any closer."

Trebor nodded. "Well, if it's a watchpole, that's one thing, but if it's a listening post or a sniffstaff, that's another. It makes a big difference how we handle it. Are you sure you couldn't discern its type?"

"It looks like all the others I've seen, but I'll tell you what," Dword said with a smirk. "I'll just go right back up there and ask him. Oh, Bosamp, yoo-hoo . . ." The barbarian started back uphill, but Trebor hissed and grabbed his arm, yanking the grinning Norlander into a seated position.

"We've gotten past such things before," Yor breezed cockily, "but we'll stay off the road."

The proximity to the object of their quest invigorated Yor; he had to fight to hold back his excitement. Once they landed in Hjarstad, they had gained rapidly on the wizard. Bosamp was stopping more and more frequently. The trip was undoubtedly wearing him down. But, Yor reminded himself, we almost lost his trail at a crossroads yesterday! That thunderstorm made a mess of the tracks, and since all of the road branches led northward over the Great Spine, we had no clue as to which to take! But just when we decided to take the middle route, that irate Munflenchian circuit rider came along down the left branch. It was clear he disliked Brets and probably would have told us nothing at all, but Bosamp had stolen his map while he was in the loo!

Helped out by a Munchie! How ironic! He turned back to the matter at hand. "It'll be dark soon," he noted, "but the darkness is no boon to us. We'll go after him right now! We might catch him bathing or cooking or something."

Nods.

"We'll have to try it on foot," Yor said. He popped a wary head over a bush, eyeing the terrain ahead. Yikes, that's steep! "There's plenty of ground cover. If we're quiet—and I mean *really* quiet!—then we ought to be able to get close enough to catch him completely off guard." Weighing the situation, he turned abruptly to the royal youth, reminded of a minor detail that needed attending to. "Prince, it might be best if you stayed here with the horses."

"Not a chance!" the prince objected. "I didn't come—"

"Shush!"

"You dragged me all the way out here, and I'm not going to miss it now!" the prince insisted. "We've got him outnumbered five to one! What could go wrong?"

"The same things that went wrong on the Escarpment!" Yor said and twisted his tongue in his mouth. "Or worse! Someone has to stay with the horses."

"Let Duddie-do do it!" the royal lad struck back. "With all that creaking armor on, he couldn't sneak up on a snoring princess! He makes more noise than a windmill in a buster-guster! Let Dudsy stay behind!"

Dumbstruck, Yor's lips sputtered to a halt.

"He's got a point," Trebor grunted.

The black-clad swordsman wavered but found no

counterpunch. "So be it," he said, regaining momentum. "Trebor and I will take the west side of the road, Dword and the prince the east." Yor stared at the teenager to underline the importance of his instructions. "Stay off the road—we don't want that pole to give us away—but don't get too deep into the woods or the brush. You can get lost in a hurry here, especially at this time of day. And try to be *really* quiet. Understood?"

Prince Rodney nodded eagerly. He checked his screamsax, the one he'd bought back in Hjarstad. A fine blade, he thought. I'm going to call it "Wizardsticker" for good luck. . . .

Yor looked away from the royal youth and held his breath, hoping for the best. This is what the king wanted, he thought. We'll try to keep the prince out of the line of fire, but if anything happens to him, I wonder how the king will take it? I hope we're doing the right thing. . . .

"Dword, did you see Bosamp's horse?"

"Tethered to the east side of the pass. Looked pretty used up."

Yor nodded with satisfaction. Bosamp doesn't know how to pace a horse! He alternates between all-out gallops and long rest stops! That tires a horse faster than a steady pace!

"Good! You and the prince keep Bosamp from getting to his horse. We don't want him to get away again! We'll get as close as we can, then when I give the signal—and no sooner!—we'll rush him! And don't kill him if you don't have to! We promised to bring him back alive if we could, and there's no telling what other mischief he's started that we don't know about yet. Okay . . ."

Yor turned to the knight and hesitated a moment, feeling sorry that the elder warrior was going to miss the battle. He smiled apologetically. "You're the reserves this time, I'm afraid, Sir Dudley."

"Understood, Captain," the prince's guardian replied. "I'll be ready if I'm needed."

"Stay mounted," Yor added. "If anyone should come along, stop him here. Tell him whatever you have to, but don't let him get by!"

"Aye, Captain! We don't want any surprises!"

"It would be a good idea to tie all the reins together," Yor decided, planning out loud. "If all goes well, I'll shout, 'Derek,' and you can bring the horses up the pass. But if it looks like Bosamp's going to get away, I'll shout, 'Charge!' Come as fast as you can. Forget about the horses. Ride over us if you have to, but don't let that troublemaking charlatan get away!"

"Aye, Captain!" the grey knight said firmly. "I'll give him a taste of Bretilyan chivalry he won't soon forget! Truckle with King Derek, will he? Fie on him!"

"Good!" Yor replied spiritedly. His face set with marble determination as he looked over the other three. "Are we ready?"

"Yes!"

"All right, let's go!" Yor stepped off, marking every footfall deliberately, keeping as low as reasonable. Veering to the west side of the road, Trebor at his heels, the two Brets faded into the brush and then into the evergreen woods, black fox and beige bear, blending into the shadows, noiseless.

"Keep a few paces back," Dword said to the prince as they paired off and went to the opposite side of the road. "Step in the same places where I've stepped. And put your sword away. It's a long walk, and it'll get heavy. We don't have to rush; speed is less important now than stealth, so take care."

The prince bobbed his head up and down in agreement. "I'll be stealth itself!" he whispered.

"Okay . . . here we go!"

They vanished into the woods.

"Good luck!" Sir Dudley said, muffling his voice so it wouldn't carry too far. Suddenly the elder knight felt very alone. They also serve who only stand and wait, he reminded himself.

Above, sunset hung in the late-summer sky, lavender robes wrapped around the auric orb, cloaking the landscape in coronation capes. This far north, the edge of night fell gently this time of the year, gradual darkening into long evenings before the night. A cold vein laced the breeze, foretelling the coming of the next season, but for now, the sheet rock between stands of trees radiated the day's stored warmth.

They climbed quietly. Gradually the ascent angled sharply. The road, furrowed with gullies of exposed crimson dirt, curved abruptly to the west as it rose up to Skandsala Summit, a major pass on the Great Spine, that broad chain of mountains separating the populous portion of Norlandia from its untamed north country. The woods here were a thicket of strapping evergreen saplings and wide frostbushes, interlaced with swatches of huge exposed boulders. A fire a decade ago had cleared the hillside and the new vegetation was in a land rush, staking overlapping claims, elbowing and shoving in the rapid growth of adolescence, bypassing stretches of stone to form a head-high rock garden.

Closer . . .

Farther up the mountain, the terrain became surly. Sheets of uneven stone, shattered by many winters' blasts, cluttered the slope, slippery rocks that slowed the pace more than even the increasing incline. The trees thinned out a bit in the stony soil, and they had to take more care to keep concealed.

Closer . . .

Smoke from the wizard's brazier drifted down from the summit, giving the dusk a pungent, seared cedar perfume, providing the nostrils a gauge for direction and distance. The fragrance of cooking meat floated in the air, stirring the glands with jealousy.

Closer . . .

Yor stopped and glanced about, checking the advance. Dword and the prince were falling behind, mostly because they were on the outside of the road's arc. Yor focused on the lad and worried; the prince was struggling. He's going too slow, Yor thought, but at least he's been quiet! Pretty good so far! He looked through the trees uphill. Can't see the pass; too many trees. Maybe it'll be all right; the trees will cover us most of the way up.

This has got to go better than it did at the Escarpment!

The climb continued, plodding, strenuous, laborious. As they neared the top, each became more conscious of his own sounds. Every move had to be calculated to generate the least noise; every muscle had to be kept on a leash while their pores flowed wet: hands, forehead, underarms, feet.

Nerves and exertion.

Whew! Prince Rodney gulped, panting. He couldn't match Dword's stride, so he had to run in fits to keep up. It didn't look this hard from back there! he moaned inwardly. And this ring mail is heavy! Perspiration dripped from his flushed face, provoking his poison acne until it twitched and, stimulated by the wizard's acrid smoke, his nose began to tingle. . . .

Don't screw up! he silently commanded his sinuses.

Closer . . .

The summit came into view. Dipping into a crouch, Yor signaled for a halt and peered ahead through the twilight.

Where is Bosamp?

The loremaster laid a hand on Yor's shoulder. "I can see the pole now," he breathed, pointing as he whispered. "Over there, in the center of the road. It looks like a vibestick. Good thing we didn't try to ride up! It would have sensed the horses a furlong back! Still, I don't know how much closer we can get before it feels our footsteps. . . ."

Yor ducked as Bosamp came into view. The wizard's cowl hung loose on his shoulders, exposing his youthful dark mane. Coal-red light from his brazier illuminated the sorcerer with a sinister aura; the once handsome face was now sallow, and the yellowish, glazed hollowness in his eyes gave him a distant, burdened look.

"He looks much older than I remember . . ." Yor said softly to Trebor. Just then a pebble bounded off a tree to the Bret's right; turning, Dword caught his eye and motioned downhill. The prince, lagging, struggling, was growing careless.

Dragon's breath! I should have made him stay behind!

Yor held up his hand and flashed hand signals; the barbarian waved back. Over his shoulder, the black-clad adventurer whispered to the loremaster, "We'll stop here for a minute and let the prince catch his breath. Now, what about the pole?"

"We'll just have to chance it."

On the opposite side of the road, Prince Rodney struggled upward, his head drooping with fatigue. Suddenly, silently, Dword was standing over him. Startled, the royal youth almost blurted out, but caught himself just in time.

"We'll rest a moment," the Norlander said, smiling. "You're doing just fine; this is a tough slope, and we're all a bit winded."

Nodding gratefully, the prince dropped down on one knee, down into a patch of bright yellow weeds, concealing himself. This is tougher than I thought it would be, but it's really exciting! I'm glad they didn't make me stay behind!

He peered between the weeds, and his nose tingled.

Dword watched with approval; good, he's out of sight. . . .

Double take.

"Prince!" Dword gulped in panic. "Not there! That's—"

"Ahhhh . . ."

"—snotbrush!"

" . . . chooo!"

What was that? The wizard cocked his head, listening.

"Kachoo!"

The rolling thunder echoed around the pass; Bosamp froze for an instant, looking wildly about, high and low, trying to figure out what was going on. "Who's there?" he demanded. "Stick, report!"

Below, Yor turned ashen and quickly glanced back uphill. He swore and made a quick calculation . . . too far! "Use the road!" he shouted and ran out of the woods onto the dirt.

No hope, no hope!

"Master!" blared the pole in base tones. "Three men running uphill! Two on the west side and one on the east! Fifteen rods and closing!"

Stumbling forward, legs pumping furiously hard and reaching only a fraction of the speed they might have on level ground, the trio charged, limbs wrenching with the monumental effort of running up the inclement slope.

"*Kachoo!*"

"Charge! Charge!" Yor shrieked.

Bosamp stared down the road and saw the slow-motion runners, impressed by the desire that drove them to torment their sinew with the pain of running up such a sharp incline, then trembled in disbelief.

Impossible! It can't be them! They're *leagues* behind me!

"Twelve rods and closing!"

Eye to eye.

"Yor, you bastard!" Bosamp ejaculated.

"The ropes didn't stop us, madman!" Yor shouted in a huff, still far from his destination. Sweat drenched his body from the effort of running in the soft, wet sand. The bouncing gait of his strides made his chain mail ride up and down, chafing his skin. "The Kundi didn't stop us!" he gasped. "The werezombie didn't stop us!"

"Werezombie? Kundi?"

"Ten rods!"

Held back by his heavy armor, Trebor couldn't keep pace with Yor. "We're still alive and kicking!" he boomed between deep breaths.

"A situation I shall soon remedy!" Bosamp shot back. Bold talk, but the wizard wasn't immediately sure how to back it up.

"Eight rods!"

For a split second, he considered fleeing; he looked at his horse and realized he had taken the saddle off. Flee—why? He haughtily disregarded the thought. *They caught me fortified with power! Not like at the Escarpment! Think, rockhead, think . . .*

*Rockhead! The Escarpment! Poetic justice!*

"Six rods! There's a fourth one coming up the road now, master! And a fifth on horseback!"

Something inside Bosamp screamed a warning that this sigil was too dangerous, demanded too much, but he choked it down and let the dragon dust buoy his blood. Spreading his orange-draped arms, yowling with self-satisfied fury, he droned like stone being tortured, like the death wail of basalt, sounds so horrid that despair gripped every living thing that heard them, and pointed his staff at the ring of stones below him.

*Runes of power.*

Summoned to battle, Skandsala rumbled. Slowly at first, then with more urgency, the hillside below him spasmed, leaping to its feet, tremors delirious. . . .

"Four rods!"

Yor cursed huffing epithets. The ground under him rocked unsteadily as the loosest, smallest boulders began to cascade downhill, gathering the mountain detritus into a rabble of rubble and opposing his advance.

*Landslide!*

Small and large, the ring of boulders at the base of the pass marched downhill, picking up speed until they careened forward, a phalanx of stone soldiers obediently hurling themselves into combat.

"Die! Die like the grist you are!" the magician whooped. Glyphs again flowed from him; he turned and faced the wall of stone on the east side of the pass and called it down with his staff. High above the summit, shelves of grandfather stone sundered at the sound of Bosamp's wizardry; the mountain slope turned into a river of lithic animosity, rushing downhill. . . .

Toward me! My gods! I've got to get out of the way!

Below, Yor bounded over a boulder and braced against a tree. It was a dead spot in the avalanche, an island of refuge; Trebor soon joined him, breathing hard. "Run!" they heard Dword urge from below. "The whole mountain's going to come down on us in a moment!"

An immense boulder bore down on the two Brets, and they leaped sideways. The tree they were hiding behind was ripped up by the roots, and they ended up on the ground. "We can't reach him!" the loremaster said to the cavalryman.

"We can't give up now! It's only a few more yards!" Yor leaped up quickly. "Bosamp!" he yelled so strongly that it rose above the roar of the rockslide opera. "Surrender! You can never win!"

"Boulderdash!" the gaunt young wizard tittered as he raced away from the avalanche and secured himself. "Boulderdash!" he repeated, instantly infatuated with his own horrendous pun. "Boulderdash! Boulderdash!"

Obeying his command, his stone soldiers descended; schist slid with increasing velocity; gravel fists pounded the hillside. Trees groaned and snapped in the onslaught; bushes lay flat and surrendered; the road was a river of stone; the rumble of the landslide drowned out all other sounds.

"We've got to go back!" Trebor shouted.

Yor bolted forward. He weaved between the boulders, managing to fight another few paces uphill, close enough to hear the trampled vibestick holler, "No, master, no!"

Leap, whirl, whirl, jump . . . not quite.

The black-clad dandy missed a pirouette and fell. Swallowed up in the river of rock, subsumed by a torrent of stone and fallen, splintered trees, Yor was dragged downhill in a snarl of bashed and bruised limbs.

Down . . . down . . . down . . .

Over and over he tumbled, desperately trying to regain his feet but caught up in a force that overwhelmed him. Then a strong arm clamped on him as he swept by and pulled him from the current. "I had to try . . ." he coughed, certain of the arm's owner.

"I know," Trebor said. "I know."

They ran downhill for all they were worth.

Boulders rained, bounding, bouncing; trees genuflected; dust and dirt turned the captains' sweat to a coarse slurry. The mountain wailed in triumph, knocking them about willy-nilly as they scrambled down Skandsala. At the behest of the orange-robed thaumaturge, columns of stone rambled forward like drilling armies, pressing together into a pile barricading the pass, concealing the sorcerer. The mound grew and grew and grew, but it did not conceal Bosamp's laughter.

"You'll never catch me now, morons! Before the next Smuggler's Moons, I will chime the Bell and doom all Leiblein! Until then—*if* you survive my magicks!—I suggest you find something soft and warm to bury your face in! Hah! I am the World Shaker, the World Breaker! Look on my works, ye feeble, and despair!"

Downhill racers, stone and flesh.

"Your horses!" Sir Dudley cried out as he rode into view, relieved to see the trio but aware that the danger had not yet passed. The panicked steeds fought his grip, but the aged knight denied them their fear. "Hurry! I can't hold them much longer!"

He held them long enough. Dword arrived first, with Yor and Trebor a few strides back.

But not the prince. "Prince Rodney!" Sir Dudley yelled. "Where are you?"

"Over here," the youth bleated in pain. "My foot's caught under a tree!"

Sir Dudley kicked his horse with a "*Hiah!*" Gamely the

courageous beast responded, and the two dashed upward through the boulders. The knight's hands grabbed a rope, and he made a loop as he rode. Suddenly he saw the prince. Tossing the rope with uncanny aim, he lassoed a limb. Tying the rope to his saddle horn, he urged the horse backward. In a second, the boy was free and stumbling toward them; the knight scooped him up and raced away.

Rout.

They rode ahead of the bounding rock, outdistancing the stone river as it dissipated farther down the slope, clumping into clots of shattered trees and boulders as the flow went out the wrong end of a funnel. Amid near misses and desperate maneuvers, it was a long ride down until they reached the bottom of the mountain and the last rock finally rolled to a stop.

Weary, breathless, they gathered together, unnerved and bleeding from countless scrapes and bruises but safe, staring at each other with lolling tongues and battered limbs, too glad to be alive for any recriminations.

Safe, mayhap, but far from happy.

"Beaten again!" Yor ranted as he looked back. The road no longer existed; in fact, there wasn't a trace to indicate that there had ever even been a road. A field of stone and shattered trees now buried the lower half of the mountain. The dust floating in the air shielded the hillside with the sinking of the sun, but it appeared that a cliff had formed as the mountain sheered away, leaving the pass high, blocked, and isolated.

"I can't believe this!" Yor stormed. "Who would have thought Bosamp could do something like this! It's a miracle we're all in one piece! But by Firefang's eye, I'll not rest until that sorcerer is in irons in a dungeon in Bretilya!" A stream of off-color verbiage gushed from the black-clad dandy until even the plants blushed at his expletives. Finally spent, his head sagged in defeat.

We're doomed. . . .

"It's just about hopeless now," Trebor said dejectedly as he sat on a boulder. He pointed to the towering pile of stone between them and the pass, then saw a thorn stuck in his sleeve and picked it out before pointing again. "Even if we could climb over that mess, the horses could never get through it. Bosamp will be gone already. We'll have to go back to the crossroads and start over. That's a day lost, maybe two!"

"There's another way," Dword intervened nervously. *I wonder if I should tell them about this?* "A shortcut I've used once or twice. There's a hunting trail that skirts Skandsala to the east, through Roskilde Chasm. It's not a good trail, Woden knows, but it's quick and saves at least a day, although there's the Roskilde to ford. . . ."

The barbarian stopped, skipping a beat. *Best not to tell them about the watervards yet!*

"The trail rejoins the main road—the road we were going to take before the cleric showed up. The trail's a league back, by the millstream. It'll take us to Holarholt."

"I saw that." Trebor frowned. " 'Trail' is a trifle grandiose, don't you think? I wouldn't even call it a Category F-One-plus footpath!"

Dword shrugged. Sizable groups of loremasters had spent substantial percentages of their lifetimes thoroughly, painstakingly classifying Leiblein's thoroughfares. There were now twenty-nine categories listed in *The Authoritative Accumulation of Alleyways* (usually called *The Triple A Guide*), which sorted venues according to the root mean square pace per nominal weather-day (vernal equinox, no rain) of the unit standard horse and rider; the seasonally adjusted probability of finding water per day traveled; the coefficient of useful plants commonly encountered; the highwaymen incidence rate; the normalized ratio of taverns per furlong; the customs inspector bribability factor; the index of proximity to points of interest; and . . .

"Trail, footpath . . . who cares?" Yor said. He stood, battered, dirty, tired. The taste of defeat hung bitter in his mouth, but he wanted action now, not solace; deeds, not bickering. "Slim hopes are better than none! I don't know about the rest of you, but I'm mad! Really mad! I want to wring that blasted wizard's neck! I'm so mad that if I had to fight watervards for the opportunity to catch that charlatan, I'd go cheerfully, with one hand tied behind my back, all the while singing the 'Ballad of Count Yor' in falsetto fortissimo, including the three-part harmony for eunuch choirs!"

Dword gasped, made the appropriate right-handed anti-hex gesture, prayed fervently that the Three Weird Sisters were off duty, and managed to keep his mouth clamped shut, shut, shut.

\* \* \* \* \*

The depth of night . . .

Tentacled emotions flayed the Bret cavalryman until he pitched the blanket back, knowing sleep would not come. Quietly he rose from his bedding and walked toward the millstream, jamming himself into a shelf by a shallow waterfall. The sound of the water dropping into the pool echoed the melancholy in his heart.

"By Firefang's eye" . . . how could I have said such a thing? The talisman.

Yor watched the moons move. For nights now, Sturgov and Ellhagen, the twin moons, had flirted with each other. Tonight—soon—they would kiss. "Lovers' Moons" it was commonly called. It was said that if the two moons touched, white and full, high in the heavens, then true and everlasting love would flourish for those who courted in their glow.

Lovers eagerly sought such a night.

His heart ached. Tonight the two moons would meet just above the horizon; tonight the third moon, Zelaven, dark and new, would shoot up out of the horizon and catch them in the act, eclipse them, cut off their celestial embrace. Such a confluence was rare. It was said Zelaven was a jealous suitor who sought to break up the lovers. Sometimes the moons would reappear still linked, a sign that love could conquer the forces arrayed against it. Other times they would reappear separated, an omen of troubled romance.

But tonight, he knew, they would drop from sight during reddish Zelaven's dark passage; their kiss would be lost in the shadows, and the sky would darken in gloom. Bard's Moons . . . Lovers who met on such a night were doomed to tragedy.

Kathy.

He remembered the first time he saw her. It was after the war. Lord Lee had prepared a celebration at the castle to honor the Light's homecoming. The town was decorated in ribbons and bunting; a troupe of players from Westwood had been engaged as entertainment; in abundance, food lay spread on tables; drink flowed like the Fairfax itself.

The parade.

The Light wore their black and gold dress uniforms, crisp and handsome: prancing ponies, tartan sashes. She watched him as he rode by. Their eyes met, linked. It wasn't really the first time he'd seen her—she was Lord Lee's daughter, after all, but she had been a gawky girl just turned adolescent when he went away to war. She was anything but now, her frame filled in smoothly, her long hair flowing off her shoulders, her flirting green eyes full of playfulness.

She bore his stare as long as she could, then blushed.

At the ball that night, he was bold, unafraid of the talk brewing in hushed corners, a moth drawn to her fire. Others she teased openly, staying just out of his reach, but he stalked her confidently, in spite of the disapproving stares of his fellow officers. The heat in his eyes cut through the protocol of society like the rapier hanging at his side.

Collision.

She was light in his arms, her skin sizzling, her silken hair sweeping against him like a spider's strands. They danced and danced and danced. . . .

They went out under the stars. He kissed her, and she toyed with him, but not for very long. They found an alcove.

Dark Zelaven ruled the night.

Bard's Moons.

Dawn did not save them.

\* \* \* \* \*

Bosamp awoke to find he still couldn't move.

The horse, injured during the stone barrage and limping slightly, stared at the supine wizard, idly wondering if he was still alive, then continued to munch on weeds.

How long was I out this time?

Agony.

The pain in his side was intense; the itching took glee in his collapse, goading his helplessness. His stomach growled like a starved wild animal, demanding its share of his attention. His head hurt. When the power had left him, he had fallen like a marionette whose strings are released.

The dust!

Salvation was in his neck sachet.

He couldn't move to reach it.

He couldn't even scream.

Fool! You are not one of the Council! You cannot throw your power around in gaudy displays and expect not to pay for it! You'll be lucky if something doesn't come along and eat you!

A night and half the next day passed before he was able to get his hands on the dust.

# CHAPTER NINE

Holarholt, two afternoons and a clutch of watervards later.

Legs hunched, Dword puffed up his chest like a firemander about to spit incendiary venom, then ducked suddenly around toward Yor and Trebor, who, twenty feet off, were watering the tired horses in a rivulet.

The red-beard grinned and winked.

What now? they thought.

Screwing back around, Dword poked a gauntleted finger into the pliant pillow belly of Holarholt's only stable master and contorted his face into a sneer that would have given umbrage even to the hermit monks of Kibquez, arguably the most unsightly visages on Lothar.

"Your sister sleeps with woollyfangs!" Dword taunted his fellow countryman. "Ugly ones, at that!"

"*Urr!*" Menthoden slavered rabidly. Livid, he gnawed his index finger until it turned purple from lack of blood, then pointed the same rude digit in the direction of the horses being offered by Dword.

"It's hard to tell which is the bigger pile of pony cakes—those nags or their owners! My dog could outrun those knock-kneed, spavined muttmeats! I—"

"Your dog," Dword challenged, jutting his face a whisker away from Menthoden's and leering like a bog serpent about to dine, "wears skirts and suckles your litter! Five fingers, our old horses, and your miserable life, you senile gasberry. This is my last offer!"

Like a bog serpent deprived of its dinner, Menthoden hissed. Then he hopped up and down as if his feet were on fire and put a hand to each ear to shut out all sound.

"*Urr!*"

When the stable master finally stopped, panting and red-faced, he kicked dirt in the direction of Dword, not quite managing to soil Dword's hide trousers, and said, "Seven, mule breath, or you can stand here and play with your tethers until there are virgins in Torpica!"

Outraged, Dword beat on his chest, driving the air from his lungs.

*Boomboomboomboom!*

His cheeks went purple; his eyes bulged ominously; he huffed and puffed to get his breath back. Feigning a dash at the stable, which made Menthoden wince ever so slightly, Dword then roared, "May Lodi send a horde of hungry in-laws to your house for the winter! May Thorogod practice bestiality with your mistress! May Woden personally escort you into the presence of Jarnarokalla of the Five Vile Odors!"

Gasp! Not that old biddy! Trembling, Yor and Trebor began to count the five: feet, underarms, breath . . .

"Five and a half, you limp-tongued hay reamer!" Dword derided. "This is my *final* last offer!"

The stable master's lip curled over; he gnashed his teeth, and his tongue made a staccato clicking. He kept this up until Dword sank to his knees and howled in mind-boggled rage.

"This—" Menthoden at last gestured to his own string of steeds, a line of six hardy fjord mustangs, stocky, long-haired, surefooted mounts well suited for the rugged Norlandic wilderness to come—"*this* is what horses look like, unbathed dung wallower! You *ride* them, not *carry* them!"

Dword's face strained with the improper urge to laugh; as much to mute it as for any other reason, he yanked on the end of his chin—the two-handed nonpersonal beard affront—pulling until his face was even redder than before. Flapping his elbows like a bird that was trying to take off, he spat with superb accuracy right past Menthoden's left ear, crowing.

"Six fingers, you cuckolded formicary! This is my *ultimate* final last offer!"

"Done!" Menthoden roared, slapping his fist in his palm.

"And done!" Dword roared back. "I'd have paid you seven, you filly-landerer!"

"And I would have settled for five, oat oaf!" Menthoden replied.

Completing the ritual of bargain sealing, the two Norlanders locked arms like long-lost brothers—they had known each other all of thirty minutes—and traded robust shoulder blows.

"A pleasure, sirrah!" Dword beamed. "Well haggled!"

"An honor, Dword Sagasmith! Yes, yes, I know who you are! I saw you once at the Ytnwald Faire years back! Many's the night your madrigals have warmed our fires! And this must be Captain Yor himself! And Trebor Manbook, no mistake!"

Groans.

Menthoden nodded cheerily at the offset duo, plainly pleased with the acquaintance. Dword unsheathed his poniard and sliced a six-finger-long strip from the argent snake coiled on his biceps. The silver passed hands; Dword retreated to his comrades.

"A marvelous monger!" Dword said happily. "Shrewd, very shrewd!"

"I noticed," Trebor drawled, adjusting the bandage on his forehead below his helmet. Watervards! he cursed. I should be okay in a day or two. "And it took only half an hour . . . almost blinding speed. Not like at Kringla."

"But," Yor injected, stealing the momentum, raising his left arm, now in a sling as a result of the battle at Roskilde Ford. Cursed watervards! Who would have dreamed that . . .

He blushed redder than a firemander's bottom and shoved the abhorrent memory from his mind. "You really had us worried when you rolled around on the ground for five minutes and ran screaming headfirst into the side of the stable."

Dword beamed with pride. "Ah—that always saves a finger of silver! It's my trademark! Many's the time I've said you Brets don't appreciate the fine art of—"

"We know! We know!"

Too elated to quibble, Dword sucked in a deep breath of northern morning. "Hair of the hoarmaidens, it's good to be back home! Smell the air! It cleans the lungs and fuels the soul! There's a promise of frost on the morrow or Thorogod's off lancing lambs! And the water . . ."

Sigh.

"Yes, well," Yor said with a smile, "there's even more of this blessed realm yet to be sojourned, so let's be going." He pointed at the stable master. "Has he seen Bosamp?"

"Bosamp?" Menthoden said over his shoulder, overhearing the query. "Sickly wizard fellow? Talks to himself and acts as if he's got this big secret or something?"

"Exactly."

"He bought a horse from me just this morning. Ill-humored, contrary coot! Pricked my spleen, he did! Had the look of a real mistreater. His own horse was near lame, so I just couldn't sell him one of my good mounts, not and still sleep nights! I sold him old McJaggar, har-har! That one's as loud and stubborn as a gravid zirii! A street fighter, that one! They're a real match, they are! No sympathy for either devil! I wonder which one of them's going to rule the roost, har-har?"

Dword beamed. "You've done us all a service! That should make him easier to catch!"

"Let's get the gear switched," Yor urged.

Menthoden and his boy began to remove the saddles and packs from the bedraggled horses and refit them to the fjord mustangs. Trebor and Dword joined in, swapping tales of their trip so far in exchange for the extra help and garnering a couple of spare feed bags for the long journey ahead.

Time: How much do we have?

Yor stared up the road as he removed his saddle. In the

distance, even above the titan evergreens ringing Holarholt, the waiting grey mountains could be seen. Vangberg! He'll be a whole lot harder to stop if he gets his hands on the Mallet! We can't let that happen!

Yor did some nervous arithmetic. Bosamp had a half-day lead. Shouldn't he be farther along? Ah, the lame horse. But do we still have a chance to catch him this side of Vangberg? We have to make up half a day somehow. . . .

Time is running out!

Just then the prince and Sir Dudley returned.

"We're back," Sir Dudley greeted the trio. "We've got some bread, cheeses, and sausages."

"Some nutsweets, too," the prince added, "and bearberries! And honeygoo! We've got enough stuff here for a legitimate feast of fives! We can have a real repast, hours of face stuffing!"

"No time for all that," Yor said briskly. "With the fresh horses, we can still make a few more leagues today. Help get the gear transferred over to the new horses. We'll be on our way in a nonce."

"But it'll be dark soon!" Prince Rodney protested. "This is a good place to stop and have dinner. After that, it'll be too dark to ride anymore, so we can sleep here, at the inn, on real beds!"

"We'll eat on the hoof," Yor insisted. "And as for sleeping, don't count on it."

"But—"

"But nothing! We ride now! Move!"

"This is stupid!" the prince mumbled. "Dumb! Dumb! Dumb!"

* * * * *

"Thwart me, will you? I want some speed out of you, and I will have it!"

Bosamp dismounted, mumbling to himself, "This is the

worst horse yet! The sorriest of a sorry lot!" He stood before the steed, a malevolent smirk warping his dried lips. "Here, beastie! What you need is a little incentive! A little desire! I think you'll find this brings back visions of your youth! Yes, I'm going to give you back your youth! I can do that! I'm a sorcerer!"

He opened the dragon dust sachet. Such a big animal . . . I wonder how much it will take? Ah, well, I'll start it on just a taste and increase the dosage until I get some action out of him!

He took a sugar cube and rolled it in the scintillating dust. "Here! Together we'll ride like the wind, you and I! And there's plenty more where that came from!"

He had to jump quickly to catch the stirrup; the horse reared half in terror, half in astonishment. The dust inflamed the equine; its body spasmed and quivered. It galloped away, with the wizard shouting encouragement.

* * * * *

North from Holarholt the party of five riders rode. The terrain thickened into pristine woodlands. Slim, straight evergreens speckled the nearby mountain grades, which were garlanded with billowy clouds. In the glacial valleys, dwarf spruces and black cedars fought over the hillocks, leaving the meadows to the reeds and thickets; ivory-ruby-topaz windflowers flourished on the myriad moraines.

Time!

Stopping by a mirror pond in the twilight, Yor looked anxiously at the chain of peaks that serrated the horizon obliquely west, intersecting with the doglegged valley beyond eyeshot.

I never thought we'd have to come this far!

Edgy, vague feelings of impending disaster fretted the cavalryman. He turned to the Norlander and asked, almost demandingly, "How far to Vangberg?"

"Beyond Odskag." The Norlander gestured, pointing to

the tallest mountain, a clenched stone fist blocking the end of the valley. "It's about ten leagues to Freissinggal, the last village in the Denali. From there to the top of the tor and down the other side into the Frozen Wastes is another day's ride, perhaps. But Vangberg is close to Odskag, less than a dozen leagues into the Wastes."

"Trebor?"

The loremaster frowned, vexed. "I doubt if he's had a single thought of us since Skandsala; he probably thinks we've given up, or at the least, that we're far behind him. No doubt he'll head straight for the volcano, cocksure.

"He'll have to find the underground passage, though."

"This *is* all just a legend, right?" the prince asked. "It's not really true, is it?"

Silence.

"Oh, come on now! All that stuff about hammers and bells and fireflies is just poppycock, isn't it? Old wives' tales! You don't really believe Bosamp can destroy the world, do you?"

"Bosamp believes it," Trebor said. "Do you want to take the chance that he's wrong?"

Silence.

"Look around you," Dword said. "When you've seen sights like this, how can you doubt the legends of the gods?"

Five sets of eyes wandered off into the timeless boreal wilds, absorbed in the splendor of nature, in the epic summer sunset, in the eldritch blue glaciers looming on the primordial mountainsides, looking like huge handprints left from forming the world. . . .

The prince gulped.

"Trebor," Yor continued, "how much longer until the sun sets?"

"Less than an hour."

"But it won't get really dark right away, will it?"

"No, not at this latitude," Trebor answered, hesitant. He knew Yor knew—they all knew—what the other nights had been like. "I hope you're not thinking what I think you're thinking. It'll be about like Juggler's Moons, but the road's much too bad for riding in that kind of light. There's holes, rocks, soft spots, streams to cross. . . ."

"We can use torches."

"Is that such a good idea?" Sir Dudley asked. "If Menthoden was right, we're only a few leagues behind Bosamp. Once he starts up the incline, he'll surely see the torches. There won't be any question in his mind who the night riders are. Might we not do better to let him think we're far behind him?"

Trebor grunted in concurrence. "If he sees the torches, he'll have plenty of time to prepare an ambush for us."

Not good at all, Yor thought with a struggle. There were risks to moving in the dark. It could prove to be utterly unnecessary; it would rob them of a good night's sleep that might be vital when they did catch up with Bosamp.

The question: Can we afford a good night's sleep?

Moody blue, the black-clad cavalryman felt their fearful curiosity as they watched him, waiting for his decision. Waffling, he glanced up at the sky for inspiration, checking the cloud pattern and the wind direction.

What will tomorrow bring?

What if the weather turns bad tomorrow? Who does that favor? Bosamp, because it slows us down? Or us, because it slows him down?

Churn.

Don't stop! an inner voice urged him. His head jerked back, acknowledging the mysterious insight with a grim nod. Turning to the others, he said, "We'll walk in the dark, ahead of the horses. It won't be as fast, but we'll still keep moving."

They didn't like it; he could see it in their faces.

He didn't much like it either.

"For now, we'll ride as hard as we can until it's no longer safe." Kicking its flanks, he put the horse into a canter, judging that to be the gait that would leave the equine spent just after the light failed.

They rode until it was so dark there were no colors. Then they walked until the ruts and muck, the stumble stones and the ankle twisters were all they could take.

Yor kept pushing them onward.

At Sturgov's Rise, they tripped a flare rod that Bosamp had secreted off the road. The rod shot straight up in the air and burst, a magnificent pyrotechnic delight that must have been visible for leagues in all directions.

And the boom carried much farther.

The prince's horse bolted at the explosion, breaking the teenager's grip, racing away in the dark.

It cost them almost an hour to find the prince's horse.

\* \* \* \* \*

"Get up!" the wizard demanded. He struck the pony with his staff. "Get up!"

The horse could not. Stuck in a critter hole, its leg was broken, but worse, the great engine of its heart was sundered. The dragon dust had given it its youth and was now giving it old age. With the second blow from the wizard, the horse collapsed, tongue hanging loose in its jaws, and abandoned life.

"Get up!" Bosamp kicked it once. "They're right behind us! Didn't you see the flare? Get up!"

It was no use, and he knew it.

He looked ahead. There was smoke emitting from a chimney not too far away—a farmhouse and a barn.

A barn!

*Groouwl!*

All right! All right!

\* \* \* \* \*

After midnight, they lost the road on flat hard rock and

missed the ford. Sir Dudley nearly drowned when he fell in a sinkhole crossing the stream.

While Bosamp slept fitfully, they marched three precious leagues, negating the distance the wizard had gained by feeding dragon dust to his horse.

# CHAPTER TEN

Dawn was bright and cold and cloudless.

Forced from their bedrolls by the testy Bretilyan cavalry-man into the nippy morning air, less than a half-night's sleep to their credit, the tired horses and riders soon resumed the chase, pounding northward toward the Norlandic village of Freissinggal.

The glorious alpine countryside quickly lost its allure as the party's fatigue accumulated; the day-after-day drain of their hunt also affected their tempers. The third spectacular sparkling stream to be waded did not make them want to cel-ebrate the soul-succoring joys of nature; it just made them wet. Likewise, the chunky swatches of volcanic lava beds, with their dapper maroon and black puffed pumice fields, their shifting floes as treacherous as ice on a broken river, pro-vided only perspiration, not inspiration. Nor were the colorful pastiches of flowers festooned in the soggy, boot-sucking bog meadows between tree-crowded ridges uplifting, nor were the road-nuzzling bearberry bushes, with their not-yet-ripe fruit and their all-too-ripe thorns, especially spiritual.

About midmorning, half a league south of Freissinggal, they found Bosamp's horse, a demoralizing image. From there, they tracked the wizard's path to a homestead several furlongs to the east, where they found a brood of irate citizens already gathered.

"I'm sorry. Could you repeat that?" Dword said in his native tongue, frowning. The local dialect was troublesome; Freissinggal's villagers spoke a peculiar variation of old Nor-landic and pronounced it strangely at that. Most of Leiblein's realms agreed to speak a polyglot hybrid of the major languages, one concocted by peddlers and sailors; these remote villagers, however, had never really seen the need to belong to the rest of the world.

Dword listened carefully while Bygdoy, the stadlord, patiently repeated his singsong saga of Bosamp's crimes. This time, though, the red-beard picked up the cadence of the dialect and was able to glean the needed information. "Apparently," he translated to his companions, "Bosamp broke into this farmer's—Hiemal's—barn last night and butchered a zux. By all evidence, he ate it raw."

"It's the dragon dust." Trebor shook his head with disgust. "The stuff burns up tremendous amounts of physical energy; it's killing him. Just like it did his horse."

"It's not killing him fast enough," Yor said hotly. "I've seen a lot of dead horses, but never one like that! Feeding it dragon dust! Anyone that could do that to a horse is a madman!"

Clogged with emotion, the black-clad dandy was unable to successfully vent his frustration. *Those who use magic have no conscience!* he accused mentally. *The glyphs of power corrupt, eroding away the sense of right and wrong! Sorcerers think they are above the laws of nature and man! Magic is inherently evil!*

*Not true!* his devil's advocate rebutted. *Magic in and of itself isn't evil. Evil begins only when one person's actions abuse another's rights. There is no evil that does not start with a freely made choice to act on a selfish desire.*

"Bosamp has a new horse now," Dword continued. "Doori, here, saw him riding away from town, toward Odskag, with Hiemal's horse, so he came to see what had happened. They found the zux and got the stadlord, Bygdoy. That's him on the left."

Yor and Trebor bowed formally at Bygdoy. They hadn't needed Dword's introduction to know who was in charge; the grizzled stadlord had the look of a cagey old mountain ram who had butted many a head, as indeed he had.

"They were organizing a pursuit when we showed up."

Bygdoy's arms flailed around in wild indignation as he reeled off several sentences, followed by grumbles of consensus from the rest of the villagers.

Yor didn't need a translation. "Tell them that if they'll swap us fresh mounts, we'll leave at once and save them the trouble."

Dword explained; back and forth the words flew. Finally Bygdoy looked at Yor's drawn, determined face, and that seemed to decide it for him. He gave in, satisfied that as long as Dword was with the Brets, Norlandic justice would be served. With a series of gestures, he deputized Dword.

"They've offered us the horses," Dword announced, "but they want them back when we return."

"Agreed."

"Ask him about the Wastes," Trebor said.

Dword nodded. He talked with the villagers and pointed toward Odskag, looming majestic in the distance, high enough to tower over even the nearby range of ridges boxing in the valley. The villagers spoke round-robin, and Dword glanced from time to time toward the distant peak.

"They haven't ventured much beyond the tor," Dword related finally. "They say there's not much out there worth the trip, other than an occasional hunt for idontcarraboo, which they herd through the Great Spine. Once you leave town, the road dwindles down quickly to a small trail. Vangberg can easily be seen from the tor; sometimes its smoke blows through the pass."

Bygdoy added a few more words and Dword tensed.

"What did he say?" Yor asked nervously.

"He says on a clear day, from the top from Odskag Tor, a golden gleam can be seen at the horizon."

They paused, absorbing it.

"Thank him. Let's go."

Hurriedly horses were brought out, and the transfer of gear

effected. The villagers helped with the horse changing; Heimal produced two haversacks of provisions and a set of woven jackets, so that by the time the party was ready to leave, it was prepared for the desolation of the Wastes.

As he recinched his saddle on a handsome roan horse, Yor heard over his shoulder, "An honor to be of assistance, Count Yor," in broken common speech.

The Bret cavalryman turned.

Bygdoy grinned ear to ear.

"Even here?" Yor wilted.

\* \* \* \* \*

Muscle and motion, hooves and sweat.

With fresh mounts below them, they rode over the valley floor at breakneck speed. Yor pushed them even harder than he had last night, desperate to gain ground, knowing that Odskag Tor would slow them to a crawl. By midday, they had reached the foot of the incline; lathered, hair matted, and feeling the euphoria of athletes who have reached their limit with grace, they halted at the base of the mighty granite paramount, near a rushing crystal clear stream and a field of wild mountain oats.

"Good ride, men!" Yor cheered. "We'll rest here before we tackle that molehill! Water your horses and let them graze a bit! Stretch your legs! Air out your clothes! Refill your canteens! We've hard work before the day is done!"

The cavalryman gazed up, scouting the steep slope, bending his neck until it hurt. *It's a couple of leagues to the top, but less than a half-day's effort, for certain.*

*Bosamp?*

The trail was overhung with trees, twisting in and out of the flying buttresses of stone. *He's up there somewhere, Yor felt, still on this side of the tor. . . .*

"Ambush?" Trebor asked, following Yor's line of sight.

Inexorably, all stared at the distant windswept col. Like a

seamstress's finest thread, the slender path wove its way along the face of Odskag, culminating in a needle's-eye pass between two titanic, towering slate bookends.

"Perfect place for it," Yor allowed.

"Ambush!" The prince blanched. It had been a few days since they'd had any trouble; the royal teenager was almost enjoying it, even the backbreaking ride until midnight last night. He'd managed to keep up, and his saddle sores were starting to get calloused. His acne had gotten a little better—probably the cool air had something to do with it—and his sinuses had cleared up. But an ambush! The prince shivered with apprehension, recalling the debacle at Skandsala. It wasn't my fault! he thought. They should have shot Bosamp on the Escarpment! We'd all be home in front of a comfy fire if they had!

"Do we have to take him alive?" the prince blurted out. "I mean, couldn't I grant you a boon or make an edict or something, so you wouldn't have to worry about it?"

"We have to try to catch him alive if we can," Trebor replied. "We don't know how he got the dragon dust, for example; that's a major concern. And we don't know exactly what forces he might have set in motion; only he can tell us that. Furthermore, though the matter isn't clear-cut, the Wizards' Guild generally frowns on the slaying of its members. They look after their own and will demand an accounting. You wouldn't want them to send a *weird* after you, would you?"

The prince was sobered. A weird was a living nightmare; it took the whole Council to create such a warp in reality, but such a spell pursued its victim, swallowing him up in his own terrifying feardreams. "So," the prince gulped, "all we have to do is catch Bosamp, tie him up and gag him, rope him to a horse, and drag him back over two continents while we watch him every second of the day and night!"

Yor and Dword and Trebor exchanged pregnant glances, not having heard it phrased precisely that way before, but . . .

"Essentially, yes. But not to worry," Trebor said, patting his bag of tricks. "I have a way of immobilizing him. I have a bit of spellbane in here."

"You do?" the other two thirds of the three most dangerous men on Lothar chimed simultaneously.

"Where did you get spellbane?" Yor demanded. "That stuff is rarer than a Munchie's honor!"

Trebor flushed but stood his ground.

"Why, you pilfering bookworm!" Yor pressed. "What did you do, and more importantly who did you do it to?"

"They'll never miss it! There were jars of the stuff just sitting around moldering in the vault."

"The vault!" Dword asked, jaws agape. "You robbed the League vault?"

"I paid it a casual visit, yes."

"*Augh!* We're doomed!" Dword said. "I might as well lie down and die right now!" Feeling the need to stretch out for a moment anyhow, the barbarian went supine and looked skyward. "Take me quickly, Lodi, while my heart is still pure. . . ."

"Pure? Hardly," Trebor retorted sarcastically. "Besides, I was very careful—"

"Hah!" Yor protested with alarm. "Every doodad in the vault is logged in triplicate! Even the cobwebs are catalogued! A ratroach couldn't leave a poop pellet in there without some scroll clerk taking a pair of calipers, measuring it, assigning a number to it, and entering it onto a ledger! When they find out what you've done, every sage on Leiblein will be after us!"

Dword crossed his arms over his chest, embracing his shoulders. "Hurry, Lodi! Be gentle! It's my first time!"

"You mean your last time, don't you?" Trebor said. He turned back to Yor quickly and defended himself. "There's only a pouchful! There won't be an audit till the winter solstice. If they miss it at all, they'll attribute it to shrinkage! I took a pinch out of each jar to make it harder to notice, and there's no way they can trace it to me."

"Hah! You'll be their first suspect!" Dword said.

"Besides, we needed it!"

"Oh," Yor said, smiling with mock benignancy. "Well, that's entirely different. You're forgiven."

"Not so fast," Dword said with a scowl. He looked Trebor over from head to foot. "And what else did you take?"

Scarlet, the loremaster bit his tongue. "Have I ever gotten us into trouble before?"

"Remember Hykon?" Dword challenged.

"That was an accident!"

"That's the point! You never know how it's going to turn out until it's too late and some gaggle of outraged victims takes after us!"

"I needed the antlers!"

"We were up to our butts in them!"

"No one was hurt!"

"Not hurt! I couldn't sit for a week! Out with it: What else did you liberate?"

"Nothing to speak of."

"Speak of it!"

"Don't worry about it!"

At that point, Sir Dudley sneezed abruptly and searched for a handkerchief. Last night's unscheduled swim had given the elder knight a case of the sniffles. His nose was already crimson, and the dampness inside his armor had given him blisters. "Captains," he said, "we've a hill to climb, and I don't relish the thought of doing it in the dark!"

Guilty red.

Revived by the break, they started the steep climb up Odskag.

* * * * *

The route to the tor philandered with the glacially planed precipice. It was the kind of path that evoked religious insights in devout sinners, the kind of path that made one wish he'd written more letters to old friends before starting up it. Below, Freissinggal shrank to a fleck that seemed about to be swept away by the Odskag's encroaching diluvium; above, two megalithic bookends waited at the tor like stone sentinels.

Scree littered the path, making every step a maneuver requiring concentration. Maypole pines, as thickly bunched as the fleece from a ram—of which they saw many—crowded the edge, jostling for positions against white-barked hoar oak and red-limbed Frieda's fir. Here and there under the evergreen boughs lay furtive patches of snow, clandestine, dying, the last remains of the bitter winter, spawning rivulets and making muck in the igneous debris. Birds of all sizes flitted noisily through the air; rodents bounded playfully over fallen trees and deliberated over goodies. Overhead, a peaceful azure sky offered no shield against the trenchant sun; the orange orb reigned supreme, basting their skins and making them squint.

It was a sinew-toughening ascent.

Hours dragged by . . . one, two, three.

They neared the tor, walking with horses in tow, feeling a little safer that way, even though the Norlandic ponies seemed infallibly surefooted.

What's that smell? Wet fur?

Yor halted. "Let's mount up," he said. "Be wary. Bosamp may have left his marker here. Another flare rod. Or worse."

Nerves tingling, they followed the cavalryman's directive. Then Odskag Tor was before them, a tapered crevice between two epochal slabs that towered unclimbably over the col, barely wide enough for . . .

"Lodi's lingerie! A snowsnake!" Dword expounded. He took a deep breath and stared, gaping actually, in a combination of concern and wonder. "I've heard of them, but I've never seen a full-grown one before!"

Sitting serenely in the sunlight, a coiled spring of fluffy white that just about filled the entire pass in loops of yard-wide cord, the monstrous reptile opened both enormous pink eyes without lifting its head and stared back at the Norlander.

"I think it's very attractive, don't you?" Dword quickly noted. Woden's furry codpiece! Did that thing just wink at me?

"*Gah!*" the prince whined. The idea of being pursued by a Council weird suddenly took a backseat to the immediate worry of the monstrous serpent planted in the gap ahead of them. He held his hands up in front of his face and howled, "Make it go away!"

"An excellent idea!" Yor agreed wryly. "Any suggestions?"

"Snowsnakes are said to be sentient," Trebor allowed, reading from a tome he produced from no apparent source. "The skin is quite valuable, with certain unique properties that . . ."

The wedge-shaped head of the serpent bobbed up alertly off its interlaced coils, and its tongue flicked.

"But, of course, that's of no interest to us at all!" Trebor hastily added.

"None!" Dword seconded.

"Absolutely not!" the prince thirded.

Did the thing just seem to relax a bit?

"The book says they make great pets when they're little," Trebor said enthusiastically, trying to make amends.

The snowsnake eyed him disapprovingly.

"He means faithful companions! Never pets!" Dword volunteered abruptly. A memory flashed through him; when he was a tyke, his father had gotten him a stuffed toy snowsnake. It had been his favorite bedtime mate—perish the thought!

The black-clad adventurer grimaced and stared at the behemoth curled up at the entrance to Odskag Tor, wondering what to do. "Dword, I don't suppose there's another way to Vangberg from here."

"Not without backtracking twenty leagues! That'd cost us about two days, enough time for Bosamp to crawl from here to Vangberg!"

"I was afraid of that," Yor grunted. He took his left arm out of the sling, then stuffed the sling in a saddle sack. Though still a bit sore, the arm was pretty much over the worst of the watervard's twisting, but as there wasn't any reason not to, he'd been babying the bruised wing. He flexed it a few times, then gestured toward the snowsnake. "That thing must be fifty, sixty feet long! And as thick around as a Torpican barrel fungus! It could probably swallow a horse whole, with room for a few footloose jesters to boot!"

"There's no report that they eat horses," Trebor observed pedantically as he browsed through the book. "They are believed to subsist primarily on vegetation, eating spruce cabbages and watervard melons, which some claim they cultivate. However, they have been reported to eat duukies, bearcats, bird eggs, mountain beetles, green and brown molt dragons, and an occasional unlucky hunter. But never horses."

Suddenly the loremaster put the book away. I wonder . . .

"So why is it here?" the prince demanded.

"Maybe it isn't."

They all stared at the loremaster.

"An illusion?" Yor asked. "Bosamp?"

"That's a possibility. Remember the *faux* Bosamp we chased?"

Yor sighed. "Trebor?"

The man-mountain watched the gentle breathing of the immense coil carefully. His eyes brightened, gauging the gap. There was about a man's length on either side of the snake, a small space but perhaps enough to slip by.

"If it's spellcast, as you know," the loremaster pontificated, "the only way to despell it is to thrust iron cleanly through any part of it. But until then, it will be real, and just as deadly. Of course, if it's *not* an illusion, a thrust might not kill it. You'd have to hit something vital, and the skin is armor tough. Presumably it would get very, very angry." As he spoke, Trebor watched the snowsnake hiss, revealing rows of razor sharp teeth and two long fangs. "But don't panic yet; I have an idea."

"I wonder if it's eaten recently," the prince blathered.

Trebor hesitated, distracted by the prince's comment. "The rest of you try to go together, in a line, on the right side of—"

"No way!" the prince gulped. "I'm staying here! Somebody has to watch the rear!"

"We should let you!" Trebor said brusquely. "Snowsnakes hunt in pairs, as a rule, so there's another one on its way up right now!"

It was a lie, of course, but well told.

"*Gah!*" the prince shrieked, swiveling in his saddle and looking behind him, panic-stricken. "Sir Dudley! Get behind me!"

Ignoring the royal teenager, the loremaster moved his horse to the side. "Keep your swords between you and it, but don't strike it unless it strikes you."

Yor and Dword freed their blades.

Behind the trio, Sir Dudley unpacked his segmented lance from its traveling kit, assembling the pieces. Though shorter and less sturdy than a jouster, it was equally deadly.

Then, as gently as possible, Trebor slid his broadsword out of the scabbard angled across his back, trying to muffle the grate of metal. The Overtoad's blade moaned a warning that made their hair stand on end; it was for just such creatures that the sword had been fashioned. Like a thoroughbred breaking through the gate, the sword surged with life, eager to be to the hunt, and the loremaster had to tighten his grip to control it.

The display of weaponry made the furred reptile perk up. Its pink eyes narrowed with annoyance and swept slowly from man to man, settling in doubt and uncertainty on Trebor's fabled blade. Its forked tongue darted, tasting the air; its nostrils puffed clouds of moisture in the cold, blustery wind whistling through the confined breaches of Odskag Tor.

"Let me go first," Trebor said. "Dword, take my horse."

Dismounting, the loremaster locked his steel-grey eyes on the serpent's. Patiently, in full control, he walked forward and to the left, one easy pace at a time, his broadsword held off to the side in as nonthreatening a posture as a well-armored titan holding a legendary blade whose embellished runes now throbbed with a faint blue light could muster. . . .

"What are you doing?"

"Move around to the right; I'll keep its attention."

Two strides closer.

Warmly the tall Bret grinned, flashing perfect teeth. "Nice kitty," he said in a mellifluous purr, with a tinge of terror to it, the kind of tone intended to beguile the chastity belt off a timid virgin.

Two more strides.

Shadows in Trebor's peripheral vision, Yor and Dword rode slowly to his right, moving up against the cold, damp granite and slate shoulders of the gap.

"Trebor, I've got your horse. I'll stay here until the prince has passed," Dword related.

"Nice kitty," Trebor soothed.

Arm's length.

The snowsnake arched its furred eyes in a mixture of amusement, concern, and confusion; uncertain, it focused on the huge Bret's defiant sword, but did not bat a tongue.

"We're all just friends here," Trebor cooed. "There's enough room for all of us, so just relax. Your eyes are getting so heavy. It's such a nice day for a nap. . . ."

In the chasms of Odskag, with the chilblains gamboling in the gusts, with small icicles hanging like pulled teeth from the slate slabs, Captain Trebor Blackburn of the Croswall Guards sweated like a Gormousian bloater in a swelterbelter.

He's going to need help, Yor thought, and steered his nervous steed to the right wall, rubbing against it, sword poised. By the sacred scribe, it's so big! I don't think we'll have a prayer if it lashes out!

Yor slipped by the snake and breathed again. Immediately he positioned himself at the opposite side of the snake, cater-corner, completing a triangle with Dword and Trebor that inscribed the great white serpent, his rapier looking like a puny sewing needle compared to the mammoth diameter of the furred white snake.

"Prince, you come next," Yor insisted.

"I'm n-not going anywhere! You k-kill that thing f-first!"

The snake hissed, blowing steamy saurian clouds in the loremaster's face; it reeked of digested meat and nearly made Trebor faint. Both its eyes opened now, changing from placid pink to ferocious rose.

The massive interlaced coils tensed for action.

Though his face remained placid, Trebor's heart palpitated. "Nice kitty," he said soothingly, his voice on the verge of breaking up. "He's just a pup . . . not even housebroken. We don't listen to him . . . and neither should you. . . ."

Gulp! I'm going to have to have a talk with that boy!

"Let's go back!" Prince Rodney shouted. "I hate snakes!"

Was that indignation in the snakes eyes? Trebor worried. "Some of my best friends are snakes!" he countered quickly.

Uh-oh! I'm going to pay for that one later!

"My liege," Sir Dudley hastened without turning to his charge, "it might be best to move on." The knight pointed his lance downhill. No one else could see what he was gesturing at. "I believe I see another one of these creatures slithering up the trail now!"

Trebor dared to spare a quick glance over his shoulder. Sir Dudley was perched defiantly on his destrier, cradling his lance, a vision of a bygone era. Good! Trebor thought. You divined my ploy! The years at court have not dulled your wits!

"Why is this happening?" moaned the prince. "We're trapped! How could they know we were here?"

"They have a keen sense of smell, Your Highness."

"Then stop making scents!" Prince Rodney gurgled. "I hate snakes! This is worse than my worst nightmare! I've got to get out of here!" Inspired by the fact that Yor had gotten by, and that the right side was away from the snake's head, and figuring it take the snake at least a minute to eat Trebor—enough time to get through the tor—the prince held his sword out with a pair of quavering arms and yelled, "Don't eat me, snakie! Eat Trebor first!"

The prince kicked his horse too hard; the edgy beast was all too happy to oblige by galloping through the gap on the right side, blowing by Dword, nearly knocking the barbarian down.

It's now or never! Trebor thought. Imperceptibly he had edged his blade forward. Steadied for the worst, he accidentally-deliberately tripped over his own feet and poked the sword straight into the fluffy white fur, trying hard to act like a clumsy clodhopper.

The Overtoad's moaning blade nicked, not deeply, the snake's thick leather, and a small incarnadine drop flowed back to the runes, making them glow brightly along his blade.

Illusions never bleed!

The snake's jaws opened with a hiss.

"It's real!" Trebor croaked. He flung his arms wide open and backward as a gesture of peace, while the blade whined a high-pitched complaint and throbbed in Trebor's mighty mitt. "Look!" he implored the snake. "No sword!" Gambling, he dropped the Overtoad's weapon, but dropped it conveniently close.

The sword hummed softly, itching to get closer.

The book had better be right! he thought.

The snake frowned, flitting its tongue in and out, coiling tighter and rising up to Trebor's face, skeptical, baffled, not quite certain what to do.

Trebor grinned boyishly. "Let me do something nice for

you!" His hands descended in a blur past the open maw. He placed them gently on the soft fuzz between the two erect reptilian ears and scratched affectionately.

This had better work! "Nice kitty! Go to sleep now!"

Did that thing just snicker?

Galloping pell-mell, the prince shot down the tor.

"Don't go too far!" Yor yelled. Futile. Well, at least he's by, Yor thought as he watched the prince ride off. He'll stop as soon as he gets afraid of being alone out there. His neck whirled, and he looked at the loremaster with consternation.

What the heck is Trebor doing?

Trebor massaged the snake's head with excruciating sensuality, his huge paws moving through the complex rhythms of the lore for backaches with luxurious tenderness, the same set of exercises prescribed and practiced with such effectiveness by the eunuchs of Pangrim.

Go to sleep, damn you!

"The second one is getting closer," Sir Dudley related. "It appears to be headed our way!"

"You can drop it now," Dword said. He, of course, knew that snowsnakes did not hunt in pairs, and he had seen through Trebor's ruse immediately. "The prince is out of danger, so—"

"Drop what?"

"You mean . . . ?"

"Alas! I wish I didn't!" The elder knight reared his horse and wheeled around. "Time, Captains!"

"But they don't hunt in pairs!" Dword asserted. "In the entire annuals of eddadom, there's no mention—"

*Snap!*

The retort of a small tree being sheared echoed through the tor, reverberating off the slate bookends of the gap like the crack of a poleaxe on an iron helm.

"Here it comes!"

The second snowsnake crawled coyly into view. It did a

double take, cocking its head from side to side as it scanned the scene and saw the loremaster and its fellow reptile of the opposite sex. What?

The first snowsnake shrugged, if it could be said that a creature without shoulders could shrug.

"Lodi's love bites! It's the mating season!" Dword erupted. Cursing in a long, picaresque Norlandic oath involving improbable copulations between species of markedly dissimilar physiologies and mitosis, he yanked on Trebor's horse, pulling it behind him, and rode by the snowsnake on the right.

As the red-beard passed by the immense white rope, he stared curiously at Trebor. Suddenly he divined the loremaster's behavior. Panic. "Not on the head! Under the chin!"

Flinching, the loremaster stared hysterically at the laughing snake eyes. "The book said the head!"

"No! Under the chin!"

"But there *isn't* any chin!"

"Close enough!"

"But it's not a true chin; that must be wrong! It—"

"Can I have your rock collection?"

"I want the geodes!" Yor echoed.

Blink.

"But it *has* to be the top of the head!"

Playfully the snowsnake licked the loremaster with a flick of its rough tongue. Rows of parallel teeth glistened in the sunlight, wet with digestive juices.

"*Eeeeeuuuurrrp!*"

Trebor's roar was so lusty, so emphatic, that it startled the snake, the three other men, the other snowsnake, a herd of nearby duukies, a flock of norgeese, and later, when it swept downhill, the entire village of Freissinggal, including their pets.

Everything froze for two heartbeats. . . .

Desperate, the tall, broad-shouldered Bret threw his hands high, welding them into a fist-club, which he crashed down on the lunging triangular head—*whomp!* The snake's jaws snapped shut with a crunch a foot in front of the man-mountain's nose; it blinked, bedazzled in pain.

Trebor jumped back and retrieved his broadsword. The Overtoad's blade hummed affectionately, like a hound eager for the hunt, tail a-wagging.

*Ssss!* the snake warned dizzily, its head wavering from the mind-numbing blast of the Bret titan's fists. The snake pulled itself up to striking height, a full torso taller than the men on horseback, and glared with disappointment.

*Zzzzz!* cried the second snake. *Hzzzz!*

It was a sound that stretched sinew taut, that curdled the ears, that whitened flesh. Even the first snowsnake was taken aback by the vindictive war shriek that now echoed through Odskag Tor like an angry army of reptiles on the slither.

"Woden's short hairs!" Dword gasped. "I hope I live long enough never to hear that again!"

"Run for it, Trebor!" Yor shouted.

Dword rolled the two horses around, straining to control the terrified equines, positioning Trebor's behind the snake.

"Hurry!" the red-beard implored.

The first snake thrust forward, jaws spread. The loremaster whacked the tender nose slits with his broadsword and the snake recoiled in anguish. I've got to get to my horse! He circled left, drubbing the reptile with the flat of his weapon to keep the blade from lodging in the snake's tough skin, trying to hold the deadly triangular head at bay.

Lunge: rap.

Lunge: parry and *riposte*.

Duck: thrash: sidestep.

"Have at you, you oversized dungworm!" Yor hurled, spurring his reluctant steed onward. "Your mother was a ball of cheap, gaudy glitter yarn, and your father was a pleasure whip that serviced pensioned nannies!"

That ought to get its attention! The black-clad cavalryman jabbed swiftly with his rapier.

Pinprick.

Yipes! Yor realized desperately. I'll have to do better than that! Maybe . . . ah, the soft underfur!

Jab!

*Hzzzzz!*

Success!

Ignoring Trebor, the snowsnake turned around, seeking the source of the sting. Its tongue darted once in rage at Yor; its tail thrust out of the coil, with a swift counterpoint banging Yor's horse back against the side of the pass.

*Whap!*

"By the blessed bard!" Yor cursed, gripping the reins tightly to keep from being knocked from the saddle. Shortly that was the least of his worries; the saurian pressed both horse and rider to the tor wall, and he couldn't have gotten off his horse if he tried. The crush of the furred coils and the scaled leather below jammed his left leg against hard, cold rock and cut the circulation off in his right.

I'm going to be smeared on the slate like chalk! Yor struck furiously with his sword, poking again and again at the huge snake's underside until he opened a small scratch. Dragon's breath, this is never going to work! I'll need to hit the head! And I'm only going to have one chance!

"Did I mention your sister is a toothless, liverish, baggy-bosomed slut bucket?" he taunted defiantly. "A varicose-veined, gamy, bowlegged hose monster!"

Bowlegged?

White rage.

Steel fury.

Trebor smote the snake's back with an awesome blow of his fabled blade. The sword bit through the hidden scales, inflicting intense pain.

*Hzzzz!*

Trebor needed a mighty jerk of both his strong arms to free the blade from the thick skin below the white fur. Huffing, he thought, In about a week I'll be able to hack halfway through it! It looked so easy in *The Illustrated Adventures of Sir Robert the Howard*! I guess his snakes didn't have skin and bones!

The second snake shot forward, and Trebor abandoned his position. Running, he hurled himself up on his horse. Soon he had his hands full keeping the second snowsnake at bay. "Yor! Get out of there!" he called out.

The coils pushed against Yor's chest and pinned him to the tor. "Forget about me! Get away from here! I—"

*Ooof!*

Dword maneuvered forward and launched stroke after stroke, but the first snowsnake hardly noticed them. It loomed up over Yor, eyeing his lightning rapier in keen determination to find a way by it.

"We're not having any effect!" Trebor cried.

Sir Dudley reared his steed, his lorica rattling impressively, a storybook picture. The lean, greying warrior whooped, lowered his deadly spear, the only weapon they had that was capable of deeply penetrating the thick snakeskin, and aimed it for the creature's skull.

"For Leyla! For King Derek! And the Dominoes!" he howled, thus naming in the traditional sequence the lady to whom the charge was dedicated, his monarch, and the nickname of his regiment.

"*Hiaaaaah!*"

*Hzzzz!*

Sensing the vibration of the charging horse and hearing the hiss of alarm from the newly arrived snake, the first snake turned away from Yor and saw Sir Dudley. All traces of its former good humor vanished; the sight of the knight on horseback stirred instinctive animosities in the serpent.

Ancient foes.

Jaws wide, braced, the snowsnake waited. It could deal with the others later.

One on one.

Steed and jouster approached the quintain. Sir Dudley kept the lance firm and steady, despite the unevenness of the terrain, pointed straight for the target most likely to result in an outright kill. He growled and stared eye to eye at the serpent, unflinching; the sun caressed his visor blindingly.

A horseshoe soliloquy.

But in the face of those rows of sharp ivory, his steed lost its mettle and veered to the left. Sir Dudley tried to compensate; he leaned boldly, dangerously from his saddle, giving full extension to his arm, but all he could manage was to slap the lance sideways across the serpent's face.

*Clash!*

Striking, the snowsnake misjudged the distance, also thrown off by the horse's change of heart. Instead of plucking the metal man off the equine, all it got was a mouthful of lance.

*Chomp!*

The segmented spike snapped like an oversized stalk of celery. Haughtily the snowsnake munched down the lance, then stopped to wonder if that was such a good idea. . . .

Follow-through.

Sir Dudley's steed was headed down the tor; Yor's mount bucked free in the melee and escaped the fluffy white trap; Trebor and Dword swung last blows and ran.

One length.

Three lengths.

Many lengths.

Huzzah!

Just seconds after the duel, they were all well away from the skirmish. Relieved, elated to still be alive, they rode side by side by side by side through the tor.

"Well done, Sir Dudley!" Yor called out. "And just in the nick of time, too! I thought I was going to be pureed snake chow!"

"I wish I had another lance," Sir Dudley replied wistfully. "And my old charger, Manfred. He had more courage than any creature I've ever known."

They understood.

"Look back!" Dword said. "There's a sight you're not likely to ever see again! Or want to!"

Behind them, a loud caterwauling arose, echoing from the tor walls. The second snowsnake crawled to the first, fluttered eyelashes in admiration, and pounced like a rescued heroine eager to reward her champion. The hisses segued into a rhapsodic fugue as the two saurians entwined in a ribald caduceus.

"Now there's an interesting position!" Dword commented gleefully. "Is that one in your book, Trebor?"

Trebor grunted. His face was sore where the snake's astringent tongue had lashed him; worse, his pride was bruised from the failure of his attempted soporific. Irresistibly he fumbled through his beige surcoat until he produced a tome.

Flip-flip-flip-flip.

"Ha! Just as I remembered!" Trebor resounded, thumbing a page. "It says right here, 'Scratch a snowsnake on the head/And it will soon be put to bed!' Forsooth! Even as I said!"

"What book is that?" Dword baited.

"Tucker's *Monsters of Norlandia*."

"Is that the posthumously revised edition?"

"The what?"

Trebor glanced quickly at the faceplate.

Then he looked at the Norlander's beatific expression.

Suckered.

Wordless, the loremaster tossed the tome far into the wooded wilderness. He cast an aspersive glare at the barbarian, as if Dword were somehow behind the unconventional nature of Norlandia's denizens.

But it was not enough to keep his companions off balance.

" 'Nice kitty'?" Yor teased.

Red-faced, Trebor rejoined, "It worked, didn't it?"

"Oh, absolutely! Confused the heck out of him!"

"Her!"

They both looked.

Suckered.

Even.

But not for long.

" 'Some of my best friends are snakes'?"

Sigh. I knew they wouldn't let that one get by!

\* \* \* \* \*

"What's that?" The royal youth gaped. "Whoa!"

The sight of Vangberg made his heart stop. Hyperventilating, Prince Rodney, alone and far ahead, yanked his horse to a halt; he flinched and dared again to look ahead. The end of the tor opened up like an inverted funnel, exposing the vast unknown: the Frozen Wastes, a pockmarked plateau, and off to the left an enormous, ugly carbuncle belching grey-yellow smoke.

Vangberg!

Snakes behind me! Volcanoes ahead of me!

He shivered, unable to go forward or backward, a dynamic equilibrium of terrors. The vision of the horrid serpents made his bones quake; their odor lingered up and down the tor and made his guts churn.

Coward! Yor's voice spoke in his head. You ran!

The prince's head fell, dejected. But it was so big!

That's not all of it and you know it! the inner Yor tormented him. Of course you were afraid! We were all afraid! Anybody would have been afraid! But Colin wouldn't have run no matter how scared he was! Nor Sean! Nor Cedric!

But it was so big!

A dozen times the scene replayed in his mind. Each time the huge saurian maw loomed over him, ready to devour him. Each time, the teenager trembled with repulsion.

You must come back! the Yor conscience demanded. We could be dying back there!

Rodney wavered.

There's still time! Redeem yourself! Save us!

I could go back, couldn't I?

He pulled the sword from its scabbard and turned the horse around.

Too late.

They were riding toward him, full of the camaraderie of warriors who had defied death together and survived, laughing, jesting back and forth, exchanging quips and teases, reveling in their continued existence.

The royal youth's heart sank. He pushed the sword back in its scabbard and hung his head to avoid their glances. Their man-to-man joshing brought sobbing humiliation to his eyes. He felt as if they were staring at him, looking right through him. They're laughing at me! And why shouldn't they? I'm pathetic! I wish I'd never been born!

They said nothing to him as they approached; the gazes the prince felt boring through him were actually cast way beyond him, beyond the tor.

"Dragon's breath . . ."

The incredible view of the Frozen Wastes and Vangberg slapped their senses and left them stunned. Sinkholes and geysers dotted the landscape from the northern foot of Odskag as far as the eye could see, thinning to the north and vanishing into the clouds covering the top of the world. Thousands of rocks, leftover stone of all sizes, colors, and shapes, covered the Wastes, the rocky remains of the many glacial traverses. Springs of heated waters burbled like scores of eternal steam flames.

Yor whistled. "What a sight! We'll be inching our way through that maze for days!"

"The rock is covered with lichens," the loremaster noted. "Tricky stuff to ride over. It's going to be slow going. . . ."

"Be grateful it's summer," Dword said. "In the winter, there're thundersnows and ice hails! The north wind is so cold it can suck the life right out of you in a single gust!"

"This is summer?" Yor smiled, huffing a deliberate cotton cloud.

"Oh, for a couple more weeks at least!" Dword persisted. "It can't be officially considered fall until the first jorlfrost, the kind that makes jorlsap thicken to pudding!"

"Wonderful!" Yor smirked. "I can hardly wait."

"Vangberg," Sir Dudley said solemnly, pointing. His arm seemed to wither in the face of that blackhead, falling back to his side, cowed. "So that's where he's headed."

They stared uneasily.

"Kind of makes you want to turn around and go back, doesn't it?" Yor said. "But Bosamp must be down there somewhere."

While the trio scanned the way from Odskag to Vangberg, searching for the wizard, Sir Dudley glanced at the prince. The youth was hunched over, morose. The elder knight saw him look quickly at the trio, a look that disappeared when the royal heir caught his guardian's eyes on him.

Poor lad. Sir Dudley edged his horse alongside the prince's, shielding the prince from the others. The knight set his reins, and his eyes shone with sympathy. "Don't be too hard on yourself," he spoke softly. "Those men are the best there is. Don't compare yourself to them. There aren't many like them on all of Leiblein."

The prince hid. "Don't patronize me," he said without looking. "I've got a dozen servants that can do it better than you can anyway. Besides, you're just like they are."

"Not quite. I ran once myself."

Rodney looked up for an explanation.

The Shield of the Prince became distant, his greying visage faraway. "It was at Rime Riche. I was about twenty at the time, I think. The dragoness Rakshawa was ravaging the Western Marches. The villagers mustered and set off into the backland to seek her cave. . . .

"We found it."

He breathed hard, eyes glazing over. "She foresaw our coming.

Exploding out of her lair, her red wings flapping fire, she flew down and attacked us on the hillside. I was too scared to run. My legs folded right out from under me. I passed out. That may have been the only thing that saved my life."

The prince looked at him in disbelief.

"A score of men died that day. Good men. Brave men. Men not afraid to face dragons. But Rakshawa still lives, somewhere in the Darklings now." He paused. "I was older than you are now and I had already fought in two battles."

"Fought in two battles . . ." the prince repeated, demurring sadly. "But dragons are even more awful than snowsnakes! I'll never be like you."

"Not everyone needs to wield steel and go around killing things," Sir Dudley said. "The world must have cobblers, potters, farmers, stableboys and laundry maids, poets and bookmakers. It even needs princes."

"I'm not any of those things! I'm not anything!"

Sir Dudley laid a gentle hand on his charge's shoulder. "You'll find your own way. There's still time. And remember, we all ran at Skandsala."

"That was my fault, too!" The royal teenager drooped in self-loathing. "We would have had him if I hadn't sneezed. I ruined everything!"

"It wasn't your fault; you didn't know about the weeds."

"You're just saying that to try to make me feel better."

"Courage," the Bretilyan knight said, "isn't the lack of fear; it's the ability to go on with what you have to do in spite of it. For now, it's enough for you to try each time to do a little better than the last. That's all any of us, even your father, expects of you."

The prince motioned at Yor. "You should hear what my father says about him. Or my sister. He's so lucky. He's handsome and he's quick. Nothing gets to him."

Sir Dudley held his tongue for a second. "Things get to him," he said remotely. "But remember, your father charged them to do two things: stop Bosamp and show you the ways of the world. There is no longer any question about which has to come first."

"I was going to go back."

"I know. I saw the sword. We all did. . . ."

Moving to a vantage point on the mountainside, Yor gazed over the vast horizon. Clouds blurred the top of the world, but for just an instant, he thought he saw a golden flash, a gleam of auric light that penetrated through the shroud.

His heart pounded.

Where is Bosamp?

His eyes fell downward, searching the land between the tor and the volcano. Below him, the tall conifers that dauntlessly defied the blasts of winter on Odskag's southern flank weren't quite so stalwart on its northern exposure. Shorter, thicker, spaced farther apart, like bathers at a frigid pond, they refused to set foot on the tumultuous tundra below.

The Wastes.

Glacial rubble matted the north country like the bleached bones of a thousand skeletons; thermal pools dotted the plateau with their ghostly effluence. Lava beds looked like ribbons on the land below: red, purple, black.

Chancres and blotches.

Vangberg . . . he can't be there yet!

The smoking cone of the volcano stood alone, hulking, a massive ecru-ebony bully that had shoved its way into the bouldered plateau and now dared anyone to knock the chip off its shoulder. Gods, what an evil eyesore! Yor shivered. And to think we may have to go down into the very bowels of that hellhole.

Where is Bosamp?

"Dword," he called impatiently to the sharp-eyed Norlander. "Can you see him?"

Leaving the prince behind, the red-beard steered his horse forward, squinting, his eyes moved rapidly back and forth over the Wastes.

An orange mote, a wisp of smoke.

"There! About a league onto the Wastes, on a beeline between the trail's end and Vangberg. He's stopped and built a fire. The smoke is mixing with the streamer off one of the hot springs. It's hard to see, but he's to the left of it."

"Cooking?" Trebor speculated. "Conjuring? Camping? It is getting on in the afternoon, I suppose. . . ."

"He probably still thinks we're back at Skandsala!" Yor snorted, unable to glimpse the wizard. He looked suspiciously at the barbarian and tried again. Anxious, he held his breath to steady himself. *I just can't see him! Knowing Dword could see him only made it worse. I want to see him! I will see him!*

Deep in the Bret's foundations, something alien rolled over and yawned as it awoke, summoned. Tugging at the end of its chains, it dispatched a surge of power through his frame, a tingling jolt, strong, febrile.

The fabric of his soul galvanized.

Disorientia.

The world blanked out momentarily.

Surreal.

Lightheaded, Yor fought the urge to faint as the world reappeared, badly out of proportion. It was as if someone had stuck a sage's looking glass too close to his face; everything was warped and expanded, ill focused, both too large and too small. His mind throbbed with the struggle to assimilate the new perspective, reeling off balance.

*What's happening?*

*Go!* something inside said.

Shadowy, Yor walked on the wind toward the orange fleck. The wizard's campsite swelled, distended, but as he came near it, it became distinct, sharp, seen and more than just seen.

*Bosamp!*

Brazier. Scorched hair.

Yor halted ten strides from the wizard, separated by a haze of acrid blue smoke. His eyes watered; his nostrils stung; his skin felt pricked by dozens of hot needles that drew the numinous inner current to the surface of his body.

Bosamp!

The wizard looked up from his trance with suppressed astonishment, as if he hadn't expected what was happening, but now that it had, it was instantly absorbed. His dilated yellow eyes keened on the apparition before him, and he stopped roasting the ratroaches he had spell-lured, swallowing the last of one with ravenous gulps.

Yor!

Yes, madman! Look at what a miserable creature you have become! Your robe is ripped and soiled! Your skin is too big for you! The dust is sucking the life out of you, sorcerer, leeching the marrow from your bones!

It hardly matters, does it? I am the World Shaker! World Breaker! And the dust will keep me ahead of you all the way to the end of the world!

Villain! I saw what you did to your horse! For this cruelty alone, I would boil you alive!

You'll have to catch me first! And you've shown no skill at it yet! I've beaten you at every turn! Your sand is nearly gone!

We're breathing down your neck, madman! Your powers are dwindling, consumed by the dust!

Words, groundling, mere words! Tomorrow I shall have the Mallet, and then I won't need my magic to beat you!

Tomorrow you shall be in irons, villain!

You'll never catch me, witch lover!

Yor gagged. The words resounded in his mind like a blow to the groin, leaving him off balance, paralyzed, out of breath. Something shattered; the vision faltered. The wizard's face cracked like glass into shards that fell from his head; miniature Bosamps were everywhere, scores of them, hundreds of them, laughing and shouting the words again and again.

Witch lover!

Blue tendrils stretched out from the wizard's brazier and wrapped around Yor's neck, choking him physically and spiritually. Yor fell . . . down . . . down . . . down . . .

Amateur! Bosamp sneered.

*Aaaiii* . . .

Nowhen, nohow, nowhy.

"Yor!" squeaked a mouse. "Yor!"

A waterfall of black inkblots splashed on Yor as he whirled around and around like a bob on a line. He tucked his arms into his sides so he would spin faster, then held his breath. He began to pulsate, first iota small, then mountain huge, strobing.

Where am I now that I need me?

"Yor!" trilled the mouse. "Break the trance!"

He opened his mouth to breathe. The air was sucked out of his lungs and his chest collapsed, but this was nothing compared to the new pain. A many-headed hydra gnawed on his shoulder, its spearlike teeth gorging on his flesh. Desperate, maddened, he slapped at it.

Reality.

In a braking thud, unreality stopped. Vacuous, Yor stared into the loremaster's face. Trebor's left hand was dug into Yor's shoulder, the metal-plated digits burrowing with the furor of a death grip. Yor's nose recoiled in horror; he batted the crushed spellbane away as if it were poisoned; his stomach flipped and made ready to eject.

Daylight.

He breathed again, sorting out the sensations rattling around inside him. "Bosamp almost had me. . . ."

Hollow.

The loremaster relaxed his grip and peered thoughtfully at his friend, a dispassionate gaze that saw through the words, watching Yor's responses carefully. "Bosamp's completely insane! The dust has warped his mind beyond anyone's ability to untangle it! It's sheer folly to link minds with him!"

Yor nodded, struggled, off-balance. A tide was running out from under him, and he was being pulled after it. "We must go," he said with great effort. "Bosamp knows how close we are now, but he's weak . . . very weak . . . and must rest and eat."

Revulsion.

"What?" Trebor said with alarm, watching Yor's face stretch pale.

"Don't ask."

Trebor pursed his lips and did not ask.

* * * * *

The five rode.

The sun waned as they zigzagged down Odskag. All at once, the enervation of two hard days dropped over them like a net, and the conversation faded. With each yard closer to the ugly vision of Vangberg, they became more introverted, more somber. Finally, in the gloaming border between the mountain's last whiskers and the sere Waste's emissaries, they halted.

The feeling of unseen eyes touched all of them when the sun vanished, as if they were being examined by the unseen magician and by the glowering volcano rising above them. An oppressive sense of exposure to evil pervaded the party.

For the first time, they set up night watches.

* * * * *

Predawn.

Uneasy, Yor leaned against a boulder, alert but leaden, taking his turn at guard. The night sky shone clearly, but it was no distraction. One phrase returned again and again to his mind: *witch lover!* It was a term of scorn, a thing you called another boy who made the mistake of showing interest in girls before the proper time, before girls blossomed from tagalongs and second-rate boys into alluring, mysterious creatures. If the other boys found out you liked one particular girl, then you had to prove you were still one of the gang; you had to do something mean to her.

He looked outward, leaving the memory incomplete. Grey phantoms strolled in the trees or skulked in the stone shoal at the edge of the Wastes, echoing shadows. He picked up a pebble and weighed it in his palm. With a raging catharsis, he hurled it into the moonlight, watching it skip and disappear.

Is all this just turning handstands, hoping she'll notice?

A footfall came up from behind him; he knew it was Dword just from the sound of the boots, so he didn't turn to face him.

"Couldn't sleep. Tough day today. More trouble tomorrow."

It sounded like a question and an answer at the same time. "It's almost dawn anyhow," Yor said. "Can't be more than an hour away."

Dword looked out toward the distant cinder cone. Not even the moonlight could illuminate it; Vangberg seemed to absorb the light right out of the sky.

This is his legend, Yor realized. It must be soul-pummeling to come face-to-face with your gods.

"What happened this afternoon?" Dword asked.

Yor stiffened slightly, not knowing how much to say, not knowing how much he understood himself. "I don't know. Bosamp's magic, I guess. He must have been searching for us. We linked minds somehow. But he's getting weaker. The dust is sapping him dry."

"He's still dangerous."

"So are we."

A bottle appeared on the tree stump.

"Krryi. It's meant for midnight peregrinations. It's later than that, but . . ."

"Let's walk around the camp."

"If you insist."

# CHAPTER ELEVEN

The Wastes: a lithic labyrinth of capillary canyons and tangled riprap; a moraine morass pockmarked with iridescent magma-stoked pools and caustic fountains. As the sun arched across the clear sky, its changing angles evoked new hues from the rock strata, frescoes of mystical inlay, redisguising shapes and shadows of the maze until even a rock mother couldn't be certain which were her sons.

Minstrels avowed that the Skolgods made the Wastes just to keep men humble, that only the wisest sage or the lowest fool could find a path through them, that every step was completely different and yet exactly the same, that a man could pass through the myriad rock-bracketed ravines over and over, again and again, and never know it. Virik Glidetongue, the greatest of the sagasmiths, vowed in "Song of the Snow Wives" that every rainbow that ever shone down on the Wastes left its spectra gamboling from stone to stone, reflected back and forth forever.

Bosamp knew none of the Norlandic lore as he looked over his shoulder. Five armored specks reflected daylight at him; he could almost make out which was which now, with the dark-clad angel in the lead. The gaunt young wizard *grr*ed, feeling trapped, wanting to strike out at the pursuers.

"Go away!" he mumbled. "Leave me alone!"

Gritch!

The itch!

Beset, he clawed the robe maniacally, raking at the inflamed flesh, up and down. His left side, armpit to thigh, sternum to backbone, was proselytized now, a conversion that was gaining momentum. The new skin was lizard-tough, scaly, green, but the robe chaffed it, galled it; the skin wanted to be naked, exposed freely to the world.

The gaunt young wizard trembled with dread. Last night, in the dementia of pain, he had taken a firebrand and tried to exorcise the spreading chancre. The results of the torching boded ill. The new flesh thrived on the heat, and the itching increased rather than waned!

Not even flame could cauterize it! He shuddered. *The patch has covered my groin and made it stiff! The pain is unbelievable! It's worse than being a Korian bird-eunuch waist-deep in feathered pudenda!*

Crazed, the black-haired sorcerer drew his dirk and scraped the blade over his thigh, poking it through the hole he had made with great difficulty in his Council cloth robe. He scratched violently, well aware that the dirk's edge was unlikely to harm the leathery new skin.

*The dust did this!*

His head snapped back with the shock of the new insight, jostling his unkempt black mane.

*The dust kills the pain of its own creating, but only for a while! Then the itch returns worse than before, forcing me to take more of the dust! And it causes the hunger, too! It wasn't a falsely cast sigil that did this to me. It's the dust! It's transmogrifying me! The dragoness said the dust would give me energy, help me cast more potent spells, help me to reach the Bell! But she never mentioned the cost!*

Chills grappled Bosamp's flesh, frigid fears; he calmed himself forcibly. *It's of no consequence. It will take a fortnight before I'm completely changed, and there isn't going to be a another fortnight! Once I have the Mallet, I won't need the dust . . . and so far, nothing the dragoness told me has proven to be a lie!*

"World Shaker! World Breaker!" he boasted to his steed. "My legend grows with every obstacle I overcome, with every sling and arrow! History will culminate at my command! The sum of all the endeavors of all the creatures that have ever lived on Leiblein won't measure up in significance to the single deed I shall perform when I ring the Bell! And then the dragoness will fly me to a world of my own to rule, to found a new order in my own image!"

*Groouwl!*

Okay, okay!

Ravenous, he grabbed his sack and slapped bread around some raw zux, now getting a bit gamy, then shoved the fist-sized roll whole into his mouth. He chewed dryly and drifted off into fantasies once more as he stuffed his face with another dose of bread and meat, envisioning his coming glory days.

A world of my own . . . what shall I call it? Bosamp's Revenge?

He tittered with glee. The horse turned to look at him. "Left, damn you, you pathetic cat's-paw!" he chided, realizing that his mount had wandered off the path again. He wiped a scrap of greasy meat from his lips with his loose sleeve. "Not that way! Follow the blue smoke trail through the Wastes! Can't you understand that? Do I have to do everything myself, you worthless mound of flea bait? I cast a spell to find a path through this maze! Pay attention!"

He yanked on the reins and turned the steed back toward the thin blue wisp left by his seeker sigil. The conjured doodlebug glyph mapped a path—one employing the right-hand search rule—until the best route through this new section of the interlocked puzzle maze was found. Then the glyph back-tracked, leaving a smoke trail denoting the shortest route. The sorcerous guide dissipated as Bosamp went by, leaving no trace for his pursuers. The only drawback was that he had to stop and wait for the doodlebug to come back.

Just then, Bosamp felt that someone was watching him. He jerked around and looked back.

They're closer every time I look!

\* \* \* \* \*

Another corner! Yor worried. Pulling away from the group by a few lengths, the black and gold rider trotted his horse forward in doubting suspense and rounded the dogleg alley.

Another dead end!

He glared ferociously; impassive, the stone wall refused to crack. The impulse to throw caution to the winds struck him—anything to break this nerve-grinding pace through the stone collage.

Impossible.

He sagged, slumped. "Stop! This passage is blocked, too!"

Not soon enough, unfortunately. They jammed up behind him.

"Not again!" someone grumbled.

His face mottled with ire, Yor stared at the stone barrier as if it were a living force that had decided to thwart him, an ill-advised action that would soon meet with his fury. He spat monosyllables at it, a gusher that made the stone blush rose but did not move it. When he ran out of scatology, Yor scowled, his boyish charm stretching taut. Mail-gloved hands over his saddle horn, the Bret dandy turned his eyes skyward, accusing, glaring stubbornly.

"The fate of the world is being decided by coin flips," he informed the gods, "right or left, east or west! Has it come down to this? What is the matter with you gods, anyway? Have you no shame? Do you conspire to aid that madman? Have you grown so bored with us already?"

Defiantly the Bret waited for an answer.

The mention of gods made Dword wince. "I'll have a look," the barbarian volunteered. Eschewing caution, he leapt from his saddle at the wall, hands grappling. . . .

Got it!

Hand over hand, the Norlander scaled up the boulders, huffing and fussing, kicking, kicking, kicking until he was topside. The brisk wind buffeted him, flapped his beard, torqued him, and almost succeeded in spinning him off the platform. Against the wind, Dword dug his boots under a slab of stone. Thus stabilized, he scoured the nearby matrix of alleys, looking for a route through the garbled geography, a rock garden badly in need of pruning.

"Well?"

Dword grunted as his eyes searched through the boulders. He realized now that shadows sometimes indicated where the paths were blocked. . . .

"There's a canyon to the right that leads to a larger passage. We'll have to back up to that big rock over there and then go east beyond the first corridor to the third one on the right. Then we'll be in another open area."

"And Bosamp?"

"Hold on a second."

The barbarian pivoted carefully, his heels crushing loose stone, sending a tiny slide of grit downward. In a daring leap, he bounded to a much higher boulder and balanced precariously, one foot on top of the other, wavering in the capricious breeze. From this pinnacle, all the land to Vangberg's base could be seen clearly by the barbarian's keen eyes.

An orange dot toddled along the horizon, bobbing in and out of sight.

"He's a little east of us, but much less than before. It seems as if we're gaining ground," Dword related as he watched the wizard pause and detour west. He considered a moment and then added, "But I think that's just because we're in an easy part."

"Easy part!" interrupted the prince with a moan.

"After the next thermal flats, the Wastes get much worse—narrower, much more convoluted—so that right now we have the illusion of getting closer. But if you ask me, he doesn't seem to be having as much trouble finding a way through this as we are. In fact, I think we're falling behind in time separation."

The red-beard checked the sun's position. "As things stand, he'll be out of the last maze about noon. And he'll have much the better of it when he hits the lava fields around Vangberg, so the distance will widen again."

"At least until we, too, get to the lava beds," Yor noted. "Then we should start to close the gap again, as we've much the better horses. At least there's no question where he's headed!"

Vangberg!

The volcano drew all their eyes. The morning's frost, unseasonably early, was a preview of the coming change of season, but it was trivial compared to the chilly indifference of Vangberg's visage looming over them as they approached it. The pumice titan, its lofty shoulders wrapped in a boa of snow, swelled before them, devouring the sky with each tortuous turn of the screw into the Wastes. Ashly grey sunlight poked through the lava pit's smoky banners, reaching out over them like a ghostly paw, giving a strange illumination to the Wastes, one that distorted the depth perception of the eyes and made even the most common objects seem unnatural, otherworldly.

Vangberg! the prince held his breath, looking at the immense black, white-headed blot. I'm going to be ill. . . .

Hey! You said you were going to try! he reminded himself.

Yeah, well, I only have to try a *little* harder. I don't have to do anything stupid, do I?

Dword scrambled down from his loft. "This way," he said as he remounted.

They turned about and veered off, maintaining a painstaking gait through the Wastes. Constant vigilance was needed, for the loose rock, slick mosses, and steaming rivulets played havoc with the footing. One false step could leave a horse lame, and there would be nothing for it now: a lost horse meant a lost rider.

The direction reversal caused by the blind glen brought Yor to the end of the pack, freeing him from the responsibilities of the lead for the moment. His mind drifted. . . .

We can't let Bosamp get the Mallet! If Dword is right about the pacing and the route, then, just when Bosamp hits the lava beds, there will come a crux, at which we'll be as close as we're going to get before he pulls away from us again.

*I'll have to think of something. . . .*

In fits and bursts, they tacked northward, a zig here and a zag there, doubling back from time to time as their luck faltered. The ground tilted up toward Vangberg, an uneven, shallow grade formed by the steady erosion of the volcano's epochal ejecta. The slope gave them a peep show of the wizard's progress on the rise ahead of them, his course twisting and convulsing just as theirs did.

At every turn, Yor recalculated the rates and distances, trying to predict the intercept point of the slow-motion race. Each time his heart sank a little further into desperation.

*We can't let him get to Vangberg without a fight!*

Finally around the last giant basalt boulder, Bosamp looked straight ahead. Unobstructed by the Wastes' barricades, mighty Vangberg reigned supreme, attended by the expansive lava field, a raised stage a man's height above the rock rabble, a straight ride to the volcano down an alley palisaded with huge slabs of stone.

"At last!" the wizard yelped, whipping his reins flank to flank. "Get up there, Gluepot, or I'll bite your ears off!"

The steed stumbled forward, then sidestepped, followed by a leap up to the shelf of lava that inclined upward to the sinister volcano's base. One jump, two jumps. A lateral seam appeared in the lava crest, and the horse loped up it onto the tilted maroon plane.

*Is that a path? Yes! I think it is!*

Elated, Bosamp glanced back at his pursuers; he was briefly alarmed to see how close they actually were. "Close, but not close enough!" he cheered himself. "I'm going to beat them to Vangberg!"

He howled a glyph of power, not a sigil, but a shout of celebration, one that rolled over the Wastes like the clamor of an incubus feeding on a virgin, one that made rocks crack in response to its vileness, one that unnerved creatures on both ends of the food chain, a sound that carried . . .

Bosamp's eruption grabbed their eyes; the orange-garbed sorcerer was plainly visible on the lava beds ahead, lording his success, a hammy thespian strutting an overacted, prolonged exeunt. The wizard's final laugh goaded Yor, but to the Bret's surprise, a kernel of pity formed in addition to the anger.

You deluded maniac! Look what love has driven you to do!

"Bosamp!" Yor hurled. "Look at me!"

The dark angel's voice sliced through the air, a whirlwind crossing the Wastes, penetrating the distance with uncanny power. Bosamp froze; geas-bound, he stared at the Bret cavalryman.

"Bosamp! Listen to me!" Yor shouted as loudly as he could, projecting his stern voice across the long yards between them. "Return with us to Bretilya and redeem yourself before you do anything truly unforgivable! If you enter Vangberg, you will have crossed the final line of demarcation! Give up this demented quest now, and there will still be hope for your soul!"

The words pounded through the magician; his blood squirmed; his temples beat. As if possessed, his hands stretched out to jangle the reins and turn the horse.

No! a voice in his mind said, taking the guise of the dragoness's distinctive rasp. They will betray you! You'll die a nameless death in this nowhere! They'll bury you out here in an unmarked grave, lost in the corridors of the Wastes! If you quit now, you'll be nothing! Nothing! Seize the Mallet and chime the Bell! It is your destiny!

Bosamp paused. He wasn't certain whether the dragoness was speaking directly into his mind or if his own subconscious was speaking, but he didn't need a dragon to tell him what to do.

"Go back yourself!" the gaunt sorcerer spat loudly at Yor. "If you hurry, you may still spend a day or two in a pub somewhere, drunk and snuggled up to some warm flesh! Hell's Bell awaits me! This is your last chance! I will offer mercy no more!"

Mercy! Yor burned in a cool rage. Why, I'll . . .

Temper!

He reined in the inner beast. Okay. I've got to try to make him make a stand here. Can I bait his ego? God knows, it's big enough!

"You caitiff galligaskins!" the black-clad dandy taunted like a court wag, waving his fist and a lace handkerchief at the distant wizard demeaningly. "You son of a worm-eating paynim! No wonder no self-respecting woman wants to be seen in public with you, you pusillanimous sheet-stainer! Stand and fight like the whimpering wretch you are—one on one, just you and me—if you've got the codpiece for it! Winner take all and the loser be damned!"

The preening challenge made Bosamp waver as it conjured up that evening in the garden when the two ladies at court had humiliated him. He blushed red and glared at Yor. His hands gripped the reins so tightly they cut the circulation off in them, and he went white with hatred. A duel? Yes! Yes! he thought hurriedly. I could finish it here and continue on to the Bell unharried!

"You put those two witches up to it, didn't you?" Bosamp howled, his yellow eyes blazing. "It's all been a conspiracy against me, hasn't it? I'll make you pay for that!"

No! the dragoness's voice countered. That's just what he wants you to do! Get the Mallet first, dolt! With that, you can pop their heads open like birds' eggs! Then you can have your vengeance on them!

But—

The Mallet, you fool!

It made sense.

"Killing you now would be too easy on you!" Bosamp jeered loudly. "I want you to know the full and awesome horror of what I am going to do! You—you are my audience! Yes, my witnesses! I want you to feel the blackest despair of all—to know that you failed, and that your dismal efforts couldn't prevent Leiblein's destruction! With the last heartbeat of your existence, you will watch me soar away to paradise!"

He bellowed and wheeled his horse, then bolted up the lava field.

In one smooth motion, Yor grabbed his flintlock and leveled it at the wizard. *I tried; I really did! Maybe—*

"It's too far!" Trebor protested. "And we're not that desperate! He hasn't got the Mallet yet! He may never get it! We need him in order to get to the bottom of this!"

Hearing and not hearing, Yor cocked his flintlock and concentrated on the pellet's flight, melding his mind with the lead ball, kenning the ball's parabolic arc and the fleeing sorcerer, visualizing the sphere piercing the wizard's back. A syllable not of this world formed on Yor's tongue, ready also to be launched, materializing from the shadows of his soul, eager to serve, knowing that it would be needed to make the shot.

*What are you doing?* his conscience blasted. *You gave Kantar your word. No magic! Do you want to be like Bosamp? Do you want to be like Kathy?*

Sucking in a breath, he remembered one particular day. . . .

*     *     *     *     *

Summer, just after the war.

Rain droned steadily on Lord Lee's hunting lodge's roof. It had dripped into the bed at an embarrassing moment, and they fled, laughing, to the safety of the floor, where they finished their tryst with urgency. Afterward, the rain still beat on the roof and windows, not relentlessly, but persistent, so they chose to be trapped in the lodge, alone—mellow, half dressed, recharging, exploring—on an island of their own while the rest of the world ceased to exist.

"Oh, come on, try it!" Kathy teased playfully. "For me! Please?"

Yor smiled and grabbed for her, but she eluded him. He

wasn't in any hurry to catch her again anyway, so he relaxed and leaned back against the wall, eying her happily.

"Kathy, it's not a question of whether I can do it or not," he said, trying not to sound too stiff, trying not to make it sound as important as it was. "It's just that I don't think I should. I made this promise, one I want to keep."

"But we already decided that repeating the Sortilege wasn't the same as making spells, not really!" the highborn lass said with enthusiasm, tossing her long hair. Rising, she paced around the room, full of nervous energy, full of the exhilaration of discovery, her smooth, lithe legs flaunted before him. She blushed at his gaze, but felt no shame at his thoughts and feigned no demurral.

"It was like reciting the alphabet!" she reminded him. "There wasn't anything wrong with that! You didn't break your promise to anyone, and you said them pretty well! I was impressed! You did more of them than I did my first time!"

"I don't think I should have," he stumbled self-consciously, managing a half-smile. "I didn't feel right about it. . . . I still don't."

"But it's your birthright, Yor! You can't help that! And you did it for me, my lord!" She turned prettily, like a coy peasant girl showing off, and devoured him with loving eyes. Dreamy-eyed, she swooned down beside him and snuggled against his chest, her body heat stirring his blood.

"I felt so close to you when you did that. . . ." She trembled, her sparkling green eyes dwelling on his, her soft hands intertwining with his. "We're so much alike. I never thought I'd find anyone like you! I can teach you! Together, no one can stop us! Just try this little set of spells. Please? They're simple and harmless, really! It's the test the Guild uses to see what element on the wheel is strongest in a potential candidate. They're not real spells! You won't be breaking your promise! I wouldn't ask you to do anything like that!"

She saw his hesitation and decided that it wasn't that

important; she was too happy to argue, so she smoothed it over. "Well, okay . . . not this time. But you can listen to me do it. That can't be wrong, can it?"

Hugging him, she crooned glyphs to him as if they were a lover's madrigal. . . .

*     *     *     *     *

Abruptly Yor jerked back from the past, flushed with the seductive pleasure of the memory, which he banished harshly from his mind. Clamping his jaws tight, he forced the eager glyph off his tongue, back into the shadows of his soul.

*What she did infected my mind, made it easier for the glyphs to get loose. That wasn't the first time—or the last—I broke my promise. But no more. Not if I have any other choices.*

"It's too far," he said hollowly. "And I might have hit the horse." He stowed the pistol. "Let's go!"

Onward.

As Dword had warned, Bosamp drew away from them, racing over the path through the lava field while they still had the tortuous last twists of the maze to wind through. Vangberg, that immense cinder cone, pulled the wizard like a lodestone. His horse, its muscles weary from the treacherous Wastes, wouldn't respond without further urging. Bosamp whipped it until its speed exceeded even his needs, galloping over the slow incline toward the volcano.

"We're losing him!" Yor fretted aloud in frustration as minutes went by and they did not reach the end of the maze.

"No, we're not!" Trebor insisted. "It's not as bad as it looks right now! Speed and distance are only relative; its time that counts! Once we reach the beds, we'll have him!"

*Maybe I should have shot Bosamp,* Yor considered uneasily. *Maybe Kathy was right. Kantar's been dead for over a century. Why should a promise I made to a ghost when I was only a boy still bind me now as an adult? The whole thing could* have been a dream, for all I know! And that story about the dragons' game and the Land of Shadows . . . how could that possibly be true? Maybe I should have paid more attention, learned more from her. . . .

He stopped the train of his thoughts cold. There was no time for recriminations. As fast as they dared, they wended through the Wastes, rushing to intersect the lava field. Every yard through the rock obstacles lengthened agonizingly as they watched Bosamp recede toward the jagged brimstone mound. When they scaled up to Vangberg's hem, their elation was short-lived.

"Look!" the prince bemoaned. "He's reached the volcano!"

"He still has to find the entrance!" Trebor said.

They shot forward with all deliberate haste, urging, swearing at their tired ponies for more speed. . . .

* * * * *

Vangberg! The entrance . . . where is it? Where? It's got to be here! I can't have come all this way to lose now! Where?

Bosamp reared his horse and halted. Ah, yes . . . the spell the dragoness gave me to locate the door! Tones of the Sortilege ripped the air as he regurgitated the spell, booming it outward toward the volcano. Blue smoke roiled from out of nowhere. He rode round to the right, circling among the lava boulders, looking, looking, looking, looking, spewing glyphs as he went. . . .

* * * * *

A wail of rapacious exultation sent shivers through them.

"He's opened the doorway!" Trebor surmised.

Another glyph creased their ears, a short, nasty retort followed by a hideous boom. Startled, the horses became fearful, fractious. They bucked on the igneous sheath, threatening to bolt.

"Quake!" Yor cried.

The ground rumbled. The smoke from the wizardry expanded without thinning, growing into a low-hanging blue cloud that devoured Bosamp and fanned outward. Cathedral Vangberg trembled, unrefined and unfriendly. Shock waves undulated from deep in the firmament, and the land convulsed. High above the sorcerer, the mountainside plunged. A stream of snow and stone showered downward and swallowed the blue cloud; dust, soot, and white rock slid, scattering the smoke.

The five man-horse pairs bobbed like driftwood in a storm. The land bounded up three times, slaps that lifted them off the ground, then rolled to rest.

Deep breaths.

Still alive!

They regrouped and stared at each other, checking everything and finding that, despite the frightening temblor, little damage was done.

"He's gone!" the prince said, pointing to the volcano, watching the last of the sorcerous smoke dissipate. Seeing a mammoth pile of rock where Bosamp had stood, the prince shouted, "Hurray! The landslide got him! That means the quest is over! We can go home now!"

They looked. Bosamp was no more; a pile of rocky rubble and snow a dozen yards high entombed his last known location.

"Not so fast," Trebor sighed. "He wasn't buried in that slide. He caused it to cover up the entrance! He's gone into the bowels of Vangberg, and we must follow!"

Crestfallen, the royal youth started to object, but looking from man to man, he knew the truth of Trebor's words. "Wait a minute!" Rodney brightened excitedly. "We don't have to go into Vangberg! We can wait right here for him to come out!"

"It won't do," the loremaster gainsaid.

"But why not?" the prince shot back. It was a good question; he could tell by the way everyone looked at Trebor that they were wondering the same thing.

"Because, for one thing," Trebor pronounced, "this may not be the only way in and out of Vangberg. Bosamp will surely choose a route out that leads north, toward the Bell, not back here."

"Well, Captain," Sir Dudley extrapolated, "why can't we just go around to the other side and wait for him? After all, we do know where he's headed. And we can gain time on him that way."

Trebor hesitated, then made a judgment. "I don't think we can chance it. Look at Vangberg! It's leagues in diameter! Going around might take much longer than going through it! And if we lose him here, we may not find him again!

"Worse, if we go around, he'll get the Mallet! We can't just let him have it! We don't know what he can do with it!"

A sobering pause. The prince started to remind Trebor that he had specifically stated that there was no way Bosamp could get the Mallet because it was guarded by the dreaded fireflies, but he decided to keep it to himself.

"It's decided."

Yor spurred his horse to the lead, and they raced toward the slide zone with ominous feelings of doom settling down on them. Vangberg seemed to sneer at them, as if the volcano were a malevolent monster waiting to pounce, laughing at their silly efforts.

They rode hard and reached the slide in a few minutes. Dust particles and wizard's smoke hung in the air, offending their nostrils, tainting their tongues with its acrid taste.

"Where, Trebor?" Yor urged. "And how?"

The loremaster skirted the slide debris, looking for clues.

What did Bosamp do? What spell would open a passage? Or did he use some thaumaturgic artifact? No! Wait! The Skolgods couldn't have intended spells to be the way to open the entrance! There was no Sortilege magic before the dragons came! Therefore, the door must open to an older power, in a more obvious way!

Think!

Trebor was aware the others were watching him intently. . . .

Ah! he smiled broadly. Of course!

He smiled at them. "I have it! A touchstone, or more likely a keystone, will open the door! And probably a summoning word! That's the way of eldritch power: like to like, coupled with an invocation! All I need is a piece of lava rock to open the portal! That piece of pumice over there should do nicely."

The loremaster dismounted. Using the hilt of his immense broadsword, he cracked off a chunk of maroon, a fist-sized rock tossed from vociferous Vangberg eons ago. With an eye toward his audience, the Bret titan moved like an actor to his mark, setting up to deliver a famed soliloquy. Facing the sheer slope with steel eyes, he braced.

"Open says me!" he pleaded, then heaved the rock at the volcano, instinctively cowering in anticipation of Skolgods knew what.

Nothing.

"Nothing," Yor noted.

"Maybe you should say the name of the god, Captain," Sir Dudley suggested, coughing, the dust and smoke bothering his lungs. "It might seem more official that way."

They all stared at Trebor.

"Apodictic," the loremaster mumbled, choosing the word that would be least likely to admit his mistake, since he was almost certain that none of them knew what it meant. Humbled, he picked up another interesting rock and faced the snowy rockslide, toe to the mark.

"Zepolinirt!"

It was a mighty heave, and it stoned the mountain with an audible, pungent *plunk!*

Zippo with Zepolinirt.

"Nothing," Yor reiterated. "Maybe we *should* go around."

"Give me a chance! Nobody said it was going to be easy!" Trebor huffed, then frowned at Vangberg like an expectant parent who has just told all his friends that a favored child was about to do something quite remarkable, but the child perversely failed to comply. Chastened, the loremaster thought out loud, watching with one eye, still hoping for some time-delayed phenomenon. "The name of the Skolgod who forged the Hammer should be the key! It's too logical to have failed!"

Dword ahemmed with an air of amused superiority. "That's not the name." No point in jumping in right away, he mused. Trebor wouldn't have listened anyway! The Norlander shook his head from side to side in mirthful admonishment. "I told you before, it's D-Ray, not Zepolinirt. Ritardando Shirr was a third-rate ink dauber whose works are only fit for lining litter boxes of diarrheic Menomian jazalcats. Try D-Ray this time."

Trebor reddened profusely at Dword's pointed censure. "That can't be it," he murmured. That better not be it!

The loremaster bent his colossal frame at the waist, spied some unusual lodestone that seemed particularly nifty and should certainly be added to his rock collection, then yanked his mind back on track and picked up instead a chunk of oddly streaked lava that seemed older than the others, out of place somehow. He hefted it cautiously, as if he were selecting a new javelin. It was oddly light in his hand, and he felt his fingers tingle slightly, even through the gauntlets.

Power.

Hmmm . . .

Returning to his mark, Trebor reared back and pitched the periapt with all of his considerable strength.

"D-Ray!"

None of them would ever quite agree on what happened next, even though they all witnessed it. Just as Trebor released the rock, it slipped off the edge of his fingertips, sailing high and wide in a comical arc, an uncoordinated blunder.

It landed far to the right and way, way up, apparently well off target.

Apparently.

Dword would always maintain that it was divinely guided.

Yor preferred the dumb luck theory. Trebor himself was never quite certain whether his old back injury had flared up and/or his invocation had been heard and/or the rock was an eldritch power stone.

Whatever.

The rock struck Vangberg high up and began to roll downward, accumulating a fall of snow and stone far out of proportion to the physics of the situation, evoking a massive chain reaction.

*Rumble!*

They dashed back a dozen yards and watched, wide-eyed.

The mountainside shook like a dog shaking off water, shedding the pile of loose rock and ice toward the five riders, while a subterranean sheath of petrous muscle undulated upward, throwing lava dust and ancient ashes into the air. . . .

*Faboom!*

The Skolgod's passageway.

"Gadzounds!" The loremaster whistled.

Never a doubt!

Three great obsidian slabs formed the entrance, one over two, mystic megaliths that no tribe of men could ever have hoped to put there had they labored for an eon. A fourth sheet of black glass formed the door, hanging above the other three like a sinister, dateless stepsister, a guardian daunting anything that dared to enter the open portal.

Arid sulfurous gases poured through the opening, gusting from the belly of Vangberg, peppery, melting the snow into puddles, which dripped downward into the curving corridor.

"D-ray's diablerie!" Dword gasped. "The sagas are true!"

Never a doubt!

A pale yellow-green luminescence glowed in the tunnel, a soft aura sufficient to see into the volcanic interior, at least as far as the curving, descending passageway allowed. The sides of the passage were smooth, marbled, as if carved out of lead glass, reflecting the diffuse light in a godly glow.

"How thoughtful of old D-Ray!" Yor teased, edgy with tension, eager to plunge into the Skolgod's corridor but at the same time, eager to get the heck out of Norlandia, a place where myths couldn't be trusted to stay myths! "Now we won't need torches! I swear, the place has all the comforts of home . . . everything but a welcome mat!"

*Rumble!*

"Hurry!" Trebor urged. "It may not stay open long!"

When knotty myths come alive, men must move gingerly. Though gripped with foreboding, they shot through the obsidian aperture—well, okay, Trebor stopped and retrieved the nifty lodestone he had seen earlier, but other than that, they crossed the threshold into Vangberg's demesne without time for regrets.

*Rumble!*

Just as Prince Rodney's horse rattled through the portal, the volcano spasmed into avalanche. Rock and snow showered down behind them, closing up the opening in a grumbling fury.

*Rumble!*

They stared backward as their eyes adjusted to the light.

Peering down the bridge of his nose at Trebor, Yor asked, "I presume you can get it open again?"

"Certainly."

"Never a doubt!" the black-garbed dandy hooted, beating the Bret titan's shoulder vigorously. "Well, that settles that, then! Onward! There's a world to be saved! Let's get that blasted Bosamp and get back to a Bretilyan tavern with cold stout and hot women!"

Yor turned his horse and pranced it around and down the eerie, glowing spiral tunnel. The others followed him, the clopping of their horses' shoes on the satin stone echoing up and down the passageway, announcing their arrival to any who cared to know.

Minutes flowed.

The tunnel descended gradually, narrowing inch by inch,

contracting until they were forced to ride single file, ducking lower and lower. . . .

And tighter.

And tighter still.

"We'll have to dismount," Yor said at last, noting the claustrophobic closeness of the icky damp ceiling to his best tam. "And if it squeezes down much more," he concluded, looking ahead in the tunnel, "we'll have to leave the horses behind. But if it comes to that, Bosamp will surely suffer the same fate. Watch your step. That floor's going to be slick."

They fell into a tight line: Yor, the red-beard, the loremaster, Sir Dudley, and the young prince, each tugging his steed behind him as he walked in the primordial underground, warmed by the forced heat, chilled by the spine-tingling oddness of the volcano's bowels.

Down . . .

     Down . . .

          Down . . .

               Down . . .

                    Down . . .

Time lost its distinctness in the strange illumination, in the wan tinkling trickle of water running down to the gods knew where. With no way to measure either the minutes or the yards as they trekked downward, they submerged in the dreamland, moving like shadowy characters in a yarn spun at midnight. They fell quiet; each dwelt with some inner voice, walking cautiously, methodically in the endless corridor.

Finally the passage leveled off.

Yor thought he heard a voice ahead of them. Bosamp? How far off the sorcerer might have been was impossi- ble to judge; the tunnel muffled, garbled every sound, carrying along only the highest and basest tones, all at the same low level, like graveyard sounds, too loud to be ignored, too hushed to be deciphered.

He can't be very far ahead of us.

Dim, dank, damp.

Yor shivered uneasily. *Why do I feel as if I've been here before?* Something crawled in his subconscious, creeping at his mind's periphery. He strove to catch it, but it eluded him.

Time flowed seamlessly as they continued in a spiral path arcing inward toward Vangberg's fiery gut. The temperature rose by degrees, making the corridor a test to be passed on the way to the Skolgod's esoteric sanctum, a test of sincerity, a test of resolve, threatening but not outrightly hostile, sufficient to separate the fainthearted and the curious from the purposeful.

*Troubled contemplations.*

Yor looked about, burdened with the unplaced feeling of familiarity. *There's something about all this that reminds me of somewhere else . . . but where?*

A scar twitched on his left shoulder.

Curious, he looked back at his companions. Dword's face was rent with his own agonizing daydreams. The barbarian unsnapped the clasps of his armored jacket, seeking relief from the rising heat. The noise of his action seemed amplified louder than their footsteps. Behind Dword, the swish of Trebor's great blade as it came off the titan's back attracted Yor's eyes. Looking at the loremaster, he sensed that Trebor, too, wrestled with some deep-rooted dilemma and clutched the blade like a lucky charm.

*We're being probed, challenged. . . .*

Yor prompted his colt through a narrow orifice in the passage. He looked back again and saw Trebor's grim face, the heavy sword in the crook of one elbow, a verdigris aura from the phosphorescence dancing iridescent on the runed metal.

*Cradled. Like a crossbow.*

Yor's shoulder twitched again, and he placed the harlequin tugging at his memory: Danby!

His heart froze. *We shouldn't have been on Lord Lee's estate,* he recalled, *but Danby said he knew a spot where we*

were sure to find a stag or two. And I agreed quickly enough!
I wanted to scout the place for an attempt to recover the talisman. I remember now. . . .

\* \* \* \* \*

Danby, a thin, lanky nineteen-year-old, stood with his
hunting crossbow in the woods north of Castle Fairfax. Yor
had known Danby since the first days of school, though since
Yor went away to the war and Danby took over his uncle's
farm, they hadn't seen much of each other the last few years.
They'd been drinking a lot of wine from their skins in the too
hot fall afternoon, and Danby's nose was a bit red, from both
the sun and the wine. It was nearing midafternoon, and
they'd had no luck. No deer anywhere.

"Hey! Over here! What's this?" Danby said suddenly.

Yor looked down and saw a half-buried stone tablet, covered
with leaves and vines. Working excitedly, they soon exposed a
rusted handle. It took the two of them to lift the stone.

A black hole yawned below.

"What is it?" Danby wondered aloud. "It looks like some
kind of a tunnel, but what's it doing way out here?"

"The escape route from the castle!" Yor realized with a
mental click. "It's probably been here for a hundred years! I'll
bet they've forgotten all about it!"

Fever hit his blood. The talisman!

"Let's try it," Yor said.

"I don't know . . ." Danby said hesitantly. "Maybe we
should go back. It's getting late. . . ."

"Leave if you want," Yor said quickly. "I'm going in."

They hacked at the tree roots to clear the entrance, stared
down ratroaches that watched them, crawled down the passage for a few yards, and found a ladder in a shaft that led to a
lower level, where the tunnel widened. Here they could stand
up and walk.

Dim, dank, damp.

The air was still and stale. They found an old musty torch and managed to light it somehow, then set off down the tunnel, Yor bubbling with adventure. The shaft stretched out for a long way, perhaps a furlong, then widened further into a natural cavern. The air was fresher here, but the passage was very wet.

They went on. The turns were marked with candles, which they lit as they went. The tunnel had obviously been used at some time in the past, and it was equally obvious that it had been quite a long time ago.

Tension rose in Yor as each step brought him closer to his goal. The castle must be near, he thought . . . very near.

Suddenly a second tunnel veered off at a right angle to the passage. "This way," Yor decided.

"Maybe we should go back," Danby said, sounding worried. He was pale, shivering in the cold underworld. "This isn't a good idea. . . ."

"Courage, plowboy!" Yor jested lightly. "After all, you have a battle-hardened veteran to protect you! The war was worse than this! Just stay behind me, clodhopper. You can have the smaller monsters!"

So they went on. Ten yards, twenty yards . . . narrow and bricked, the passage finally ended at an oaken door set in a shambled brick inlay.

Yor inspected the door carefully; he spied and removed a small dagger trap, one he wasn't even sure would have worked after all the years. Satisfied, expectant, he drew a deep breath and clutched the handle to the door. With a stiff jerk, he freed it from the time-warped jambs. . . .

*Creak.*

There was a flash of scarlet light, and Firefang's eye glowed so brightly it blinded him. She was standing there, waiting, torch in one hand, her full lips pursed, dressed in a haunting black gown, in her other hand a deadly chryst, a poisoned crystalline dagger.

The talisman!

Their eyes locked. In a dazzling flash of the red gem, he saw it all.

Betrayed.

"Kill him, Danby!"

Whirl, shove, run—*zing!*

Danby's expression was a bucket of cold water thrown in Yor's face. The crossbow bolt buried into Yor's shoulder as he ran, but it hurt less than her laughter, less than seeing his friend rush to her side like a puppy to its master, reloading the bow as he went.

"So false, my lady fair!" Yor flared, his blue eyes darting in wildfire pain as he pulled the bolt free and hurled it at his friend-no-more. "Is there no end to your treachery?"

"You're too dangerous!" she lashed back, her long dark hair draped down past her swelling cleavage, the chryst raised high. "I knew sooner or later you'd try to get the talisman back! I haven't had a good night's sleep since—" She bit the thought off. "But I'll sleep well tonight, my love! Though not as well as you will!"

He had no more words.

Dive—*zing!*

The second bolt grazed Yor's flesh as he dropped to the dungeon floor. Off balance, he hurled his hunting axe, scattering both of them. She dodged as it went by, but it rebounded off the wall and back at her, tearing into her dress, slicing across her calf, leaving a thin red wound. She screamed, and the spell forming on her lips was disrupted. Her eyes filled with hurt disbelief, then dread as she watched the aborted glyph come to life, a deformed child of magic.

Not that easily, witch! Not that easily!

Danby stumbled over a chair in his haste to charge, but Yor's dagger caught the farm boy in the side; Danby fell, reaching out for her, dragging her down as he went.

Blood, scramble.

The *crack* of sorcery.

Quicksilver.

The tunnel. The loose brick yielded, collapsed at Yor's insistence: rotted mortar, rotted masonry.

Rotted memories.

\* \* \* \* \*

Yor's teeth gnashed as the memory faded. He struck Vangberg as he walked just to feel the pain, to verify that he was real. Poor Danby, he thought. There are times, my friend, when I wish you'd been a better archer. . . .

"There's a red glow in the passage up ahead," Trebor said suddenly, forcing the morose mood from Yor. "Looks like there must be a cavern of some sort."

They moved forward carefully, clinging to the sides of the corridor, their pulses accelerating with each step. As the passage flared wider and wider, heat and fumes accosted them; bravely they persisted, moving into an antechamber.

Brimstone.

Awesome, terrifying bas-relief figures stared down at them from the top of an arched portal that undeniably led to the volcano's inner sanctum. In the flickering light of the grotto, the figures were the final nail in the coffin of doubt as to the veracity of the legends.

"Woden's wonders!" Dword shuddered. "They're ghastly!"

Indeed they were: grotesque shapes carved life-size in the stone, forms that could only be the likenesses of the Skolgods themselves. There was Om, the bejeweled toad with the massive planet-sundering hind legs; deadly D-Ray of the burning eyes; ferocious Aga of the starfire breath; nine-tusked Kluute, with his many pairs of hoofed legs; treelike Yggadrasil, with his doomball swung on its globe-spanning chain; Hrssula of the four delights, her blonde mane draped around her curvaceous form, the heads of her lovers hanging from a chain around her waist; slavering Fenrisa Wolfbitch, with her fanged jaws and double row of teats; paired Allinir and Magnus, fair and terrible, hand in hand, a peace branch in Magnus's free hand and a whirling starslayer in Allinir's; Tyrdrep, with his paintbrush of comets and his skirt of moons; voracious Rugayrokstaar of the dreadlocks; Hrathgar of the lightning limbs. . . .

The urge to flee back through the corridors was palpable. Each of the five felt as if his head had been pulled off like a cork and his soul dumped out of his body like thick honey from a bottle so that it could be examined by the inhuman sculptings, and then found to be unworthy.

"Must be some kind of primeval fear spell," Dword gulped as he studied the Skolgods. "Meant to keep the riffraff out. They won't harm us."

At least, I don't think they will, the Norlander silently qualified. I wonder if our new gods—Woden, Frieda, and brood—hold any sway here?

"Come on, then!" Yor encouraged. "Make way, you moldy old gods! You've caused us enough trouble already! Stand aside, I say!"

The fright lessened to merely unbearable. Through the portal they ran, if three hurried steps can be said to be running. Immediately they stopped again, standing at the edge of an immense domed underground pavilion. The god-forged grotto dwarfed them.

A roar off to their right trapped their gaze. More than a hundred yards away, the boulder-littered floor of the oblong cavern dropped away, as if mighty Vangberg had chomped a jagged bite out of it, leaving a precipitous abyss, a gaping, burbling pit that fell straight to the planet's fiery core.

"I take back what I said about Ritardando Shirr!" Trebor whispered. Impulsively he pulled out the book taken from Bosamp's tower and quickly reviewed the passage written by the overwrought bard. "There isn't any way even he could overstate it!"

Emanating from the chasm, a reddish orange aura bathed the chamber, strobing irregularly; the light from the lava pit cast gruesome shadows on the cavern's tapestries, distorting the many-edged tufa formations and stalagmites into flickering scarlet outlines of supernatural horror.

"It's him!" the prince cried. "On the ceiling!" The royal heir pointed up at a wraith overhead, its arms spread outward over the abyss.

Ceiling to floor.

"There!" the prince shouted.

Across the grotto stood Bosamp, statue-stiff, catatonic, exposed to the firepit. Just in front of him was a massive obsidian altar, glossy black, a megalithic rectangle waist high, etched with arcane symbols; on each end of the slab was the towering, hideous statue of a Skolgod: D-Ray at the right, Om at the left. The wizard swayed slowly, oscillating, his palms resting on the ebony slab, his words too low to be heard across the vast cavern.

"Stop, villain!" Yor hurled.

The thunder of Yor's words resounded off the sides of the underground enclave. The gaunt Bosamp's concentration snapped. He stopped chanting, and his sallow eyes opened reluctantly. He turned and looked past his horse and across the cavern.

"Impossible! You couldn't have gotten in!"

"Wrong again, madman! The time has come at last!"

Yor looked over the field of battle. The disjointed floor and tufa were worse than the Wastes themselves; riding was unthinkable. "Leave the horses in the anteroom!" he shouted. "They'll be no good in this cluttered mess!"

It was done at once. Charging forward on foot, the five vectored through the field of hydra-headed tufa, five streams diverging, but all leading to the same place: the altar.

Panicked, Bosamp flung his arms away from the slab, his shadow flailing viciously on the ceiling. Pirouetting, snarling, he shook off the torpor of his pitward summoning and folded his arms together, reaching deep into the blossomed sleeves of his battered robe.

My last trick! It had better work!

"You've no time left! The Mallet is as good as mine!" With that, the magician tossed a shiny metal sphere into the air and began to call forth the runes of the Sortilege.

The path to the wizard was a long run—if running were possible, which it wasn't. The bizarre stands of limbed rock were everywhere, as sharp as scythes, a must to avoid, so there was no straight route to the black altar.

While they approached, Bosamp raved, his orange-draped arms spread high and wide. Glyphs of power sundered the cavern, rising above the roar of the volcano, above the sound of the five rushing hunters. To the top of the cavern the gilded sphere flew, whirling like a top over the sorcerer, who returned now to his previous evocation.

The sphere sizzled, crackled.

"Bremstrahlung's bad breath!" the red-beard swore, taking the Norlandic god of lightning's name in vain. "Isn't that B. G.'s Orb of Deadly Dancing Darts?"

"It couldn't be!" Trebor shot back. "That's much too advanced for a novice like . . . sure does look like one, though, doesn't it?"

They ran onward.

Too late! Yor thought. We're not going to make it!

High in the enormous grotto, the shiny metal ball whirred into a blue blur, absorbing the wizard's runes like a flywheel and giving off vapors until a thick, swirling storm surrounded it, hiding Bosamp from their sight. The storm grew in diameter until it filled the cavern from top to bottom, a furious mass of rotating gas.

The five stopped.

Maelstrom.

"Wedge!" Yor shouted. "Sir Dudley! Prince Rodney! Get

behind us! Take cover in the rocks!"

"But—"

"There's no time to argue! Let us handle this! We've done this before!"

Instantly the three melded into a triangle with the rapid sureness of a practiced drill, Yor at the point, Trebor right, Dword left, swords held before them, gleaming in Vangberg's crimson gloaming.

"Forward!" Yor shouted.

The steaming cloud scintillated with sharp flashes of light; tiny sparks zapped the surface of the ball, racing around the contour of the cloud. The first light dart jumped, a slim bolt of arrow-swift energy, unerring. . . .

Swifter still was the black-clad cavalryman. Electrified with adrenaline, Yor deftly deflected the dart off his rapier, steering it into a nearby tufa shaped like a coatrack. When the bolt struck solid matter, it exploded in a flare, searing a small, perfect hole into the rock.

"Here they come!" Yor barked. "Use these weird formations as cover!"

Slowly they advanced.

Dartwheel.

At first it was only a trickle, one bolt every few seconds, then every other second, then every second, building into a torrent of missiles, a mandala of flashing light. Frantic, the trio dodged, weaved, and slashed at the rain of bolts, each defending against the beams boiling out of the storm in his own style: Dword's screamsax with intuitive fury; Trebor with parsimonious use of his broadsword, not a flinch more muscle than was needed; and Yor, a whirling dervish, his rapier striking faster than light itself, daring and double daring.

They pressed ahead, step by step, indomitable.

Swords and sorcery, *son et lumiere*.

Smoke rose off the rocks from the sizzling darts, making it hard to see. Trebor stumbled over in a pothole and lost his balance. "Ow!" he growled. A bolt slipped past his guard and bored through his armor, singeing the cloth below until it smoldered. His skin was scalded, cauterized.

"Damnation!"

Off stride, the loremaster was struck again, his armor punctured, absorbing the sizzling energy of the streaks, and his surcoat caught fire. "*Augh!*" He fell to the ground, rolling on the crusted rock.

"Trebor! Over here!" Dword yelped. Dropping down to the struggling loremaster, the red-beard's hands sought his water bag, heedless of the darts. One glanced off his helmet in a brilliant blast of light, setting off a ringing in his head.

I'm glad I brought that thing. . . .

The barbarian found his bag.

Splash!

Maddened at the danger to his friends, Yor popped up onto a flat rock. He twirled his blade in slaughterhouse fury; faster and faster it went round, frenzied, drawing all the magical gale's animosity to himself like a lightning rod.

Flick-flick-flick-flick.

"Is that the best you can do?" Yor taunted the storm. "Pathetic! I can spin better magic than that myself! More I say! More! More! More!"

The cloud flashed with rage.

The lithe Bret moved like a berserk dancer, a wriggling, ducking, twisting, well-honed machine revving with fey laughter. His iron blade-wand was alive with light, scattering bolts in every direction until it seemed as if they radiated from him and not from the storm, as if he were steadily sucking the pulp out of a piece of fruit and arrogantly spitting the seeds away.

Fasterfasterfaster.

Bolts singed by him, coming too quickly now to be aimed; he could only parry with short jabs. A slash across his gauntlets— ouch! That hurts! A nick on the edge of his ear—yeow!

What have I gotten myself into?

The pain drove him to even greater speed, until it seemed as if he were more than one man, more than human, a set of simultaneous Yors separated by strobes of time, daring the sorcerous storm's tirade.

A pair sprang up from the grotto floor. Trebor, his scorched surcoat burned away to expose his cuirass, and the supple Norlander both reentered the fray, drawing off the assault from Yor, forging forward with cries of victory.

And so the storm sputtered, despairing; the bolts dwindled in intensity, bursting into splinters of timid candlepower, slowing in frequency, sluggish, enervated. Then, with a whine, the metal sphere stopped spinning and fell to the ground.

"It's done!" Yor cheered. Lathered with sweat, he drew in a deep breath, happy-tired, denying the cramps in his legs, the bee stings on his hands and limbs, the fire on his head. . . .

"Your cap!" Trebor cried. His huge hand sprang and knocked the flaming tam to the ground; he stomped on it a trifle over-hastily, his immense brown boot crushing the cap to a lifeless ort.

"My tam!" Yor's striking blue eyes widened; his lip curled into a sickle.

Men had died for less.

Trebor reacted instinctively. "It's not my fault! "Bosamp did it!"

"*Grrrr* . . ."

"How unfortunate," Dword bemoaned. "And to think you only brought two more."

"But that was his favorite!" the loremaster mocked.

Yor was inconsolable. "That cap was given to me by Lady—" He stopped short of indiscretion. "Bosamp, you anile famulus! If I have to chase you to the end of the world, I'll—"

The unfortunate choice of words left him groping; the metaphor went incomplete. Instead, he bounded forward.

Bosamp did not, could not, hear. Spellbound, the ragged, hollow-cheeked wizard stood enthralled before the black altar.

Something droned in the pit.

Bosamp returned to life at the sound; his eyes, wildly maniacal, filled with the reddish glow of the pit and the terrible yellow of dragon dust.

"Ah!"

The five were halfway to the sorcerer when the portentous humming stopped them in their tracks.

"Keee-ripes!"

Fireworks rose from the pit, a thousand snooker balls of flame swarming up. The buzzing became deafening, ear-popping, high-pitched, piercing the grotto with frightening sonorance. The crimson corona shone more brightly, until it hurt the eyes.

"The dreaded fireflies!" Trebor trumpeted.

Scarlet shards of living lava vaulted up from Vangberg's pit, magma modules that had waited untold eons for this summoning. In blazing congress, they swept around the magician and the megalith.

"Aaiii!"

Jaws agape, Bosamp howled as if ripped apart at his seams, then disappeared in the fireflies' sea of fury.

Trebor sighed righteously. "I told you he'd never get by the fireflies! His sorcery just isn't powerful enough; he overreached. He was only an apprentice, albeit a talented one, and this was simply too much for him. Thus be it ever with wizards!"

"But this has nothing to do with magic," Dword countered. "It has to do with the Skolgods! The potency of Bosamp's spells isn't the issue—just his desire to ring the Bell! D-Ray never made any requirements about that!"

"But he must have!"

"Why?"

The theological debate ended; the draconic cloud of fireflies engulfed the sorcerer only briefly; then the red sea parted. On the obsidian slab lay a magnificently crafted, platinum-leafed Hammer of surpassing, exotic beauty.

"Aha!"

Swiftly Bosamp clutched the Mallet of Doom. Though

oversized for his hand, it was light to his heft. A dizzying sense of well-being excited the sorcerer as he held the god's tool to his bosom, then lofted it high above his head.

Recharged.

"Behold!" Bosamp railed with the pomp of the circumstances, invigorated by the flush of new energy provided by the Hammer. "The Doomsday Pealer! Even as it was foretold! With this Hammer, I could—dare I say it?—rule the world!"

He stuffed the Mallet of Doom in his sash.

"Death to the infidels!" he then roared. "World Shaker! World Breaker! My name shall ring through the galaxy forever! Go, my fire fiends! Attack the unbelievers!"

Pivoting, the wizard dashed to his tethered steed and climbed aboard. "Hah!" he incited the horse, which was only too happy to be leaving.

Stunned and amazed, four faces fell on one loremaster.

"What?" they all said.

"You said the fireflies guarded the Mallet! You said he'd never get the Mallet from them!" Yor berated.

"But the legend said . . ." Trebor stuttered. "His legend!" He pointed at Dword accusingly.

Dword balked. "Don't blame this on me! You know how devious the eddas can be! And I'm not responsible for Ritardando Shirr's lousy translation!"

Yor moaned. "I don't believe this! Couldn't you people just worship the sun or something?"

"Well," Trebor postulated rapidly, "I suppose the fireflies guard the Mallet from theft. Bosamp, however, didn't really come here to *steal* it; he came here to use it for the purpose for which it was secreted in the first place. Ergo, it seems logical that the fireflies might indeed simply hand it over to him."

"So much for the dreaded fireflies!" Yor snorted.

"Not quite, Captains!" Sir Dudley interrupted. "It looks like we're in for it! I guess they've sided with Bosamp!"

The knight's observation brought them around. The fog of

floating lava balls had wafted within hailing distance. The warm swarm grew closer leisurely, as if unsure what to do— go back to Vangberg's fiery bosom, or attack the interlopers as Bosamp had requested, or be satisfied at just placing itself between them and Bosamp's escape.

This wasn't in their instructions. . . .

Finally a solitary firefly broke from the pack and buzzed by the five in warning. The herald swooped so low over them they could feel the heat radiating from it.

Yor slashed decisively; his rapier cut through the firefly, cleaving it into two nearly even pieces.

*Gizz!*

The divided lavaling wailed, and the two fragments looped drunkenly around the grotto, bouncing off tufa. They finally stabilized, two flaming dots high above Yor, and to the Bret swashbuckler's dismay, re-fused in a new, if slightly diminished, magma ball.

"By the blessed bard!"

Annoyed, the volcanic courier dived at Yor again. The terrible swift steel of the cavalryman lashed out at the fire packet.

*Gizz!*

The two pieces rejoined a second time, reduced still further, but still sizzling potent. It buzzed overhead, but this time, the cloud droned along behind the herald, ambling closer, closer to the five.

One last time, the head firefly dipped in admonition.

Yor struck savagely, throwing the weight of his body into the slice, not a fencing move, but maddened butchery. He splintered the firefly into a fusillade of fragments, fiery raindrops, which left bubbling molten lava spewed on the cavern floor.

Boyish grin. "Hey! This might not be so bad after all! They can be stopped! Maybe—yeow!" Yor shook his hot hand up and down, then pitched the torrid blade back and forth between his hands. "My sword's getting too hot to hold!"

"What did you expect?" Trebor rejoined. "Earth—iron—is

not the counter to the fire element! Water is!" The man-mountain had a sudden insight; his haughtiness returned. "But you can also fight fire with fire! That is the way to defeat this kind of sorcery!"

"But—" Dword tried to say.

Too late. The loremaster had already sheathed his broadsword. With one eye peeled on the firestorm, the Bret man-mountain pounded in giant steps across the cavern floor. Quickly he removed a torch from his pack, lit it, and returned, swinging the flaming limb around his head.

"But this isn't sorcery!" Dword warned. "You'll—"

Heedless, Trebor dashed past his companions with a war whoop, courageously lunging into the fireflies.

"Go get 'em!" the prince cheered. Hey! That doesn't look so hard to do! Maybe I can do that too! "Fire with fire!" he echoed and raced back to get a torch from his horse.

Trebor charged. The volcano's brood whined shrilly, complaining, decrying the loremaster's assault. Around and around they whizzed, angry red wasps; he waved the torch, strong-arming it through their midst, scattering them with flame and muscle, while the fireflies whined in anguish.

"It's working!" he cheered.

Pause.

"It's *not* working!"

Back out of the red cloud scurried Trebor. His torch was afire—not just the oil-ragged end of it, but *all* of it. He threw the tinder snake from his grasp and beat his gauntlets together to stifle the incipient fire.

"Are you all right?" Yor asked, worried.

"I think so. . . ."

Good! Yor grinned. Although it was entirely possible they were all going to die shortly, he certainly wasn't going to pass up an opportunity to get off a cheap shot! "So—have you got any other hot ideas?"

Trebor frumped. "Well, we can go back out the way we came

in, but the odds are we'll never catch Bosamp in time. Or we can try to break through the fireflies and hope some of us make it."

"Some of us!" the prince gurgled as he rejoined them. He pitched the useless torch to the ground.

"Dragon's breath!" Yor cursed. "Dword! This is your legend. Doesn't this go beyond the fireflies' charter?"

"It seems like it ought to," Dword replied. "They're supposed to be guardians of the Hammer, not its protagonists."

"So talk to them!"

"What?"

"Talk to the fireflies! Tell them to stop interfering in the destiny of mankind! That can't be what D-Ray intended!"

Okay . . . but how?

The red-beard wasn't allowed the time to think; the veil of fireflies rolled toward them. Fivesome formations of lava pilots broke off from the holocaust. In intricate aerial maneuvers, they harassed the five, not decisively engaging them, but upping the ante, reluctant to use any more force than was necessary, uncertain as to what their role should be in this unforeseen conundrum.

A show of arms, a test of wills.

The five were soon busy batting away the fireflies with their weapons, five metal flyswatters. The prince was in the thick of it, side by side with them, breathing hard, legs wobbly.

I won't run! I won't run! he thought.

A firefly flashed by.

He swung his short sword.

*Gizz!*

Wow! I hit it! The royal lad recovered from his disbelief and lashed out at the next buzzing ball.

Missed.

Flinking ogre pus! What was it Yor said? Balls of the feet! Balls of the feet! He stole a quick glance at the black-clad adventurer and aped his stance, his body remembering. . . .

Thickening, the fireflies met determination with determination. But they still were merely harassing; they hadn't yet decided on an all-out assault.

"We can't stay here any longer, Captains!" Sir Dudley advised. "Sooner or later they'll overwhelm us! So, forward or backward? It's time we faced the music!"

Music? Dword looked at the statues of the two Skolgods. Did Om just wink? It could just be the light. . . . Why, yes, of course! "The Song of Solvang the Flautist!" Music! The only way Solvang could communicate with Om!

Dword plopped down on his derriere, sitting cross-legged. Laying his screamsax aside— but not too far!—he pulled his flute from his heavy metal jacket.

"Dword! Are you hurt?" Yor asked with desperation.

"No! Stay put! Cover me!"

"*Cover* you? If you don't get up, we'll have to *bury* you!"

A few practice scales cleared the barbarian's throat. His fingers flew over the holes as he threw everything into the recorder, its fipple vibrant on his lips. The acoustics of the chamber were superb; they distilled and enhanced the recorder's tone, the slight echoing effect adding depth to Dword's overture.

Notes flowed. . . .

The horde of fireflies paused, confused, touched by the chords. The loose terriers of the red cloud buzzed back into the mass, and the cloud stepped back from the five adventurers; this quelled the steel-armed band's melodies. The fireflies themselves quieted respectfully as they took an aerial perch above and beyond the five, hovering, with awesome Vangberg's caldron at their backs.

Dword went into *arpeggio* to close the overture, a dozen or so bars of lighthearted, attention-grabbing fluff, then segued into the first movement of his impromptu symphony, a pastoral paean to the manifest joys and sorrows of human existence, recounting as an undertone Magnus's great gift of life. It was nothing less than an unabashed tribute to existence itself, with all its bittersweet facets.

"Should we run for it?" Yor bothered. "We're losing time."

"Let's hear the lad out," Sir Dudley suggested. "Maybe he can convince them to let us pass. That would save hours! And the fireflies do seem to be listening."

Indeed they were, for it seemed as if the fireflies now moved to the music. Dword's *adagio* first movement speeded to *allegro*; the new theme conveyed the momentous import of their quest to stop Bosamp. Full of verve and bravura, the new theme delineated their heroic struggles to catch the sorcerer, whose own theme was off-key, off-timbre, implying—but not too heavy-handedly—that it was questionable whether or not the wizard could still claim to represent humanity after all the dragon dust he had consumed, dust provided to him by—whom? Who dabbled mischievously in the sacred contract between men and gods? Who dealt from the bottom of the deck? What mountebank interfered?

Who?

The questions fluttered in the grotto without answers. The fireflies buzzed, swarming fluidly, caught up now in the musical debate and rebuttal.

Ominous, Dword's third movement overlaid the second, corrupting it into cacophony. This discord shattered the upbeat lilt of the second; it was Bosamp's theme perverted to its ultimate goal. Strains from the second theme sallied vainly to counter, but the impending destruction gained momentum.

*Sturm und Drang.*

Somehow Dword made the recorder sound like the thundering of an enormous bell. Once . . . twice . . . and then a third fatal time.

Silence.

Almost. All was not lost, the fourth movement whispered. It need not be! For all its many faults, life was preferable to oblivion. Magnus's theme returned, a saucy *scherzo*, a raunchy but heartfelt mood of optimism, conjuring the pleasures of just being, an acceptance of the pain that living caused, the heartache and the physical perils, the sadness and the sorrow, but underlined with a strong desire to continue to roll the bones, whatever else, to play the game and take the risks, all of them. . . .

Rambling, gambling Man.

Concinnity.

Dword's tune celebrated life. Why should one man, gods or no, speak for all? They were five to Bosamp's one! The theme intensified, challenging D-Ray's premise: if the gods could not agree, who were the fireflies to take sides? By their interference, did the fireflies deem to decide the fate of men themselves? Was this what D-Ray intended?

And who else was interfering in the Game itself?

Suddenly Dword just stopped. He let the question hang in the chamber, an inappropriate ending to the work, incomplete, a thwarted symphony.

He stood. He would play no more.

He put the recorder in his jacket.

The fireflies were incited to riot. The mass of red swarmed in debate, warring with the purpose for which they had been formed, questioning and trying to remember their exact instructions, whirring in a brightening crimson.

Hysterical vacillation.

*Boom!*

Everyone froze. Dust rose from the far side of the chamber; rock cascaded down from the north end of the oblong cavern.

"What was that?"

The fireflies seemed to know; the blast precipitated their debate into conclusion. The red cloud drifted back to Vangberg's pit.

Consensus, reprieve.

"You did it, lad!" Sir Dudley rejoiced in Dword's ear. "They're going to let us pass!"

"Nice going, Dword!" the prince cheered.

Dword flushed with their unreserved kudos. He turned to his two companions.

The loremaster cleared his throat and coughed, then managed a weak, "Not bad."

Dword wilted. He looked to Yor.

"Sir Dudley! Prince!" the cavalryman said, turning away from the expectant look of the barbarian bard. "Bring the horses! We've got to got to get moving!"

Pause. Yor knew he couldn't postpone it any longer. "You know I'm tone deaf!" he pleaded. "But it sounded okay to me. . . ."

Oh.

Dword sagged, turned away. The third movement was too abrupt; I could change the pacing a bit, add a few bars. . . .

Two hands pounded his shoulder.

"An epic performance!" Trebor said stoutly.

"No doubt it will win the Eisteddfod next year!" Yor added.

Life returned to the Norlander's ruddy-sheathed face. "Only if there *is* a next year! We'd better hurry before the fire-flies come back for an encore. How about 'The Ballad of—' "

"No!"

The castle duo brought the horses posthaste. Hustling, all rushed toward the black altar. When they reached the obsidian megalith, they hung back from it, fearful of the ancient black slab, and gazed north to the cavern wall.

No sign of Bosamp.

"He must have taken one of the exits," Yor guessed. Pointing around the chamber where the greenish ovals obviously demarcated other tunnels leading in and out of Vangberg, he fretted, "But which one? There's a dozen of them. . . ."

"Shouldn't there be one more?" Sir Dudley observed. "There's a gap there; all the others seem evenly spaced."

"If there was a passageway there," Dword added, "it'd be opposite the one we came in! It would lead due north!"

"Zounds!" Trebor erupted. "The Mallet! That's what that boom was! He's sealed the egress!"

"The Mallet sealed it up?" The prince's newly found confidence wavered. The feeling of being in a cage overtook him.

I've got to get out of here!

Vangberg spoke.

Loudly.

The cavern bounded up and down, as the center of the volcano yawned after an eon's slumber. Chunks of the ceiling shook loose and dropped, small ones for the most part, weighing in the low tons; tufa toppled.

*Thud! Grumble! Thud! Thud! Belch!*

The ominous sound of burbling lava.

"We've got to use the same exit he did!" the loremaster implored. "We'll have to clear it!"

"But we'll be buried alive if we stay in here any longer!" the prince wailed. "Can't we use one of the others?"

"No!" Trebor countered. "They're only rods apart here, but this is the center of the pinwheel! They'll be leagues apart on the surface! Ten minutes here could be worth hours up there! We've got to follow him!"

"Trebor's right!" Yor decided quickly. "We don't dare lose his trail now! Let's go!"

They shot over the uneven underground, dodging the intermittent droppings from the cavern ceiling. Immediately the trio tackled the larger rubble; the elder knight and the royal teenager rolled away the smaller stones.

Vangberg hiccuped.

Ten hands, one thought.

Lava bubbled up in the pit, casting a fiery glow on the walls; the temperature soared. A stream of molten earth dribbled into the grotto.

"Faster!"

They worked furiously, clearing the wizard's debris, tossing it into a small dam to protect themselves from the approaching lava. Smoke from sulfur fumes filled the cavern; the heat was incredible. The lava stream reached the edge of the dam.

Then just one last immense boulder blocked the exit.

"We'll have to use another way out!" Prince Rodney moaned. Terrified, he stared at the approaching lava, then back at the gargantuan boulder. "No one can move that!"

Yor stared at the boulder, feeling the press of defeat. "No *one*—and perhaps not all of us . . ."

The horses!

"But we aren't alone!" he rallied. "Prince! Sir Dudley! Get some rope and make a noose for the rock! Tie our horses to the other end of it! We'll pull it away! Trebor! Dword! We'll dig a hole at the base of the boulder with our swords and use them as levers! Hurry! There's not much time!"

The lava was a spectator to their frenzied actions, rising slowly, inexorably toward them.

Equine muscle and mechanical advantage.

It took all five of their steeds and their combined strength to move Bosamp's plug; even then, they were only able to move it a few feet from the spot but . . .

Enough. Just in time.

*     *     *     *     *

In a cavern high in the Darkling Mountains, the chrome dragon grew angry, vengeful. He grabbed the gold's head and lashed it with a sweep of his tail, inflicting insulting pain.

*You should not have linked minds with Bosamp! I never dreamed you'd be so audacious as to try it in my presence! How could you be so stupid as to try to communicate with him so close to the Bell! Now I'll have to—*

A glyph of godpower exploded over them; they froze in trepidation. Then the chamber was filled with music, glorious music. It filled their ears and minds; they wondered at it, but they did not comprehend it.

The dragoness Drachshiska trembled. *The music! It's beautiful, yet horrible! Where did it come from? How did it get here?*

*The question is not how or where! The question is who? And why?* The chrome craned his neck, searching with his mind and sorcery, but found no answer—or rather, feared the answer so terribly he was afraid to say what he knew must be true.

The last refrains of Dword's concerto echoed off the limestone, lingering, marking the end of the magically piped piece, and then there was a moment of ominous silence.

*WHO DARES INDEED?*

Instantly the chrome was struck down flat, unable to move any of his limbs even a fraction of an inch, not merely paralyzed but also inanimate. The chrome slumped uncontrollably across the helpless gold, who herself was agonized with pain beyond description.

*The eyes of D-Ray have fallen on us!* the gold cried into infinity. *O mighty Magnus, save us, we beseech you! Spare your children from the wrath of D-Ray! Hurry!*

Both gold and chrome screamed sounds that made the rock itself shake in abject terror as the Skolgod gnawed their minds. And screamed. And screamed.

And screamed . . .

\* \* \* \* \*

Later, as they neared the end of the lava tube passage, they discovered that Bosamp had also sealed the exit to the surface. They lost half a day clearing a path out of the volcano.

Yor lost his voice, hoarse from cursing.

The wizard was nowhere in sight.

\* \* \* \* \*

Nightfall, snowfall.

The air was decidedly colder. Once the five tired riders fought their way down from Vangberg's sprawling lava beds, a snow squall came up on them very, very fast, blowing thick graupel—damp, hail-like snow pellets that melted almost as fast as they hit the carpet of tundra. The unseasonable weather was more a nuisance than an inclemency, dampening their horses and themselves. They soon lost visual contact with their surroundings and with their quarry's trail.

They stopped to set up a cold and gloomy camp.

"Dword?"

The Norlander glanced at the loremaster, waiting for the question. Trebor was nearly conspiratorial, so the red-beard resumed assembling their tent without undue obviousness.

"Which way is north?"

Dword lowered his scarf so he could speak. He closed his eyes and let the feeling come to him. "There."

Trebor nodded solemnly, then reversed to steal a quick look at the beclouded southern sky. Dword joined the loremaster's gaze casually.

A scarlet cloud backlit the grey ether.

It wasn't the sun.

Dword secured his tent post with a pound through the loose surface soil into the permafrost and handed a rope to Trebor. "It's the fireflies. They're following us," he said.

"Or Bosamp."

"Or Bosamp," Dword agreed. "It's their legend, too."

Trebor brooded as he raised the tent pole, threading a stiff leather strap through an eyelet. "I think they just want to see how it's all going to end. They chose not to go beyond the letter of their instructions, but I wonder. . . ."

The Norlander shrugged silently.

The whipped snow blustered in the dark.

It began to stick.

# CHAPTER TWELVE

Snow.

From the west, a thicket of frosty flakes roared over the Wastes, a cloud monster impelled suicidally, horizontally by a blustery whip. The airborne white crescendo bore down on the five riders with the rapidity of a diving sea hawk, catching them in bottomland between ridges on the sprawling tundra.

Yor looked ahead to reconnoiter the terrain, his mood as stormy as the weather. Snow, he thought grimly. Just what we needed! Dword said Norlanders have twenty-one different words for snow, defining its size, wetness, and texture! Dragon's breath! Trebor's loremasters only have ten!

Whatever you call it, it's still a pain. . . .

An ankle-deep blanket of mush lay in broad patches on the tundra like a herd of white throw rugs. Beyond Vangberg, the Wastes were no longer a maze of rocky roads. Except for a series of bony ridges running east to west, cutting across their path, the land was flat and swampy.

The ridges, however, were a godsend, providing shields against the preemptive weather. On the southeast side of these barriers, vegetation congregated, huddled together for protection, short, gnarled spruces mixed with sturdy alpine bushes. The leaves of the latter were turning pale yellow and purple, ready to drop before the next Button Moons. On the exposed northwest slopes, nothing but stalwart wild grasses claimed the rocky soil, wavering in the wind gusts. In between the ridges, streams flowed like veins across the steppes, dotted sporadically by thermal vents that filled the air with steam streamers.

Back in faraway Lothar, hot summer days still strutted through their last act and scene on the stage; here prima donna autumn had bullied in ahead of cue and was playing puckishly to the crowd. No sooner had Yor seen the storm cloud than it plastered his face, sticking to his mustache and green cape like dandruff. He tried to shield his cobalt eyes from the furious flurries, but it was no use. Either way, he was visionless.

"Another squall!" he complained. "I'd hate to think even the weather is against us! If that vomit-eating pustule of a wizard caused this, I'll—"

"Bosamp can't control the weather," Trebor said from a few yards back. "Not even the entire Council in spell meld can. The Storm Wraiths claim to, but even that is dubious."

"Woden knows, it's a little early in the season for snow," Dword said, stroking his ruddy beard in contemplation. "But it's an altogether natural phenomenon. I've seen it snow farther south even earlier than this. Why, I remember The Year Without a Summer; we—"

"Curse these arctic climes!" Yor snapped at the barbarian. It was supposed to have been funny, harking back to Dword's comment at Teckwood, but Yor's voice was too strained, his temper too close to the surface, and it came out harshly.

"The weather's slowing him down, too, Captain," Sir Dudley said calmly. "Nobody can ride very fast or very well in this. And the tracks have looked very fresh of late."

"Finally!" Yor lamented, exposing his raw mood fully.

His comment killed conversation; without waiting for any response, Yor rode on, brooding over the events of the last few days. Many long hours had they labored under Vangberg after Bosamp collapsed the exit from the volcano, long dreary hours digging out. For the next two days, they chased the wizard's trail, closing in on him, shrinking the half day's lead until now they felt that they were within striking distance again.

We might have had Bosamp by now if Rodney hadn't got caught in the quicksand around that geyser! Yor sulked. Worse, he got some minor burns—we all did!—when it spouted while we were getting him out! And now the prince has the worst case of saddle sores I've ever seen in my life! Trebor's poultice helps, but the prince keeps falling behind! Maybe I should cut Sir Dudley and the prince loose, and the three of us make a run for it.

No.

All of us or none of us. I can't explain why it's right, but I know that it is. . . .

Yor threw aside his cape to shake off the snow that had blown through his defenses and impaled itself into his chest, on the comfortable jacket that Hiemal back in Freissinggal had foreseen they would need. The five were all layered in clothing now, even though the temperature wasn't all that uncomfortable. It was the dampness that was dangerous, and the extra layers helped keep them dry. The cloud's white barrage was wet and heavy and in many places melted on contact; in others, the tundra permafrost made the snow stick.

And it was accumulating.

Yor traced the tracks up to a rill. Bosamp's course was plain enough: north, over hill and dale.

He must know where he's going, though I couldn't swear to it myself in this weather! I don't know why, but I presumed the Bell would be closer to Vangberg than this. Thank heavens it isn't! He'd have been there by now!

Flinch: psychic hangover.

For a brief, awful moment, Yor wasn't sure if he was awake or dreaming. The vision of the wizard's trail plundering the white-clad Wastes triggered *déjà vu*, a flashback to last night's dream imagery. The nightmare images flooded over him again: titanic bells ringing so loud that the brain stopped; continents heaving, jumbled like butter in a churn; people being ripped apart by the thunderous sound until their very molecules could no longer cling together.

I don't think I was the only one who had such dreams! Everything seems different since Bosamp got the Mallet! And this morning, I think we all feel that today will see the end of it, one way or another.

A gust of wind blew in another storm cloud. Snow fell quickly, swirled by the wind, cutting visibility to only a few yards. Without discussion, the riders pulled up, huddled together, pointing downwind, just as they had when the last two short squalls blew over them, ready to wait it out.

All but Yor.

He grimaced at the enemy snow. Without conscious thought, words erupted from him. "We'll ride through this one," he said, his heart pounding. "Time is running out! Try to stay close together! I don't want anybody getting out of the sight of the person in front of him or behind him. Is that clear, Prince?"

They stared at Yor in surprise at the outburst.

The tension's getting to him, Dword thought. It's getting to all of us, but he's taking it personally. . . .

The Bret cavalryman pricked his spurs into his steed's flank. The horse jolted forward, straining up the ridge with a lurch. Behind him, slowly, the others followed his path, running parallel to the lines left by the wizard, through the falling snow.

The squall continued; it was persistent rather than violent, determined rather than abusive. It coated them with a thin white dew as they rode, sucked into Yor's determined wake. Across the valley floor they trudged silently, then upward, sheltered from the worst of the squall by the ridge.

The respite ended minutes later at the ridge crest. Yor strained to see in the renewed assault of snow. Where's Bosamp? The white glaze was almost impenetrable. Objects lost distinction in the diffuse, shadowy light; shapes lost their edges to become white contours, overlapping, hiding their depth relationships.

He shook his reins, and the horse paced ahead, but the difficulty of riding in the squall soon absorbed all his thoughts. Down the opposite slope he rode, then veered north, tacking along the incline.

We can cut across that gully and pick up the trail over there, he decided. That narrow crease, a creek bed probably, a path down . . .

Creek bed!

Below the ivory patina, a smooth slipstone tripped up the fjord colt; the horse fumbled for footing. For one split second, it seemed to keep its balance, but then a rear foot came down on a second slipstone.

Horse and rider toppled, both crying out.

"*Uff!*"

Answering gravity's summons, Yor barreled downward through the snow, unable to control his fall on the slippery hillside. Over and over he flipped, feeling the cold slap of snow-crested stone on his face. He lost his tam; his hair aged to premature white with graupel. Swearing, Yor struggled against his momentum on the slick decline. Eventually he braced against something with his feet and stopped his headlong slide.

His face was full of weather droppings.

Clown! he thought as he wiped the gunk from his face. A creek bed! What did you expect would happen? Like an acrobat, he popped back up briskly, jauntily, trying to act as if nothing had happened, his firemander boots buried ankle-deep as he rose to his—

*Urk!*

Arms gesticulating wildly, legs shooting sideways, he slipped and landed on his firm butt, then coasted about ten yards before he came to a stop, scattering a foraging clan of mottled ice mice back to their holes. One of the feisty rodents paused at its lair, standing up on its two hind legs with its forelegs poised, chattering abusively at Yor.

"You're absolutely right," he told the outraged mouse. "I deserved that."

He got up slowly, wary of the treacherous footing of rocks and snow, and peered through the white, gauzy veil. Packs had fallen off his horse, strewn along the ridge haphazardly, dark shapes in the fading visibility. He picked up his rapier—his baldric had been torn in the fall—and looked uphill.

The horse! Oh good, he's already up. He looks okay from here!

He scolded himself bitterly. Jackass!

Mercilessly the squall chose that particular instant to abate and part the white curtain concealing him from the others. They were staring down at him from the crest of the ridge. "Go on!" Yor growled without blushing. "Sir Dudley, take the lead—and don't follow that flinking gully! I'll catch up in a minute. I've got to pick up some of this stuff. Go on, I said!"

"Don't be long," Trebor warned. "The next squall could come along any minute."

"I can follow the trail the horses leave!" Yor barked back. "Bosamp isn't going to wait around for me, and you shouldn't either! Get going!"

He turned his back on them and walked uphill toward the horse, not an easy climb in the slush. I'll leave most of the stuff—I'll pick it up later . . . if there *is* a later.

Feeling utterly alone, he ascended the slope, passing up a bag that was yards off his course, but picking a canteen on his way to the horse, which was in no hurry to join him. Humbled, sullen, grumbling, he reached his steed. The roan horse snorted and shook its head, turning away from him. The Bret cavalryman apologized and took a quick look at the horse, soon satisfying himself that other than a bruised foreleg, no harm had been done.

Awful lucky! If I had manure for brains, I'd be twice as smart! I can't push the horse too hard, though, not with that bruise. . . .

He turned and watched the four riders reach the bottom of the ridge and curve to the left, vanishing in a ground-clinging mist now washing down over the ridge and over him. He recinched the saddle and checked what supplies he had left to ensure they were securely lashed. Nothing really important was missing . . . a haversack with spare tack, a hand axe, a rope.

He glanced around for anything else that might have fallen free in the tousle. Walking the horse back down the path he had gouged in the hillside, he reached the end of the gully and recovered his tam. Then, for no reason other than to make himself feel better, he pitched a piece of bread out for the ice mice.

Enjoy it while you can. Who knows what tomorrow will bring?

He remounted. The horse shied away from putting full weight on its foreleg, and Yor didn't press the matter, confident that a few minutes easy riding would loosen up the leg.

The clouds reconvened, big pillows of white and grey with narrow vents of sunlight plunging through them. The next squall hit and swallowed him whole. The snow fell in immense wet flakes, blown sideways so vigorously they seemed never actually to touch the ground. The terrain was rough, with matted grass making riding difficult. Minutes later, he lost the party's tracks, filled with blown snow.

Whiteout: snow, fog, and steam.

I won't admit I lost them!

He rode toward what he thought was north.

A few minutes later, he heard a voice, but could discern no speaker.

"Captain Yor!"

It was Sir Dudley, not far away, from the sound of his
voice, but completely obscured by the translucent shroud.
The Bret cavalryman oriented himself in the direction of
the voice, standing high in the stirrups.

"Captain Yor!"

"Over here!"

"Captain, there's a hot spring here! And a sward for the
horses! Might be a good place to wait out this squall!"

"Okay, Sir Dudley! I'll meet you there!"

A gleeful honk carried to Yor as he settled back down
into the saddle. Ah! That's the prince's laugh! he thought.
Carries well . . . for once, I'm grateful! Over this way . . . I
wasn't too far off! Should be just over that rise. . . .

* * * * *

Prince Rodney gaped at the ivory mulch in wide-eyed
ecstasy. "Snow! Look at it all! It never snows at the castle.
This is neatest thing I've seen since we left home!"

A primeval urge struck the royal youth; irresistibly he
stepped away from the hot spring and trotted off toward a
foot-deep drift. Chuckling gleefully, the teenager packed a
couple of handfuls of snow into a ball and spun about for a
suitable target, turning, turning. . . .

Whoa!

He stopped, lightheaded, half out of breath. You can
really get dizzy fast out here! Everything looks the same in
every direction! Whew! Well, what about that rock over
there?

*Smack!*

Got it! Now something a little harder, a little farther out
. . . That tree blowing in the wind at the top of the rise?
Why not! Packing another shot, the prince reared his gangly arm and unleashed a full-bodied toss, hurling the spher-
oid with unswerving accuracy at the moving green patch.

Moving?

"Duck!" the prince called as the heedless horseman emerged from the lacy shroud of mist and snow.

Duck? Yor wondered. *Whomp!*

Perfect pitch.

The snowball splattered with chilly impact on Yor's right temple, breaking into frigid pellets that stung his face and made a mess of the green cape encasing him. Angered, he cantered his horse down the hill within a few yards of the prince, gyrated in the saddle, and leaped out of the stirrups, bounding to the ground.

The din of boots on fire. I'll teach that snot-faced—

*Urk!*

*Thump!*

Too angry to be embarrassed, Yor was on his rear less than a second. "Like a brother!" he said churlishly. "Well, little brother, here I come!"

"Sir Dudley!" the prince wailed, paralyzed with fear.

Yor dived, flying through the air at the dodging teenager, and knocked him hard to the ground. Popping up, Yor grabbed the yowling youth by the collar and jerked him off the ground, despite the fact that the prince wasn't much shorter or lighter than he was.

"When I get done with you, you'll know your manners!" He shook the overmatched prince from stem to stern with barely concealed roughness, venting his accumulated spleen with a hostility that surprised even himself.

"Sirr-rr-rr Did-did-didly!"

"Captain!" the elder knight protested. "This is—"

"Did you hear something?" Trebor quizzed, laying his giant hand on Dudley's armored shoulder and looking about blankly, deafly, daftly. "I don't hear anything! I especially don't *see* anything!"

"Helhelhelphelpppp me-ee-ee-ee . . . *uff!*"

"It's the wind," Dword said scholastically, his gauntleted

palm clenching Sir Dudley's opposite shoulder. "Makes strange, almost human sounds. We have a word for it: icesighs. Woden's whimsy, I wouldn't be surprised at all if this were the perfect weather for it!"

Sir Dudley glanced from man to man, wrestling with his sense of duty. Teach him the way of the world, the king had said, but— "Aye, Captains. Icesighs . . . they play real tricks with a man's senses. As long as it doesn't get out of hand, that is."

"It won't."

Sir Dudley decided his packs needed checking; he went back to his steed, whistling lightly.

"*Augh!*" the prince wailed as he was whirled about, then propelled forward by Yor's boot, making a face plant, nose first into a soft, wet pile of snow.

*Urk!*

*Thump!*

Losing his balance in the kick, Yor's dignity suffered a third spanking for the day. Grounded, out of arm's reach, they glared at each other.

"Pretentious poseur! When I tell—"

"Pockmarked brat!"

"Zux-breathed bully!"

"Flatulent dandiprat!"

Handfuls of snow joined the pitching of insults, both flung with growing alacrity.

"Preening pantywaist!"

"Unweaned runt!"

"Baggy-trousered buffoon!"

"Acned albino!"

"Priggish clotheshorse!"

"Chancred crybaby!"

"Crybaby?" The prince froze in hurt, the word an arrow sticking in his soul. His lip trembled compulsively, and he wanted to run, but there was nowhere to run to, no door to slam, no secret passage to hole up in, no one to hide behind.

Crybaby . . . Cedric always called me that. . . . They're all so much better at everything than I am: Colin, Sean, Cedric . . . always laughing at me. I can't do anything right.

The prince folded his arms over his legs and worked the word-arrow loose from his soul with a tear.

Clotheshorse? Yor bounded up. The two Brets were covered in snow until even a yeti couldn't tell them apart. Courtly, he yanked the prince up to his feet, brushing him off with officious protocol. "My liege!" he fussed obsequiously. "Be careful! It's very dangerous out here, very dangerous! The snow can bury a man in seconds! Where's your muffler and your mittens? Haven't I always told you never to go outside without them?"

"Indeed you have, Count Yolk!" the prince retorted. Half hurt, half ashamed, he groped for words. "I didn't see you. I was . . . I'm . . . I'm . . . sorry."

Rodney beamed crimson. Never before had he ever uttered that particular combination of syllables.

Yor blinked. Recovering, he bowed graciously. "That is what I should have wanted my younger brother to have said. But, of course, no normal mother's son would ever say such a thing to his older brother!"

"Never!" the prince agreed.

"Look!" Dword said. "The squall's dying!"

"Huzzah!" Trebor cheered. "We'll be back in the saddle in no time!" Hustling to and fro, the five men remounted.

Their levity evaporated as soon as they hit leather and the ominous nature of their quest regripped their hearts.

\* \* \* \* \*

"Faster!"

Totally blinded by the blowing snow, the wizard jangled

his reins and used the whip again. Fearful, the horse responded. Bosamp growled. His skin was stiff from the cold; his stomach was empty; his eyes glowed bright yellow. Worse, the itch clawed at his knees and underarms like thousands of tiny pincers, and the weight of the Mallet chafed at his side, irritating the lizard skin now encasing his abdomen and thighs.

But not even these annoyances could pierce his euphoria. His mind was a bonfire of dragon dust and adrenaline.

The Bell! I can feel it, even if I can't see it! It's just ahead! The Mallet is guiding me! It's glory time!

"World Shaker! World Breaker!"

He grabbed the Mallet. The god-forged tool tingled in his grasp, its magic more powerful even than the dragon dust. Visions flitted through his mind: scores of voluptuous women lay at his feet as he sat on a shining platinum throne whose arms were shaped like the Mallet; row upon row of impeccably attired servants bowed before him; far-flung worlds worshiped his image in immense shrines filled with creatures that had magically followed his life unbeknownst to him, religiously recording on golden tablets every word he had ever uttered, debating endlessly over the punctuation alone!

I'm practically a god now! And the dragoness will come and take me to my worshipers! At the chime of the Bell, she will come, and we will fly away together. . . .

*Clink!*

The horse shied, stumbled, hopped, tripping over the root of a bush in the white fog. Bosamp was thrown; only luck saved him from having the horse fall on top of him.

\* \* \* \* \*

Silence netted them. The days on horseback had worn them down; they'd heard enough of each other's stories,

had enough of each other's foibles, seen enough of each
other's faces. The monotonous sterility of the snow-garlanded
Wastes was a clean canvas for their imaginations, providing no distractions from their helter-skelter thoughts; they
painted their hopes, their histories, their secret fears on it.
And ever below their consciousness was the knowledge
that at any moment the tintinnabulation of the Tocsin of
Terror might bellow in their ears, the last sound they
would ever hear.

Time.

Midday came and went; not even the prince asked why
there was no break for lunch. Yor glanced from rider to
rider, looking at their faces, seeing their hushed concern.
Riding down the ridge, he suddenly noted that the ridge's
dwarf forest of short, black, gnarled spruces marked the end
of all growth; they were crossing the tree line now. And the
next bank of blown snow gave him a start, for the depth of
the loose, powdery fluff was boot deep.

But the last of the set of squalls had blown through; the
wind had quailed. The falling snow now mimicked the
sands of an hourglass, dwindling down to a few indecisive
flurries. Every minute now seemed exorbitantly precious to
him, like the last drops in a waterskin, to be used as effec-
tively, as efficiently as possible, a priceless, but hazardously
finite, resource.

Time: it's really the only thing we own, isn't it? Yor
reflected. We trade it for money, hoping to buy it back
later. We burn it up on the mundanities of living. We
squander it pursuing things we can never have and things
not worth having. . . .

At the top of each ridge, they looked through the misty
curtain in anticipation of what they might see, wondering
if Bosamp would be within sight, or worse, the legendary
Bell. Ridge by ridge, they despaired of not seeing Bosamp,
again and again, disheartened by the accumulation of tiny

terrors.

Yor stopped to let the party catch up, as Prince Rodney had fallen behind again. Guiltily the cavalryman realized he was pushing his own horse too hard, especially after the fall they had both taken.

I should let Dword or Trebor take the lead, he thought. But I just can't!

The wizard's trail was now plain enough, laid out in the snow for all to see. True, they might lose the trail for a few hundred yards on some swampy morass stoked by geothermal ovens where the snow did not stick, or on the sheltered leeward sides of the ridge, where the snow blew past, but it was easy enough to recover. It was a beeline north.

Yor examined the tracks and knew.

Soon!

"We can't be far behind him now," he announced as they grouped together. "We'll probably see him from the next ridge. Be ready to ride hard. And don't bunch up together."

Yor hesitated for a breath or two, looking from man to man in the mists. Their faces were grave, joyless. Trebor's jaw was set with that immutable look of his, his tall, muscular armored frame on alert, his calm intelligence and determined strength a breakwater on which storms had dashed their hopes. Dword's keen pale blue eyes shone with irresistible wonder and excitement, yet they probed through to the essence of things, his common sense a catalyst they could depend on. Sir Dudley of Manchester sat atop his charger, lost in thoughts of battles past, his armor dulled by the weather and battles, but his heart and mind still on fire, ready for duty, as if the fate of the world was a daily chore he had grown accustomed to performing.

Yor's eyes fell on the prince last. The teenager was nervous and withdrawn. For an instant, the royal lad seemed to Yor a symbol for all the aspirations of mankind, an allegory for their pursuit of the base wizard. Still innocent, still fumbling for the path his life would take, the prince was a blank scroll to be written on, with all the hopes and fears of adolescence, with all the futures yet to be decided.

There are only so many firsts in a lifetime; use them preciously, lad, Yor thought with a twinge of envy.

"There may not be time to plan anything," he said solemnly. "So do what you have to do. If we can take him alive, fine. If not, there's too much at stake to worry about politeness and etiquette.

"And watch out for the Mallet. I don't like the looks of that thing at all. Bosamp's completely deranged, and the Mallet's a power beyond anything we have of our own."

Onward. The pace quickened relentlessly until it seemed that even their horses understood that the steeplechase's final hurdle was about to appear. Up and down the tundra dunes in the valley between the two ridges they rode, wading through the beveled landscape. It began to snow again, not a squall this time, as there was little breeze, but the grey, gloomy cloud overhead foretold of a long, slow, stubborn siege to follow, a steady drip of cotton puffs, not overwhelming but tireless, the kind of snowfall that can go on for hours without stopping, falling nearly straight down, large, loose, and wet.

"What's that?" The Norlander's voice broke the spell. Dword squinted, spying something on an outcropping of slate near the top of the ridge ahead. The snow there was disturbed, exposing the icy grey sheet, and something glinted in the sparse sunlight.

Anxious, they rode toward it. Near the outcropping lay a curled metallic ribbon. Two sets of tracks diverged from the slate.

"That's a horseshoe!" Yor exclaimed. "Bosamp must have tried to gallop over the slate! Look—you can see the marks where the horse fell! There some of his gear! Look at that set of tracks; the horse is lame for sure! We've got him now!"

The Bret cavalryman nudged his maverick uphill, weaving cautiously; he passed the horseshoe with a knowing nod and went over the top. "There's the horse!" he cried out to the others, turning in the saddle to face them, then turning back again, eager to pursue the vision.

Bosamp!

Abandoned by his horse, beset by the barrage of weather, Bosamp struggled on foot in the snow.

"There he . . ."

Stunned, Yor couldn't complete the thought. Beyond Bosamp, the cavalryman saw shining a brilliant golden gleam, a dazzling auric aura so spellbindingly powerful that he felt like a beggar ant standing before the gates of Cathedral Heaven.

The Bell at the Top of the World!

Full palette, emotions daubed through the black-clad adventurer: green-yellow sickness, ivory-pure terror, metallic-grey foreboding, beige humility, purple-angered shock.

"By the blessed bard, there really is a Bell!" Yor raged indignantly. "What kind of imbecilic irresponsibility is this? Do the gods suffer from amentia? If I ever get my hands on that D-Ray, I'll—"

Bosamp's going to make it there yet!

"Charge!"

Five across, earnestly whipping their tired steeds, they galloped downhill into the valley of the Bell. The icy air, intensified by the horses' speed, abraded their faces red; the huffing vapor of horse and rider coursed from their lips, looking as if the life stuffing was slowly leaking from them.

My gods! Yor realized. It's all come down to a simple horse race!

The noise behind him made Bosamp turn. The sere sorcerer stared without surprise. Snarling, he gauged the distance between himself and the looming metallic dome.

A lot of snow to wade through . . . fight or run?

He hesitated. His new lizard hide throbbed maddeningly; it yearned for killing, seethed for it. Visions of cracked skulls and bleeding, twisted bodies flashed through his mind; the transmogrified skin itched insanely for the sight of blood and viscera.

Yes! the skin whined.

No! the Mallet hummed. The Bell! That's all that counts now!

The gaunt young sorcerer pulled away from the bloodlust. He spun around—or was spun around; it was hard to decide which—as the Mallet magnetically homed in on its destined lover. Pointing the Mallet ahead of him like a divining rod, he felt his body surge with raw, renewed energy. Growling with a sudden idea, he swung the Hammer hard into the snow blanket.

*Kaboom!*

White explosion.

The sea of snow parted before Bosamp, leaping away like cats off a bed, clearing a trench all the way to the plaza of the Bell.

Aha!

What was that? Slack-jawed, Yor stared at the snow carpet jumping out of the wizard's path. Dragon's breath! Have we no luck at all?

Then Yor's eyes snapped upward, reacting to a gut feeling that something was about to happen.

And so it did.

Mysteriously, as if someone above had thrown open a window to see what was going on below, the wind ceased abruptly, stopping dead, as if commanded to be still, and the clouds parted. Flurries dropped to the Waste like lead sinkers in a pond, inanimate white dust, unmoving, and received no reinforcements. Orange and oblique, the sun now bored a hole through the grey ceiling and lit the Tocsin of Terror like a sacred torch, and in the southern sky, the scarlet cloud of fireflies reappeared, murmuring low.

Spotlight: white and gold.

The Bell!

What Yor had seen before, as awesome as it was, was but a minuscule fraction of the Bell's true grandeur as revealed in the shaft of resurrected starlight. The shimmering Bell was a gargantuan lantern that illuminated the snow matte with a glow beyond comprehension. Two massive white marble pillars supported the Bell like slaves bearing a litter; this timeless duo labored atop a stupendous ivory stone ziggurat; scores of concentric disks, each one man-sized step above the other, raised the Bell tower high above the rabbled tundra in fearsome majesty.

The Bell!

Bedazzled, Yor could look at nothing else, wanted to look at nothing else, would never again see anything as fantastically, fearsomely beautiful.

The Belle Dame Sans Merci smiled down, waiting for her suitor, and struck a chord of dread inside all six minds.

The five plunged their ponies ahead, fanning out across the ridge. Dword's steed proved to have the most run left in it; the red-beard drew ahead of his comrades, gaining as he rode over each of the shallow rises in the concave amphitheater of the Bell, rises like the ripples formed when a stone hits still water, until he was a dozen galloping strides in the lead.

A cry of joy stabbed the silent Wastes, and Bosamp began his ascent of the ziggurat.

Endless seconds later, Dword, too, reached the steps. Frantic, he leaped from his steed, unsheathing his screamsax on the run, jangling as he ran. He's so far ahead! the red-beard fretted. I don't think I can catch him!

*Rap-rap-rap-rap-rap.*

The barbarian's armored jacket seemed like a coffin, a hundred stones. He pushed himself, muscles overstraining,

and was able to match strides with the Mallet-fueled madman, even gaining a rung or two as he flung himself up the
yawning steps.

*Rap-rap-rap-rap-rap.*

A third of the way up, dreadfully in arrears, Dword heard
boots behind him: Yor and Trebor, a tap-dancing *pas de deux*
of dashing harmony; then, moments later, another duet, the
prince and Sir Dudley, a staccato chorus.

*Rap-rap-rap-rap-rap.*

Dword's muscles ached; his breathing came in giant
gasps as he dashed up the steep ziggurat, rung by rung.
Sweating, lightheaded from exertion, he nearly tripped, but
somehow he kept moving higher and higher, as fast as he
could go. His eyes focused on only one thing: the shining
Mallet.

Woden's perversity! Bosamp's going to beat me there!

"Hah!" Bosamp cheered as he leaped up to the last step,
his flogged body on the verge of collapse. He bent over to
catch his breath, realizing with apprehension that when the
Mallet no longer sustained him, he would collapse. Resolute, he looked back down to see Dword, far below on the
immense marble ziggurat, then glanced at the Bell.

I'll probably make it, but why not? The *pièce de résistance!*
Let's see . . . what spell would work well right now? Ah,
yes!

Spreading his arms wide with the Hammer held out, the
sorcerer stood and dug deep inside his soul, summoning a
sigil, spewing the runes of power in a hoarse, crackled voice.

Off-key.

The glyphs came out warped, contaminated. Horrified,
he squelched his casting, fearing what the misshapen spell
might do, his lips curling in dismay.

It must be the presence of the Bell itself! he abruptly
understood. Spells won't work here! But I won't need them!
I have the Mallet of Doom! That is power enough! Grin-

ning like a matador before the five charging bulls climbing the ziggurat, Bosamp held the Mallet defiantly high above his head.

"World Shaker! World Breaker! My time has come!"

Turning, he raced for the Bell.

Heartbeats.

*Rap-rap-rap-rap-rap.*

When Dword reached the top, he saw the orange-clad magician running across the broad plaza with the fulgent hammer held high over his head, ready to strike the Mallet downward on its appointed task. I'm too late! the Norlander feared.

The Bell! The Bell! The Bell!

Then Bosamp reached D-Ray's doomsayer. The sallow, yellow-eyed sorcerer paused at the top of his swing, savoring his victory. He looked back at Dword, still running, still a dozen yards away, and taunted, "I've won! I've done it! It shall be just as the dragoness said!"

It takes three peals! Dword reminded himself. Run, damn you!

Vengefully Bosamp struck the lip of the Bell with the Mallet, a resounding wallop that cost him his balance. He tumbled down to his knees with the effort, cringing away in anticipation of the peal to come.

*Creeeeak!*

The massive, mighty Bell rocked on its titanic bearings, nearly locked tight from eons of unuse, nearly immobilized by the frigid weather's offerings. With a horrid metal-on-metal grinding screech that made their ears wither in anguish, the Bell swung toward its clapper, seeming to move in slow motion while time stood still.

*Creeeeeeak—thunk-thud-ud-ud-ud-kathud . . .*

Inside the sheltered alcove of gargantuan metal, a batting of snow had accumulated for millennia; with the rocking of the Tocsin of Terror, tons of packed, chunky snow fell down,

piling up on the plaza like a small avalanche. Ice shards slid
off the outside of the Bell, forcing Bosamp to jump backward to avoid being impaled. Both cascades continued as a
waist-deep mound of snow and ice accumulated below and
around the enormous Bell, while the god-forged golden
sounding bow touched the clapper.

*Binnnng!*

The interior snow avalanche muffled the sounding blow,
resulting in a chime that somehow failed to convey any
sense of impending disaster. Nonetheless, something must
have been paying attention, for the very foundations of
Leiblein stirred.

*Rumble!*

Over, under, sideways, down, the earth trembled, a sig-
nificant convulsion, but more of a wake-up call than a clarion trumpet of doom. It lasted for several seconds, then
quieted with a bump, waiting, waiting, waiting for gods
knew what.

Bosamp decreed, "That's one!"

"That's all!" Dword interrupted. He reached the wizard,
screamsax ready, and, remembering the admonition against
killing sorcerers, he brought the blade down flat on
Bosamp's shoulder just as Bosamp reached the apex of his
second backswing.

*Whap!*

The blow buckled Bosamp's legs from under him; toppling forward, the ball peen of ruin just missed the Bell;
instead, as the wizard broke his fall in the deep snow-ice
mound beneath the Bell, the force of the errant stroke carried the Mallet down to the Plaza, slicing through the
mound of ice and snow like a knife through butter.

*Crack! Hmmmmmm! Hmmmmmm! Hmmmmmm!*

Glistening, D-Ray's Hammer shocked the marble as if it
were a river of ice; shatter lines fanned out swiftly across the
plaza, an explosion of thunder that numbed the ears. The

vibration transmitted up Bosamp's arms from the blow was so severe the wizard released the Hammer like a hot utensil.

And still the plaza hummed. A frightful massage rang through all feet in contact with the ziggurat, shaking them to their knees, rendering their legs jelly. The quavering stopped Yor and Trebor in their ascent; they wavered dizzily on the ziggurat, several rungs below the plaza. Farther down, Sir Dudley and Prince Rodney were knocked from their feet, as they had the misfortune to be in a resonant node for the transmitted energy.

Flatfooted on the plaza, Dword had the better of it. Bounding forward with a Norlandic war cry, the red-beard, his thick forearms curdling with sinew, grabbed the sorcerer's cowl as firmly as a cat grabs a mouse, jerking Bosamp forcibly up and away from the Bell. "Got you, villain! Your days of troublemaking—"

Too soon.

Hissing, with hideous dust-augmented strength, Bosamp turned in the barbarian's grasp, his battered, abused robe ripping apart to reveal the ugly scaled skin below and freeing him momentarily from Dword's clasp as the barbarian was left with a handful of rent robe.

The horrid display of inhuman flesh made Dword's gut jump.

"Woden's bruited calumny! Is that a tail?"

Bosamp pushed away from the barbarian, swept up the Mallet while Dword lurched after him, and whirled about like a child's top. Contact!

"*Argh!*"

The Mallet's blow landed on Dword's right side. The impact of the numinous Hammer, far in excess of the sinew of its wielder, broke ribs and lofted Dword high off the ground in its arching follow-through. Electric pain radiated through the red-beard's brigandine to every ligament in his body, telegraphing the incredible throbbing that would follow if he survived the impending crash.

"Die!" Bosamp sneered as Dword sailed helplessly over the plaza, a dozen feet above the hard marble floor. Like a discus hurler, the wizard stood and watched in delicious anticipation of the bone-crunching agony the red-beard was going to experience when he hit the marble. "Die, you barbarian bastard!"

Dword fought to stay conscious in the tumult of pain assailing his body and dropped the wizard's robe fragment as he tried to get his hands below him to brace for the landing.

*Bam!*

Dword collapsed with a sickening snap on impact. He rolled over the marble plaza, over and over, finally stopping near the edge of the steps. Clutching his side, he tried to stand.

Impossible. The pain in his side was incredible. "Oh . . ." he moaned and sagged down to his knees.

"It won't hurt for long!" Bosamp gloated maliciously. "Spend your last seconds worshiping me from a distance! Be grateful you will see the final scene of the end of the world from a front-row seat!"

Then Yor and Trebor popped into view, running, flintlocks in hand. Bosamp's eyes lit with fury when they came into view. "You're too late!" the sorcerer coolly informed them, then reared the Mallet back above his head. "Watch me and despair!"

*Pshk! Pshk!*

Two lead rockets sliced through the air. Instantly D-Ray's diabolical gizmo responded to the threat. Plunging backward, nearly yanking the startled sorcerer off his feet, the Mallet sank to intercept the deadly spheres, a blur of shining metal.

*Ping! Ping!*

The lead balls flattened against the malevolent Mallet.

"Bosamp," Yor growled as he ran, "I'm going to rip your face off and use it for a boot buff!"

Off balance, Bosamp shivered with understanding and tried to regain mastery of the Mallet. The shriek of swords being drawn from their scabbards and the fury of rushing feet urged him on; before Yor could reach him, the wizard finished his stroke.

*Bonnnnnnngggnnggnnggnnngg!*

This time there wasn't a shred of doubt about the Bell's potency; a world-rattling peal trumpeted loose, a call to harms, a colossal chime that tolled in no uncertain terms the imminent demise of Leiblein and all its creatures. The sound wave flattened them, flinging them all to the frigid marble, where they were caressed mercilessly by the reverberating Bell, overwhelmed, prostrated, humbly cognizant of their utter cosmic insignificance.

Then Leiblein death-spasmed violently: backward, forward, round and round and round. The foundations of the world quaked, leaping in reflexive, puppetlike obedience to a god's legendary decree.

Terror infirma.

They were driftwood in an earthen tsunami that was as different from the first chime's evocation as a balled fist's blow to the midsection is from a gentle tap of reminder on the shoulder. Finally, just when it seemed that the very fiber of the world would unravel, hurling every rock of the planet away from each other at a speed that defied the mind's ability to comprehend, the brink of disaster calmed.

Not quite yet.

"That's two!" The loremaster shuddered.

Body tingling, Yor rose first, Trebor paces behind, fumbling with his belt pouch. Behind them now came Sir Dudley and the prince, each at the ragged edge of his physical endurance, the former past his prime and the latter nowhere near it. Boot and huffs, the four Brets raced across the plaza.

Writhing, grasping the Mallet of Doom to his chest, Bosamp unbent slowly from the fetal fold brought on by the power of the Bell's titanic peal. He staggered to his feet and reared for one more fell swoop and looked skyward.

*Where is she? She promised to take me away to a world of my own to rule! I have to wait for her!*

*Hurry!* the Mallet shouted in his mind. *Do it now! I'll save you until she gets here!*

He started downward.

"Stop!" Yor yowled desperately. Without thinking, he threw his rapier like an underhanded dart, a maneuver he had practiced at length for use in barroom brawls. The slim metal arrow glided accurately through the air.

"*Argh!*" Bosamp bleated as the rapier pierced his back, and but for the lizard skin sheath now encasing him, it would have gone clean through him. Instead, the blade stuck in only point deep, painful but far from fatal. The wizard wobbled, the stabbing misery making him forget everything else. He let the Mallet fall limp in one arm as the other reached for the searing steel.

Mercurial, Yor was there. He grabbed the hilt of his rapier and yanked, tugging the sorcerer toward him, with a shudder freeing the blade from the lizard flesh.

Bosamp pivoted, possessed and obsessed, his mind scrambled. In a roundhouse recoil, he swung the Mallet.

Deftly, Yor parried.

*Shinnnk!*

On impact with the Hammer, Yor's rapier shattered to smithereens, fragments showering around the two combatants. Horrified, the Bret stared blankly at the remaining hilt.

Growling, Bosamp reversed the sweep of the Mallet.

*Yipes!*

Yor jumped to avoid the backhanded blow. Missed! His heart started beating again. Then he saw Trebor dive past him, ducking under the perihelion of the Mallet's orbit, throwing himself at the wizard's legs.

*Whomp!*

Down Bosamp and Trebor went, rolling. The collision carried them under the shadow of the Bell, into the loose, chunky snow piled beneath it, burying them in a white whirlwind of snow, which was still showering down from inside the Bell like sifted flour. Yor watched, his dagger drawn, trying to sort out who was who in the roiling white confetti as the loremaster and the sorcerer wrestled in the snow pile, gyrating, churning, glimpses of legs and arms and torsos.

*If I can just get this spellbane in his mouth!* Trebor thought as he popped the vial's stopper. But he wrestled blindly in the snow, his massive size a hindrance at close quarters, unable to turn and twist as quickly as the maniacal wizard, never quite getting a grip on the slippery sorcerer.

Yor heard footsteps coming up from the rear, announcing the prince's arrival. *There's Bosamp!* Yor dived; Prince Rodney followed him into the snow. Four bodies floundered, a convoluted, twisting gnarl of limbs, metal, snow, and ice, a kicking, shoving, pushing, groaning, grappling morass with the tempest-tossed snow concealing them all in confusion, shouted curses, and mistaken identities.

Now came Sir Dudley, puffing, armor clattering. Sword ready, the elder knight poised beside the seething snow and grimly watched, determined that no arm would reach out for the Bell.

*There he is!* Trebor realized. He lunged and tried to hold Bosamp's Hammer arm, but the arm hurled him back with frightful power. *The Mallet's helping him!* the loremaster thought. *There's no other way he could have gotten the strength to— Got him!*

Trebor crushed Bosamp's face to his cuirass with his left

arm, then he smashed his right palm into the magician's mouth, pouring powder from the vial.

"Eat this, runeslinger!"

The young warlock jerked with a spasm. Spellbane coursed through his veins, chaining his inner power, negating the dragon dust in an electric discharge. He screamed, a noise the others would never wipe from their nightmares, and flailed, kicking Yor well away from him and knocking the prince across the face with a blow that drew blood from his oversized nose, the Mallet ominously close to everyone.

Bosamp's skin was on fire with anti-magic, his soul attacked at the core of its existence. Paroxysms of superhuman strength erupted, breaking the wizard from Trebor's grasp. Bosamp shoved the loremaster from him, swishing him across the face with his tail while he whirled the Mallet.

*Crash!*

The Mallet grazed the loremaster's rear end; Trebor went spinning out of the snowbank like a pinionless pinwheel, turning, turning, turning, shooting across the plaza, unable to control the spin.

He collided headfirst with one of the massive pillars supporting the Bell.

Trebor was motionless.

"Trebor!" Dword cried and crawled toward him.

Loosed, Bosamp was unchained fury. With a growl, he clawed the prince's face and shoved the royal teenager aside. He kicked Yor in the groin when the cavalryman latched on to his arm, and then suddenly broke free.

Now! the Mallet demanded.

Bolting upright, empowered by the doom-lust energy of the Mallet, Bosamp emerged uncontested and unmolested from the white pile.

Lunge!

Sir Dudley skewered the wizard's wrist. Transfixed, Bosamp growled, baring his teeth. "You still lose!" he brayed. Despite the pain, the wizard pitched the Mallet at the Bell, a feeble toss, but . . .

"Oh, no!"

The elder knight was unable to stop it. At the very lowest edge of the Bell, a fateful fraction of an inch from missing, the Mallet of Doom struck the inside of the Bell.

*Bonnnnnnnnnnnnnnnnnnnngggnnngggnnnggggg!*

Death knell.

Every last biological iota on Leiblein offered up hastily confessed sins. The sonic discharge of the Bell at the Top of the World blasted all those near it like leaves in a thunderstorm; they fell, crumpled, around the plaza, paralyzed by the trembling din, unable to stand or even think in the sonic fury.

"Doomsday is here!" Yor cursed. "Die all! Die merrily!"

*     *     *     *     *

The Bell?

Om stirred, and the force of his motion made Leiblein shudder. For forty million years, Om had lain in the radioactive hell at the planet's core, resting, meditating. Om, birthed in the superheavy white hole, the elemental yegg; Om, who had grown bored of the other eternals in the five thousand thousand thousand thousand sunrises since the yegg hatched them; Om, who to get rid of that incessant pontificating, philosophizing, moralizing D-Ray, had agreed to this silly wager. . . .

Well, what else was there to do after thirteen billion years?

Now—so quickly!—his peace and quiet was disturbed by that clanking noisemaker of D-Ray's. Twice had he heard the Bell chime, just the way D-Ray had demonstrated it when the wager was set, when the Mallet was hidden, when Om had crawled to the bottom of Leiblein just to get away for a billion years or so. . . .

Or had it really been three chimes?

Om wrinkled what passed for his nose and furrowed what passed for his eyebrows, scratching his jewel-encrusted skin with a suckered claw, while continents heaved at his contemplation.

That first peal certainly didn't sound like the other two, not the way D-Ray had chimed it when he tested it. Should it count? Must I lose the bet on the basis of that possibly unintentional peal?

Hmmmmm . . .

*  *  *  *  *

Eternity.

Actually, it was more like a minute, but to those stricken by this apocalyptic peal—even more deafening than the previous, only mind-sundering, bone-rattling chime—it seemed forever.

Then it stopped.

The ringing stopped, the landscape ceased throwing up, and the glue of the world sprang taut, relaxed, resettled. The amalgam of pebbles that was Leiblein remained in one piece—a chastened, badly unnerved piece, perhaps; a tenuous, shocked, numbed piece, for certain; but basically, one humbled, thankful piece.

Soiled undergarments.

As soon as each of them had two brain synapses to rub together, each reached the same conclusion:

One more!

Yor struggled to his feet, reeling dizzily, legs enervated by the shock waves. Where is Bosamp? he thought. His eyes flew this way and that, but so badly bruised was Yor's being that he had trouble focusing. Moans directed his glances, and he tried to assimilate the groaning, limp forms scattered about the plaza like leaves in the autumn wind. Over there, the prince was on his hands and knees in the snow pile, and somewhere over there, Dword tried to get up. Over there . . .

The Bell!

Its eye-searing brilliance flashed in Yor's face as he turned toward it. Then he saw Bosamp at last, despite the Bell's glare. The Mallet had returned to the wizard's grasp, serving as an anchor in the sonic chaos, keeping the stunned wizard within a few strides of the Bell, while Yor had been pushed far away across the plaza.

Bosamp stirred, eyes blinking, body uncurling.

My god! He can still do it!

Bosamp shook his head to clear it. I'm still here! he thought. But why? Were the legends false? Is all of this just a cosmic joke? And where is the dragoness?

You must strike it one more time! the Mallet demanded.

But—

Hurry!

Bosamp rose, or perhaps was pulled up to his feet, the Mallet held high in triumph. Then he saw Yor's weaving, reeling attempt to run, and he laughed savagely at the cavalryman's futile rush. He paused, deciding to drag it out to the maximum horror, to wait until Yor was but a stride away before swinging, tormenting him, both knowing how it had to end. Bosamp relished it. "You haven't a snowball's chance in hell of stopping me, Count—"

A white snow bolt whizzed through the air: *pow!*

"Got him!" the prince cheered.

The rock-hard, icy snowball pelted the thaumaturge like a feral fist square on the forehead, tipping him on his heels, dazing him, filling his nose, his eyes with freezing ice and grit. He tied to rub his forehead, but it only made it worse, grinding in the grit and snow until he was blinded.

Maybe! Yor thought. Just maybe!

Panicking, Bosamp whirled sightlessly around, sweeping the Mallet waist-high, missing the Bell by a foot. Then he stopped and felt the power of the Mallet home in on the Bell, jerking him left toward it.

Now! the Mallet hummed.

But Yor's arm struck like lightning, a snake coiling around the wooden haft; inexorably he jerked the wrist and Mallet back. Power flowed from deep within both men's souls, but one was far the emptier.

*Snap!*

Bosamp's wrist broke; Yor seized the Mallet. Bereft of the Mallet, without the dragon dust, without his sorcery, Bosamp collapsed in an unconscious, twitching heap.

But the Mallet tingled maliciously in Yor's grip, holding him as tightly as he held it.

"Saved from the Bell!" Rodney exclaimed.

"You stopped him cold, lad!" Sir Dudley agreed. "Now let's make sure he stays stopped!"

"I'll get the rope!"

Meanwhile, Trebor stood wobbly-legged, moaning from his ungodly headache. He removed his dented helm, which had saved his life, and threw the now useless armored hat away. Holding his throbbing skull, he walked unsteadily toward Dword.

"Are you all right?"

"Of course." Dword coughed bravely. "This happens to me every other week."

"Yeah. Me, too. I won't be able to sit for a while, though."

"Hey—what's with Yor?"

Yor's reality blinked; their whispers were a trillion miles away. Where am I now that I need me? . . .

Transition: years backward.

*  *  *  *  *

Twilight, late summer.

The hunting lodge on the castle estate.

Unlacing from their tangled slumber, the girl beside him slid to the edge of the bed, her silken brown tresses brushing against Yor's cheek, disrupting his sleep. Lithe, naked, she rose and stretched coquettishly, like a kitten limbering, stretching, yawning.

Motionless, she breathed a deep breath. Then her hands dipped to the bedstand and her purse. A small grey candle appeared, and she set it in the candle holder, removing the previous half-spent occupant, then used the old soldier to light the new sentinel. Leaning down, holding her fine hair back to deny it its peekaboo flirtation with her grey-greenish eyes, she mated the flame to the wick, and the candle flickered, strobed.

She watched it burn until she was satisfied that the fire had taken hold. Good! Now . . .

She paused but a moment, then turned quickly in place, profile to the bed. Deftly her delicate hands fell on something on the bedstand, her graceful frame flowing catlike as she clutched it up and turned her back to the bed, pacing a stride or two away toward a chair. Like a satin waterfall, her hair cascaded from her bare shoulders down to the supple curves of her back, and she placed a gold chain around her neck, securing the clasp.

Deadened with sleep, Yor fought his eyes open and blinked them heavily. The husky scent of passion lingered in the shuttered room. The amber aura of late daylight filtering through the gabled windows cast her in a sensual, tawny glow. Then, as he lay mute, immobile, leaden, unwilling to let go of sleep's hold, his nose twitched with an odd odor, not unpleasant, but unplaced.

He stared as if frozen. The newborn candlepower lionized

her, silhouetting her trim, high breasts and smooth legs, fawning on her flawless skin. God, she's beautiful! he mused. There's fire and passion there; we're a perfect match. . . . Well, things would be a lot easier if she'd been born a peasant girl instead of heir to the manor proud, but still . . .

"Come back to bed, wench."

He patted the bed suggestively.

Startled, she felt her nostrils flare. No man had dared call her that before, but this wasn't the cause of her panic; it was the fact of his voice, not the words, that made her eyes widen in fright. Her highborn hauteur evaporated; she forced herself to keep her back toward him and calculated furiously.

It's too soon! I must stall him!

"You're awake," she said uneasily, without facing him. "I have to go now. They'll miss me soon; Daddy's expecting guests from court tonight. But there's no need for you to get up."

She searched for her undergarments; the panties were missing, so she ignored them, picked up a petticoat, and put it on.

Yor frowned and abandoned his effort to lure her back to the bed. "Daddy" was Lord Morgan Lee, Master of the Fairfax, to whom he owed allegiance. Boldly Yor decided to press the issue that had to come to a head sooner or later.

"Kathy, don't you think it's time you told your father about us?"

She paused, carefully considering her words, then just let her emotions rule.

"He already knows."

Parry and *riposte*. His heart stopped, dumbstruck.

There was iron in her tone now. "This was the last time for us, Yor. It's over."

Yor fended off the dagger hurt. She can't mean that! She's said it before . . . what to do?

Flash.

She turned sideways, and metal jangled meekly. Scarlet rays radiated out from the dragon's eye hanging around her neck; its facets reflected light directly into his eyes. Firefang's orb hung down randy in her cleavage—the slim gold chain was too long for her neck—drawing his eyes where they needed no incentive to go.

The talisman.

Yor frowned. "Kathy, I've told before you not to wear that. It's not jewelry; it's—"

The candle scent laced the air. Now! she thought.

"It's over!" she said forcefully. She turned, finally ready to face him. "We're just too different, and too much alike in the wrong ways. You've taught me a lot, and I'll never forget you, but it could never work."

My god! I think she really means it! Yor's mind reeled, trying to think what to do next, paralyzed and yet running rapidly down the possible choices.

Moving to the end of the bed, she picked up her brocaded gown and stepped into it, pulling the dress up over her in an unconscious reverse striptease. She snapped the clasp with finality. "We will never see each other again."

"No more games, Kathy," he said. Blood pounded through him again; he struggled with the covers. "I—"

The blanket seemed to be made of stone; he could barely move it. When he tried to sit up, some unseen barrier blocked him, and he bounced back with a thud.

What?

It wasn't hurt or fatigue that forbade him; some unseen cords bound him to the mattress, a smoky wisp that descended and coiled around him like a constricting serpent, binding him to the bed.

"This is no game, Yor." She dropped her slim, athletic legs one by one into her tall, black riding boots. Aware of the power in him, she froze and poised her forefinger to her full lips, rasping a rune she had prepared. The glyph formed, and the air became thicker, heavier. "Stop me if you can, my love."

"Kaa . . ."

His tongue wouldn't budge in his mouth.

*She's used her sorcery on me! I've got to get up!*

Twisting with adrenaline, Yor pushed upward and pressed against the unseen barrier. The bonds yielded slightly, whining in protest. He bounced off the mattress once and impacted the barrier, but it refused to buckle, and he was pitched back flat onto the bedding.

She stepped quickly to the door and paused, unable to leave without one last look. "I could have taught you spells!" she said sadly, angrily, with a tone of betrayal. "You could have been as great as Kantar. Maybe if you had . . ."

She banished the thought.

The words slapped him, and a lump formed in his throat. Gasping, he wrestled to rise, struggling against the inexorable bondage. Her redolent perfume still clung to the bed, taunting his helplessness, mixing with the smell of his tremendous exertion.

Comprehension came in a burst.

"The candle!" he croaked hoarsely, straining against the glyph choking his neck.

She reeled as if slapped and felt a loss of power as he shattered the glyph with his own inner, raw wildfire magic.

*If he could break one spell . . .*

She whirled. "It's over!" she insisted, as much to convince herself as him. "Over!" She watched as he struggled against the smoke, trying to reach the candle. Quickly she reached for her chryst.

His grasp was short by a yard; she smiled in victory.

"No! It's not over, witch!" he growled, his words warped by her silence spell. *The talisman! She has it!*

Understanding crushed him, took the wind from him.

He was coerced to the mattress, trussed beneath the coils of
her witchcraft. His muscles fought back, and he stared in
hurt disbelief, tears in the corners of his eyes.

"I don't love you anymore!" she shouted, fist clenched.
She sighed to relieve the tension, almost disappointed that
he had been so easily snared. "Don't try to see me again!
You'll never get past the guards!"

She crossed the threshold and yanked the door shut.

He heard the sound of her horse's hooves fading into the
distance. . . .

* * * * *

Transition: back to the present.

Her sorcerous bonds were still imprinted on Yor's flesh
and on his emotions; her perfume was still in his nose, the
cruel candlelight still in his eyes. He hadn't simply remembered that afternoon; he had been forced to relive every terrible second of it.

The Mallet hummed with power in his hands.

Cold, cold sweat.

Fool! the Mallet of Doom said in his mind. Did you ever
really believe you could win a woman like that? I can take
the ache away from you! The humiliation, the haunting! I
can give you oblivion . . . sweet oblivion!

And you will have revenge on her!

Yor wavered, riven to the bone, memories flashing
through him faster than the speed of time. He remembered
escaping from the bed; he remembered Danby, and that
night in the tower.

You're wrong, Kathy! he said to the ghost that had
haunted him for seven years. It's far from over! Our fates are
entwined, interlocked . . . lover to lover, nemesis to nemesis!

You lost the talisman! the Mallet jeered. You failed your

stewardship! You must destroy her and the talisman! Strike the Bell—now!

Yor hesitated, trembling, and looked at the terrible, beautiful Bell.

I can give you peace, the Bell cooed.

A hand settled on his shoulder. Trebor's. Intuitively the loremaster read the nature of the Mallet's seduction in Yor's face. Friendship stayed the man-mountain's broadsword, but fear kept him from grasping the Mallet, afraid of what demons within himself might be loosed.

"Drop the Mallet!" Trebor whispered. "Please!"

Yor looked at the Mallet, then looked back at Trebor, then at the shining Bell.

"She will never love me again!" he vomited, weak in the limbs.

"She wanted the talent you possess, to channel it for her own base purposes," Trebor said. "You would have been her consort, her champion, but never her equal."

Yor blinked and gripped the Mallet with determination to control it and himself.

"I promised I wouldn't use the power. The ghost of Kantar told me something about a Game the dragons play and the Land of Shadows. I didn't understand it. But Kathy couldn't . . . ."

There were no words.

"She loved me once, I think."

Catharsis.

No, Kathy. This is not how it will end.

Hostile, the Mallet sent stinging shocks racing up his arm. Yor's inner reservoir came to his aid. He turned and threw the defeated Hammer. It sailed far, far away, off the plaza and far out into the Wastes, and Yor was convinced that the Hammer was flying away from him on its own.

"Where there is life, there is hope," Trebor said.

"Hope? I think not. But there *is* life. And the gods shall

not take it from us this day!"

"Look!" The prince's cry made them turn.

The fireflies swarmed down from the sky, surrounding the Mallet in a buzzing swirl of lava. When they rose up, the Mallet was gone.

"They're taking it back to Vangberg," Dword said.

"I wonder, Captains," Sir Dudley said as he watched the crimson fireflies wing southward. "Does it take just one more chime? Or does the count start over?"

"Hey!" Prince Rodney said, interrupting the thought. "I have Bosamp all tied up. What do we do with him now?"

Trebor looked at the wizard, who was indeed under wraps, tied with enough rope to rig a frigate, leaving only his head and hands exposed. "I'll tend to him," he said, "but only after I have a gander at Dword's ribs."

"Me?" scoffed the Norlander, hunchbacked, backpedaling, grinning. "A mere scratch! But I do think we should have your head examined."

"There's nothing wrong with my head."

"That's easy for you to say!" Dword smiled. "Look at your helm over there! Ruined!"

"And that was his favorite!" Yor needled.

Trebor took a quick look at all of Bosamp's wounds and the knots binding him, pronouncing both travel worthy.

"You're going to develop a real taste for spellbane," the loremaster said and hefted the wizard up to examine him. "And the fainli would like word or two with you. . . ."

Deprived of the power of the Mallet and the dragon dust, Bosamp was now only a limp marionette. Trebor stopped long enough to bandage the wizard's bleeding wrist while Bosamp, delirious, gurgled unintelligibly, something about dragons.

"Come on, Bosamp," Yor said. The memory of what the Mallet could do to a man was still harsh in his mind; it softened him to sympathy. "It's all over. I'll buy you an ale when we get back."

Oh . . . one more thing.

Yor turned to the prince and smiled at the royal youth. "Good work, Your Highness! Neither Colin, nor Sean, nor Cedric would have been the right man for the spot we were in! And you did it your own way. . . ."

Rodney blushed happily. "*Now* can we finally go somewhere where they have mounds of disgustingly sweet pastries and real soft beds with huge, fluffy pillows? Do I have to make it a royal order or something?"

"Follow me!" Dword said, hobbling, one hand bracing his side, using his screamsax as a crutch to hold him up. "I know just the place! It's in the village of Frostgard, where I grew up—Frostgard on the Hardansfjord. We can visit my mother for a few days and recuperate!"

The red-beard winked wickedly at them all. "Let's see if you Brets can handle some real women, like my sister Brunehilda!"

"What?" Yor leered like a Gormousian flesh peddler. "What does she look like?"

"She has a terrible personality."

"That pretty, eh? We'll see! We'll see!"

They laughed and straggled across the plaza.

At the ziggurat's steps, Yor looked back over his shoulder at the Bell, shuddered, then stared at Dword, finger pointed. "You and your lousy legends! You people will be the death of us yet! The Bell at the Top of the World! Really!"

"You know, of course," Trebor leaped in with both nit-picking feet, "that it's not actually at the top of the world. I mean, geographically speaking, this isn't the pole. There must be hundreds of leagues from here until the real top of the world!"

" 'The Bell Almost but Not Quite at the Top of the World'?" Yor conjectured. " 'The Bell at the Top of the

World, Metaphorically Speaking'?"

" 'The Gong with the Wind'?" Trebor offered. " 'Dooms-day's Chime'?"

" 'Shirr's Trou-bell?' 'The Clapper Trap'?" Yor countered.

Dword's face seized up; he would truckle no more, not in the shadow of the Bell itself, at any rate! He made a one-armed, two-fingered anti-hex sign and fied back at them, "It's 'The Bell at the Top of the World'! It has a nice ring to it—now leave it well enough alone!"

Laughter.

\* \* \* \* \*

Om keened what passed for ears, waiting. He had decided not to count that first insipid chime. D-Ray had said three times true, and he was holding him to it. Three clean, crisp peals! If D-Ray didn't like it, that was just too damn bad!

Quietude.

After a few hours, Om shrugged what passed for shoul-ders and went back to his dreamy stupor. After all, it had only been forty million years.

Oh, yes, let's see now. Does the count start over, or . . .

\* \* \* \* \*

A god glyph thundered in the dragoness's lair.

Judgment.

It was a few seconds before the chrome saurian realized that he wasn't going to die, that they had both been allowed to live. In a flash of understanding, he knew what D-Ray had decided: death for the dragons if their interference affected the outcome of D-Ray's wager in his favor; death for a dishonorable win.

But reprieve—with a warning—if Bosamp failed.

*Honor . . . there will be honor! Just as the gods decree!*

He growled arrogantly at the helpless gold and licked his abrasive tongue over her with deliberate and playful ruthlessness.

*This matter is decided, daughter! Bosamp's quest has failed! You are to remain in this cavern until I send for you, Drachshiska! You will continue to recite—*

*I only did it for my son! To spare Firefang . . .*

The chrome lashed her viciously.

*Firefang's fate lies with Kantar and his descendant! You will do nothing whatsoever to interfere, do you understand? Firefang must do or not do on his own! He has already lost his eye! Unless he can reclaim it honorably, he will never molt gold!*

Drachshiska did not reply. Better the world be destroyed and you should die, my son, than to let you serve Kantar's plan! But I have not failed completely; you will still have a chance!

A sadistic smile crossed her reptilian lips. Kantar is dead, she thought, and the eye lost!

*Kantar is not dead!* the chrome bellowed in her mind. *And you cannot save Firefang from the cusp of destiny! You tried to destroy this world before its time! To end the Game on a technicality! You interfered with designs of the gods themselves! But you have failed! The Game resumes! Lore and magic must war until one wins! The world will be consumed by the Land of Shadows or sorcery banished! Only then will we fly—if we survive!—to the next world!*

The chrome stared a long time without speaking, weighing his words.

*I am the Gamesmaster, first among those who came here! You do not know the ecstasy that comes with watching a race destroy itself with the tools we have provided! That is the Game, daughter! And if your son, or any other dragon, fails to molt gold before the Cataclysm, there shall be no mercy for him!*

He paused ominously and composed himself.

*But there will be honor!*

Smiling evilly, he decided he could spare a few more days torturing her, then felt compelled to speak again, admiring even in admonition.

*The tainted power dust was a nice touch, daughter. A pity he wasn't completely transformed. So very deliciously cruel. And the world you chose for him . . . so gorgeous, so splendid . . . and the gravity, so crushing . . . the air so fatally unbreathable. . . .*